KRINGLE

THE STORY OF A YOUNG TOYMAKER

D.P. MCWANE

KRINGLE

THE STORY OF A YOUNG TOYMAKER

D.P. MCWANE

EDITED BY
EMILY ROGAN
JOHN MCWANE

WONDERING CAT

Kringle
by D. P. McWane

For more written works by David McWane visit:
davidmcwane.com

ISBN: 978-0-9914919-5-7

DEDICATED TO MY GRANDFATHER
GEROULD ROBERT MCWANE,
THE TOYMAKER.

ACKNOWLEDGEMENTS

Thanks to my father John, Emily and Marc.
And to Brianne Finn McWane, my magical new bride.

BE THE ANSWER TO THEIR LITTLE PRAYERS

INDEX

FALLING FLAKES,
THE FAWN AWAKES
& THE TRAIN COMES
BARRELING BY

STORY 1

＊

TWO SNOWFLAKES

Two snowflakes
struck up a conversation
on their mid-morning descent to earth.

"This is wondrous.
Look! Look how beautiful we all are,"
said the bigger of the two.

"Yes, but aren't you scared?
I am.
Where will we land?
Oh, we are all so bright
I can't see where we are falling to,"
replied the smaller snowflake,
trying desperately to catch a glimpse
of their leisurely approaching earth.

The bigger snowflake smiled and reached out his hand,
"Here, stick with me.
I hear we are coating a glorious mountain."

The bigger flake
went on calming the smaller
until they became one.
Until they became
a glorious mountain.

＊

Story 1:

FALLING FLAKES, THE FAWN AWAKES & THE TRAIN COMES BARRELING BY

*

What we all love most are the big snowflakes. We spot one and we chase it. These bigger snowflakes simply stand out to us among the smaller wild ones that whip by. Hovering, they slowly canopy down, rotating above us with sunlight illuminating small rainbow prisms inside their tips. Magical twinkles of yellow, orange and red sparkle. Purples and blues allow the fluffy flakes to be perceived wet inside, as if small droplets are keeping them healthy and happy. The big flakes we chase allow us time to get under them with our eyes up, squinting and tearing. Arms out like a ballerina in *attitude en point*, we have time to call out to friends how beautiful our choice flake is. We dance under these saucers of snow almost tripping, almost crashing, laughing at our silly display and at our friends who are twirling with us.

Some say the reason there are snowflakes bigger than others is because the brave snowflakes take the hands of the smaller ones who are nervous and talk to them, reassuring them that they are on a safe and wondrous journey down. These brave snowflakes hearten the nervous ones that each and every one of them is to become something grand, something beautiful. Others say that the wisest snowflakes just find the view below so gorgeous that they want to slow their descent. These friendly flakes take each other's hands, talk about the beauty below and decide together where they would most like to land.

This particular snowflake was the biggest that New England had seen in years. It moved up with the wind; then fell slowly, rotating slightly. All of the chatty flakes, hand-in-hand, sparkling yellow, orange and red with small droplet like twinkles of purple and blue, looked down with big eyes and all cheerfully agreed to fall ever so softly on the forehead of a newborn baby fawn, whose fur was snow white, still sleeping, snuggled warmly within her mother and father.

Poof.

Kringle

It's a sound and smell *we* wouldn't have noticed. In other times the father deer would have ignored such a distant sound, such a distant smell. But now with the birth of his white fawn and her new shaky legs, he decided to raise his nose and eyes far north, past Montgomery Lake, past Mr. Donnelly's out-of-season corn field and even further north where the white tops of birch trees blurred into the white snowing sky. The father deer squinted his eyes. His ears fluttered. He could see it now. Smoke. Black smoke. Not a lot, but enough to discolor the New England sunrise.

He kept his breath slow, so not to startle his love. Yet, as his ears turned northwest, she awoke for she could feel the change in him. The distant sound came once again. His love and he locked morning eyes. Devotion. She looked to where he was focused. He gave her a morning touch with his nose. She closed her eyes. Together they let out two slow breaths. Understanding one another, the father and mother deer spoke through their eyes. The mother put her nose in where her baby was the warmest. Her nose moved her baby's small front leg from over her eyes and nudged her awake. The white fawn's eyes slowly opened to see her mother rising.

The white fawn recognized her mother and already loved her; she thought her graceful. The mother and father deer bent low and touched their baby signaling her it was time to stand. Wobbly, but determined, she rose. Once stable, she looked to her mother. Her father was focused north. Her mother stepped beside her white fawn to keep her assured. Maybe there was a time the faint sound and smell would have been overlooked, but things were different now. The father deer took in a deep breath and as he let it out, he shook off the puffy snow that had collected on his colossal antlers. And, as the morning snow fell, the three, at her pace, slowly walked deep into the trees - just to be safe.

The five o'clock train heading to Boston barreled through the newly layered snow at sixty-seven miles per hour. The four thousand pound manmade comet blew the snow up so high it looked like a blowing geyser was sliding across the countryside. It was pure locomotive power. Thunderous.

Billy sprung up. The steam whistle jolting the Boone boys from their morning dreams with authority. Groggy, with blurry sight, Billy scratched his static hair, smiled from the remembrance of his dream of flying though the sky piloting one of his and his brother's rocket-ship sleds, then scurried to his bedside window to watch the distant black smoke make it's way closer. Johnny, a bit still in dreamland, put his pillow over his head, moaned and desperately tried to go back to the very same dream. But Billy watched the black smoke wiggle it's way through the distant white pines.

Inside was Old Man Harrigan, smoking his pipe while chomping away on sunflower seeds. "Them seeds keep ya alert," he'd always say to the younger conductors. Old Man Harrigan wore thick, dusty glasses and his long dusty beard flowed out the locomotive's window. In younger years his dusty navy blue uniform, with dusty conductor hat, fit Old Man Harrigan well. But as he's grown older, he's shrunk a bit, so now his uniform looked to be about two sizes too big.

Sitting beside him was Old Bootsie, a big brown, slobbering Czechoslovakian bloodhound, howling away as he does whenever the snow is fresh and flying. The two were true buddies. Old Bootsie was just about the only thing Old Man Harrigan brought back from the war. He was just a pup then and was known as simply Bootsie. He got the name because he tore up every pair of Old Man Harrigan's war boots. And to this day, he attacks all kinds of boots with everything he's got. Not shoes though. Not heels or slippers. Strictly boots. That's why Old Man Harrigan wears those silly loafers year round. The two were practically the same soul. Their heads seemed to always look in the same direction. They would cough, sneeze - even yawn at the same time. The two buddies blasted forward, with dusty beards and flapping ears.

Inside, the locomotive smelled of fresh coal, burning coal and old burned coal. The bouncing metal rattled as if every screw in the locomotive was loose. Old Man Harrigan was taking short pulls from his pipe and blowing the whistle of the locomotive with each puff. Old Bootsie would howl every time the whistle blew. When Old Bootsie got a good howl going, Old Man Harrigan would spit his seeds out and join him and the two would just be screaming away cruising like a rocket. And this morning, that's exactly what the two were doing - howling and howling away.

Betsy Bound it read on the side of the locomotive. Betsy is the name of Mrs. Harrigan. Old Man Harrigan had his nephew paint his wife on the side of the locomotive. She's now up there dressed in a futuristic red hood and cap, shooting a ray gun with a big smile, riding a rocket-ship that Old Man Harrigan once saw in a *Buck Rogers* comic strip in the *Worcester Evening Gazette*. "That's my out-of-this-world girl," Old Man Harrigan would tell you, even if you didn't notice.

Betsy Bound is a shipping train. No passengers. The first five cars held coal for the city - Boston. The four cars after that held timber and steel for the city and the growing towns around it. The four green cars in the middle held Duesenbergs for the fortunate automotive enthusiasts. And the train cars near the tail were full of miscellaneous merchandise that would change with each load and fad. But the last car that was supposed to be empty, today held something very special, something that was *not* supposed to be there.

Kris Kringle with his eyes wide, red hair whipping and cheeks as rosy as anything, hung outside the last boxcar with a big smile looking for the right place to jump off. Kringle is a tall man, a thin man. Young and new to traveling, Kringle had been taking care of his sick mother after his father's passing. Before she moved on and lit the lamp of her new world, she told her son to leave their small northern village and go have a life filled with "love and joy". So Kringle hung outside that boxcar searching for just that.

His boots were scuffed, burned and too big for him. His overalls were the same - stained, a bit burnt and too big. His loose belt was taken from the strap of a black horse saddle and seconded as his tool belt. Yet the only tools Kringle owned were a carving knife, a hammer, and a broken pencil. With his tan shirt sleeves rolled up, Kringle held onto the top of the last train car's doorframe and hung out looking with wide eyes for the right place. That's when he saw them.

"Well, now ain't that something," Kringle said aloud, yet inaudible under the power of the wind, as he saw two strong deer with a young white fawn walking deep into the forest. As the cold air rushed into Kringle's nostrils, freezing his brain and icing his hair, he began to fall in love with the town. Everything looked fresh there. The trees seemed noble; the hills proud. He liked the stonewalls that bound the land, for they told the history of focused men. He over-romanticized everything, because that's what his father had told him is – "The secret to being happy." He looked toward the distant town. It was quaint. Small. Something there was calling to him. Something important. And he was listening. He was sure to not let all these new colorful feelings pass him by. His logic and instincts agreed; it was stamped "approved".

"Sure is something swell boys. That there, those deer there. You see the

small one, the white one? Well that's what it's all made of. Yup," Kringle looked
to see the three men he had met a week earlier still sleeping off the rugged
drinks from the night before. They lay on one another sharing an old burlap
potato sack as a blanket

Kringle looked back outside, "*Welcome To Hamilton, Massachusetts*", he
read fast, on an old sign that flashed by. Heading back inside the boxcar smiling,
Kringle reached into his red sack. "Now wait-wait, where's everything?" Kringle
moved cautiously toward his sleeping travel companions. "Ah-ha, for you Mr.
Rustle, and I wasn't sure, mind you, but I think you would find this keen - a
new pipe." Kringle gently placed a handsome pipe he had been whittling for the
past few days under Mr. Rustle's hand. Mr. Rustle's old cracked pipe moved up
and down in his mouth as he snored. "And for you Big Tony, a new wine sack."
– Kringle took the open bottle from Big Tony's hand and poured what was left
into a wine sack he had made from leftovers -- a drawer knob, some string
and a piece from that old black leather saddle -- and placed it under Big Tony's
arm. Now, bumping up and down in the boxcar, Kringle turned to the last man
sleeping with a Civil War hat over his eyes. Kringle pulled out a small pouch
from his sack, reached into it and looked over seven small Civil War soldiers he
had whittled and painted. "And lastly for you Colonel, here are the stories you
told me. May you fine gentlemen see better days; joy to ya."

Kringle stepped up to the boxcar's door, brushed himself off, rubbed
his face muscles loose, put on his red wool hat, red gloves and dirty red jacket,
slung his red sack over his shoulder, took a deep breath and leaped out of the
boxcar.

"Well, what d'ya know about that? Johnny, Johnny a man just leaped off
the train there. Boy he just jumped right off, tumbled right down there. Where'd
he go? Well, what do ya know ab…"

"Are you boys up?" yelled Miss Eleanor Boone, known as Ellie - the
Boone boy's mother. She was in the kitchen smearing marmalade across
buttered toast. Ellie is slender, a dark Irish. She has long black hair that she
often tied up or wore in a babushka. When she was younger, Ellie wore her
hair down, but now that she was in her twenties and times being as they were,
she seemed to have endless work for herself, so she found it wise to just keep

it up. Her clothes were nothing too exciting. Ellie's clothes were mostly from her childhood that she had mended throughout the years. She hadn't owned anything new for some time.   Ellie's tall for a young woman, six feet, and was endlessly made fun of as a child. When the schoolboys and girls saw her coming they'd sing, "Boom, Boom - Boom, Boom" as a death march to her steps. The school children would also sing a song that Ellie still sometimes accidentally sings in her head while she walks:

> *"Here comes the mighty giant,*
> > *Run, run - here she comes*
> *Here comes the mighty giant*
> > *Big 'n' huge - she'll step on you!"*

The endless teasing made it so Ellie could always take a verbal punch. Ellie is a smart one. An observer. She grew herself up to be as kind as a storybook and as loving as a new mother. Her overall approach to life is that she doesn't want anyone to feel like she did when she was young. She wanted others to feel happy, because Ellie thought being miserable was out of style and simply overrated. One would often hear Ellie say, "you gotta make your own sunshine, don't ya?" Ellie just wants to help all of those who struggle. People who didn't know her would say she was shy, but Ellie isn't shy.

"Momma, I just saw a bank robber jump off a train. He jumped off right before the bump track. Wow Momma, you should'a seen him," Billy hollered down from the bedroom, which was just a small loft with a ladder to get up into and to where Ellie slept in the one big bed as well.

"No time for masked bank robbers Billy Boone. No time. You and your brother are gonna be late if you don't break outta that mind of yours. Now come on down; the marmalade is warm," said Ellie.

Johnny slowly sat up. Yawning, he pulled a rope that hung above his head. A small bell chimed. The rope gave tension to a large sailing pulley, oddly nailed to the ceiling boards. The other end of the rope lifted a beaten brimmed hat. Emerging from under the hat was a rocket-ship whittled from an old candle stick. The rocket-ship had acorns for wheels. Seeing the rocket launch, Billy quickly crawled back in bed and put his arms straight up into the air the way his brother now was and stared with wide eyes. The rocket-ship wobbled halfway down a plank that was also oddly nailed on the wall. When it reached the end

12

of the plank it tapped a massive book labeled, *How To Build A Rocket-ship*, that fell, slamming down on a small board that rested like a seesaw across an empty can of beans. Once the book slammed down on the board, the counter weight shot two piles of folded clothes into the air. With both brother's arms in the air, their socks, underwear, pants and shirt rained down on them. Johnny's hat landed on his head, but he only got one arm into one of his shirt sleeves. Billy's pants and shirt hit the window, his socks landed on his hands like mittens and his underwear plopped down atop his head covering his face.

"Pretty good Johnny," said Billy encouragingly, muffled under his underwear.

"Yah better than last time huh," agreed Johnny.

The Boone boys dressed and took the ladder down to the first floor of the makeshift home.

The Boone home was only one room. It was sectioned off into two sides - one side being the kitchen with a small eating table and the other side having a retired church pew in front of a fireplace. All around the house were Johnny's inventions. The Egg Cracker - which was two small nails tied with twine to a pair of old scissors. The Wood Splitter - which was a saw blade attached to an egg beater. And of course the famous - Doorbell - which was a small hammer rigged to a rat trap, nailed to the outside of the door with an old cracked bell hanging from the inside of the door. When company arrived, and the Boone's seldom had company, they would pull the hammer back, which would hit the bell through a small hole in the door, making a clanky clang that anyone and everyone would hope to never hear again.

"Now if this snow keeps up…boys pay attention. Eyes here. If this snow keeps up, you know it's gonna be a deep walk home so be careful. Mind yourselves. And no stopping at the clubhouse neither."

"It's Central Command; it's a Space Station Ma," Johnny corrected, scarfing down his warm toast.

"Fine. A Command Station then. You two come right home. Are you hearing me boys? Are you boys on memory record?" Ellie continued dressing them tight. "I need you to check the bump track for the fallen coal on your way home too. We're low. And brush off the log pile. And do whatever work Miss Magnolia gives you from school. You hearing your mother now boys?"

Both brothers pulled their scarves from their mouths and stared at their mother.

"Ah Ma, you know we gotta Battle Cruiser to build. Ain't that right, Billy?"

"Yah, Momma, we got a new rocket-ship ta build," Billy chorused.

"We gotta go down to Pete's and look for parts even. We only got a month 'til the Red Robin Race. And we gotta…"

Ellie's demeanor changed. She does this whenever the boys get snippy; she calls it her – "Papa Stance". Ellie developed this stern character after the boys' father got a pamphlet reading there was work out west. Mr. Boone packed a suitcase and headed that way by train and hitching. He left with the purpose to make money for the family. However, all he found was another woman, and all his family got was a note saying that he wasn't ever coming back. So now Ellie plays the Mother *and* Father and she does it quite well. She stood up straight, took a big breath to puff her chest out and placed her hands on her hips.

"I know you boys ain't moanin' to your Momma. I know you ain't. And I know this because, why? Because Boone's don't moan. No we do not. What *do* we do Billy Boone?

"Ah c'mon."

"Tell me."

"We strong people Momma."

"That's right we are. Go on. What else?"

"We take care of each other Momma."

"Well, *why* would we do that?"

"Because family comes first; family's something you always got."

"And what else, Johnny? Tell me Johnny Boone, why do we help each other?" The Boone boys began to shuffle. They had to answer these questions from their mother about five times a week. "Boys! Look-a-here. Eyes up."

Johnny Boone fixed his posture and said, "'Cause we love each other and 'cause we strong people."

"Billy already said we're strong people."

"I mean 'cause we, um, love each other and caring for each other is more important than caring for just one's self. 'Cause if we care for each other then we have the strength of three people in one."

Ellie then switched back to her mother mode. It went against Ellie's core to be so constantly stern with her boys and it went against her soul to pretend to be their father. Her "Papa Stance" always left Ellie feeling tired and thinking about things she didn't want to think about anymore. It always left her feeling a bit open. Raw.

Ellie tweaked the last tweaks of her two boys' patched up winter clothes.

"That's right. Good. You remember that." Ellie looked over her bundled boys. "Okay. Lookin' good. Just get this here; put your arms up Billy. And okay. Yessiree, good lookin', warm boys we have here."

The Boone boys wore a lot of their father's old clothes that Ellie tailored to fit them. She told them they were *her* father's clothes and jazzed the boys up to feel proud of that. Ellie promised the boys that they'd get some fine, new clothes once they were seventeen and slowed their growing down. At eight and ten they just changed too-too much for Ellie's small nest egg to keep up with.

"I'll see you as soon as Miss Winkelplex sends me home. I love you, young men – like the Sun loves the Moon. Now go on, don't be late for the bell. Johnny, show your brother where the path is."

An attention seeking wind screamed through the trees and down to the snow floor, an angry wind, which enjoyed shattering the morning coat. Johnny and Billy trudged a mile to school and a mile back each day. They glamorized their winter walks, envisioning they were on a groundbreaking expedition to the Arctic. The Boone boys often imagined the world was watching them from above and taking notes on how courageous they were.

There is no real road to the Boone home. Bridge Street is just an old horse path. At one end of it is the Boone's home and the town's junkyard where their neighbors Pete Smit and James Riggelsworth work and live. The other end of Bridge Street connects with Commonwealth Street. Everything is found on Commonwealth Street: all the homes, the shops, the library, police station, *Bonne Affaire*, *Home Cooked*, the once tavern but now the only restaurant in Hamilton. And at the end of Commonwealth Street is the big three: the school, the church, and the town hall. The town of Hamilton is like many early colonial towns. It has one road heading into town and one road heading out of town. It's a toy train set model town, save the train doesn't go around Hamilton; it goes through it.

Before heading up Bridge Street, the Boone boys went over to the junkyard. Each morning the boys stopped by Pete's because his dog, Rudy, liked walking to school with them. Rudy was discovered five winters back living in the junkyard. Pete was organizing the piles of junk when he found an abandoned brown puppy with black ears - one sticking up and one flopping down, hidden in the crevice of an old blown-out tire. The little puppy waited there, a bit confused, and a drop hopeful. When Pete grabbed the tire to patch it up, the pup fell out; plopped right on Pete's foot. Pete picked him up with his big calloused hands, rubbed him, cleaned the cobwebs from his eyelashes and snout, kissed him and kept him. Ever since then Pete and the Boone boys shared Rudy's love.

Pete lives in a rickety shack that he grew up in with his mother and father. They long since passed. Pete is a tall fella. He is great with his hands and loved by the church, not the church at the end of Commonwealth Street, that's the white church; no, the church that loves Pete is the one held in Mr. Thomson's old red barn. The church people there call Pete – Honest Pete.

When the kids approached the junkyard, Pete was standing with his head down along side Mr. Riggelsworth, Mr. McManus and his assistants, Elmer and Lloyd. The Boone boys call Elmer and Lloyd the *Dunce Brothers* because they are brothers and because they are frankly dense. They're big and oafish; they're muscle and gut. Johnny said, "If you put their dinosaur brains together, they still wouldn't be as smart as our Rudy." Mr. McManus is pretty much the mayor of Hamilton. Hamilton didn't have a mayor anymore, not after Mr. McManus petitioned the old Mayor to leave town over some false accusation that he was a Communist. These days, everyone just acts like Mr. McManus is mayor, for no one has the courage to challenge him and be the next one Mr. McManus gets a witch hunt on. And because Mr. McManus owns most of Hamilton, the town had now become too dependent on him. He owned most of the homes people lived in, all the small shops, even *Home Cooked* and, of course, Mr. McManus' New England famous and most profitable business of European imported furniture called *Bonne Affaire*, where Ellie is a sales lady. He even owns the junkyard. Someone said he recently bought up Little Island Pond, but no one knows how a man could buy a pond if the pond isn't for sale. Those same people say the sheriff's looking into it, but most think Mr. McManus will own that pond; he'll make people pay to skate and swim, pay to boat and fish. He's criminal. Piggish. Mr. McManus had become larger than a man; he'd become a cloudy sky that the town now lived under. He had become an American King.

Dressed in his fancy clothes, with a black top hat, holding that silver pocket watch of his, Mr. McManus was just about shouting.

"Don't care, don't care; I do not care! Sing it to the birds; pray it to Jesus," Mr. McManus was having a good go at Mr. Riggelsworth.

"Eight years I worked for you," defended Mr. Riggelsworth. That Mr. Riggelsworth, he's a good man. Not many women can see it in him, because of his rough complexion. Chickenpox had left his face scarred and cratered. His features make many women uneasy; they often step back from him, tighten their muscles and hold their breath. But all types of men know that Mr. Riggelsworth is a top man - someone you could truly count on.

"You stole from me, so *you* don't come around *here* ever again. Never Riggels. Never! You hear me? I'll call the sheriff. You'll see. You'll be locked rrright up. Slam-click."

"I didn't steal a dang thing and you know it," Mr. Riggelsworth stepped forward, losing his composure. The Dunce Brothers, then stepped forward as well, doing what they're paid to do. "I'll tell the sheriff what you're doing here. I ain't scared of you, or you two neither, I'll…"

That's when Rudy let out an excited bark, ran in two small circles like he was chasing his own tail and bolted to the Boone boys covered in snow.

Mr. McManus brought his voice down and his white-gloved finger up.

"You say one word and you know that'll be the last word you're ever gonna say. You too, Pete! You say one word and I'll get both of you locked up, slam-click. You go on and put *that* on your conscience then, Riggels. See how *that* jacket fits. Now get off my property. Get!" Mr. McManus turned to Pete who was now looking up at the Boone boys. "You, hire someone, anyone. First man who comes looking for work. Hire 'em. Today Pete! Get it done!" With that Mr. McManus checked the time on his pocket watch, shook it, groaned, snapped it shut and stepped into his Duisenberg – the only car other than the sheriff's in all of Hamilton, mind you. Lloyd got behind the wheel as Elmer began to push, to give the Duisenberg some traction in the new morning snow.

The boys approached with Rudy smiling.

"Johnny and Billy Boone, the famous Boone boys," said Pete proudly trying to disguise the argument.

"Hey Pete, hey Mr. Riggelsworth," the boys spoke under scarves.

"Hey boys. Well…I'll be seeing ya, Pete. So long pal," said Mr. Riggelsworth under his breath as he sadly headed down Bridge Street.

Pete shook his head watching Mr. Riggelsworth make his way up to town. Pete knew there was nothing he could say and he knew that Mr. Riggelsworth wouldn't for a second allow Pete to do anything for him anyway. It was just another recurring injustice that the men of these times were getting used to. Pete turned to the boys.

"You boys coming by later? Be looking for new parts for building that Spaceship then?"

"*Battle Cruiser,*" Johnny corrected.

"Battle Cruiser that is. Mm hm. It'll be fast as anything," cadenced Pete back.

"Naw, can't, Ma said we gotta do things. Maybe tomorrow. That'd be okay with you Pete, we comin' by tomorrow and all?" Johnny asked.

"That'd be fine. I'll be here. I'll search with ya." Pete loved the Boone boys. He thought Johnny was becoming a fine craftsman. He'd build all types of "flying spacecrafts" and "underwater space-submarines". Johnny and his gang would come by the junkyard every weekend with just a comic strip torn out from the *Worcester Evening Gazette* of Buck Rogers' newest spaceship. Johnny would go into the junkyard and build it as best he could. His ships would have oil cans for rocket boosters, ironing boards for wings, old phone receivers for radio communication. He even found his gang old leather football helmets and goggles to wear as their space/underwater suits (that all depended on if the ship was to explore deep space or the deep ocean). Yes, Pete thought, Johnny was becoming a fine builder.

Billy, well, even though he was the youngest of the gang by about two years, Pete thought him the wisest of the lot. Billy had a knack for noticing things, things other people would never see. He's perceptive. An observer. Often Pete will hear Billy's little wise words, under the gang's commotion, but the rest of the gang usually just ignores Billy, just because he's younger. Billy is a very bright boy if you'd take the time to listen. Pete was curious where that talent would take Billy one day.

Top to bottom, Pete liked them Boone boys. He enjoyed their visits. And he thought it damn rotten their Papa never came back.

Brushing the snow off, Kringle looked up to see the most peculiar looking home. A small barn, probably once used to store a tractor or bound hay, sat shyly up a small rise, almost embarrassed of itself, hidden among a few adolescent trees. The front entrance to the barn had been clearly enclosed by a different type of timber. A proper sized door with a screen door was built in the new wall, making the barn now a home. A modest but charming porch was also built out from the new entrance, giving it a more cottage look. But the porch looked dubious to stand on. All its railings were a bit crooked, Kringle thought, but brushed the thought of feeling he was being an over-analyzing carpenter. One of the front windows was small, the other was of normal size and both windows were slightly uneven with one another. A questionable chimney pipe that looked as if it could come down from one great gust poked out of the rooftop. Kringle tilted his head because the entire home, save the porch, seemed to be sinking to the left. And the porch to the right.

The house fascinated Kringle. He loved all its different colors. The red barn, the new yellow front, the orange door, the one blue and one blue-purple front window frames with the multi-colored planks that made up the porch; the home brought a new talent to the idea of quirkiness. It all made Kringle smile. The house looked fun. Happy. He headed toward the home.

Ellie was just locking the front door; she was about to start her mile long walk to work.

"Miss! Say Miss!" shouted Kringle.

Startled, Ellie turned around. She squinted her eyes, puckered her lips, caught sight of Kringle, then rolled her eyes. She did not have time for an out-of-work, nagging man.

Kringle approached the bottom of the porch.

"She sure is something swell," Kringle said, shaking his head back and forth.

"Excuse me?"

"Oh, um, the home, I mean. This home you got here. She's something swell. She's a doozie all right. You do all that work on it, Miss?"

"My husband and myself."

"Wow. Sure is something," Kringle repeated looking around and behind Ellie. "Nice work you two done. Different than I've seen". He then put a hand on the porch rail to test its durability. It was strong. His thoughts of it being wobbly were wrong. Kringle started ascending the porch. "Well I just…"

"Excuse me!" Ellie said sharply and then took a big breath up into her chest, stood up straight and put her hands on her hips. Kringle stepped down and took his hands off the porch rail. He then took off his hat, combed his hair with his fingers and held his hat in front of himself like he was at church.

"Pardon me, Ma'am, I just come…"

"Is there something I can help you with? Because I have to get to work now and my husband inside don't like strangers lurking around, startling his wife, especially ones dressed like a lost fireman. That what you are? You a lost fireman?"

"No Ma'am." Kringle looked at himself and noticed how much red he did have on and how most of his clothes did have burn marks. "No, I'm not a fireman Ma'am, I'm a carpenter." Kringle pointed to his unimpressive tool belt. "See, I just come off that train, the train that just come by. And I…"

"You jump off that train?"

"Well, yes I did. I jumped off it, Ma'am."

"Lordy, lord. Billy, Billy Boone," Ellie murmured to herself, shook her head back and forth while she blinked slowly, then said a bit louder, "Well then you better not be train robber."

"Oh no Ma'am. I…I just came to town today, hoping to find work. Was wondering if you knew if there was any, um, well, work around here, around these parts?"

"Work's tough these days," Ellie said as she tied her babushka up under her chin and started down the steps.

"Yes it is, Ma'am."

Ellie kept up her stern posture. When she reached the bottom of the porch, she took a pause to look Kringle square in the eyes. Ellie was now keen on seeing the seed of undependability inside a man.

Kringle stayed silent. *This woman was as original as her home*, he thought.

Face to face, the pause continued.

Getting a better look at this stranger Ellie noticed how his attentive eyes and almost boyish smile made her uneasy; she didn't like it. Kringle noticed this woman's long red velvet jacket with white puffy cuffs and thought she looked like a starlet. Ellie didn't understand how this man could have so many burn marks on his boots, pants and jacket and not be a fireman; *he must be a klutz*, she thought. Kringle could tell this woman didn't have the best eyesight, because she kept squinting and puckering her lips while sussing him out; *they were very kissable lips*, he thought. Ellie didn't like his hair or hat. Kringle liked how she had bags in her boots to keep her feet dry – *thrifty*, he thought. Ellie didn't like that they were both wearing the same color. Kringle liked that she had two scarves, the yellow one for the inside of her jacket and the green one for the outside – *inventive*. He didn't look responsible to her. Kringle could tell a smart woman when he saw one. *Why was he just standing so quiet?* she wondered. *Her eyes are bluer than most blue eyes*, Kringle noted as he followed the falling flakes reflecting in them. Ellie didn't like him. Kringle thought she was something swell.

"Mm, well…" Ellie pointed north to Pete's junkyard just down the little rise, easily visible from her home. "Well, I don't know if they need work or not. I mean I'm not the all seeing whatever you call it, but there's a man there, Pete's his name. Good man. Honest. He has one fella working along with him, maybe they need another."

"Just there?"

"Just there. It's the town dump, but work's work and Pete, well, you go give him an ask. If he don't have work maybe he can help you just the same. Gettin' work's tough these days. Now *I'm* gonna be late 'cause of *you*. So you head down that path there. Town is that-a-way. One mile. And don't be hanging around here; my husband will have the itch to shoot at you if you be hanging about."

Kringle put his hat back on, slung his sack back over his shoulder and did a clumsy half bow to Ellie. "I appreciate it Miss, you're a kind one. And you got a lovely home too."

Ellie rolled her eyes. Kringle put out his hand. "Name is Kringle, Kris Kringle Ma'am."

Ellie squinted her eyes and shook his hand quickly then said,
"Boone, *Mrs.* Boone."

The snowfall had lightened. A new white layer covered the junkyard making the grounds look as if you were coming upon Shackleton's Arctic sinking ship. Different angles and edges now coated white, hued bright, lit from the emerging sunlight. Kringle moved with a straight-line of vision. The day was proving to have promise the higher the Sun rose.

Ahead, Kringle saw a man lifting things that looked to be heavy for him and, by the size of the objects, they looked heavy for most men. The man turned around, sensing his approach.

Pete dropped the old basin he was moving down to a pile for plumbing supplies, clapped the snow off his gloves, let out a tired breath and waited for the distant man to approach.

Kringle dropped his red sack on the cushioning snow.

"Alright," said Pete, to get the man talking.

"Well hi-ya, name's Kringle, Kris Kringle," Kringle took off his glove for a handshake, then Pete as well.

"Pete Smit. Nice to meet ya."

"Oh good, you're Pete. Nice to meet *you*, Pete."

"What can I do ya for, Mr. Kringle?"

"Oh Kris is fine, some people call me Kringle too. Both fine."

"Alright."

"I just come from Mr. Boone's house just there and…"

"Mr. Boone's not around no more, that there is Miss Boone's place. Yup, I know the one."

"Oh, okay, um, Miss Boone's place, right. Well, I come off the morning train there, head up to her home, Miss Boone's home, ask her if she knew 'bout any work around this town. She said to come look for you, Pete, ask you if you knew of any work. I'm a good worker. Solid worker."

"Alright, I see. Ya good with your hands?"

"I am. I'm a carpenter. I can build, make anything really."

"Well, then you're hired Mr. Kringle. Kringle I mean."

"I am? Well what do ya know about that? Thank you Pete Smit, truly," said Kringle and the two men shook hands once again. "What's the job?"

Pete looked over the junkyard, then back at Kringle and said, "We make everything people want."

As all men and women knew during these times, if you were lucky enough to get a job, then you started right away. Pete and Kringle walked the junkyard side by side.

"I first sort it so it's easier to find things. That pile, that's just junk, can't do much with that, and that pile there is what I'm sorting through - plumbing parts. That's a few car parts, that's home things, like, ah, furniture, bed frames, busted bureaus, desks, that kind of stuff." Pete went on pointing to each pile.

It was an open field filled with piles of sorted junk. Some piles had blankets or tarps over them, which Kringle assumed was because of the falling snow. Other piles were buried in white. Five busted bureaus lined up, four cracked sinks lined up, four bathtubs lined up; it was all well organized.

"We fix things up?" Kringle asked.

"Well, I'll be gettin' to that," Pete said as he picked up an old shoe that was poking out of the snow, then held it to his foot. "What size shoe are ya?"

"Eight and a half."

"I'm a nine, let me know if you find a nine. This looks like a seven." Holding the shoe, Pete headed toward a small shack. "I assume by you being new in town you need a roof with a bed too, that right?" Pete asked.

"I would, I mean I do, yes." Kringle knew to feel lucky to have met Pete. He tried to show Pete that by being attentive, short-spoken and polite.

As the two men entered Pete's small shack, Pete dropped the shoe in a barrel outside the door filled with old shoes.

"Well, I call this, The Workshop," said Pete proudly.

The Workshop was warm inside. It was small; a simple place. The smell of fresh sawdust came upon entering. There were two workbenches against opposite walls. In between them was a small table. "I work here, you'll work there. And when we're done, you just spin your stool around and look - dinner table, card table. Right there." Pete let out the first laugh and the first smile.

Kringle noticed Pete's eyes first. They were green and watery. They gave off a mystical sense. He didn't have a jacket; he had layers of sweaters on to keep himself warm. His overalls were worn. He had two different shoes on – one black boot and one loafer that looked to have once been a Sunday service shoe. The loafer was split at the sole and flopping. His brown leather brimmed hat had grease stains all around it, but looked comfortable to wear. Pete seemed to be a young man, yet his grey whiskers and hair also made him look to be a bit older. He had a calm posture. He seemed very comfortable and committed to each place he stood. But it was those green eyes that really told Pete's story. You'd never forget those watery green eyes. They were mystical.

The two men sat down at their workbenches and turned their stools to face the small table and one another. Kringle could feel the small shack tilt and bend by the subtlest of movement.

"I have the bed on the right, left one's yours." Opposite the entrance were two old war cots pressed against the wall. A window between the beds rayed in dull sunlight. Sawdust floated in its rays. Between the two cots was a heap of blankets - *probably for a dog to sleep*, Kringle thought. "We get paid for each item we make. Our boss, his name is Mr. McManus, is a bit more than just a bit of a bastard – you should know that. Fancy type man. He makes a list from people down in the city, things they want and we make what's written on the list he gives us. Simple. Here's what I'm working on."

Pete handed Kringle a folded piece of paper.

It read:

> *High Boy (flat top)*
> *Cabriolet Chair (gold trim, white fabric)*
> *Cage Chairs X4 (Swiss Alps Region)*
> *Swiss Buffet (200 cm high, 173 cm wide)*

"Cage chair, Swiss buffet, this is overseas furniture; deluxe stuff. So we make replicas then?" asked Kringle as he handed the note back to Pete.

"Not exactly," Pete said as he took off his hat and set it down on his workbench and then scratched his head with both hands. "I mean, yes we do, but…well, let's start with this, you a church man, Kringle?"

"Sure," responded Kringle as he followed suit and placed his red hat on his new workbench as well.

"Well, what we do ain't exactly…it's, well…what I mean is…shoot, let me tell you like this. Mr. McManus he owns a furniture store downtown, see? It's got a French name for it - *Bonne Affaire*. Well, that's where most of what we make goes to be sold off. Mr. McManus also has us do specialty jobs, orders from rich types that live down in Boston, Cambridge. That's what this list is. So, Mr. McManus goes and tells people that he knows all these fancy folks over across the big ocean in Europe. Places like Switzerland and France. It's a lie. Mr. McManus don't know any European folk. He goes and pretends that what we make for him is from there. Says he gets shipments off a boat that come down on the train line. He then goes and marks the price up more than a hundred times what it should be. Maybe more. He makes a king's fortune I tell yah. Them rich people, they think they're getting fancy stuff when it really just be stuff me and…well, the man who's job you be taking, make, from this here junkyard. It's wrong; I know. That's why I asked if you're a church man."

"What happened to the man before me? If you don't mind me asking?" asked Kringle.

"Oh, well, me and Riggels, that's him, we be dropping off some pieces to the store, *Bonne Affaire*. Riggels sees a friend of his with his wife. Just so you know, I wouldn't be telling this story around town. Ya?"

"I won't tell it."

"Anyways, they're looking at a crib, she's pregnant you see, and the crib they be looking at Riggels made, made it right there. So Riggels' friend's wife wanted that crib bad, really centered on it and all, but the price, the price was way too big for any normal man. Riggles whispered to his friend not to buy it and that he'll make him one just like it. Riggels be saving that man. Saving the family if you ask me. Anyway, the manager, Miss Winkelplex, scary woman, reminds me of some kind of mean, sick bird. I'd tip-toe around her if I was you. Well, she overheard Riggels whisperin."

"She told Mr. McManus," Kringle added.

"She told Mr. McManus, that's right. Mr. McManus fired Riggels. Done it today. Done it 'bout an hour before I seen you. Threatened Riggs with jail time even. Slam-click."

"Lord."

"Lord is right. Psst. You still want the job?" Pete laughed and smirked in a way that only hard working men do to communicate – "It ain't right, but that's what it is."

"I need it."

"I know you do. Same with me. Okay then. You can use that trunk for your belongings. And the basin is just there. You said you're good with your hands then, ya?"

"I am. My father was a carpenter. He taught me."

"You got specialties? I'm mostly a furniture maker as you could guess. Hat racks to bookshelves; bureaus to beds. I can replicate, like you were sayin', just about anything."

Kringle sat up straight on his stool, smiled and said, "I make toys."

Hamilton, Massachusetts shares in the start of America. It's a place where the first settlers' graves are still visited and their flowers are always replaced. It's a place where a man can remember his grandfather who told him stories about fighting in the Civil War and who *his* father heard family stories from the Revolutionary War. It's where every road was a horse path first; a town that is home to many heirs of the first settlers. Hamilton, like her small cousin towns beside her, is the heart of New England, which paved the way for America. Like many New England towns, Hamilton did bear lackadaisical men and women, but not many. And they too chipped in, more so than those who are driven, born from lackadaisical lands. Hamilton is an American town that was built on merit alone.

Hamilton is also filled with children. These children mold themselves after their hard working parents and often try out the same strong language they've heard *them* use.

"Heeey what's the big idea? Put your paws down, Charlene. I ain't gonna hit no twisted dame," hollered Johnny Boone standing in a circle of kids at recess.

"I'll knock ya, pally. You wet sock! You grease ball! You…you! And don't think I won't! I'll punch your head! Now put you're dukes up you sissy egg! Put 'em up! You flop! You…you! C'mon then!"

Johnny Boone was knee deep in an all too often, screaming match with his nemesis Charlene McManus. Mr. McManus had twin girls – Marlene and Charlene. Charlene was an outspoken spoiled menace; Marlene was fairly quiet. Marlene could always be found standing right by her spitfire of a sister Charlene waiting for a cue. Even though Marlene didn't join in her sister's daily arguments, her quiet presence gave Charlene more clout. Day in and day out, Charlene was verbally setting fire to something. The most mysterious happening with Charlene though, was that for some reason, she never liked the Boone boys - Johnny Boone to be specific.

Like always, Marlene and Charlene were dressed alike. They had on grey wool winter jackets, buttoned to their necks, black scarves, black gloves, black boots with black buckles and black bonnets tied with a bow. The two stood before the gang, challenging them to a one-on-one sled race down Patton's Hill, a month preceding the town's official Red Robin Race down Robin's Hill. The whole school of twenty-two tatterdemalion children were standing around them listening to the challenge.

"Awe tell it to Sweeny. And put those meat hooks down you...you... Dumb Dora," hollered Murf, and all the kids readjusted to get a better look. Murf was chubbier than the rest of the kids at school and a bit shorter. He always wore red overalls with a red and white-checkered scarf in his back pocket to wipe his brow if he got himself over heated. Some people think he always wore those red overalls because that's all that the entire county had that could fit his size. He looked like a snowman without the middle piece. Murf had one missing front tooth and often felt the gap with his tongue and fingers for the incoming tooth's progress. He had brown hair that was always sticking up like a street urchin and always said, "We'll show 'em," under his breath like his father says to his mother after talking about something important.

Murf got his schoolyard reputation for being the toughest of them all just last year. Marlene and Charlene were giving Ramona a run through about her height. They were razzing her about if she ate the leaves off the trees like they saw giraffes doing in an African safari photo their teacher, Miss Magnolia, had tacked up that morning. Murf, not being very agile, stepped forward to defend Ramona, but tripped on an old birch tree's root and crashed into Charlene. His head slammed right into her nose. Knocked his front loose tooth right out. Everyone thought he did it on purpose. Even the gang did. From that day on everyone at school mistook Murf's extra weight as pure muscle. He was considered the roughest, toughest guy in school. "Strongman" - some of the kids called him.

After Murf shouted for Charlene to "put her meat hooks down," she took a step back and brought her hands right down. Then she scowled something ugly at Johnny. Ramona, standing with the rest of the gang, gave Murf a nod and a smirk as she now does after the day he defended her. Ramona is one of the guys. She wears a pair of denim britches to match Murf's overalls. She's got long red pigtails and her face and body are covered with a sprinkle of orange freckles - another reason Marlene and Charlene call her "giraffe". She had the worst mouth of the lot. Spat a lot. And her mother and father, Mr. and Mrs. Grey, were right off the boat Irish, and hadn't calmed their speech down yet. Mr. Grey used to clean up at the local restaurant but got fired because of a complaint Mr. McManus had about the way he spoke, a year past. "That is not what English sounds like," he said. Now the Greys eat mostly by their garden in the warm months and by hunting small varmints in the winter ones. It's said that Mrs. Grey's father was a well-to-do businessman in metals back in Ireland. But Mr. Grey was a proud man and told his wife's father he was going to go to America and make his own money. Mrs. Grey didn't mind that though, her side of the family always took a shine to men who stood against the world. That's why Ramona takes a shine to Murf. And Ramona, like everyone else, was certain Murf popped Charlene on purpose that day - for her. Since then Ramona always tried to stand or sit close to Murf. He became her champion that day.

"We best split. The bell's g-g-onna ring soon, we b-best break th-this up or Miss M-Magnolia w-w-w-will…w-w-w-will, well who knows, but sh-she'll be up-s-set," stuttered Terrance, the nervous one in the gang. Terrance McKool wore his pants up to his ribs like his father. And like his father, had a stutter, poor eyesight, big glasses, a frail body and gaunt cheeks. Mr. McKool works at the town pharmacy. His mother, who spoke mostly with smiles and head nods, was pregnant, but helped out at the pharmacy as well. You didn't see the McKools that often, that is unless you visited the pharmacy. They were very quiet, almost fearful people.

"Ahh bah, your sled don't have a chance anyhow. Made from junk. Made from scrap-trash. Ahh, you're just bumping gums Johnny Boone," said Charlene looking straight with a narrow squint into Johnny Boone's big blue eyes.

"Oh yah? Friday! Patton's Hill! We'll race your crummy Flexible Flier," challenged Johnny Boone. "It's on!"

The crowd of kids all erupted in cheers. Winter was getting boring and they all needed some excitement.

"FINE!" said Charlene. "Let's go, Marlene, we don't need to be talking with these wet socks." With that the bell sounded and the two girls spun around and stomped back to the classroom.

"FINE!" hollered Johnny back.

"We'll show 'em," murmured Murf to the gang with a wink.

"Okay class sit-sit, sit-sit. Like I said we are going to finish up the last of the oral reports," said young Miss Magnolia as she stepped close to the front row of desks and pointed at every student not yet seated. "Down-down; sit down. Yes you too. Down we go. Alice, turn, scoot. There we are. Aaand fine."

Miss Magnolia sure was pretty. She had a light frame and seemed to always have sunlight on her cheeks. Her healthy long hair was always wrapped in different ways and slung over her left shoulder. Miss Magnolia wore the same five dresses in rotation, but they were nice dresses. Colorful. She had a small one-bedroom apartment above the post office. The town had fixed her up that space quick after Mr. McManus fired the old teacher, Mr. Cook, saying something about him being a Communist. Miss Magnolia wasn't even fully a teacher yet. She was living a few towns over in Salem studying to earn her teaching degree when she was asked by the Hamilton school board to come in for an interview. Miss Magnolia still doesn't know who recommended her. She was only in her third year. But that didn't matter. The town thinks she's lovely. All the parents in Hamilton appreciate Miss Magnolia and are extra kind to her when they see her sitting outside the post office reading. Miss Magnolia can't believe how delightfully people treat her; she's not even sure she's teaching correctly.

"Johnny Boone, please step forward and speak to the class," instructed Miss Magnolia as she took her seat. "And please Johnny Boone, take off your hat and lose that straw of yours." There were four things Johnny emulated from his father after seeing a photo of him posed, leaning like a proud young man against the front of the school with a few other men who helped build the new addition. Those four things were: he always wore his father's old boots, always wore his father's old beat-up tan newsy cap and often chewed on a straw like his father was doing in the photo. The fourth thing was that Johnny looked quite like his father, and all the girls in class thought him something handsome.

As Johnny walked to the front of the classroom all of the girls' eyes followed. They were wide-eyed and smiling. Lashes fanned slowly. Breaths were let out heavy. All but Charlene, she had her mouth in a pucker, head down, eyes up and arms crossed.

Johnny Boone cleared his throat and began, "Betsy Ross is a great American because…"

*

Mr. Riggelsworth joined the men who walked up and down Commonwealth Street looking for work. A few years back, Commonwealth Street was pretty still during work hours, but now with so many men looking for jobs, the "Pacers", as they were called, walked up and down Commonwealth Street, day in and day out waiting for any 'Help Wanted' sign to be posted.

Mr. Riggelsworth peeked into shop windows with his hands cold in his pockets.

Coming up on the Police Station, Mr. Riggelsworth saw Sheriff Jones scratching his head, standing in front of his police car.

"Problem Sheriff?" Mr. Riggelsworth started.

"Dang thing won't even pretend to start. Been trying everything. Now I think I've flooded it. I checked the radiator, the oil, the battery, everything. I think she's just dead."

Mr. Riggelsworth knows cars. Machines were his specialty in the junkyard. He took a step back and inspected Sheriff Jones' car like it was the *Mona Lisa.* He walked around it scratching his chin and giving it looks as if wanting a confession out of her.

The sheriff went on.

"I parked outside of the garage during the storm last night."

"I saw you did," said Mr. Riggelsworth.

"Yah, I knew I shouldn't have. I just thought it'd save some time shoveling out my parking spot if I had it out."

Mr. Riggelsworth continued circling the car. A few Pacers stopped, because men often like to gather when they are bored.

"Car broke, sheriff?" asked one of the Pacers, but Sheriff Jones didn't have time to respond to the always-bountiful suggestions of bored men.

They began…

"Probably the battery."

"Got gas in it? Check that did ya sheriff?"

"Maybe you got gloppy oil."

"No, I bet it's the battery."

"I heard sometimes these models just die. Boom. One day – dead."

The suggestions from the Pacers continued. Sheriff Jones just kept his eye on Mr. Riggelsworth as he leaned over near the gas tank.

"Say how long this hinge been like this sheriff?" The latch covering the gas line was faulty and didn't shut properly.

Sheriff Jones hustled over to Mr. Riggelsworth followed by the whispering Pacers. "Oh ya that. Um, well that's been a bit stubborn for 'bout a few weeks now."

"Weeks?!" Mr. Rigglesworth said surprised and then knelt by the small hinge.

"Yah, about three," answered Sheriff Jones, embarrassed among the judging Pacers.

All the men knelt behind Mr. Riggelsworth.

"Well, you see here?" Mr. Riggelworth pointed to the gas tank. "Dented. This latch, as you know, won't lock now. It's easily fixable. But ice, see, has built up all around here and inside here, near the cap. You say you kept it out during the storm. Well, I'm not the kind of man to say I know all, but…" Mr. Riggelsworth knew he was right, he was just being polite to Sheriff Jones in front of the crowd of kneeling Pacers. "I'd say some water from the snow leaked in your gas tank, here sheriff. Maybe even some frozen water in the fuel line. That's possible."

All the Pacers grumbled to one another about how they had said the same.

"Dang it all. I knew I should'a had that fixed," admitted Sheriff Jones.

"I'd siphon that gas out to be safe and toss a hot water bottle over the fuel line to melt any possible ice inside. Then siphon that as well."

The Pacers grumbled in agreement as everyone stood back up.

"Okay. Sure thing. Will do. And I'll fix that latch up. Say, thanks Riggels," said Sheriff Jones.

"Welcome sheriff. Ma always said I was good in a jam."

And with that everyone dispersed, each man taking credit for the evaluation and everyone, save the sheriff, went back to pacing up and down Commonwealth Street.

✳

"Woo-wee, I'm just sayin', you are luck-key my darling girl. Whoosh, you still got me all scared and fidgeting all over this place. I'll say it again, you be one luck-key ho-ney-bee. I mean it Ellie girl, if she caught you being so late, you would'a been hung like drippin' laundry. Oo-oo, I'm-a need to sit down again."

Taking a seat on a false French art deco bridge chair, Florence Anne Miller, known to the town as Flo, took an elegant Southern pose sporting her West Virginia smile. Flo moved to New England when she was twenty because she couldn't stand her rich family's politics any longer. She told her Daddy she was gonna go to Harvard University and be one of those "clever Yankees" like her father would always cuss out at the dinner table when politics was the burning topic. And Flo's father was not using "clever" in any good sense mind you. Flo never did go to Harvard, but she sure is a Yankee now and she sure is clever.

"Oh, I know, Flo, I know. Now stop making it such a *such to do* already," Ellie was repositioning the furniture. She was happy Miss Winkelplex wasn't in yet because she was two minutes late. Being late was a big deal to Miss Winkelplex. Even if you were on time, that counted as being late. You had to be at least five minutes early to be on time. Miss Winkelplex once timed how long it took Ellie and Flo to take off their jackets and hats when they came into work and told them, "I don't pay you girls to change your clothes. You both be in position with jackets off by eight o'clock." That never made too much sense to the girls because no one came into the shop before ten.

"I just do not think Miss Winkelplex would believe that a fireman went and jumped off a speeding train to ask little old *you* for a job. You must have a guardian angel or somethin', my beautiful friend." Flo sat with her legs crossed with one of her elbows cupped in the palm of her other hand. She had quit smoking cigarettes just a few days ago, but still pantomimed the habit. While watching her fidgety friend slightly reposition the furniture displayed on the show room floor, Flo took long drags of an invisible cigarette and politely blew the pretend smoke to her side. Ellie and Flo were best friends - real best friends. They had the kind of relationship girls have with one another when they're young, before they notice boys and learn to be tactful women. Flo always wore dresses with bright flowers on them. She had a skip to her step and always swung her left arm as she walked. Flo had an all around bounce to her. Her short red curls were tight curls that stopped just at her shoulders. They almost looked like she had sprongy tentacles coming down off her head. She never cussed, but would often re-shape cuss words and used her own language to express herself: *Hell = Big Helpings, Damn = Dancing,* that sort of thing. She had luscious lips and bang-snap hips. And had sharp devilish eyebrows and a sharp devilish smile. If Flo heard any exciting or mischievous news, she'd bite her bottom lip while smiling, raise those pointy eyebrows and say, "Well, break a dish and kiss a frog."

"Why you still so jumpy, you done didn't get caught. You're safe. Everything's Jake," said Flo as she threw her invisible cigarette on the floor and stamped it out.

The front door bell chimed and Miss Winkelplex exploded into *Bonne Affaire.*

"Flo, sweep the front! You girls shoveled, I see that, bravo-bravo, that alone is front-page news, but how many times do I have to explain to you? You don't stop there. You need to *keep sweeping* the snow that continues to fall. Let's try *this time* to remember that, shall we girls?" blasted Miss Winkelplex.

Flo grabbed the broom, looked out the window and said, "I don't believe it is snowing anymore Miss Winkel…"

"Lord girls don't question me, we are not in court; I saw a patch of snow. Sweep it," Miss Winkelplex began to take off her long fur coat, scarf, fur hat and slammed down her briefcase. Then she continued under her breath, "I go and almost slip and break *my* neck and this Southern dingy dingbat of a girl tells me that it's not snowing. Lord, please save me. Please Lord? Please?"

Once outside Flo noticed the path was clean and there wasn't a flake coming down any longer. She swept the path anyhow.

"Okay Ellie, tsk-tsk, this way." Miss Winkelplex pulled out five official documents. "Okay, here are the Letters of Authenticity for the new inventory. As you can see they are signed and stamped by all the distributors and all the craftsmen. Mr. McManus will be by later today to sign here and here on each document. Then you stamp "approved" here, on each."

"Yes, Ma'am. I know. I will," said Ellie as she took Miss Winkelplex's things to hang up. Ellie knew how to fill out the documents; she did them every week.

Mr. McManus' and Miss Winkelplex's racket was meticulously detailed. Mr. McManus would type false Letters of Authenticity at his home, then Miss Winkelplex would sign them with fake names and stamp them with fake crests counterfeiting that the letters came from Europe. Miss Winkelplex had much better handwriting and could fake many more different signature styles than Mr. McManus. The two swindling partners knew that the more details their fake imported furniture company had; the fewer questions about it would arise. "Keep the people busy with tasks and complications and they won't have the time or energy left to question us," explained Mr. McManus to Miss Winkelplex. And after five years, no one had questioned them. The two dishonest merchants had become quite rich in these hard times. Quite rich.

Two days a week Miss Winkelplex would take a train and a few trolleys into Boston and Cambridge, to rub elbows with potential buyers. Over decadent luncheons she'd consult these buyers on what exactly they would like to furnish their fortunate homes with. She'd mesmerize buyers with stories about her many made up romantic villages in Europe, where their nonexistent craftsmen lived and crafted for only a special few. Miss Winkelplex would speak of heart-warming old men who worked endlessly with great skill and care to bring these one-of-a-kind pieces of home art to select, elite Americans. She'd say, "It's their darling little dreams to share their true art with us. It makes them feel important. How simply beautiful, don't you think?" She wines and dines, coos and woos her potential buyers into very profitable sales.

The orders are then brought back to Mr. McManus who then puts Pete to work on them. Once Pete is finished, Mr. McManus tells Miss Winkelplex to let her buyers know that their order has finally come in by boat and is packed on a train and will be ready for pick up soon. In between orders, Pete is instructed to make other replicas of European furniture to fill *Bonne Affaire's* showroom and meet the demand of the weekend buyers that come up from the city to see the hidden gem furniture shop.

It's detailed, it's all the rage and it's a lie.

The Sun had proved her strength. High in the sky she burned through the passing clouds. Her rays bestowed upon the overexposed white snow. Once hidden squirrels and rabbits emerged cautiously and sniffed the melting air. Tree limbs began to drip rainbow droplets. There were many new worlds, in many new puddles.

Kringle and Pete both pulled long sleds down Bridge Street. The sleds carried new pieces of replica European furniture; each piece wrapped in big red sacks.

"See, my folks, they had eight kids. I'm the oldest of seven younger sisters. My folks both worked hard for us kids, but never had the left over lettuce to pay for any toys for the girls. All my parents' folded green went to food, clothes, mortgage, taxes," explained Kringle.

"Mm hm," answered Pete.

The two men were just passing Little Island Pond, half way to Commonwealth Street. They had a natural conversational pace. Similar souls.

"So my Daddy tells me, 'son make the girls some toys would yah?' So I did. But the thing about seven sisters is, you can't just go and make one toy and just hand it to one of them. It'd be skirt riot."

"Sure would."

"So what I would have to do is make them all separately something special and give it to them all at once."

"Mm hm, smart man Kringle. No riot then. A birthday for everyone."

"It don't even stop there, 'cause you gotta make sure each doll, toy or what have you is of equal quality or the girls will fight over the best one. So I'd really have to think about what each sister would like most. I'd tell them to write down a dream gift for themselves and we'd put that note in the fireplace cauldron. I'd tell my little sisters that their words would go up with the smoke and travel to a place where wishes are answered. That the smoke would spell out the words they write over the night sky, lit by the Moon himself."

"You are a creative man you are Kringle. I like it. That is definitely a bit of what it's all made of right there. 'Lit by the Moon himself', I like that."

"Yah they loved it; each one of my little sis's is a slice of something sweet."

"Go on then. Then what?"

The two men reached the end of Bridge Street and rounded the corner, starting down Commonwealth Street. The Sun was burning bright; she was compelled to hold the grim winter back.

"Well, for each gift to be right, it'd take me most of the year to craft all seven. And truthfully, I did fourteen, each girl getting two in case one wasn't what she was truly hoping for. Avoid them tears ya know? Then I'd give them the gifts on the coldest, darkest winter night when their spirits were at their lowest. That day, like no other day, would brighten the whole family up. My Daddy would be mighty grateful, my Mum too. He'd say, 'That a boy.'"

"Your sisters know it was you?"

"Oh no, no, no. See I thought about that. Lord, if they knew it was me making them dolls and such, then they'd go and be asking me to make more and more and even more! I know my sisters well. Sweet, but smart; they'd never stop hounding me. So no, I told them that an elf must have brought 'em. I said, an elf far away must have read their notes written in smoke on the parchment of the sky, lit by the big round star; he must have jotted down their wishes, made them their toys, then come in the night and leave 'em by the fireplace. I called the elf - the Little Red Man."

"That's nice Kringle. I like that too," Pete was smiling, caught up in the tale.

"It was nice yah. It sure was. My little sisters are swell girls; they love that day of the year more than all their favorite days of the year combined. So what about you Pete, you got any loves other than making furniture?"

"I do, I do. I got a fine dog named Rudy. He's a good helper. He fetches things I need in the yard."

"You don't say?"

The two men walked in the middle of the road. You could follow their fresh sled tracks for miles. The Pacers would stop to look at the two men hauling their big red sacks up Commonwealth. They were envious of the work.

"Yup, I'll go 'Rudy boy, you get me a plank this big boy', or 'Rudy you go and get me a piece this big', he'll go and fetch. Bring it right back to me."

"I don't believe it."

"It's the truth, I taught him. Rudy's a smart boy. Can't seem to find a size nine shoe though. I can also play the guitar some. The blues. Uppity-blues. I enjoy that something, well, something big I guess."

"You don't say? Well I play something of a harmonica myself."

"Truth's truth?"

"Sure do. I used to listen to the radio and play along to Blind Willie Johnson until, well, until I recently hit the rails."

"That's fine, that's fine. Blind Willie Johnson sure can play."

Kringle and Pete started their friendship like most men do – naturally. They sure did have similar souls.

Bonne Affaire's door chimes rang and all three ladies' heads turned with a smile. Once Miss Winkelplex saw it wasn't a customer, but actually Pete with his hat in his hands, her smile immediately dropped and her orders burst out.

"Flo, go make room by the front window for three new pieces; we'll put the other two in the back. They're getting picked up Friday. Ellie, help the boys not scratch or bang anything. And don't you track any snow in here boys. You hear me?" Miss Winkelplex headed to the back to make room for the incoming furniture to be picked up that Friday.

"Yes, Miss Winkelplex, no tracking no snow," responded Pete.

"Got a few new orders do yah Pete?" asked Ellie approaching Pete to welcome him and help who she thought was Mr. Riggelsworth holding a chair over his face, approaching the door.

"Hello, Ellie. Yes Ma'am, I have four orders; eight pieces", Pete handed Ellie the order.

"Okay, we'll be putting the high boy and buffet to the back for pick up and the cage chairs and cabriolet can go by Flo there," helped Ellie.

The unseen man holding a cabriolet chair entered. Pete took the chair from him. "I believe you two have met already?" said Pete to Ellie.

Ellie and Kringle were left standing eye to eye in front of one another.

"Why sure Mrs. Boone. Sure, her and me are old friends," charmed Kringle. Kringle knew not to say, "Miss" instead of "Mrs." until he was instructed with the correct way for him to address her, he'd stick with what she told him. Flo curiously looked over hearing the mistake and new voice. Pete walked the cabriolet over to the section Flo had opened up near the front window.

"We are not old friends," corrected Ellie. "We are strangers who happen to be seeing one another again."

"Strangers?" questioned Kringle. "But Mrs. Boone you gone and got me a job. Pete gave me a job like you said he would. That makes you my *very best* friend."

"We are not *very best* friends, Mr. Kringle, that's not how adults do things. They don't make friends by just arbitrarily talking to random strangers. That's nutty talk. You made me late today. Did you know that? Could have lost *my* job. Did you know that? And that ain't something light," said Ellie. Flo and Pete smiled at one another and pretended to position the new chairs as they listened.

"Oh, I'm sorry Mrs. Boone. Truly. Well, how can I make it right so we *can* become friends then?" asked Kringle.

"You won't. That's how. I don't make friends with strange strangers," said Ellie frankly.

"Well, how do people make friends with each other if they don't talk to strangers?" asked Kringle. "How would I make friends with you, if I wasn't me?"

"You don't have any friends do you Mr. Kringle?" asked Ellie as she took a deep breath, puffed her chest out and put her hands on her hips.

"Well, I think you're my friend," answered Kringle.

"Well, no I am not. We just went over this. We are strangers that happen to be in a conversation," corrected Ellie.

"Pete's now my friend. You my friend, Pete?" asked Kringle to Pete as Pete headed cautiously outside to bring in the rest of the furniture. Neither Flo nor Pete wanted to interrupt the verbal tennis match. It was too fun to watch Ellie get bothered, because she was so unnatural at getting upset.

"Sure we friends Kringle," said Pete as he reemerged with a cage chair. "Kringle's gonna join the church band. He plays the harmonica."

"Congratulations," said Ellie dully.

"See, Pete's my friend, Mrs. Boone. Now, don't mind me for asking, and I know it's tacky, but ain't some strangers just best friends who haven't met yet?" Kringle smiled; he was somewhere in between teasing and courting. Kringle then went outside and grabbed a cage chair as well. "I'm a good friend, Pete - I know jokes, I can dance, like you said, I can play the harmonica, I'm a nice fella. Mrs. Boone I think you need a friend like me."

"No. I disagree. I know for a fact that I do not need an odd charcoaled hobo who jumps off trains, bothers strangers making them late and tracks in snow like they were told not to, like yourself, as a friend," said Ellie as she turned around to grab a mop to clean where the men had been tromping.

"Well, I'm not a hobo per say, I..."

"Well, break a dish and kiss a frog, you that lost fireman aren't you?" interrupted Flo as she looked over at Ellie who was mopping the floor. Flo held her elbow in her hand bouncing an invisible cigarette off her lips. Kringle set down his cage chair by Pete's that Flo was sitting in.

"Is this your friend?" asked Kringle to Ellie. Then Kringle turned to Flo, "If Mrs. Boone says I am a fireman, then yes I am one."

"It's *Miss* Boone," Flo corrected and Ellie gave her a look that spoke volumes.

"*Miss* Boone, is this your friend? How'd you meet her?" asked Kringle inquisitively as he and Pete went outside for more cage chairs.

Mopping behind their steps Ellie said, "Work, of course. Now clean them boots off before coming back inside. This ain't a barn."

Kringle and Pete came back in with the last of the chairs.

"So you skipped being strangers and just became friends?" asked Kringle.

"Yes," said Ellie.

"Lucky," said Kringle to Flo.

Flo smiled with raised eyebrows.

"Now please stop asking me trivial things. Ugh, what did I say? Now you clean it," said Ellie as she handed Kringle the mop. Kringle mopped up Pete and his wet tracks and handed the mop back to Ellie.

"Won't happen again," said Kringle.

"Mm hm," Ellie said inspecting Kringle's mopping work.

Ellie went to stand next to Flo. Now standing by her grinning friend, Ellie positioned the chairs in her "Papa" position. The boys headed outside for another load.

"Stop talking to him," whispered Ellie to Flo.

"Why?" asked Flo. "This is fun."

Both Kringle and Pete were coming back in sharing sides of the high boy. They tapped their boots against the step before touching the floor.

"How'd you two become friends? Did you both just know you liked one another right away," Kringle asked Flo as Pete and he cautiously walked the high boy through the shop.

"Whoosh, big *hell-pings* no, we didn't like one another at first," said Flo.

Struggling a bit with the high boy Kringle says, "Well it seems you don't like me too much neither Miss Boone, maybe we're friends."

"No, Ellie liked me. I didn't like her," corrected Flo.

"Oh, then, what did Miss Ellie Boone finally do to get you to like her Ms...um,"

"Miss nothin', I ain't got no last name 'till I'm properly noticed. Flo," Flo tossed her invisible cigarette away and shook Kringle's hand.

"Nice to meet you Flo, name's Kris Kringle. People just call me Kris or Kringle."

"Well Kringle, she was just so *dancin'* nice to me and so *dancin'* pretty, that I eventually broke," Flo smiled at Ellie, but Ellie didn't smile back. She was getting annoyed and red.

Kringle and Pete headed outside; they only had the Swiss buffet left to bring in. Slow coming back in, struggling a bit from the weight of the Swiss buffet, Kringle said, "Well, I'll just have to be extra nice to you then Miss Boone."

"I'd rather you not. We are *strangers* Mr. Kringle and *we will* stay that way no matter what verbal dance you spin about," Ellie wasn't sure what was happening, but she knew she wanted to win. And she felt she wasn't.

"By that brave logic...."

"Button this up Kringle, I'm at work," said Ellie without eye contact.

Miss Winkelplex emerged from the back.

"Pete, this way with that. It's coming back here. Put it in *pick up*," instructed Miss Winkelplex as the boys squeezed by her and headed to the back, holding the Swiss buffet. Miss Winkelplex stroked the piece as it passed her by. "Oh that looks lovely, just lovely." She headed over to Ellie and Flo to look over the other pieces. "Who's the new guy with Pete?" she asked as she ran her hands over each new piece.

"That's Ellie's new friend," Flo answered biting her bottom lip and smiling.

The long day at school had finally come to an end. The Airlords - Johnny, Billy, Murf, Ramona and Terrance approached the massive oak tree that stood behind the Boone home. From a distance, when its leaves have fallen, the old oak tree looked as if Mother Earth was reaching up to taste the vanilla scooped clouds. The Airlords climbed the boards nailed like a ladder to the big oak. Central Command was their clubhouse, their home base. It's where they escaped to discuss their most important matters. It was a rickety room and not secure in the least. It was placed in the palm of the oak tree. Central Command would pitch and sway to whichever side held the most weight. Outside, different size boards of all styles were nailed to the tree, keeping the shack in place. But what truly secured it was that the small clubhouse had the awesome oak's main branches all around it, cupping it in place. *That's* what kept it from falling. Central Command had square openings on every side so that the Airlords could keep watch on the happenings below. Inside were piles of pinecones under each window, used as ammunition to throw at potential attackers. They had had a lot of "code yellow" drills concerning attacks, but no actual "code reds" just yet. Covering three walls were comic strip clippings of *Buck Rogers* and *Amazing Stories* ripped out from *The Worcester Evening Gazette* that Terrance was allowed to tear out of his father's copies at the pharmacy. The remaining wall read the Airlords' name that Ramona wrote in chalk:

Airlords of Hamilton.

Under that was the Airlords' sled helmets (leather football helmets), scarves (torn bed sheet) and goggles of all different kinds hung from bent nails.

The Airlords sat in a horseshoe. Rudy kept watch, barking at any squirrel that got too close. Terrance unfolded the newest comic strip of *Buck Rogers*, placed it on the floor and they all moved in and began reading.

Silence took to Central Command.

After ten minutes, the discussion began.

"Boy, oh boy, that's what we need, Johnny, we need 'Rocket Tubes," said Murf. "How 'bout we put *Rocket Tubes* on the new *Battle Cruiser*. Could ya do that, huh Johnny?"

"Sure I can."

"Oi brotha, racket teebes v'ould be swell," added Ramona. "V'hat v'ould de dew?"

"Well, I suppose they'd be powerful rockets that would launch the sled to fantastic speeds," Murf was almost quoting the comic strip they had just read.

The Airlords moved over to where Johnny kept his blueprints; Billy was still reading.

Johnny laid down older sled blueprints and schematics.

Murf was the Airlords facilitator, "Okay Airlords, now let's put our noodles together. What's on our front burner?" he asked.

"Beatin' de socks off dem damn dead ducks," said Ramona with conviction and showing her best stink face.

"Oh, we'll show 'em alright. And how. Them sink Twins ain't gonna beat the Airlords of Hamilton this time. No way, no how. So, gang, here's the low down, we're gonna have to go though all of Johnny's blueprints here and figure out what went right and what went wrong. Then we'll know how to build the *Battle Cruiser*. And then we'll go and show them Twins. Right, Airlords?"

Billy was finished reading and took a seat with the rest.

"Right," cadenced the Airlords.

Johnny Boone spun his hat backwards and placed the straw he was chomping on in his back pocket that already had three other straws sticking out and said, "Ya, you said it. Now look-a-here, gather round. I figure that the problem with *The Ship To The Unknown* was the *Stern Rocket Gun Turret.*" Last summer Johnny took a door from the junkyard, souped it up with a couple of small wagon wheels and added a few couch springs to the bottom to represent *Buck Rogers' Spring Landing Skids.* The springs acted as softeners in case the ship ever took off into flight and needed to land hard. Then Johnny added *Radio Phones* to the bow and stern, which were actually rutabaga cans tied with a twine so the *Captain* and *Stern Rocket Gunner* could communicate. But, like Johnny Boone said, it was the *Stern Rocket Gun Turret* alone that did the ship in.

To make the *Stern Rocket Gun Turret,* Johnny had nailed together a giant slingshot using pieces from an old picket fence and an old torn inner tube. The slingshot was as tall as Billy. Then the Airlords collected mud clumps from Little Island Pond for bombs. When *The Ship To The Unknown* was stationary, the mud clumps could be fired a full ten feet. However, when they launched down Patton's Hill, with Johnny as captain and Murf manning the *Stern Rocket Gun Turret*, the weight of Murf combined with the giant sling shot and pile of mud had the *The Ship To The Unknown* up on its back wheels. It spun like a tornado, hit a rock, and crashed covering both Johnny and Murf in mud clumps.

"Yah, we don't need that, no how. But the *Radio Phones* were a smart one Johnny," complimented Murf.

"Okay write this down," instructed Johnny.

Terrance grabbed his school notebook and a pencil. "Sh-sh-shoot, J'J'Johnny," Terrance got out.

"Lose the *Stern Rocket Gun Turret.* Keep the *Radio Phones,*" dictated Johnny then he pulled out another blueprint. "What about, *The Mystery Ship*?"

"De *Vertical Fin* looked swell 'n' the *Electroscope* v'as sure swell too Johnny. I jest dink de *Cloaking Device* wasn't fully developed yet," said Ramona pointing at the blueprint of *The Mystery Ship.*

The Airlords were in full agreement. Johnny made the *Mystery Ship* out of a small wooden horse trough. The entire gang could sit inside *The Mystery Ship* including Rudy. Johnny slapped wagon wheels on it as well and the *Vertical Fin* was actually an oar Johnny found; it was used somewhat as a rudder. Johnny poked a hole out the back of the trough so the fin of the oar could scrape on the ground behind them. While sitting inside, the Airlords gripped the other end of the oar and tried to steer. It didn't work too well, but that wasn't the problem. *The Mystery Ship* was to fly down Patton's Hill at night with its *Cloaking Device* activated. The *Cloaking Device* was an old black horse blanket that they put over the entire ship with them under it. Billy sat in the bow with the *Electroscope* poking out of the blanket. The *Electroscope* was really a busted telescope and Billy Boone couldn't see a thing through it. The Airlords rushed down Patton's Hill, blind, until boom-smack they slammed into Mr. John Robin's barn.

"Okay, then, I say we keep the *Vertical Fin* and lose the *Electroscope* and wait until the *Cloaking Device* is more developed. Agreed?" asked Johnny.

"Agreed!" shouted the rest of the Airlords. Everyone was getting excited, because they knew this was to be the ship of all ships.

Johnny unrolled last summer's blueprint.

"Now, *The Submarine Rocket Ship*, equipped with a *Stabilizer Wing*, *Torpedo Tubes*, four *Torpedoes*, the *Spectrometer* and, of course, the *Lifting Element*. Any thoughts?" Johnny looked up to the Airlords, spun his hat back around and pulled the straw back out of his back pocket and started chewing again.

The Submarine Rocket Ship was a sad topic. The Airlords had spent a lot of time on that ship and truly thought it was their best work.

After Sheriff Jones busted up a group of men making beer in the woods bordering Hamilton and its neighboring town, Ipswich, he had all the brewers' equipment tossed into Pete's junkyard. That equipment was what Johnny used to make most of *The Submarine Rocket Ship*. He took three big barrels, big enough to hold two Airlords each, and tied them together with rope. Then he took two broken ironing boards and secured them to the middle barrel – like wings. Attached to the ironing boards were two tin tubes each. The back of the tubes had a collection of rubber bands stretched and secured, and inside the tubes were empty beer bottles with sassy notes from the gang written inside. *The Lifting Element* was one red balloon tied to each barrel and both ironing boards, given generously by Mr. McKool's pharmacy. Johnny said, "This makes the ship lighter."

Manning the first barrel was Billy and Rudy. Billy had a glass bowl they called the *Spectrometer*. He was to lean over the front barrel, place the bowl in the water and plant his face inside the bowl to monitor the evils below. In the middle barrel were Terrance and Johnny. They manned the *Torpedoes* by pulling the elastic bands back and shooting beer bottles out. And in the last barrel, Murf screamed the orders as Ramona did what she could with the only oar.

The Submarine Rocket Ship didn't stay afloat that long. Using his *Spectrometer*, Billy Boone flipped over his barrel and Rudy jumped in after him. Terrance and Johnny Boone both got one torpedo launched before also falling over board. The ropes loosened and everything but the third barrel sank. Murf was left screaming orders as Ramona paddled them in circles while all the balloons, save Murf's and Ramona's, lifted to the sky.

"Maybe save nothin' from the *Submarine Rocket Ship*, Johnny," Murf said defeated.

"V'ell we're using de oar, which v'as dee *Vertical Fin* of *Da Mystery Ship*," Ramona said hopefully.

"That's true," said Billy.

"Oh yah," said Johnny."

"Good point," said Murf.

"I-I-I'll j-j-jot it down," said Terrance.

Ramona glowed a proud Irish red to have saved the morale of the Airlords and to have saved *The Mystery Ship* from being a total disaster.

Johnny began to sketch out the *Battle Cruiser*.

After the Airlord's meeting had concluded and everyone had headed home for supper, the Boone boys headed to the Bump Track to collect the coal that falls from Betsy Bound when she hits the bump in the track. However, they forgot to bring their coal pails from the house so they stuffed their pockets with the wet and runny coal. When their pockets were overfilled, Billy had the idea for them to use their socks as small sacks. Now hunched over, sockless, with bulky pockets and dirty hands and coal smeared faces, the Boone boys collected the day's fallen coal beside the Bump Track. The Sun was setting. The Moon was peaking. The sky dimmed. A few geese squawked as they flew south. The wind was subtle. And it wasn't too cold. Under it all, the Boone boys talked softly about spaceships and sled races.

"I suppose so," said Johnny. "But I'm not sure where we can find skis. We'll take a look tomorrow."

"What about skates?" brainstormed Billy.

"Yah that could work too. But skis would be better. Skates are for ice and unless Patton's Hill is iced over like it was last winter, we'd best stick to skis to stay on top of the snow. If the snow ain't light and is packed down good, maybe hand railings could work, like the ones at the school's entrance. We best check Patton's Hill; see how the snow is settling."

Billy held up his two coal filled soaked socks and noticed a man walking a few yards down the tracks, a man dressed in red.

"Holy cats, Johnny, that's the man I saw jump off the train this morning. Just there. See 'im?"

Before looking, Johnny too held up his wet filled wet socks, checking his bounty.

"I see him. He looks to be coming this way," remarked Johnny.

Kringle noticed the two boys while he was taking a walk around the junkyard getting a lay of his new land.

"Hello boys," said Kringle.

"Hey Mister, I saw you jump off the train right there this morning. You go jump off that train Mister? Huh Mister? How come you do that? How come you jumped off the train, huh? You running from someone? You a train robber? You go rob that train did yah? How much you get?", spat out Billy until his brother elbowed him to shut it.

"No it was just my stop," smiled Kringle.

"That ain't a stop," said Johnny.

"Yah, that ain't no stop. Train stops down at Beverly Crossing, next town over," said Billy. "You rob that train Mister? You got a sack a money? Jewels even?" Again spat Billy and again his brother elbowed him to shut it.

"No, no. No money, no jewels. I ain't no bank robber. It simply was just my stop that's all," said Kringle. "What are you boys doing down here by the track, hm?"

"Aw, we just take the coal that falls off the cars at the Bump Track. It ain't stealin'," explained Billy. Johnny stood quiet looking over Kringle.

"What's the Bump Track," asked Kringle looking about.

Quietly Johnny joined the conversation, "You see where that bit of land dips? Well, when the train comes by all the cars take a big bump there. If the coal cars ain't got no snow on the top of them, well then, some coal comes rolling off. See? Look-a-here."

Both Billy and Johnny held up their socks.

"Say that's something. You two are true entrepreneurs," said Kringle.

"Who's Aunie Pen Your?" asked, Billy.

"Aw, no one. Entrepreneur - that just means you make your own rules," explained Kringle. "Live around here?"

"Yah, there," Billy pointed to the converted barn behind them. "Live with

45

our Momma."

"Miss Boone?" asked Kringle.

"Why you know our Ma, Mister? She don't know you," said Johnny. Kringle could tell he was getting sized up a bit by the older brother.

"Oh, she helped get me a job over there. I'm working with a guy named Pete. You know Pete do yah?" asked Kringle.

"'Course we know Pete," cadenced both boys.

"What happened to Mr. Riggelsworth?" asked Billy.

"Never met that man, but I heard the man who had the job before me lost that job. Heard he was a fine man though," said Kringle.

Johnny squinted his eyes while Billy opened his wide from the surprising news.

"Mr. Riggelsworth got canned?" started Billy, but his brother elbowed him one last time.

"Well, we're off Mister," said Johnny, then spun his brother around and started them both towards home.

Billy hung his neck back and hollered, "Don't be jumpin' off no more trains, Mister; you'll get smooshed." Then he smiled at his brother, but his brother's face was tight in thought.

Kringle gave a small wave and both parties, along with the Sun, the geese and the weakening wind, headed home for the night.

It only takes one candle to light Pete's workshop. The shadows it casts pulsate the happy home's heartbeat. Kringle and Pete sat facing one another playing dominoes on their small split wood table. They drank hot tea with small dollops of Pete's rugged rum. Pete would make "rugged tea" for "calm occasions" as he'd say. Rudy had been sitting by Kringle staring up at him getting new kinds of rubs. The hopeful dog was getting to know his new roommate and was kindly memorizing his ways. Finally content and tired, Rudy walked over to his blankets, circled them a few times and lay down for the night. He let out one long breath through his nose that signaled all his muscles to loosen. Rudy melted into the blankets. Sleep. Outside the snow fell and the stars and Moon wavered. The diminutive shack smelled of saw dust and nice spiced cinnamon. The wood stove spit and crackled.

"Sure I know it, I went and showed the Boone boys the Bump Track 'bout, hm, 'bout a year ago I'd say. Good boys; help their mama like they ought. I like them boys. Kids are good for a man." Pete thought over his next move, "Kids see, they snap a man out of his head. Snap out a man's forever looped thoughts of his hard life. Little ones, it's the little ones, kids, children, toddlers, even babies - they remind men of magic after they've forgot. Like they remind him of who the man *was* and what a person *should* remember to be more like. That's what I think. I like them Boone boys coming around. Rudy likes 'em too. It's good for Rudy. It's good for him to be part of the gang they have going there. Good for when I get borin' and have to work all day and night. Hear this Kringle," Pete looked up smiling, "the gang calls me The Scientist. Something about how I provide the parts they be needin' for the ships they build. I'm somehow in the story they got going there in their lil' heads. Rudy and me are official members of the gang, ya know that? The leader, the bigger one, Murf's his name; he tells me they're called *The Airlords of Hamilton*. I like that quite a bit," said Pete, as he finally and slowly laid his domino down. "I do."

"So what do they build? Go-karts?" asked Kringle as he thought over the game.

"Well yah, but no. Don't go be calling them that to them. You'll get corrected snap-quick. They're *spaceships*. Oh here, take a listen," Pete spun around to his work desk that had a small radio hanging on a nail. He switched it on.

CLICK.

There was static, then a low and serious voice came to The Workshop:

"Meanwhile, the Mystery Ship had drifted past Mars – and was now speeding on toward the Asteroid Belt."

"Oh good it's on," Pete turned the radio show down a bit. "This is one of them programs they listen to. Seven o'clock every night. Riggels went and fixed up a radio for the Boone boys just like this radio here, so they could listen to this show, Buck Rogers it's called, like their schoolmates do at school. I listen too. It's a bit complicated for me, a lot of space gibberish. I never know really what they are talking about, but it can get exciting. There's ray guns and this space woman; Wilma Deering's her name. I like Wilma's voice. She sounds like she looks like a pretty deer, elegant you know, and as if she smells like sweets. I don't know."

Pete blushed a bit. "And I like to try and know what the kids are talking about before they start yipping at me about the parts they be looking for. It can get very cryptic. You'll see."

"What about their mother Ellie? What's her tale so far?" Kringle asked as he set his domino down and flaunted the power of his move with his outstretched arms lifted over his shoulders. "There ya go."

"Oo that's good. Dang," Pete saw that Kringle was now ahead. "Hm. Well, if you ask me I noticed you flirting up a good one with her."

"No, no, no. I was just being friendly."

Pete laughed, "'Friendly', oh, okay. I think you, Kringle, think she's hotsy-totsy. You weren't a bit dizzy? Bah. You didn't notice you were courting her up a good one then?"

"I didn't really even notice myself until today actually. I mean, I got a job, a home, a bed, a dog," Kringle looked up at Pete unsure if he should have said Rudy was his as well.

Looking down at the game, Pete gave him a nod of approval.

"I got a friend. You. I've got a warm drink here. That's somethin' alone. I've done more today than all last year. But yah, she is something swell. I like that long black hair and how she wraps it up in that cloth. That's skill. And her being so serious all the time. Jeesh. Never met a girl like her before. I really gotta think hard before I talk. She seems like she catches and squishes any wiggling word she don't like. She that stern with everybody? I do like her hair though. She got a fella? She's nice and tall too. Yah, I don't know." Pete smiled noticing Kringle talking up a good one to himself. "I feel lucky I guess. Good day you know? Never really knew this type of me before, to have all of this and all. Guess I'm just getting to know this new me. I thank you for that Pete."

And with that Pete looked up and put his domino down.

"Domino!" Pete said and won the game. "Come get your jacket. I'm gonna show you something." Pete took his hat and sweaters off the coat rack and layered them on. Kringle grabbed his red jacket off the rack and slung it on too. Rudy awakened from the moving shadows, yawned, stretched with a squeak and was ready for the excursion.

The men headed out into the cold, into the junkyard. It was now much colder. Kringle and Pete's breath rose up to the night sky and followed the wind's current. The Moon was half, but bold and wavering with a blurry ring around him. And the clouds were thin; stream like. They flowed swiftly over the Moon and stars.

Pete stopped and looked far and wide. Rudy sat and did the same. Once Kringle understood there would be no conversation for a while, he settled into his own natural instincts.

It was quiet.

Sometimes the men and Rudy would look in the same direction. Other times, each soul centered on something different. A Snowy Owl flying high circled the junkyard hunting. A few branches snapped deep inside the woods to the west and there was a scuttle underneath the plumbing pile. But the silence was the best thing that could be heard. Kringle felt himself truly being accepted by the land as they stood without words. Rudy took a few steps forward, leaned against Kringle's leg and sat close by him. It had been such a new day. Not one thing was like it used to be. Kringle put his hand on Rudy's head. The branches of the trees were leafless and beautifully wicked. They creaked with the sway of the wind. Then Pete spoke.

"My parents, they, they bring me up here. I's born here. My Daddy worked for Mr. McManus too, but that was a different kind of time. I used to look out over this junkyard and be ashamed a bit. Not a bit, no…I was just plain ashamed. My Daddy goin' and pullin' me out here, telling me to look through other peoples' don't cares, and try and go make something useful with 'em for us, for the family. I mean every gift I see him give my Ma'ma and give me, was something he gone and made out of other peoples don't cares. I thought that something rotten. Like it was wrong of him, like my Ma'ma, she be deservin' something new, something only for *her*. Not people's don't cares. No, I didn't look at my Daddy right in those days." Pete turned to look at Kringle. "I remember just there, well there was no pile there then, but just the same, right there my Daddy worked on this hat rack and bureau, 'bout so tall. He'd have me looking all around for specific things he'd need. I'd bring him the things and he'd say, 'No, boy, see that there is regular wood, we be looking for cherry wood for your Ma'ma.' And I'd just not listen. I didn't care. I just thought it wrong and then he'd go and find clothes, *clothes*, other people's clothes, in this here junk pile and put 'em aside for Ma'ma." Pete shuffled his feet some. "But on her birthday, when she was out working for a woman in a different town, my Daddy and I brought that hat rack and bureau inside. He go and hung all these hats he'd cleaned up for her and washed and folded all them clothes he found for her and set them all in that bureau. Set it all up nice like. I thought it rotten of him; I's embarrassed of him. I's

49

just embarrassed my Daddy was like that." Rudy laid down, but kept his shoulders and head up and at attention. "My Daddy then tell me to run off for a bit. 'Boy don't get into no trouble, but give your Ma'ma and Pa some time to themselves,' he told me. I didn't go nowhere. I just went behind the house to sulk I guess. But when my Ma'ma come home, when she go inside and saw all them things my Daddy get her." Pete looked up at the wavering half Moon with his green watery eyes. "Well, she done cried. Not sad. She was happy crying. Happy my Daddy is the way he is; do the things he'd done. I look through the window of her trying on all them hats, clothes, dresses. She looked like a little girl that night. My Ma-ma spinning around in them dresses, doing funny walks like she was a fancier type a woman. My Daddy he just sat watching her, applauding and smiling. Whistling. They danced and danced, there was no music, but they danced and danced. I could see she really loved my Daddy there. And I could see the same in him for her - 'course. Seemed the only rotten one was me. But not after that, that was the night I learned my Daddy knew magic. That's right, my Daddy, he knew magic. He could make miracles here. I love this here junkyard, Kringle; I love this here junkyard with all my heart. I just truly do."

The two men and Rudy continued to look in the silence that their souls shared. Pete was a good man to stand with.

By the fireplace hung the Boone boys' socks, each filled past the ankle with coal. They dripped while drying. The floor became stained. The home was cold, save if you stood right in front of the fireplace or stove. Johnny boiled potatoes. The only recipe Johnny could make on his own when his mother was late coming home was mashed-potatoes. He was proud of his one culinary ability. Billy set the table and filled three glasses with water. *Buck Rogers* played on the small radio.

The low voice spoke:
"Wilma and I, in the latest type of observation ship, set out to find and destroy the terrible Mongol-machine."

"Hey Johnny, that's what we should call the Twins' sled - *The Mongol Machine*," spoke Billy.
"Shh," responded Johnny.

Then a softer voice spoke:

Wilma: "*That looks like the spot. We'll cruise around until night.*"
Buck Rogers: "*Hold that altitude, Wilma, we don't want to be seen. I'll float down now. Be sure your radiophone is in tune with mine.*"
Wilma: "*I'll circle until I get your message.*"

"Johnny, they're using the radiophone like you made us," said Billy as he threw on his jacket to get more wood stacked on the porch for the fire.

"Shh," said Johnny, then realizing he had shushed his brother three times in a row. "Yah, Billy, you said it. *The Airlord of Hamilton* vs. *The Mongol Machine.* That's what we'll call it. Good idea."

Billy went outside happy his brother heard and agreed with him. Johnny mashed the potatoes with a fork, buttered them a little, salted them a little, and peppered them a good deal. The radio had gone to commercials so Johnny turned it down and scooped them both out a sharing. When Billy came back inside he set the new logs to dry by the fire. They were for warming their mother up for whenever she came home. Feeling his mother would be late, he took the last two sugar cookies and placed them on the fireplace mantel to warm - 'They would be a nice surprise for Momma later,' Billy thought.

Each night Ellie came home at a different time. It all depended on when Miss Winkelplex decided the girls were finished. Flo says, "All them bluenoses are the same, I tell ya. It's a *dancin'* control thing, she's got going with us Ellie, a *dancin'* control thing."

That night, Miss Winkelplex kept Ellie later at the store than ever, so Billy and Johnny sat at the table eating dinner and listening intently to the radio show without their mother. The Boone boys only looked up from eating at one another during the exciting parts of the radio show. After dinner they cleaned up their dishes in the basin, repositioned their mother's place setting, kicked the fire up, got into their red and white striped pajamas; Johnny warmed two cups of milk, one for him and Billy to share and the other cup Billy placed next to the cookies to stay warm - Billy knows that his mother, like he, likes warm milk with cookies. Watching Billy, Johnny turned the radio up a little, both brothers climbed the ladder to their bed-loft and quietly lay together sharing the milk and listening to the radio, while imagining themselves beside *Buck Rogers.*

Ellie forgot to put her bags back in her boots to keep the insides dry, so her feet were now wet, frozen; there was no feeling in them. Even though the day had warmed, the night became a dismal story. The half Moon had tried to calm the new agitated clouds for Ellie, but they were too agitated to be soothed. It was eight o'clock now, cold with a heavy sleet coming down. Earlier, Ellie had picked up a few groceries. The brown paper bag she gripped was now pulping. She held the bag from the bottom with frozen mittened fingers.

The sleet abused Ellie in the face as she walked mirthlessly home. It also made the path home slippery. Cautiously trudging across the snow covered pitfall, her boots would kick out from under her with every step and her scarf became frozen over her mouth. It was dark. Ellie had to brave the walk home by blind memory. Squinting with a hidden pucker, Ellie looked over the tree line to where she could see the faint smoke from her boys' fire.

But Ellie slipped.

The ice, on purpose mind you, slipped Ellie's left ankle out. She fell hard to the ground banging her chin, crunching her teeth and scraping her elbow in a few places. But that's not what made Ellie begin to cry. The bag had torn and three of the eggs broke. With lifeless fingers, Ellie, as carefully as one could, self pityingly scooped the broken eggs into her frozen scarf and stuffed it in her coat pocket. She took the sugar and flour bags that were also getting wet, wrapped them in her other scarf and placed under the armpit of her jacket. The tomatoes, potatoes and onions were stuffed in her other pockets and she held on to the cheese and meat.

Ellie walked feeling her heart beating in her scraped chin. She no longer was tearing, but her body was still crying. The sleet, wind and ice were cruel to her. When Ellie was weak, her sad thoughts came to her more easily. Ellie believed in the story that the church taught her as a young child - that the devil stood on your left shoulder and an angel on your right shoulder. But she more believed that the devil was just her emotions and the angel was her true logic. The church had told her the devil speaks loudest and that the angel is usually late with talking to you because it's helping others somewhere else. Ellie thought more that her emotions came *first* and she'd often have to calm herself down and ignore those emotions until her true logic could catch up with her. It took a lot to overpower those dreadful thoughts though. The church was right, that her helpful logic, her angel, was always late. So, as she walked on, Ellie decided to stop singing that mean old song the school girls used to sing to her in her head, she'd stop thinking about cussing out Miss Winkelplex and she'd stop thinking about why that Hobo kept on her so much about being her friend. Instead she thought about the future of her boys. She thought about them older, married and happy, strong, successful and with babies of their own. She forced herself to think good thoughts, as she walked hunched over, wet and cold, following the smoke from her boys' distant fire.

It was difficult.

When Ellie got to the door her fingertips were ashamed of their mittenless impedance. But eventually Ellie worked her house key into the iced latch. Once inside Ellie put the three broken eggs in a coffee mug, covered it with a saucer, placed it in the icebox and then looked around the room. The fire was still going and she saw that Billy had brought in a few logs for her. *Good boys*, she thought. Ellie walked over to see what was hanging by the fire. She took the coal out of the crusty smelly socks and put them in the coal pail. Then Ellie hung up her wet jacket, turned the small radio off and placed her boots by the fire. She looked up and saw on the fireplace mantel two small sugar cookies next to a glass of milk. Ellie smiled. She popped one of the cookies halfway in her mouth, went over to her clothes trunk, changed out of her wet clothes and into her long grey nightgown as she nibbled and sipped. Ellie then quietly climbed up to the loft, saw the boys in bed, took the empty mug out from under Billy's hand and tucked the blankets tighter around her boys.

The boys were awake, pretending to be asleep. They were usually cold until their mother came to bed; she provided the heat they needed to sleep. They missed the time when it was the three of them bundled in bed waiting for their father to come home from work. Billy actually didn't remember this too well, but Johnny would tell him about it if Billy asked. Johnny only once volunteered his memory, one night when they were both exceptionally cold and their Mother was exceptionally late coming home. Johnny doesn't like talking about it too much; it makes his heart feel young. However, Johnny understood that Billy needs his memories sometimes.

Ellie went to the stove and heated up her peppered mashed potatoes. As she stirred the heating pot she looked out the window to the half Moon. The thin clouds moved swiftly across the dotted sky. The sleet continued its abuse on the land. She noticed how pretty a square of moonlight framed her place setting. She muscled a nice thought out from under her creeping dreadful ones - Ellie liked to believe the light was a sign from her mother and father up in heaven or maybe it was the Lord himself reaching out to her. Ellie sat down at the table. Her muscles pulsated and ached. Her chin and elbow hurt and throbbed. She tried to move her frozen unfeeling toes. With her eyes closed, Ellie sat quietly eating her warm mashed potatoes. It was quiet in the colorful barn-home, other than Ellie's quiet breathing. When Ellie was finished, she washed her plate, checked up on the fire and quietly went up the ladder to nuzzle in with her awaiting boys.

BOYS & GIRLS,
DOG & CAT,
CHASE ONE ANOTHER ON
DANGEROUS TRACKS

STORY 2

DECEMBER DREAMS

As little boys dream
        of space and flight
Warmed by their mother
        on a cold December night
A white fawn walks;
        mother and father in sight
Lit like milk
        by the half moon's light

✻

Story 2:

BOYS & GIRLS, DOG & CAT, CHASE ONE ANOTHER ON DANGEROUS TRACKS

The young white fawn was becoming aware; she knew who her parents were. Her mother was always close by, beautiful, long and loving with her. Not once did the white fawn look up at her mother when her mother was not already looking down on her. Her father invariably stood in front of them both, robust and gazing far, far ahead. She wondered what he searched for, but she knew she would always follow him. His antlers were august. They reminded the white fawn of the mighty trees around her. She felt her father looked to be part of the land. He was her God. The white fawn began to notice the difference between her mother and father, physically and mentally. She also noticed that they were different with each other than they were with her.

The family stood atop Patton's Hill looking down at John Robin's farmlet. The sleet was lightening, but still not healthy for the white fawn to be out in. She had endured an unhealthy amount that night. She needed to be warmed. The father deer moved the family down the hill. The three walked closer than usual. The mother and father deer tried to shield their young one from the unkind weather. Scanning the farmlet, the father deer recognized a secure place to take the family. A small lean-to with a few bundles of hay sat ten yards from the Robin's home. It was John Robin's hay house. They would rest there.

The family walked onto the farmlet. The sleet sizzled still. The white fawn was tired; this was her most enduring night. Her legs began to shake from being cold and exhausted. Once on the field, the father walked them directly to the lean-to. Even in the lousy weather, while feeling very low, the family looked angelic as they truly were.

The lean-to shielded them from the sleet. It was nice to finally be covered. The mother crouched down and the white fawn followed. The hay felt nice under their tired legs, tummies and over all bodies. The father still stood, gazing - listening. Washing her baby, the mother deer kept an eye on the father until a long white haired cat decided to make herself known.

The McManus' cat, Periwinkle, was Marlene's cat. She was spoiled, fancy and quite mischievous. She loved the presence of herself. Periwinkle's biggest defiance to the world was that she always walked too far from home. Intentionally, mind you. Caught in the storm, she, like the deer family, hunkered down in John Robin's hay house. Periwinkle let out a chirp and the charms on her collar jingled. The ears and the eyes of the three deer went to the sound. Periwinkle trotted out from her warm spot. She was confident and curious. Bouncing, she walked over to the small white fawn. The white fawn became paralyzed. Her heart raced. Curious themselves, the mother and father allowed Periwinkle to approach. They too were taken aback by the confidence of such a small thing. Periwinkle let out little chirps with every step while her collar reflected the moon and chimed with every step.

When she finally reached the white fawn; the white fawn pulled her head back unsure. As did her mother. The white fawn had never seen another walking creature before. Her heart continued to race. Her eyes widened even more. Periwinkle went in for a sniff. Instinctively the white fawn did as well. And when the mother too decided to investigate with her nose, Periwinkle felt confident enough to circle three times, let a final chirp out, tuck her white paws in and lie down looking like a loaf of bread beside the family of deer. The mother and white fawn continued to sniff.

The father deer was not so interested. He let a powerful breath out of his nostrils, that looked like two whirling white tornados. Then he stomped his left hoof down. Hard. Periwinkle sprang up and dashed out of the hay house. 'Little white creature, you will have to find a new place for the night' was his message.

The father deer lay down by his family. Warming slowly, the family layered upon one another. The white fawn fell right to sleep. The mother deer horseshoed around her baby and laid her chin down on her love's back. 'They would have to move on once the weather lightened,' the father deer thought as he stared out onto the dark sleeting farmlet.

When Kringle found out that Pete and he were to get paid differently by Mr. McManus, because Pete was a black fella and Kringle a white one, he wouldn't have it. Kringle told Pete he'd give him the difference out of his pay, so they'd be "straight". Pete refused, "It is what it is Kringle, and I ain't gonna be taking your money." But Kringle wouldn't drop it. Persistence is a gift. All day they worked in the yard and all day Kringle wouldn't let it go. It exhausted Pete. "I have never met a white man so determined to give me money," said Pete as he laid his elbow down on the small wood split table across from Kringle.

"Deal is, I win, we pool our pay. Equal. You win, well you ain't gonna win so," explained Kringle. He had finally annoyed Pete enough to agree to an arm wrestling match over the subject. Rudy didn't know what was going on, but he liked it. He could tell there was a playful energy in the air. Rudy kept dashing in and out of The Workshop bringing in different things, like old shoes from the barrel and scrap wood, dropping them down, chasing himself in a circle a few times, letting out a few excited barks and then bringing the items back outside, once Pete would let out - 'No, no Rudy. Out, bring out. Yard. Yard.'

"No way. Say what we said before. If *I win* you drop this here subject," said Pete.

"I don't remember agreeing to that," laughed Kringle.

"Oh you don't? You're a swindler Kringle, a swindler," said Pete.

"Stop stalling old man," Kringle liked teasing Pete. Pete was only a little older than Kringle, but he had that early grey hair coming in. Kringle took Pete's hand and the men settled into that grip. "Hey, hey no cheating, keep your arm straight."

"My arm is straight, you just don't think so 'cause *you* keep bending yours. You keep *your* arm straight," said Pete and both men shuffled their arms and bodies.   "Okay ready, here we go, One..."

Rudy came in, growling, dragging a broken lamp in by its chord. "No, no, Rudy. Out, out. Yard, yard." Rudy barked three times at Pete and spun around and then barked three more times. "Rudy, out."

"...two, three, Go!" said Kringle quickly, smashing Pete's hand down on the table with feeble resistance. "I win," smiles Kringle then raised his arms triumphantly.

"No, no. You're a cheat. That don't count you swindler. I wasn't ready and you know it," said Pete. "Rudy, no! Out, out! Go on! Take it out!" Rudy bit the chord of the lamp and dragged it back out, growling menacingly at it. "Protest. I protest. You just lost 'cause of you're cheating. You're disqualified."

"I am not. You're just a sore looser, you sore looser. I won fair and square;

I said 'ready'" laughed Kringle as he turned around on his stool to face his workbench. Kringle couldn't contain himself.

Pete grumbled. "I protest. I do. It's silliness, the whole dang subject. You play a lot Kringle, you do."

"I may be guilty of that there. 'Play a lot', sure thing, I may rightly be guilty of that."

Kringle and Pete didn't have a new list from Mr. McManus so they spent the morning outside sorting the junk into piles. Pete showed off to Kringle how Rudy could fetch different objects and different size lumber. Kringle couldn't believe it.

"Rudy. Wood. This big, by-by, this big," Pete would say, pantomiming the size he meant. Low and behold, a few minutes later Rudy would come back with the right size wood. "Good boy, good boy."

Rudy loved making Pete happy.

The men had agreed to spend the rest of the day talking about how Kringle makes his toys. While sorting through the junk piles, Kringle took different odds and ends and stuffed them in his red sack.

Back in The Workshop, Kringle turned the sack over and emptied it on his workbench. Pete came along side and stood over Kringle. He was eager to learn Kringle's trade.

"Okay, so what we are gonna do here is make a *toy-box*. A toy-box can have any theme really. They are open to creativity. Let's say this one will have you, me and Rudy working in the yard." Kringle picked up a drawer he found earlier that day and set it down, upside down, on his workbench. He waved his hand over the flat top and said, "Now, usually you'd make a scene, a scene of something nice like a ballerinas twirling, or, for instance cowboys riding horses. But for this one, it'll just be us." Kringle took a pencil and made some marks on the flat bottom of the drawer. "We'll put you here, me here and Rudy here. We'll put The Workshop here and all our piles, here, here, here, and here."

"Okay," said Pete as he got more interested and grabbed his stool to sit down beside Kringle.

Kringle flipped the drawer over, "Now all our work, all the gears that is, all that will move our characters, will be hidden under here, inside this drawer. We'll cut holes around our three characters, connect them to our gears hidden underneath and connect the gears to a crank cut out about here on the right side."

"Alright," said Pete. "So when you turn the crank, what happens, our little pieces move?"

"Mm-hm, that's right. That's the fun part." Kringle readjusted, he was getting deeper in the project. With his pencil he drew. "When you turn the crank, we can have Rudy here run in a circle around this pile here. Put a size nine shoe in his mouth." Both men smiled. "We can have you here, so that Rudy can bring you the shoe."

"Would I move?" asked Pete.

"Yah, but not your body, we'll just have your head move to follow Rudy runnin' and we'll have your arm move up as if it's reaching for the shoe," explained Kringle.

"You can do that? It seems pretty intricate. Small pieces and such," said Pete.

"Oh yah, we can do it. I've made some swell ones: horses racing, fish jumping, even firemen puttin' out a fire," said Kringle.

"What will you be doing then?" asked Pete.

"I don't know, you tell me," answered Kringle handing him the pencil.

"Hm, we could have you go in and out of The Workshop. Maybe you could come out, then circle this pile here and go back in. Like gettin' supplies. Could the door open and close too?" asked Pete handing Kringle back the pencil.

"Yah, I like the door idea. Sure. Never done that before." Kringle started measuring his cut markings and Pete followed his logic carefully.

"I just worry about how small everything will be. I never worked on something so small; my hands are, well, pretty big, pretty roughed," said Pete.

Kringle continued making his marks. "Well, you know what you do about that?" asked Kringle as he put down his pencil and walked to his trunk at the end of his bed.

"What's that?" answered Pete spinning around on his stool to follow Kringle.

Kneeling at his trunk, Kringle took out two small wrapped bundles. He then closed the trunk and began to unwrap what he had placed on top. "My Pop had me build a miniature ship to steady my hands." Kringle handed Pete a fully detailed model of *The Santa Maria*. It had everything: masts, sails, ladders and was painted with minute detail. The small ship was no bigger than the size of an apple. Kringle then unwrapped another bundle. "This one's my father's, it's *The Nina*." He handed that ship to Pete as well. Pete gazed at the miniature masterpieces. Silent, Pete's mind worked deducing all the details. "You can make

The Pinta."

"Oh my, Kringle. Oh my indeed. I sure will try. Might end up looking like a blown-to-bits pirate ship," said Pete with boyish excitement.

Outside Rudy let out warning barks. Following was the sound of Mr. McManus' Duisenberg pulling up. Pete handed Kringle the ships, to which Kringle set them on his workbench beside the future toy-box. Pete opened the door. Rudy rushed in alarmed and warning. The three walked out to meet Mr. McManus.

As the car pulled up, Pete could see that Mr. McManus had the Twins with him. Marlene and Charlene sat in the back seat on either side of their father. Elmer drove and Lloyd sat passenger side. The group had been out all day looking for Marlene's cat - Periwinkle. She was found chasing the chickens inside John Robin's chicken coupe, John Robin wasn't too happy, but it was Mr. McManus' cat, so what could he do about it? Periwinkle now leisurely slept on Marlene's lap.

"I wanna get back home, Daddy," Charlene whined.

"Now, I'll be just a moment, angel. You girls stay in the car," said Mr. McManus as he scooted Charlene back into the car and closed the door behind her.

"But Daddy," Charlene continued.

"Just a moment my little lamb. Daddy will be only a moment." Sternly, Mr. McManus turned and addressed the Dunce Brothers. "Elmer! Lloyd! Let's go! Bring my papers," he barked as he approached Kringle and Pete standing outside The Workshop with Rudy by their side.

"This the new guy?" Mr. McManus was looking Kringle up and down as he approached the men. "You the new guy?"

"Yes Sir, Mr. McManus. Kris Kringle's my name," Kringle put his hand out and the men shook hands.

"You good with your hands Kringle?" Mr. McManus asked.

"I am," Kringle responded.

"Pete catch you up on what we do here?"

"All caught up, Sir."

"You a wise man Kringle? Huh? 'Cause the only rules here are my rules. You want this job, you follow 'em. See a wise man, he doesn't follow any rules; he makes his own. I don't need that. So I ask you; you a wise man Kringle?"

"No Sir. I'm just a man that's happy to have this job and happy to follow the rules."

"Correct. Okay, good. You're hired. Okay, now let's get this done," said Mr. McManus. "I don't have all day. I have a darn cat in the car and two girls that are ready to scream their heads off if I don't get them and that - more than I asked for feline - home." Mr. McManus turned to Pete, "I got a few new orders, but most important, I have the outline for what we need for the Winter Auction."

Mr. McManus, along with Miss Winkleplex, held the annual Winter Auction in the Hamilton town hall every season. People would come from all around: Boston, Rhode Island, New Hampshire, Maine and even New York City to bid on what Mr. McManus would advertise as his 'Finest Imported European Furniture In All America'. Mr. McManus would make a bundle and poor Pete would be worked right through his rough hands and down to the bare bone.

The group of men headed inside The Workshop. Rudy stayed, staring south. He could see the Airlords approaching; they were slowly making their way to the junkyard.

"Then it's settled - Johnny and me will man the *Battle Cruiser*," said Murf officially, holding up the new sled's blueprint that Johnny had finished. The Airlords were heading to the junkyard to collect the needed parts. "Agreed?"

"Agreed!" cadenced everyone.

The Airlords felt good about the new design. They had spent many hours discussing and researching how to make a ship that could beat the Twin's Flexible Flier, which they all agreed to call – *The Mongol Machine*.

"V'ell, v'ould ye look at dat," said Ramona, then spat in the snow. Everyone looked where she was pointing. "Dat dere is da Twin's car. 'N' I dink I c'n smell Charlene. See brothas, she's hanging' out da window even. Looks like she's hollerin' someding, someding fierce tew."

Charlene had seen The Airlords approaching and was already hanging out of her father's car shouting. As The Airlords got closer they could better hear Charlene's taunting.

"What a bunch of flops! Hey Marlene, get a load of these jellybeans. Say you wet socks come to dig in the trash. Pathetic." Charlene was pretending to be in hysterics.

"Ah, shut your trap Charlene," Johnny blasted back as the Airlords approached the car.

"A bunch a garbage rats we got here, Marlene. A bunch a garbage rats here to play with all the other garbage rats," Charlene made a rat face at Johnny.

"You're the rat Charlene, you and your sister too," Johnny said back. Marlene leaned forward a bit to see out of the car, she didn't want to disturb Periwinkle, but did want to see who had called her a rat.

"No, you're the rats!" yelled Charlene back.

"No, you are!" screamed the Airlords back.

"Nooo, Yooouuu!" screamed Charlene as she became red hot.

Inside The Workshop the men leaned over Pete's workbench looking over Mr. McManus' list, discussing what was needed for the Winter Auction.

"Sure is more than last year Mr. McManus," said Pete.

"Dang it Pete, you say that every year," said Mr. McManus back.

"Well, Sir, that's only because every new season there's more than the year before. I just wish you could have maybe let me known all these here orders earlier. This is just a big order here to fulfill in four weeks. That's all I'm sayin'."

Mr. McManus turned toward Pete. "Look Pete, you moan this same story every year. Sing it to Jesus, not me. Speaking of which, how's the Pastor's cross coming along."

Mr. McManus knew he could never outright buy the land that the town's church stood on, but if he wanted to continue expanding his kingdom he'd have to own it somehow. The police station and the church were next on Mr. McManus' list to own. He had told Pastor Finn that he personally would finance the purchase of a cross more magnificent than he had ever seen. Mr. McManus told Pastor Finn that he was a dear friend of a celebrated convent in Italy, where he said the priests agreed to craft Pastor Finn a cross seven feet tall. But, none of that was true. The cross was actually in The Workshop under Pete's cot. He had crafted it out of a tree that had come down during a storm the previous summer. A lightening bolt struck the tree, breaking it right in half. Pete believed that that tree should have fallen on The Workshop and on Rudy, Riggles and himself, but that the Lord chose differently. He believed that the Lord was telling Pete to use that tree to carve the cross for some greater purpose Pete had yet to know.

Pete walked over to his cot, got down on his knees and reached under it. He pulled out the cross that was wrapped in many torn blankets. The men horseshoed around him. As Pete unwrapped the cross, he spoke.

"Almost finished Sir. Looking good if I do say so myself," said Pete proudly. And it did look good. The cross wasn't finished, but you could already see its impressive design. "It's a fine cross and it'll sure look mighty holy hanging high."

Mr. McManus, grunting and puffing, uncomfortably bent to his knees. Running his hand over it he said, "Oh my, Pete, this looks fine. And when it's finished, it'll look exactly like I promised?"

"Sure will, Mr. McManus."

"Exactly. Pete? I can't have it look anything but perfect. You understand me?"

"Yes Sir, it'll look exactly like you instructed," said Pete as he folded the newspaper clipping that Mr. McManus gave him to model the cross after.

Mr. McManus stood and checked and shook his silver pocket watch. "Dang it all! Tell time you second-rate watch! Kringle, you fix things?" asked Mr. McManus.

"Well, sure."

"Here, see what you can do with this. My pocket watch stopped working a week after I purchased it down by Harvard. I was having lunch with the mayor himself," said Mr. McManus showing off. "Pete here says he can't find anything wrong with it. Here take it, see what you can do," Mr. McManus held the watch out for Kringle.

"I'll try, Sir," Kringle took the watch and carefully placed it on his workbench. Once Kringle opened up the line of sight to his desktop, Mr. McManus could see the small ships and the outline of the toy-box the two men were working on.

"What's all this?" Mr. McManus asked.

"Oh, this is just some stuff I made and a small project Pete and I are working on. I'm originally a toy maker you see Mr. McManus, but I can do furniture just as well."

Mr. McManus approached Kringle's workbench and picked up one of the small ships. "Toy maker you say? Well I'll be. Holland is big with toy making, so is Switzerland. Germany too. Toy making, huh? You make what, dolls, cowboys, toy trains, that sort of thing?"

"Yes Sir that's right. Things of that sort. See just here," Kringle went into his trunk and pulled out a wooden man with a rope through each of his hands and feet, parallel to each other.

"Say Pete, hold this end and hold it above your head. Yah that's good, a bit higher if you could," Kringle knelt down and began pulling on each rope: left, right, left, right, as if he was milking a cow. The little wooden man began to climb his way up the ropes until he reached Pete's hands. "I call him The Mountain Climber."

Excited with a new light air, Mr. McManus said, "You made this Kringle, you didn't buy it? This is *your* invention?"

"Well sure, Sir. I got lots of them."

"Lots you say? Toys, huh, yes toys. Not just adults, no we can get the kids too. It's a new market see? Toys…yah, that's it, it's perfect, we'll make one-of-kind, special, rare toys. You can make more money off kids than the adults, because the kids will whine for it, like my Twins do, see?" Mr. McManus turned to Lloyd, "Lots of little brats come into the store."

"They sure do, Mr. McManus," said Lloyd.

"Lots of them little brats go to the Winter Auction," said Mr. McManus to Elmer.

"That there are, Mr. McManus. Tons," said Elmer with a devilish smirk.

"Toys…it's so simple. Can you feel it? We will double our sales. Maybe triple them. Toys…of course from all over the world. Toys from Germany, toys from Italy, toys from France. All of those fancy little city women will want their fancy little city girls to have fancy little dolls from fancy little France. We'll make a killing. We'll charge them a fortune. Oo, oo, oo, I can smell the lettuce." Mr. McManus grabbed Kringle's shoulders, "Toys, Kringle - You make toys?"

"That I do sir."

"And you will make *me* toys Kringle. Come, what is this, tell me what you got here." The group of men surrounded Kringle's workbench. Kringle began to explain to them how the toy-box is built.

"Ah, go chase yourself. At least I *have* a brain. You're all a bunch of no good junk rats. A bunch a wet blankets out here building a sorry excuse for a sled. Psst. Which, by the way, will most likely fall apart like all your other stupid inventions," yelled Charlene pointing at Johnny, leaning more and more out of the car window.

"Your *Mongol Machine* will have nothing on our *Battle Cruiser*," screamed Billy.

"Who are you calling a Mongol, you half pint of spoiled milk," yelled Charlene. "You're just stinkin' like green cheese you are."

"You don't call my brother stinky cheese, you Mongol," defended Johnny.

The Airlords and Charlene were becoming riotous; Marlene just sat still trying to calm Periwinkle from the ruckus.

"Oh sit on scum. I ain't afraid of you Johnny Boone. I'll knock yah. I'll punch all your heads. I'll…" screamed Charlene, as she reached out the window and poked Johnny in his chest with her pointer finger, making Johnny take a step back, slip on a patch of ice and fall down on his butt. "See! Ha!"

All of the loud sounds had already unsettled Rudy, but when he saw Charlene knock Johnny to the ground, Rudy leaped up on the car putting his two front paws on the window and barked in Charlene's face. This action just about scared the claws out of Periwinkle. Her hair poofed out, she leaped off Marlene's lap and bolted out the open window.

All of the Airlords' jaws dropped. Marlene screamed. Charlene was silent. Rudy jumped down from the car and made chase for Periwinkle.

Cat and dog dashed. They headed down toward the train tracks. Marlene and Charlene hopped out of the car and came around the side.

Marlene just kept screaming.

"Someone help her!" she screamed. "Someone save my Periwinkle."

It had just struck 3:58PM and *Betsy Bound* with Old Man Harrigan and Old Bootsie were howling down the tracks heading south. Seeing the train coming, Periwinkle turned a hard right with Rudy close behind. The two came parallel with the locomotive. As Rudy gained on Periwinkle, Periwinkle did what she felt was her only choice. She looked to her left at the approaching train car; its door was slid open. Periwinkle jumped for it. She landed in the car, slid, set her claws down into the floorboards, then sat and licked her paw nonchalantly. Periwinkle then looked back at Rudy who had stopped running.

"OH NO PERIWINKLE! NO! SOMEBODY PLEASE SAVE HER! ANYONE! PLEASE! SHE'S…SHE'S…ON THAT TRAIN!" Marlene turned to Terrance, grabbed his shoulders and said to him, "Please save my little Periwinkle please." Marlene then fell to her knees crying.

Terrance thought for just one moment and then sprinted toward the speeding train.

"What is all the commotion about?" said Mr. McManus, as he and the other men came running out of The Workshop.

Sobbing, Marlene pointed to the train, "Periwinkle jumped on that train, Daddy."

"The train?" asked Mr. McManus baffled.

"Yah, and I think Terrance is going after her too," said Billy to Pete and Kringle. Marlene stood back up and they all stared at Terrance as he approached the passing train. Without leaving a moment to think, Terrance snatched the passing metal ladder bolted to the end of one of the train cars and jumped on. It was an act of courage that no one knew lived inside Terrance.

"We gotta save him," said Kringle to Pete as did Johnny to the Airlords.

Kringle sprinted toward the fast moving train. Terrance was climbing the ladder and was just getting to the roof of the middle train car. If Kringle sprinted hard enough he would have a chance at grabbing the ladder of the last empty car.

Murf sounded the alarm, "Airlords of Hamilton, red alert, red alert, man that Space Car." Murf pointed to Mr. McManus' Duisenberg. The Airlords jumped into the front of the car. Johnny sat behind the wheel, Billy crouched down to where the pedals were, Ramona sat in the middle and Murf took the passenger seat. And before Mr. McManus could stop them, Marlene grabbed Charlene's hand and dragged her into the back seat with her. "Blast off!" Murf screamed. Billy slammed the clutch down with his feet and the gas pedal with both hands. Johnny jiggled the gear shift, then grabbed the wheel tight. The Space Car launched forward.

Dumfounded, Mr. McManus, Pete and the Dunce Brothers just stood with their jaws dropped, while snow mixed with dirt spit out from behind the Duisenberg, slopping up their pants.

Kringle's legs burned as he ran. To his right he could see Terrance up ahead on the side of the middle car climbing. To his left he saw the last car quickly approaching. Kringle leaped, but slipped as he did and as he fell, he stretched his body as much as he could, managing to grab the last step of the last ladder of the last train car. Gripping the step with all his strength, Kringle was dragged by *Betsy Bound*.

Mr. McManus' Duisenberg's sped wildly, bouncing up and down. Johnny gripped the wheel, Billy pushed the gas pedal down as hard as he could and Murf screamed for - "More Power!" Ramona faced the back screaming at the Twins.

"Oi yew stuff it Charlene," she said.

"I said get down you flagpole giraffe, I can't see," Charlene yelled back.

"I ain't naw steepid giraffe Charlene," screamed Ramona. "Jew say dat one more time 'n' I'll knock yah, jew dead duck."

"Ah go on then you, you stupid *GIRAFFE*, lets see yah try," yelled Charlene.

"Periwinkle! My Poor Baby!" cried Marlene.

"Billy, we need more power," ordered Murf.

"I'm doing all I can," said Billy as he began to bounce his butt up and down on the gas petal making the car jerk violently. Everyone inside bounced and flipped; flipped and flopped.

"I gotta take her down the hill Airlords," screamed Johnny. "Hold on!"

If the Airlords were to keep up with *Betsy Bound*, Johnny would have to drive down the small rise and drive parallel with the powerful locomotive. They would have to hurry too if they were going to do any good, the train tunnel to Beverly Crossing was only a half mile after the Boone home, so time was scarce.

"Okay Johnny, I'm gonna give you more power," screamed Murf. "Get ready."

"How are ya gonna do that? Billy stop bouncing!" Johnny put his foot on Billy's head to keep him from bouncing. He pressed Billy down. The Duisenberg resumed its speed. Johnny cut the wheel and the car ran down the small rise and came parallel with *Betsy Bound*.

"Like this, Johnny!" said Murf. "Billy, when I say get out'a there, you get out'a there" Murf crawled down under Johnny's feet where Billy and the pedals were. "Okay Billy One, two, three! Get-get out'a there!" Billy jumped up on Johnny's lap and Murf sat down on the gas pedal. The Duisenberg lurched forward. Ramona and Billy tumbled to the back seat and landed on the Twins.

Periwinkle turned to see two questionable looking hobos smiling at her, "And where-o-where did you come from my little white dinner plate?"

"Looks like we're having cat for supper," said the other hobo and the two men laughed sadistically. One of the hobos pulled out a dirty sack, the other pulled out a rusty fork. Then the two men launched at Periwinkle. The three of them began to run in circles in the empty train car.

Terrance had made it to the top of the middle train car. As the train bumped and wobbled, Terrance cautiously walked across the top of the car until he got to the ladder at its front. He climbed down. Now, balancing on the hitch connecting the next train car, Terrance secured his glasses, looked down squinting to see the tracks rushing by below him. Terrance carefully balanced himself over the hitch. He inched forward. A whirl of fresh snow came up between the two train cars like a small white whirlpool. This made Terrance slip. As his feet slid out from under him, Terrance made one last reach. He grabbed the next car's ladder and began climbing up. Once on top of the next car, Terrance cleaned his glasses and saw that it was full of coal. He began to carefully walk over the coal to the other side. Old Man Harrigan blew the train's whistle as *Betsy Bound* hit the Bump Track hard, knocking Terrance off balance again. He flipped over the side of the car. Hanging, he gripped the top of the train car. He held tight for his life. Coal bounced out of the car and ricocheted off Terrance's head. It was hard to keep his grip from the train's vibrations, but Terrance held on. The edge of the train was freezing to the touch. "Gotta save Periwinkle. I must do it, I promised. I must save her," Terrance said aloud, as his body swayed back and forth and as he searched for the strength to pull himself up. He didn't stutter once.

Betsy Bound was dragging Kringle. "Well, aren't you a bucking bronco," he said as his boots bounced off the tracks and as he slowly pulled himself up the ladder. "But I'll wrestle you, you metal bull. I'll wrestle you good." Kringle pulled himself up the ladder to the top. Now, standing on the top of the vibrating train car, Kringle looked up ahead and saw Terrance hanging on the side of the coal car. "Oh no!" Kringle said as he began to run atop the train car. Kringle leaped over the gap of the two cars, landed, slid, slipped, collected himself and continued running. He leaped over the next car, and the next, but before he could jump again, the car he was on top of reached the Bump Track and hit hard, sending Kringle over the side as well. Like Terrance, Kringle hung on, hanging over the side gripping the frozen edge of the train car while his body swayed this way and that.

Up ahead Ellie was splitting firewood. She looked up for a tired moment to watch the 3:55PM train barreling by. Drained, Ellie leaned a bit on her axe, exhaled a few cold labored breaths, then squinted and puckered, focusing on the passing train. First she thought she could make out a little boy hanging off the side of the train car, followed by a man also hanging. The man looked to be pulling himself up. Once up, he began running atop the cars, leaping from one car to the next. Then Ellie looked down the rise. Following the train, Ellie saw Mr. McManus' Duisenberg driving wildly. She squinted and puckered even harder and could swear she saw in the driver's seat her oldest boy Johnny at the wheel. "It can't be," she said to herself. "Now Lord, I know that isn't Johnny there, tell me that's not my boy in there." But Ellie's eyesight just wasn't good enough for her to be certain.

"Ellie!" Pete shouted. Ellie turned around to see Pete followed by the Dunce Brothers, followed by a tired Mr. McManus running up to her house.

"Come quick. One of them boys is stuck on that train. Kris Kringle's gone after him. And your boys, they be driven that car there."

Ellie dropped the axe and started running with Pete. "What do you mean they're driving that car? My boys don't know how to drive."

Now, running side-by-side, Pete said, "They sure can Ellie, they sure can."

"How we doing Johnny?" screamed Murf up to Johnny Boone while sitting on the gas pedal.

"We're gaining Murf, we're gaining. Keep it up." Johnny looked to the train and saw Kringle jumping from one car to the next. He looked further up the train and saw Terrance hanging on the side of the coal car. "Boy-o-boy, Murf, Terrance is hanging off the train there and that Kringle fella is leaping the cars like he's got Buck Rogers' *Lifting Element*. He looks to be goin' to save 'im."

In the back seat, Marlene stared intently outside the car window at the train, processing all the happenings. Billy Boone, Ramona and Charlene sat beside her screaming at one another.

Back in Periwinkle's train car the hobos were becoming frustrated.

"Get that damn cat!" screamed one of the hobos.

"What you think I'm doing Frank, you see me doing it," the other hobo said back. "Heck, you so smart, you get it."

Periwinkle wasn't having any trouble making these hobos look like a couple of clowns in a traveling circus act. They'd leap, they'd dive, and they'd crash. Periwinkle ran the hobos in circles. She took pride in her skill.

"Get her!"

"You get her!"

"I'm trying!"

"Well, I'm trying too!"

"Well get her anyway!"

"Dang you, you smirkin' whisker."

Periwinkle dashed under the two hobo's legs every time they'd make a grab for her.

By the time Terrance had pulled himself up to his elbows, Kringle had reached him. "Take my hand kid, kid, c'mon take it." Terrance reached with all his might. Kringle pulled fast and hard and brought Terrance back on top of the coal pile.

Both their faces were smeared in black soot. Both lay panting. But just for a moment.

"We gotta get Periwinkle!" Terrance screamed to Kringle.

"We gotta what?"

"Marlene's cat, she's in that train there," Terrance pointed to two cars up.

"Cat, right? Okay! Well, if we gotta, then we gotta," said Kringle back.

With wild driving, Johnny brought the Duisenberg to the side of the train car where Kringle and Terrance stood.

"JUMP, JUMP!" Johnny screamed to them.

Terrance squinted to make out who was driving the car.

"JOHNNY? YOU'RE...YOU'RE DRIVING A CAR!" Terrance screamed back.

"TERRANCE, THE TUNNEL IS COMING UP YOU GOTTA JUMP!" Johnny screamed.

"I GOTTA GET PERIWINKLE FIRST!" Terrance shouted. Terrance's stutter was completely gone; Terrance screamed back. He was even over articulating his words.

"ASK HIM WHERE PERIWINKLE IS!" Marlene yelled to Johnny.

"WHERE IS IT? WHERE'S THE DANG CAT?" Johnny asked.

"WHAT TUNNEL?" Kringle screamed to Johnny. Johnny tried his hardest to keep the car along side the train. Johnny pointed up ahead. Far in the distance Kringle could see a train tunnel. "We have to get out of here kid!" Kringle shouted to Terrance.

"We gotta get Periwinkle first!" repeated Terrance as he leaned over the coal train car to count how many more cars ahead Periwinkle was.

"ASK HIM WHERE PERIWINKLE IS JOHNNY!" Marlene yelled again.

"WHERE'S THE CAT TERRANCE?" Johnny asked again.

"TWO CARS UP!"

"Murf, we need more power. You got any more?" Johnny asked Murf.

"I'll see what I can do," Murf grinded his butt into the gas petal and the Duisenberg lurched forward.

"Okay let's go!" Kringle agreed. "You're name's Terrance then, right?!"

"Ya Mister. Periwinkle is in that car there!", said Terrance repositioning his glasses, pointing and squinting.

"Okay we gotta get there before that tunnel guillotines us!"

Kringle and Terrance moved fast. They climbed down the ladder and up the ladder to the next car.

Pulling the Duisenberg up beside the train car that Periwinkle was in, Marlene could see the horror. Periwinkle was cornered and hissing while the hobos were moving in.

"OH NO, PERIWINKLE. DON'T YOU TOUCH HER!" Marlene screamed.

Billy, Ramona, and Charlene stopped their bickering and everyone stared out of Marlene's window.

The two hungry hobos dove in for their attack. Finally they sacked Periwinkle. The cat hunters could hear Marlene's scream over the sound of the train. When they turned around they saw a little boy driving a Duisenberg and in the back seat were four kids hollering and screaming. It made the men pause, but then uncontrollably laugh out loud. They held up the wild sack.

"Well that sure is something", said one of the hobos.

"I bet yah three gold watches this here is their crummy rat catcher."

"You don't say," the two hobos began to laugh a dirty tooth laugh as they swung the sack in front of the kids.

Kringle and Terrance made it to the top of Periwinkle's train car. All the kids in the Duisenberg looked up screaming and pointing. But, with the sound of the train combined with the Duisenberg, Kringle and Terrance couldn't make out what they were saying.

"Terrance, you stay up here, I'll get the cat and throw her to you!" Kringle shouted.

"No way, no how Mister, I gotta make sure Periwinkle is safe! It's gotta be me Mister; I mean what if you don't get her? Ya see it's a promise I'm in to get that cat back!"

"Rrr okay then c'mon, we gotta hurry, that tunnel is coming up fast!" Kringle pointed ahead and the tunnel was coming closer. Both Kringle and Terrance lay down on the train car and looked down. The two hobos were laughing while they waved the sack that held Periwinkle in front of the Duisenberg, teasing the kids.

The kids saw Kringle and Terrance above looking down. They pointed to the sack.

"Oh no, there's men in the train car. I think they got Periwinkle, I think she's in that sack they got there!" screamed Terrance.

Kringle

"I'm gonna lower you down - you grab the sack! Then you hand off the sack to your friends - then we'll jump! Okay?" said Kringle as he looked ahead and saw the train tunnel approaching even faster.

Terrance stood up and tightened his belt, "Okay! Let's do it Mister!"

The hobos continued to laugh, dangling the sack in front of the kids. Marlene looked up hopefully with both of her hands over her mouth, watching Kringle and Terrance readying their plan. Johnny looked ahead, the tunnel was coming up; he'd soon have to pull a hard right to avoid it.

One of the hobos began to sing:

"Hiya little brats
I got yer cat, I got yer cat
I got 'im right here
in my sack, in my sack
I'm gonna eat 'im up
just like that, just like that
I'm gonna eat right up
yer yummy cat, yer yummy cat"

Kringle had Terrance upside down holding him by his legs. Marlene covered her eyes and the rest of the kids got silent. This made the laughing hobos confused. They could see that the kids were looking above them, but it was too late. Kringle dipped Terrance down. Terrance grabbed the sack with one hand and poked the hobo holding it in his eyeballs with his other hand. The hobo jerked back in pain, bumped into his companion and knocked them both to the floor. Kringle swung Terrance forward. Marlene reached out of the Duisenberg as far as she could.

"If you're gonna get that dang cat get it nooooowwwww!" screamed Johnny, as the tunnel was upon them.

"JUST A LITLE FURTHER!" screamed Terrance. Marlene reached out of the Duisenberg too far, her legs flipped up; Ramona, Billy and Charlene grabbed her legs before she somersaulted out. Kringle swung Terrance forward one last time; Marlene kicked her legs free, stretched even further and grabbed the sack from Terrance. Ramona, Billy and Charlene grabbed her loose legs now half way out of the car. Marlene hung down from the Duisenberg holding the sack.

"GOT IT?" asked Johnny.

"GOT HER!" screamed Marlene back.

"HOLD ON!" screamed Johnny as he pulled the Duisenberg a hard right to avoid hitting the train tunnel. Marlene lifted horizontally as the Duisenberg swung right - her nose just one inch from the tunnel's stonewall. Ramona, Billy and Charlene pulled Marlene back into the Duisenberg.

The Duisenberg skidded out, spun in a circle three times, but avoided the deadly crash.

Before Kringle could pull Terrance up, the hobos collected themselves and grabbed both of Terrance's arms. It was a human tug of war.

"LET HIM GO! QUICK! LET HIM GO!" screamed Kringle to the hobos.

"OR WHAT?!" screamed one of the hobos back.

"OR THAT!" Kringle motioned with his head. The train tunnel was seconds away. Both the hobos screamed, let go of Terrance and jumped back into their train car. Kringle pulled Terrance up, grabbed the collar of Terrance's shirt and screamed, "JUUUMP!" Both Kringle and Terrance leaped off the train just before *Betsy Bound* began to disappear into the train tunnel.

Murf sat on the brakes sweating. Johnny gripped the wheel; his eyes were wider then they had ever been.

"He saved my Periwinkle. He saved you, my Baby Princess," said Marlene as she undid the tie of Periwinkle's sack.

"No, wait don't open that yet," Johnny could hear the hissing and growling from within the sack. Periwinkle leaped out of the sack clawing everyone but Marlene. Johnny, Billy, Murf and Charlene all jumped out of the Duisenberg.

Kringle and Terrance brushed the snow off and walked over to the Duisenberg. Pete and Ellie with Mr. McManus and the Dunce Brothers lagging behind also approached the Duisenberg.

"Johnny Boone, Billy Boone what in the high heavens do you think you're doing?!" said Ellie with her arms on her hips and her chest pushed out.

"Oh hey Ma. It was a code red. We had to, we just had to. We had to save Terrance," said Johnny back. Johnny and Murf both had their chest out as well. "And we did it." Both boys looked and nodded to one another. They were proud of their successful *Space Car* flight.

"And what do you think you were doing riding on that train, young man?" asked Ellie sternly to Terrance.

"I had to Miss Boone, we had to save Marlene's cat. I promised," said Terrance with his chest out too and still without a stutter. Terrance had never stood so proud. He glowed.

"Thieves, Thieves!" screamed Mr. McManus, the last to approach. "I'll have you all arrested. All of you. Slam-click, for all you little thieves."

Marlene with Periwinkle purring in her arms stepped out of the car and approached Terrance. "But Papa-Papa, Terrance is a hero, a brave, brave hero. He saved my Baby Princess from those train robbers." Then Marlene planted a big kiss on Terrance's cheek. "He's my dear-dear...*dear* hero."

Ellie was setting down dinner. Johnny and Billy had been going over the adventure from start to finish and then back again. Ellie wasn't happy about what she kept hearing over and over, but she did want to know the details about what had led her boys to drive Mr. McManus' Duisenberg.

She finally spoke.

"No going over to the Junkyard. No building any spaceships. No building anything for a while."

"But Ma?", started Johnny.

"But Ma nothing Johnny Boone, and don't be talking to that train jumping hobo, Kringle fella anymore either. We don't know him. Do you boys understand what I'm saying? You on memory record? You both almost got yourselves killed today. Really killed, you hearing your Momma? And I can't have that boys. You should have let that cat go. It was probably just trying to escape that incorrigible family anyways." Ellie looked at her boys more sternly and spoke more softly, slowly. "Boys, you *should* have let that cat *go*. Now I don't wanna hear any more about it. Finish your plates and go on up to bed. We got church tomorrow."

You can bet your two mittens that at 9:00AM on Sunday mornings everyone in Hamilton is doing the same routine. And that's squeezing into their finest clothes for Sunday service. Church wasn't just a place to hear Pastor Finn speak and remind us of the divine Creator and of Providence that awaits us. No, it was also a time when the town could come together as one. The men of town could catch up on the hearsay of possible work opening up, while fortunate men could flaunt with one another their most recent investments. The women of town could come to church to catch up on their gossip in the hope of learning about how the mechanics of the town were truly working, while fortunate women could flaunt their most recent gifts. But for the kids of Hamilton there really wasn't much going on at church. They were all dressed too nice to be allowed out of their mothers' sights, for a quick game of marbles or a quarrel that ensued to a fight. No. The only thing the children of Hamilton got out of Sunday service is that they learned the value of patience: patience to wear those tight clothes, patience to stand with their parents as they talked their boring talk, patience to smile to the adults they are told they should know and patience to listen to the sermon and wait for it all to be over. For every child in Hamilton knew that after church - the Sunday fun began. Patience is what the kids get out of Sunday service, and fortunately it was patience that Pastor Finn was teaching them that Sunday morning.

Ellie thought it more sensible to sew the rips in the boys' clothes while they were wearing them. Too many mornings did she sew patches on armpits and have them again rip when her boys modestly reached up to scratch their noses. Johnny held his arms in the air while Ellie knelt down sewing his right sleeve back onto his right shoulder. Billy practiced lifting his arms; they were tight; he could only lift them a foot above his hips.

With pins in her mouth and thread set on her knees, Ellie finished Johnny's sleeve.

"Billy don't go tearing that again. Momma doesn't have time to sew it back together. Keep them arms down. Down you little octopus, down," said Ellie as she wound up the rest of the thread and got up from her knees. "Feel good Johnny boy?"

"It's kinda tight Ma."

"Well, it'll have to do for now. Eh-eh, both of you keep them arms by your side. Lordy-lord boys, please do not test it."

The same was going on all throughout Hamilton. Usually, Terrance would be dragging his sleepy self all around the house in a sulking objection to get changed for church. But on this Sunday morning not only was he dressed first, but his mother had to fight him for the bathroom.

"Your hair looks fine Terrance. What has gotten into you?" Mrs. McKool asked her son.

"You think so?" Terrance was still trying to flatten down a few cowlicks as he finally gave the bathroom up to his mother. "Marlene's gonna be there that's all Mom. A hero's gotta look the part, right?" Terrance walked down to the kitchen and poured himself a cup of hot coffee.

Mr. McKool, sitting in his chair, looked up from *The Worcester Gazette* upon seeing his son sipping the hot mug. He shook his head and went back to reading.

"Honey, your stutter sounds better, don't you think?" Terrance's mother yelled down from the bathroom.

"So it does, so it does. I hadn't noticed," said Terrance as he sat on the couch by his father. "Say Dad, could you spare the comics section?"

Murf's mother, Mrs. McCullough, was never sure on how to tackle her son's or her husband's button problem. Every time she sewed a button on their Sunday slacks, their big bellies popped the button back off.

Pop! - And another button rolled under the icebox.

"Okay boys, stay there. Don't wander away," Mrs. McCullough told her men. Both Murf and Mr. McCullough stood in the kitchen holding up their slacks looking at one another perplexed. Mrs. McCullough shuffled back into the kitchen sliding her slippers on the smooth kitchen floor. "Okay let's try this." Mrs. McCullough took a bit of twine, wound it around the replaced button and tied the other end to the button loop allowing Murf an extra two inches to his waistline. "There. Perfect. Now you." Mrs. McCullough patted Murf's bottom signaling he was finished and then tended to her husband's uncooperative waistline.

"Bet Meh, I v'ook like a stooopid grrrl," Ramona never liked wearing dresses because the other Airlords always razzed her about it when she did. She stood in the living room in front of both her proud parents wearing a light green, white polka dotted dress.

"Bet Petal, y'rr *a'hhre* a grrrl," said her mother pleased as anything. Mrs. Grey could only get her oldest daughter into a dress one day a week and she basked in the sight every Sunday.

"Yu ll'ouk darlin' mi li'll Irrr'ish orchid," said Mr. Grey as he smoked his pipe and brought his wife in closer to him.

"Bet I den't wanna ll'ouk *darlin'*. And I den't know vhat a crummy orchid even *is* - bet I know I'e den't wanna ll'ouk like one," Ramona was sulking, standing with her arms crossed and her eyes down. "Stoopid, I'e ll'ouk stoopid."

"Jahst darlin," Mr. Grey said as he looked proudly at his wife.

"Isn't sh'eh?" Mrs. Grey said back as she looked up to him.

On Sundays Mr. McManus would drive his family in the Duisenberg to church, but something happened to the car after the train incident. Once he got it home, it wouldn't run anymore, so Mr. McManus asked the sheriff to drive them. Sheriff Jones didn't like the idea at all and resented Mr. McManus for even asking him. But Sheriff Jones knew it was always wise to do what Mr. McManus asked and unwise to turn him down.

Mr. McManus liked sitting up front with the sheriff; it made him feel even more like a true mayor. But Mrs. McManus didn't like being in the sheriff's car one bit. She felt as if the Twins and she had been thrown in the back of the police car for some crime they hadn't committed. She was red faced embarrassed to show up for church in this way.

"I don't see why we couldn't just walk," Mrs. McManus said.

"And I don't see why we couldn't bring Periwinkle," sulked Marlene.

Without turning around, Mr. McManus said, "Look we're not walking because it's too cold out and Sheriff Jones offered us a ride" – which wasn't true – "And we're not about to bring a cat to church Marlene. Jesus doesn't like cats."

"But then how am I supposed to show my hero that she's okay? If we don't get married it's your fault." Marlene kept on.

"Yuck! Who cares about that wet sock," said Charlene with as much attitude as she could muster that morning. "Garbage people," she said quietly under her breath.

"Terrance is not a wet sock, Chaaarleeene."

"He is too."

"No. You're a sock."

"Ah, *no* I'm not. And uh ya, he is too a wet sock."

"Both of you cut it out," Mrs. McManus interjected as she looked out the window to gauge how far they were from church. "We can't bring a cat to church, it's simply God's rule, not ours. Just tell this boy she's fine. That's enough. And Charlene stop pestering your sister, I swear you're becoming more and more like your father every day." Mrs. McManus straightened up. "Sheriff Jones, could you possibly drop the girls and me off a little bit before church; it's not healthy to be so showcased. Honey, you can stay with your friend if you like riding in this swell police car so much."

"How's here Mrs. McManus?" asked Sheriff Jones.

"I wanna stay with Daddy," Charlene said. "Can we turn the siren on?"

"No!" said all the adults at once.

"My people come to you, as they usually do," spoke Pastor Finn reciting Ezekiel 33:31. "And sit before you to listen to your words, but they do not put them into practice. With their mouths they express devotion, but their hearts are greedy for unjust gain." Pastor Finn looked up at the congregation with solemn eyes. "Now what does that mean to us? Hm? What are *we*, living *today*, in *these* times, supposed to take away from that? Well to me, I find this passage *most* important. I feel it is saying that *all* of us shall not simply just *hear* the words of God, but actually…"

Pastor Finn had been talking for thirty-five minutes. Like every Sunday, all the children were in the front pew dozing off. Each one of their little heads took turns falling backward, falling forward or falling onto the shoulder of another sleeping child beside them. Their parents spent most of the sermon staring at the behavior of their children more than actually listening to the important morals Pastor Finn taught. Ellie was the most nervous parent of them all; Pastor Finn's voice always put Billy Boone down right away. Even when the congregation stood to sing, Billy would either be found half lying on the pew or being held up by his brother. But this Sunday service, when Johnny went to turn the page, he let go of Billy's collar and Billy fell right down, fully collapsing on the red carpet with a thump.

BLAMP!

All the children broke from their sleepiness; they snickered with sleepy eyes and giggled at Billy. When Johnny helped Billy back up, Billy's eyes were glazed and he looked confused of where he was and what had happened. Pastor Finn only paused for a moment before resuming the sermon.

"It is not enough to *say* you are one of God's children. No, you see the Lord wants you to actually conduct yourself, every minute of every day, in a good, peaceful, caring, manner, free from all the temptations of sin. You must *be* one of His children, not *say* you are one of His children. It is only the Good that are good. It is only the Good that shall see Providence. Our Lord can see the wolves that walk among us, throughout our days, hidden under sheep's clothing. Carry that with you, and with you, you will not only *hear* God's word, you will *be* God's word."

Biting her bottom lip and bouncing an invisible cigarette, Flo nodded her head in agreement; she thought Pastor Finn was handsome.

Mr. Thomson's congregation met every Sunday in his old red barn, which he and a few close friends had cleaned out seven summers back after Mr. Thomson's last horse Frosty lit the light to his new world. Now the red barn was used on Saturday nights as a dance hall for the teenagers and on Sunday nights it was used as a place of worship.

Some simpletons call it - "The black church", but Mr. Thomson's church is welcome to white folk too; Mr. Thomson was white, but mostly the few black folks of Hamilton attended it. Mr. Thomson is a jolly man. He's big and plump and loves music. He plays a self-taught piano and Pete plays the guitar along with him. They're in the church band. The people call them, The Uppity Boys, because they get everyone up off they're seats, singing and dancing.

There wasn't any proper pastor leading the sermons, but everyone there was a true person of God, so the place of worship functioned just the same. And this Sunday, Mr. Thomson's barn-church was in full swing.

Kringle stood with Mr. Thomson, five other white people and the few black men and women of Hamilton – about eleven. Everyone wasn't just standing either; they were clapping along and stomping their feet, singing along to Pete and the four other men playing the uppity blues beat on a small makeshift stage that stood where Frosty used to eat.

Pete sang the verse:

"Sixty feet stomping
Music be playing
People be singing
Lord be smiling"

Even Rudy had a few friends he could visit every Sunday at Mr.

Thomson's barn-church. Mr. Thomson had two dogs himself named Toothache and Sarah and Pete's drummer Eddie always brought his small hairy black dog named Mr. Handsome. The four dogs chased each other drooling and smiling all around that place.

Pete sang the verse to the people and the people answered the words right back, stomping and clapping:

> "Worked all day – *Go on then*
> Didn't get paid – *Go on then*
> Walking ten miles home – *Go on then*
> Tomorrow I'll be doing-it-again, hit me - *Amen*
>
> Got five mouths to feed – *Go on then*
> So in this field I'll bleed – *Go on then*
> Devil be digging my grave – *Go on then*
> Lord knows that I'll-be-saved, hit me - *Amen*

Joy. Everyone danced. Everyone smiled. Everyone was friendly and wanted to meet Kringle. The Sun came in bright through two big windows. The light lit the barn floor in the shape of the window frames only much larger. The boards of the barn made a great boom sound once you stomped your feet – it'd shuffle the dust. The dancing kept everyone warm. It smelled of cakes and coffee that Mrs. Thomson had set out, and which many of the other women added to.

"Living with Honest Pete huh? That's fine, that's fine. Pete's a good man to stand with ain't he? Good man to stand with that Pete is. He was a fine boy, Honest Pete I'd call him, and a fine man he is now. Truth's, truth," one older man said to Kringle.

Pete was the rare man that listened to the vices of your life without any suggestions; this was appreciated greatly by women and also by men, but men never knew exactly what it was they were appreciating.

"I hear you're from way up North. That true? Lord I don't know how you could live somewhere that gets even colder than here. Woo-wee. You must have polar bear blood there son," one older lady said.

"Kringle huh, hm…Kringle…mm…is that Dutch? I hear I'm part Dutch. Holland's where my Pappy's Pappy was born. Kringle, yah I think that may be Dutch," another man started.

When the band had first kicked up, Kringle was nervous because he felt he wasn't the best dancer. But after the first tune Kringle thought he was keeping up with everyone just fine. It's hard to be bashful when girls want to spin with you. After a few songs Mr. Thomson came on stage, said a few words and everyone prayed; they prayed for what this small congregation that met in Frosty's old barn felt was the most important prayer for each and every one of their Sunday services - they prayed for others' prayers to be answered.

"Amen," spoke the seventeen sweaty dancers.

"And now Lord I have one more request, may you please, *please* get this new skinny fella Kringle up on this here stage, 'cause I hear he plays an uppity harmonica and I am not changing my shoes until I dance to it."

Everyone cheered Kringle to the stage. Pete was laughing at Kringle's shyness, but then quickly kicked up an uppity blues so Kringle could show the people what he's got.

After church Pastor Finn was making his rounds. The men grumbled, the women gabbed and the kids did their best to leave their parents' side and meet up. As Sheriff Jones stood with Mrs. Robin, he caught sight of Mr. Riggelsworth standing a bit away from the bustle, buttoning up his jacket and starting down Commonwealth Street. Riggels had come to this church ever since he was a boy. As a young man, for private reasons, Riggels had declared war on those who step on or over others.

"Riggels, hey Riggels, you got a moment?" Sheriff Jones called out. "Pardon me, Mrs. Robins I have to have a word with Mr. Riggelsworth."

"Sheriff's work is never done, I understand, bless you. But like I was saying, anything you can do to keep that cat out of our chicken coop would keep more food on our plates and be much-much appreciated Sheriff."

"I'll speak to Mr. McManus," said Sheriff Jones, but he was more interested in decreasing his involvement with the McManus family than increasing it.

"Say Riggels," Sheriff Jones called out and then jogged over to Riggels. "May I ask you another favor?"

"Sure thing Sheriff, Ma always said I was the dependable one."

"Mr. McManus' car..."

"The Duisenberg?"

"Yah, it got a little banged up the other day. Won't run anymore."

"Yah, I hear them Boone boys took it out for spin. Kicked it up a good one. Wish I could'a seen that."

"Well, that's just another headache I gotta get to, but that Duisenberg, no she isn't running anymore. Do you think you could take a look at it for him?"

"Well, I could, but I already did. I was walking last night; saw it where he parked it outside *Home Cooked*. I noticed she had some extra mud and undesirable marks on her. I was curious. So I checked her out."

"What'd you find wrong? Can yah fix it?"

"I can't fix, or I guess I should say, I won't."

"I understand. It's a damn shame he canned you like that Riggels. He told me the story too. I know you didn't steal anything from him. He's a crummy man that man - don't be repeating."

"Appreciate the words Sheriff. I won't. I don't hold no grudge on him. And it ain't completely his fault that I be rubbin' wooden nickels fer heat these days. A fool holds grudges on bad men. Bad men are just that, bad men. Ain't no reason to wait for them to be good. Can't wait for water to light your stove neither; can't wait for the incorrigible to be reformed. No, I won't fix it because, well, like Pete says, 'Fortunate men at least gotta figure out the easy ones.' See Sheriff, that car probably ain't running, 'cause it's out of gas. That's all. Mr. McManus is gonna have to figure that one out himself. And like you know best Sheriff, a man has to believe in justice even if it's small justice."

Both men smiled. It was a private victory.

"Out of gas. You don't say. Well, do you mind if I *lead* him to that discovery? I keep the peace around here and if he asks me for another ride I'm afraid I may un-keep the peace."

Both men laughed and kicked around the snow a bit.

"Sure thing Sheriff. I wouldn't wanna sit that close to him none-neither. Just don't be telling him I had anything to do with untangling his kite."

"You're an understanding man Riggels."

"That's how my Ma described my Pa, Sheriff. Alright then, you take care," said Mr. Riggelsworth as he brought his brimmed hat low and turned down Commonwealth.

Mr. Riggelsworth always left the sheriff thinking.

"Oo-oo it *is* swell when you *really* get it going huh? Just hums and makes yah feel so alive don't it?" said Flo. She loved the story of the Boone boys having a ride in Mr. McManus' Duisenberg.

"Yah, we were going about five hundred miles an hour I think," said Billy. Johnny and Billy were excited to retell the story. "We almost flew."

"Well, it probably was more like thirty-five or forty. But, biiig hell-pings yah, it sure is exhilarating. Once I seated myself in my Daddy's hoopdee and before I crashed it, I think I was going at least…"

"Flo. No-no. Eh-eh. Don't. Don't be telling the boys that. Boys, Aunt Flo is making this up," said Ellie as her eyes rolled.

"Oh yah, no. I was just spinnin' you mini-men around. My mind, it just, woosh, make-believe all the time," said Flo as she gave Ellie her best 'whoops' face. "Awe big *hell-hell-hellpings,* here comes the firing squad." Mr. McManus and Miss Winkelplex were pointing and waving at Ellie and Flo to come to them as they approached.

"Boys you go find your friends, Momma needs to talk work talk for a few," said Ellie as the boys smiled and ran off. "Don't go too far."

"Ready?" asked Flo.

"Ready," Ellie said. "Let's see what kind of damage is coming our way."

"Ugh, I just hope these wolves don't blow our straw-houses down," said Flo and the two girls straightened their postures and put on practiced smiles.

Mr. McManus and Miss Winkelplex stopped walking once they saw the girls saw them, making the girls walk the rest of the way.

"Ladies," started Mr. McManus.

"Girls," said Miss Winkelplex.

Ellie and Flo stood straight with kind faces.

"Why hello Mr. McManus, hello to you Miss Winkelplex," both women said.

"Lovely sermon, don't you think," added Flo.

"Yes, lovely," said Mr. McManus.

"Yes, lovely," said Miss Winkelplex.

"Oh yes, lovely," said Ellie.

"I did like the part when Pastor Finn said, 'To understand how one treats…'"

"Yes fine. It was lovely. Ladies, I need you to redesign the showroom today," said Mr. McManus.

"Today?" asked Ellie.

"Yes, we are having new products coming in tomorrow and we need to make room for them," Mr. McManus continued.

"New products?" asked Flo. "What new products?"

"Toys," said Mr. McManus directly.

"Toys?" asked Ellie.

"Yes girls - toys. Now pay attention; no more questions."

"Pete and that skinny new fella have a shipment of toys coming in on the late train tonight. I need you to have a special spot ready for them. Special, you hearing me? It must catch the eye."

"The front window, girls. Open up the front window. Push everything back and to the sides, but make it so you can still walk through. It can't be cluttered again."

"But today, Sunday? Could we do it tomorrow morning?" asked Ellie.

"No!" both Mr. McManus and Miss Winkelplex said with pointed fingers.

"Absolutely not, we must have it ready to go by the time we open the store tomorrow." Mr. McManus was talking to Ellie and Flo like they were children. "You can't be moving things around when customers come in? That's sophomoric. I want us to be looking fine *tonight*. Looking more than fine. This is to be our big new release for the Winter Auction. Toys! Tell everyone too. Be specific - they are from Holland, Paris and Milan. The toys Pete and, and that new, spindly fella..."

"Kringle," Ellie helped.

"Yes, that one, are bringing to the shop tonight are *not* for sale just yet. But they *will* be up for auction. These are to *tempt* the buyers, see? Are you getting all this ladies? You look baffled."

SNAP-SNAP!

Miss Winkelplex snapped her fingers in front of Ellie's and Flo's faces. "Do you girls understand Mr. McManus? Front window - push things back - make room for people to walk - make it look nice – catch the eye - toys! Okay? Good. So head there now, because the toys are coming in around five o'clock..."

"Five o'clock?" Flo let out.

"Yes. Lordy is there a problem Flo? You seem to always be shocked."

"Well, Miss Winkelplax, I-I don't have my key on me."

"I don't either Miss. Winkelplex. If you want us to go home and then come back, well then we could just…"

"No. No. Lordy girls. Okay, here take my key." Miss Winkelplex handed Ellie her shop key. "Don't lose it. Ellie…don't you lose it; it's the master."

"I mean you could just lock us in and then later let us out Miss Winkelplex," suggested Ellie.

"No, no Sunday is my day to relax. Just lock it up and don't lose that key. Okay are we all set girls?"

"Yes Ma'am."

"Yes Ma'am."

"Toys ladies! Great, wonderfully fun toys for all the kids. Be happy. Be joyous. Be excited. Tell everyone all about them, starting now. Imported too, remember that, that's the bait. *Imported.*"

"Yes Sir."

"Yes Sir."

Mr. McManus and Miss Winkelplex headed over to Pastor Finn to catch him up with the progress of his imported cross from Italy and to discuss its grand presentation to him and the town at the Winter Auction. Ellie and Flo were left looking at one another, disappointed to have lost their Sunday.

All the kids in town who succeeded in getting away from their parents stood in a small circle listening to another juicy argument between Johnny Boone and Charlene McManus

"Yah, but Charlene, we didn't get to build our *Battle Crui*…I mean our new sled, 'cause of that stupid cat of yours," said Johnny.

"Who is doing just fine by the way," said Marlene to Terrance.

"I'm glad," said Terrance holding a hero's stance.

"That doesn't matter. You made the challenge, so if you forfeit *you* forfeit; *you* lose. So, are you forfeiting? Huh?"

Charlene was right and all the kids knew it. If you make a challenge and don't show up – You lose!

"No, we don't forfeit," said Johnny quietly.

"What was that?" I didn't hear you. Did you just say you forfeit?" teased Charlene.

"NO! I said we DON'T forfeit! We'll be there," said Johnny a bit worried. He wasn't sure if he could build a sled in one day, let alone a few hours.

Ellie and Flo entered the circle of children to tell the Boone boys about the change in the day.

"Oh, it's you. Ramona right? So tall, like a starlette. Lucky. Didn't you look nice in there? That's a pretty dress you have on under there Darling. I used to have one much like it. It's lovely. I like the bottom; how it's loose and free." said Flo to Ramona. Flo could tell Ramona had a bit of a liking for Murf; Flo's good that way. "Didn't you think she looked nice in that dress there?" Flo said to Murf.

"Um, what? Me?" asked Murf.

"That's right, you," said Flo back.

"Um. Yah, sure," said Murf, confused to be pointed out.

"Nice dress isn't it?" Flo continued with Murf.

"Hm? What? Ah, ya I guess," Murf looked at Ramona who was wide-eyed and immensely embarrassed to be on display to the whole group of kids.

"That's right it is. You're a smart one. *You* can tell it's a nice dress. Smart mini-man. Murf right?"

"Yes ma'am. Murf McCullough."

"Well, Murf McCullough. Your lady looked very nice in there."

"My..."

Neither Ramona nor Murf knew what had just happened, but they were both full of fireworks.

All the kids were ready to tease, but they'd have to wait on account that there were still grown-ups present.

"Boys, Momma's gotta go into work now. I'll be home for supper though. You boys head home without me and do your Sunday chores," said Ellie to her boys.

"We got a race at four o'clock, down Patton's Hill. We, we gotta go Momma or we'll have to forfeit," said Billy to his mother.

"Ma?" Johnny looked longingly at his mother.

Ellie looked at the kids around. She could tell the race was with the Twins by how Charlene was stink-nosing her boys. "Well, ooookay. Your chores first. Deal?"

"Deal," said Billy and then Johnny appreciatively.

Ellie kissed her boys on the tops of their heads and Flo winked at

Ramona and shot her with her finger gun. Then they both headed down Commonwealth to the shop.

"Four o'clock. Don't be late, ya garbage pickers!" said Charlene.

"We won't, you dumb Dora's," said Johnny back.

Kringle and Pete walked back to The Workshop talking about the many toys they would have to create that day. Kringle was good, but not so good that he could make ten toys in one night. To fulfill Mr. McManus' unreachable order, the two toymakers would have to keep things simple. Pete went out and collected twelve table legs, that he would later carve to look like bowling pins – Rudy helped fetch the legs along with him - Kringle finished a simple toy-box of a ballerina twirling atop an iced pond that was modeled after Hamilton's Little Island Pond - Pete and Rudy collected nightstand legs that Pete would later carve to look like police and firemen standing at attention - Kringle took an old cabinet with swinging doors, nailed a roof on it, and built the insides of the old cabinet to match the insides of a real house with floors, walls, rooms and a staircase, then later, he'd have a five foot tall dollhouse. Pete sawed out horse profiles from a brown and black plank board, stuck them onto broom poles and attached wagon wheels at the bottom and had two functioning racehorses - but it still wasn't enough.

"Mr. McManus said ten items; we only have eight," said Kringle as he finished the shingles on the dollhouse's roof. "I don't think we should start anything new."

"I don't neither," said Pete as he finished the horses' heads.

"Right, okay…so let's finish what we have here. These are the most important cakes to bake. I can add the ships my father and I made. If we add those, that'll make ten."

"Yah, but Kringle, you don't wanna be giving Mr. McManus your father's and your ships. He'd sell them right out from under you. I know this to be true."

Kringle was done with the shingles on the dollhouse roof. He stood and stretched long.

"Well, he said these toys here are just for display. They're just to put up in the store to get the people interested. I'll explain it to him. I'll tell them they ain't for sale. They'll be safe. And for now adding them can buy us some more time."

"I don't know Kringle. Let's keep working and try not to commit to that there idea."

"Fair."

The two toymakers worked on.

"Dis iz one pimple spittin', dead leg runnin' mess wez ge'ot ourselvez into heh?" It was different hearing Ramona's Irish slang come out of her when she wore a dress. Ramona did have her winter jacket on over her dress and the Airlords were used to seeing her in that, but it wasn't buttoned anymore, so you could see that light green and white spotted dress and it simply made Ramona look more like a real – girl. The Airlords had only a few hours to build their *Battle Cruiser*. They all sat on the floor of Central Command still in their church clothes, but now with their racing scarves and racing helmets on and their racing goggles secured to their foreheads. "Sow v'haht 're wez ganna do heh? Wez ain't ge'ot a launch'able ship d'ere Johnny. I dink ve're at a code red again, ye?"

"She's right, this is officially another code red," said Murf. This was the second code red of the weekend and of the Airlords entire history. "What do we need Johnny?"

"Well now, hold yer horses, we do have one thing to take care of before anything else," said Murf very officially. "Everyone please rise and stand at attention." Murf had asked his mother a few months back to make *The Airlords* medals like his father's war medals. He wanted to have them ready in case there was ever a real 'code red'. Mrs. McCullough used the tops of her raspberry jam jars and her good ribbon. She really got into the craft, and after her daily lunch she would spend an hour painting the medals meticulously so to look as official as her husband's medals.

The Airlords were lined up at attention: Billy, Ramona, Johnny and Terrance. Murf pulled out two medals with blue ribbons.

"Billy Boone, I give you and me, Murf McCullough, these medals for our acts of courage, bravery and above all…being really good at getting Johnny the power he needed in that Space Car. Boy that was somethin'." Murf placed the medal over Billy's neck and then his own. All of *The Airlords* took the ceremony seriously. "And to you Johnny Boone, I present you this medal of courage and bravery and above all…for driving that car and going so dang fast and getting it so close to that train that was going, like VRR-RUM-RUM-ROOOOOM fast. That was really something, and doing that thing you did when you cut the wheel and we spun out and it was all just so wild." Murf placed the medal around Johnny's neck and then stepped down the line. "And to you Ramona, I present you this metal for courage and bravery and above all…for keeping those Twins out of our hair and saving Marlene when she leaped outa the Space Car, grabbing her legs and all, jeesh, oh, and for telling those girls to shut it." Murf brought his voice a little lower, "'cause you don't look like a giraffe Ramona. I checked my Dad's encyclopedia, giraffes look mighty different. Those girls are just jealous. My Mom said when you grow up you'll be all happy you're so tall, I wish I was tall, I wish I was tall like you, I think it'd be swell to be tall. Anyways she made your medal with a pink ribbon, I told her not to, but she did anyway. I hope you still like it." Murf had to get up on his tippy toes and Ramona had to lean forward and down a bit, but they got the medal on. Murf brought his voice back up, "and finally to our big-big hero, a man we always knew was great, but just didn't know how great. All of us Airlords present you Terrance McKool…" Murf pulled out an extra special medal that was made from a bigger raspberry jam jar lid and had all the different colored ribbons dangling from it. "…This swell medal is for your acts of courage and bravery and above all… boy, I mean wow, you were like a real life space hero. You were like Buck Rogers himself." That was as big a complement as you could get from the Airlords. "You all running after that train and even just getting up on it was fantastic, I never seen anything like it." The other Airlords shook their heads in agreement. "Then when youz were climbing that ladder and then when youz almost fell off, I saw that, I thought you were gonna get smushed like a rotten tomato Terrance, or get stuck on that train and swoosh, we never see yah again or somethin'. I swear I thought, 'well there goes Terrance, I'm sure gonna miss him', but you didn't and then you got back up and how you grabbed that sack all upside down." Murf tilted his body to look more upside down. "That looked really scary and then when you slung that sack with that cat to Marlene, I mean, boy oh boy, that was somethin', wasn't it Airlords?"

"Sure was Terrance."

"'ure vas some-ding Turrance."

"I mean I thought your head was gonna get smushed right off Terrance," said Billy with wide eyes.

"And then...and then...right before that tunnel you and that Kringle fella leaped off the train just in time. I mean who does that? I'll tell yah - heroes do that! Boy. Wow. Faaantastic Terrance. Boy-ooooo-boy." Murf placed the medal on Terrance's neck and started clapping; the rest of *The Airlords* joined in. "Three cheers for Terrance. Hip-hip."

"HURRAY!"

"Hip-hip."

"HURRAY!"

"Hip-hip."

"HURRAY!"

The Airlords had never had such an official ceremony before. Morale was high, but there were still important tasks at hand.

Murf passed up and down the line of Airlords like he was a commanding officer.

Johnny pulled a straw out of his back pocket and started chewing, "Well, I've been thinking. We can make most of the ship right here, from parts we already got. But we gotta find skis, Airlords, that's most important. We'll nail them to the bottom. She'll work fine, just fine. It's all on how you pilot the ship anyways."

"Okay. Yah hear that Airlords? That's the plan. Now let's get building," said Murf, then he saluted the Airlords. "Dismissed."

The Airlords climbed down the ladder of Central Command. There were pieces of past ships and ship parts organized in different piles, like the piles Pete made, at the bottom of the massive oak.

Terrance grabbed the base of *The Ship To The Unknown*, which was an old door, and Johnny nailed the sides of a baby cradle that they'd been saving to the sides of the door – the bars of the baby cradle would keep the pilots secured in the ship - Billy brought over the *Spectrometer* - this would help plow through any tall fluffy snow they might encounter and help them see through the spray - Ramona found the oar and tossed it inside – Murf and Johnny would use the oar as a steering rudder – but how would they attach the skis to the bottom? That was the daunting question that had all the Airlords pacing back and forth in the snow.

"I know," Terrance said. "We'll take some boots, then nail them to the bottom of the ship and then nail the skis to the boots."

"Naw," said Johnny, as he thought hard, then turned his newsy cap around and put the piece of straw he was chewing back in his back pocket.

"We could nail some bricks to the bottom of the ship and then nail the bricks to the skis," said Murf and then everyone looked at him oddly.

"Well, first we ain't got no bricks and second yah can't nail bricks," said Johnny.

"Well, why not?" asked Murf.

"Because they're bricks Murf," Johnny thought on.

"Wez cnnn't jast nail dem skis to da bottom of da derr?" Ramona asked.

"Naw there needs to be something in-between them. We need to lift it up a bit; about a few inches."

"Well, why don't we use the bottom rockers of the cradle?" asked Billy. "The curvy part."

The Airlords looked to the cradle. It was wobbling back and forth without its railings. Johnny squinted, puckered and thought.

"That's it Billy! Yah the legs of the cradle. Perfect. That's all we need; that's what we'll do. Good thinking Pal." said Johnny as he gave his brother a pat on the shoulder. It wasn't every day that the Airlords, let alone heard a suggestion from Billy, but actually gave him credit for one of his ideas. Billy was shocked.

The Airlords diligently went to work.

Kringle and Pete glowed orange as they pulled their two sleighs into town. They had finished all the toys they had started that day, but, regrettably, they did have to add Kringle's small ships to make it an even ten. The toys were wrapped inside two massive red sacks. Rudy led them into town.

Kringle and Pete were passing the Boone home and came upon the old oak that held the Central Command in its palm. One bark from Rudy made five small heads turn. With their goggles now on and their scarves flowing long in the wind, each of The Airlords gave Pete a wave.

"What do we have here; what yah working on? New ship?" asked Pete as he repositioned his red sack, steadied it better on his sled and then walked toward The Airlords. Rudy's eyes widened at Billy's long flapping scarf; he ran at Billy, bit at the flowing fabric and started up a game with them both. Kringle checked the positioning of his sack as well and then stood by Pete. "Is this the *Battle Cruiser* Johnny?"

"Naw we didn't have time to make it. We call this the *Earth Cruiser To The Nine Moons Of Saturn – Earth Cruiser* for short."

Kringle approached the sled; The Airlords stepped back to give him room. Billy was running around the old oak, laughing, while Rudy chased him growling in play. Kneeling in the snow Kringle inspected the *Earth Cruiser's* design. He didn't know that young kids could build to this imaginative caliber. Even though crooked, rusty, bent nails were obviously used and most likely pulled out from some old wood, they were nailed in with determination and that kept the sled fairly sturdy. The door was nailed to the curved legs of the baby cradle - this made the ship two feet high. The sides of the cradle were nailed to the sides of the door - this made the ship look like a baby cradle for adults. The glass bowl was secured at the ship's bow with rope and the oar was locked with boards and rope to the ship's stern ready to steer. Kringle wasn't sure how it was supposed to work; without the skis attached the ship looked like it would just tumble down Patton's Hill, not sled down it.

"You made this?" Kringle said to Johnny. Now on his knees as well, the two were eye level.

"Yup."

"It's good."

"Yah," Johnny wasn't so proud. The *Earth Cruiser* wasn't his best work, so he was a bit embarrassed to talk about it.

"I have a question though. How is it supposed to coast on the snow? You try it out yet?" asked Kringle. He didn't want to be nosey or rude, but he did wonder the question just the same. "She might topple forward if you all get in and point down hill."

"I know," said Johnny, "What you take me for Mister? I ain't a dumb Dora. We gotta get some skis of course. Gonna nail them skis down here. Then she'll coast just fine."

"Hey Pete, you got any skis in the junkyard?" asked Murf. "We were hoping so." Pete smiled before answering. All The Airlords looked fantastically imaginative dressed in their leather football helmets, goggles and scarves. Murf's goggles were the largest; they looked to be hard for him to see out of.

"Skis, hm. I'm not sure I do children," said Pete.

"Awe nuts," said Murf. "You got anything similar to skis?"

"Well, I do have an old white picket fence. Its wooden posts are shaped like skis."

"You could nail those to the bottom. Sand 'em real good. That'd help it coast," suggested Kringle.

"We don't need no more help, Mister," said Johnny to Kringle. "I mean, thanks for the help with Terrance and that cat, but all the same Mister, I got this here covered just fine." The Airlords liked Kringle after the big train adventure, but Johnny didn't like outsiders giving their two cents about how to build *his* ships. Pete knew not to make a building suggestion to Johnny unless asked first. They didn't know where Johnny learned it, Ellie would say "probably from his father," but his usual response to a building suggestion was – "Advice should only be given if it's asked for or if it's life threatening." These wise words usually shut people up quick. Kringle backed away from the ship. Pete patted his shoulder with a smirk.

"Sorry Johnny. Sure thing, I know you got it," said Kringle.

Panting, Billy and Rudy approached the group.

"Hello Mr. Train Man-Bank Robber. Hey Pete," said Billy as he wrapped his scarf back on. It was wet with drool and a bit ripped.

"Sure Murf, you can go for a look. Take what you need," said Pete as he got his sled ready to pull down to town.

"Swell. Well, we better hurry if we're gonna make it in time for the race Airlords. See yah later Pete. See yah later Mr. Kringle," said Murf. The Airlords headed up the ladder, which was just loose boards nailed poorly to the old oak.

"Kringle's fine. No need to call me Mr. Kringle," Kringle said back while watching The Airlords climb the loose boards and pile into the rickety Central Command. Pete and Kringle watched the clubhouse pitch left and then sway right as The Airlords walked about inside. Back and forth the clubhouse rocked, back and forth, with the pattering sounds of little feet.

"That ain't very safe up there is it?" said Kringle as the two men began their trek to town.

"Bit wobbly huh?" said Pete back.

Rudy was unsure who to stay with. He barked at Pete to let him know he was thinking about staying with the Airlords. Pete waved back to Rudy, "Okay Rudy, see you later. Have fun. You take care of them Airlords."

"The older boy Johnny, he don't like suggestions too much huh?" asked

Kringle as they walked.

"No, and I should have told you that. He's a proud boy. Wants no help from others. It's a good character trait, but it can often butt-bite yah back sometimes. But that boy Johnny wasn't always that way. No, he was a lot like his brother. Happy. Trusting. Enjoying life and all. After Mr. Boone left, Johnny got a bit cold inside. Builds a lot now. Keeps busy. Those ships I mean, and that clubhouse they got. Guess he's handling his Papa leaving like a man handles his woman leaving." Pete looked over his shoulder at the clubhouse and then at Kringle. "He's got a broken little heart."

"So Mr. Boone, he just get up and go huh?"

"He get one of them yellow fliers, saying how they got all kinds of work out west – farming, picking, that kind of work. You seen 'em?"

"I've seen 'em."

"He found a lady there. Married her pretty quick. Even sent an official document, like a contract, home, saying that Ellie had to sign, saying it was all right him marrying a different woman and everything. Riggels told me – well he heard from Mr. Robin that Mr. Boone's new Mrs. Boone's daddy owns a big farm. The enormous kind. Acres and acres of peach trees, I heard. And so, I hear from Riggles, Mr. Boone manages that farm now and when the new Mrs. Boone's daddy dies, he'll own that farm. He'll be rich. Real rich."

"There's two Mrs. Boones?"

Kringle and Pete took the turn off Bridge street and headed down Commonwealth. They pulled their sleighs slower as the long day and the long walk had made the men tired. The only glow was from the Moon that reflected the remembrances of the Sun. Yet the horizon still held a line of pink. No one was out. The town was still. The two men once again walked in the middle of the road.

"Yah, Ellie never changed her name back to her Papa's. Don't know why. Don't know if it's an off shoot of pride, embarrassment or what; she probably does it for the kids or for some reason we don't understand."

"When I met Ellie, she told me a Mr. Boone was inside the house. Inside with a gun."

"I thought she stopped doing that. Ellie changed a lot too when her man left."

"Yah?"

"Sure. Ellie's very focused now. She's like how her boy Johnny is now.

98

See Ellie, well, Ellie *lived* life more then, now it seems she battles it."

"Makes sense though."

"Makes sense though."

The two men continued down the road pulling their sleds with red sacks filled with toys.

Ellie and Flo had been working for hours getting *Bonne Affair* ready for the new toys. Everything looked as Miss Winkelplex had requested. For the last hour Ellie and Flo waited for the toys to be delivered. The two friends sat in cabriolet chairs: Ellie inspected a tear in the bottom seam of her Sunday dress - she had caught a snag earlier while the two ladies shared sides moving the High Boy back a few feet. She wasn't happy about the clumsy move. It left her feeling defeated. Flo sat with her legs crossed painting a sign advertising the coming toys. She was also feeling weary; her muscles ached from the extra work. She was looking forward to getting home, looking forward to a hot bath with her book *Love Bandit*, looking forward to seeing her cat Virginia, wondering if she had left enough food out for her and feeling bad for Ellie; she knew the rip in her Sunday dress would be hard for her to shake off. Both ladies often felt each other's disdain for the world when the world was being rotten to them. Seasonally, New Englanders settled into their winter blues and when they did so, they usually did it with a friend close by.

Flo's curls were pointing in all directions, especially in front of her face; she blew the thick curl, but it wouldn't budge so she had to use the pointed end of her paintbrush to try and flip it back because all of her fingertips were now blackened from the paint.

"Ah *crackers.* Now I don't know what I'm writing anymore," Flo said.

"What do you mean? What do you have?"

"Well, I started with, '*Coming Soon*' and was going to write, 'Hand made toys from across the sea, at the Winter Auction December twenty-fourth', but I wrote the first bit too big. The rest won't fit."

"Let me see." Ellie tossed the bottom of her dress down and turned to Flo. "Lordy-lord Flo, you don't have room for half of that." The girls laughed; they needed a third wind. Flo's words "*Coming Soon*" took up half of the sign she was painting.

"Ugh, I know, I know. What do I do? I ain't startin' over."

"Just paint 'TOYS' in big capital letters and then 'Special From Europe' a bit smaller and then 'D - E - C, twenty-four' even smaller."

Flo held up her sign.

"Yah-think that'll fit?"

"You can try, or just 'TOYS' really big."

"I always start things off too big. And then I'm left with a mess."

Knock – Knock!

Kringle and Pete were outside *Bonne Affair*.

"That's it; let's get this done," said Flo as she set her project down and headed to the door, wiping her fingertips with a rag.

"Good evenin' Flo," said Pete with his hat in his hands.

"Good evenin' Miss," said Kringle with his hat in his hands.

"It could'a been a good evening, it should'a been a good evening and you know what Pete, Kringle, there will hopefully *still be* a chance for a good evening, that is if we can get this finished up. C'mon in." The men slung their sacks over their backs and headed into *Bonne Affair*. "I got me a reading date with little Miss Virginia and she'll be one prissy kitty if I don't get home soon."

The men could tell the air of the store was one of tired women. Kringle didn't dare talk up Ellie; her expression told him so.

Ellie walked over.

"Careful, lordy-lord what kind of toys do you fellas have in there. Bring it this way. We'll be setting things up here," Ellie instructed as she stepped out of the way of the two big red sacks being placed on the floor by the front window.

"I saw your boys; they got themselves a new sled Ellie. Some race going on right about now," said Pete.

"Did you notice if them boys changed out of their Sunday clothes? I forgot to tell them that."

"I didn't notice, no Ma'am."

It was about then that Ellie noticed how silent Kringle was - Flo had noticed the moment he got quiet. Kringle had never seen Ellie dressed nice. Her Sunday dress had him speechless. If it was said, Ellie would never agree, but Kringle thought she looked like true art. Ellie stood beautiful and strong with

100

her hands on her hips, her long black hair full, wavy and now down, her chin up, her demeanor calm, her long light blue and white Sunday dress hanging on her small shoulders by two straps that had light blue bows lining it. The dress hugged Ellie's doe-like frame. It bellied out over her hips. Kringle was smiling at Ellie. He wanted to dance her. He wanted to know what her waist felt like in his hands. He realized a bit too late that she was talking to him.

"I don't think he heard you," Flo laughed as she walked over. "Kringle yoo-hoo. Can we see what you got? We really want to get home soon'ish Honey."

"Oh sure," said Kringle. He shook his head, snapped himself out of his daydream and untied his sack. Pete looked at Flo and they both smiled – "Puppy love."

Pete and Kringle pulled out each toy one by one: The dollhouse, the police and firemen, the riding horses, the bowling set, the small ships, the climbing man, two wooden dolls, a carving of a boy catching a fish, the racing horse, and the toy-box of a ballerina twirling on a small pond.

Flo and Pete set up the front window display while Kringle and Ellie set up the display table behind it.

"These sure are something. Where'd they come from? Switzerland?" Ellie asked Kringle as she positioned the toys.

"All over Europe they tell me. This one here is from Germany they say and they say this one here's from Switzerland. You were right with that. All sorts of places I guess. They tell me that the people who make them are old men from small villages," said Kringle as he handed Ellie the toys she would point at and then place meticulously on the table.

"How wonderful. Mm exquisite. I'll say these are just beautiful." Ellie stood up straight and combed her fingers through her long black hair to make sure that her hair wasn't knotting. "Beautiful though. I mean look at these ships. Look at the detail," Ellie said to Kringle.

"You think so?"

"Well, sure. Just look."

Kringle picked up the toy-box and set it on the display table.

"I like this one," Kringle said to Ellie. "Look what it does if you turn this lever here." The ballerina twirled as she skated around in circles. Small carved birds stood on a small carved fence; they flapped their wings and followed the ballerina with their heads. A small fish jumped out of a circular hole in the pond's ice and disappeared again.

"Oh my. What a tiny fantasy. Well I say…this is the most wonderful thing I have ever seen. May I?"

"Sure thing, just twirl it."

Ellie brought the toy-box closer and slowly turned it's crank. She watched all the happenings play out in front of her and she smiled and giggled like a younger Ellie did.

"Oh I love this. This is darling. I didn't even know something like this could exist."

"It's not too hard to build, you just have to know how."

"Psst. I could never make anything like this."

"Sure you could."

Ellie stared and smiled at the ballerina.

"No I could not. Not in a miiiiillion years. Such a tiny fantasy." Ellie held the toy-box further out from herself. "But you know what? Hm. I bet you Mr. McManus charges a fortune for them. Ya, I bet. These toys here, these toys are just for children with fancy folks. I bet you this alone costs three dollars. No real person can buy that. And you know what, now that I'm using my mind, now that I'm actually thinking about it, I think that's rotten."

"What's rotten?" asked Kringle, confused to see Ellie's smile fade so quickly.

"This toy here. You don't see the bottom line of all this Kringle? It's rotten that we grown-ups have the power to make something this wonderful, something that'd make children so so happy. These would simply make little eyes glow. But we don't. Mr. McManus will put huge price tags on them all. See we put a price on every single thing these days. Even the happiness of a child. See Kringle, I'll be telling *most* of the children – 'You don't get this 'cause your Momma and Poppa can't afford to buy it for you. Nice though isn't it; now give it back?'"

"I never thought about it like that."

"That's the problem, people never think. Look-a-here Kringle, just think about this, it's barely a law that you have to feed children, let alone keep them loved. There are orphans all over this silly country right now and little ones are just dying - dying 'cause they don't have any food or they're just too cold. And they don't know why? It seems most people have just missed the whole point. We should know enough to *give* to children all the magic and happiness that we can easily provide and not charge them for it. No. You know what?" Ellie was getting pink in the cheeks. "It's just that, us adults pray for help, don't we?"

"Sure."

"Right, but why would God help someone, us who don't even answer the prayers of little children. When *we* could? I think it's all terrible."

"I see," said Kringle as he lightly touched the toy-box Ellie was holding.

Ellie was deep inside her words, as if Kringle could have walked away and she would still have declared her awareness to her hypocritical world.

"Me, I say these toys here are crummy. Mean little things. Crummy, crummy, crummy *and* criminal."

"Crummy? I thought you said you thought they were beautiful."

"No, they're crummy," Ellie put down the toy-box and scowled at the toys on the table. "All these toys do is show little boys and girls, good boys and girls mind you, magic that they can't have?"

"They could buy them."

"No real person has three dollars for a doll Kringle, you know that."

"You really think they'll be sold for that much?"

"Oh sure, probably more. Probably start at five. Flo, how much you think this here will be?" hollered Ellie to Flo.

"Probably start at five, six maybe. Three at the lowest."

"See, three at the lowest," Ellie said to Kringle.

"Wow. I never thought about it. It's not worth six, 's only about a few hours of work."

"Well, whatever it is, it'll show children something they can't have. Heck, to a little child, it'd be like if colors cost money, but grey was for free."

"Sheesh."

"Look-a-here Kringle, I'll tell you, truth is truth and if I could make something like this…" Ellie began turning the crank of the toy-box and became lost in watching the ballerina twirl. "I would make one for every child in the world. Every single one."

Silhouettes of long legged children atop Patton's Hill were cast down the snow-covered crest. The curious Moon hung over them. They looked organized. They looked purposeful. A wind came up the hill like an invisible punishment and lifted everyone's racing scarves. A light snow began under the grey clouds above while the black clouds behind them spoke of something much more authoritative on its way.

The Airlords, the Twins and the rest of the children from Miss Magnolia's class stood in a circle, ten feet from their sleds that sat ready to be manned. The children were going over rules for the race. The two sleds were parallel at the starting rope, which lay in the snow.

The Twin's expensive *Flexible Flier*, that the Airlords now called the *Mongol Machine*, was sleek, shiny, tan and red; unscratched, un-smudged, it could hold four, but only Marlene and Charlene ever raced it. The red metal railings looked smooth. Strong. The sled sat still on Paton's Hill, but you knew it was fast.

The Airlord's *Earth Cruiser To The Nine Moons of Saturn*, was enormous. It stood two feet higher than the *Mongol Machine*. The Airlords didn't find any skis at the junkyard, but they did find a broken white picket fence. Johnny took two pickets from the discarded fence and tied them with twine to the curved bottom legs of the cradle. It was clumsy. It was crude. It didn't look fast, or sleek or strong. It looked like trouble.

Elmer kept watch facing the children; the sleds and Lloyd were behind him. Lloyd bent over and pretended to retie his boot strings. Getting a better view of the Earth Cruiser Lloyd smiled, and when he laughed out loud, he spit and his nose leaked and his face became wet.

"Hurry up", said Elmer. "Them kids look like they're wrapping their little pow-wow up."

Lloyd took out his small yellow pocketknife, its blade was red stained and rusty, and cut at the twine fastenings the fence pickets to the cradle legs. The twine was tight and cold, so it snapped and popped apart as Lloyd committed deeper into his sabotage.

Rudy, standing by Billy in the circle of children, turned around hearing the twine pop and looked deeply into Elmer's eyes.

"Um Lloyd their dog, is ah, their dog is looking at me. And err-ah, and he doesn't look happy neither," said Elmer. "You best finish up with what you're doing there, as in - right now!"

"Wait just one more moment, I'm almost through."

Rudy showed his teeth.

"Lloyd, finish it up. Really, no foolin', like now. That dog's got smarts and does not look happy."

Rudy turned his body all the way around. He let out a low growl.

"Now Lloyd! I'm begin' ya. Go get-get up now! Now!"

Billy looked at Rudy and then followed Rudy's line of site to The Dunce Brothers.

"Uh-oh, them kids are all done with their huddle or whatever you call it. They're coming back Lloyd!" Elmer pleaded.

Pop!

One of the last loops of twine was cut through, but Lloyd didn't get all the loops; the fence-skies were still secure by a few loose loops. The Earth Cruiser still had a chance to stay secure through the race. A small chance.

Elmer pulled Lloyd to his feet just as all the children turned around and began to make their way back to the sleds.

"I-I-I think I got it. These garbage pickers have one wild ride in store for them," laughed Lloyd.

The Dunce Brothers drifted back from the sleds as the children flooded in. Billy stared at Elmer and Lloyd as Rudy continued his stare and growled low. Billy knew something was wrong. He was certain The Dunce Brothers must have been up to no good. And he thought it wise to check over the Earth Cruiser before Johnny and Murf launched. But the excitement had started and the surrounding kids crowded the best viewing positions. There was no way they were letting Billy nudge through to the front. Billy tried, but Billy's small.

"Wait, let me through. Wait don't go just yet. Let me through," Billy pleaded, punched and pushed.

Johnny and Murf sat in the *Earth Cruiser* with their helmets and goggles on and their racing scarves wrapped around their necks that blew as if they longed to fly. Murf held the oar with two hands; Johnny gripped the sides of the ship and looked competitively to his right at Charlene. Charlene stared at Johnny as she gripped her steering ropes, Marlene sat behind Charlene and stared at Murf, who just noticed her confident glare and gave it right back - when it came to competitions, Marlene was just as competitive as her sister. Billy kept trying to get through the crowd of kids, but it was too late; the race had begun.

Oliver, the butcher's son, was the tallest and best reader in Miss Magnolia's class, so he always refereed games and races. He was chosen not only because he was the tallest and best reader, but also because he was extremely uncompetitive and didn't care much for games.

"On your marks," started Oliver. Marlene dove her mittens into the snow and slid their *Mongol Machine* back and forth, ready for a powerful starting launch. That's when Johnny and Murf realized they had no way of kicking off. They were too high off the ground for their arms to reach the snow.

"Get set," Oliver took off his blue pom-pom knit hat and held it over his head. Elmer and Lloyd smirked at each other a few feet back. Billy and Rudy ran around the side of the crowd.

"Go!" Oliver threw his hat in the air and the race was on.

The Twins launched out.

WHOOSH!

Charlene snapped the steering ropes as Marlene dug in, paddling for extra speed. The *Earth Cruiser* didn't move, so Johnny and Murf began to hop up and down trying to scoot their sled over the hill's ledge.

All the children cheered.

The Twins were already at full speed, weaving though trees with a great lead when Johnny and Murf eventually got moving. At first the Earth Cruiser moved slowly, but it steadily picked up speed. Murf wrapped his arms around the steering oar. Its vibration shook Murf so violently that it made him look as if he was having a fit. Johnny gripped the sides of the ship and screamed from the excitement of seeing his craft in flight - Rudy chased them down the hill - Billy, Ramona and Terrance watched nervously at the top - the rest of the kids cheered and jumped excitedly, while Elmer and Lloyd were nowhere to be found.

Murf held on tight. His pudgy cheeks jiggled. He wasn't doing any steering just yet, but Murf knew he had to hold the oar centered if the ship was to stay on course. The Earth Cruiser blasted down Patton's Hill. It was wild. It looked monstrous. It looked unstoppable. And it still looked like a heap of trouble. Johnny scouted a tree at twelve o'clock.

"Muurf! Treee!" shouted Johnny as he moved to the stern of the ship to help Murf steer. Both boys pulled the steering oar hard and toward their chests sending the Earth Cruiser to a hard right. The Earth Cruiser shook as it turned.

Murf looked over the side of the ship to see both fence pickets dislodged and continued straight down Patton's Hill as they went right.

"Jooohnny! The skiiis!" shouted Murf to Johnny. Johnny looked to his left and saw both fence pickets passing the tree on either side of it. Rudy's instincts told him to chase after the fence pickets, but he stayed with the boys.

"Whoaaaa!" screamed both boys as the Earth Cruiser rocked back from the exposed curved cradle legs. The steering oar snapped hard on another snow covered rock and dislodged. The ship was now going top speed down Patton's Hill, but the curved cradle legs made the boys' weight distribution most crucial if they were going to make it to the finish rope. The Earth Cruiser toppled back and the bow was almost sticking straight up.

"Quick to the bow!" screamed Johnny and both boys crawled their way up to the front of the ship. This only made the Earth Cruiser dip forward, tumbling the boys once again. The Spectrometer's nose planted down, blasting the boys in the face with snow. Under the new blizzard, Johnny screamed.

"You go to the stern and I'll stay at the bow!"

"Aye-aye!"

Murf climbed back to the stern. The Earth Cruiser slowly became level, but with Murf being so much heavier than Johnny, the ship gradually rocked all the way back again, but Johnny held on to the Spectrometer dangling vertically from it.

"Ahh!" Johnny held on for dear life. His boots were inches from Murf's nose.

"What do we do?"

"I don't know!"

"We're gonna crash!"

"I know!"

Rudy barked along side the boys, loving the game.

"Let's switch!"

"Okay!"

The Twins had already crossed the finish rope; they stood by their sled staring at the horrendous happening. The rest of the Airlords and Miss Magnolia's class stared wide-eyed with mouths open. The boys struggled to switch spots. Rudy was still keeping up. The Dunce Brothers snorted and laughed hiding behind a few birch trees by the finishing rope.

Once the boys were both in the middle of the Earth Cruiser it became more stable.

"Wait, wait, let's both stay in the middle," Murf screamed.

"Okay!"

But it wasn't easy. The ship would pitch and sway and the boys would have to correct their weight distribution by climbing over one another. The boys knew they had lost the race, but the new mission was to get the Earth Cruiser to the finish rope.

Everyone on the top of the hill began to run down. This was more exciting than even the race itself.

The Earth Cruiser pitched and swayed, swayed and pitched.

The boys tumbled and crawled, crawled and tumbled.

"Wait, you come this way!"

"I'm trying; you're standing on my scarf!"

"No wait the other way, the other way!"

"You're choking me!"

Johnny and Murf were just coming to the bottom of Patton's Hill, but to make matters worse, the Earth Cruiser hit a patch of ice once they hit level ground. This sent them spinning in circles. Both boys held on for dear life. Both racing scarves twirled above the ship like a colorfully knitted whirlpool. And both Marlene and Charlene smirked at the silly sight.

"Whoa!" the boys screamed. "Ahh!" the boys chorused. Sliding on the ice, the Earth Cruiser spun, slid and spun some more. Rudy barked, slipped and slid as well. They were almost to the finish rope.

Charlene nudged Marlene and pointed ahead of the boys.

"Look."

"Oh no!"

"Yup."

A square bale of hay left over from the harvest season lay half hidden under the snow. And the boys were spinning right at it.

"Here it comes," Charlene said, as both girls tightened up their bodies.

BLAM!

The Earth Cruiser smashed into the square bale of hay. The ship flipped over, while the boys held on tight. The Earth Cruiser landed hard. The ship was now completely turned over, crunched deep in the snow, leaving Johnny and

108

Murf trapped inside. They held onto the bars of the cradle, looking like baby prison inmates - helmets and goggles half on, while tangled in each other's scarves.

It was a rough first flight.

✻

Each of the Airlords held a piece of the Earth Cruiser as they walked home. It was dark now. The Moon was missing. The Airlord's boots made fresh prints in the new snow. Rudy was tired. He held one of the fence pickets in his mouth. Johnny and Billy pushed what was left of the Earth Cruiser. The rest of the Airlords held on to the broken pieces of the ship and looked down at the ground when they spoke. It had been a pretty lousy Sunday.

"There was nothing we could do," said Johnny, deeply disappointed that one of his designs, once again didn't bring the Airlords glory.

"Awe hellz, wez knaw brotha," said Ramona.

"Ya we know Johnny," said Terrance, as he approached his house. "W-well see yah tomorrow?"

"Yah," cadenced the Airlords back.

Terrance placed one of the fence pickets back in the ship that still had the curved cradle legs and sides attached.

"Don't sweat it Johnny. That ain't th-the important race," said Terrance with a slight stutter as he latched the gate to his house and waved 'so long' to his friends.

"Yah," said Johnny, as he kept his head down and waved Terrance a 'goodbye'.

The Airlords walked on.

Billy scooped some snow and made a snowball, then handed it to Johnny. Johnny placed it on a scrape on his forehead. He had a deep black eye as well.

Ramona did the same and handed it to Murf; he had a black eye too and was limping just a little bit.

"It just came apart," said Murf. "The skies and then the steering oar. There was nothing I could do. Honest. Honest!"

"Wez knaw Murf," said Ramona and then put her arm around his shoulder. The act had surprised her – it was her instinct to console Murf. The act had also surprised Murf – he straightened up and tried to limp less. Ramona left her arm there, but was now so jostled from the act that she wanted to take it back. It did comfort Murf.

"There was nothing we could do Murf. It just came apart. I mean I fastened everything so tight. I really did. I just don't know how it could have happened," said Johnny still looking at the ground pushing the Earth Cruiser.

"You know what I think?" said Billy.

"We know you're the best ship builder Johnny," said Murf. "We'll double secure the Battle Cruiser; it'll be the most powerful, most fantastic ship ever."

"Oi yah 'n' it'll blast dem twisted Twins out of da sky," added Ramona. She took her arm off Murf and handed him the few broken pieces of the Spectrometer she was holding in her other hand. They both tried to smile at one another, but each one of them diverted their eyes to the ground when the other flashed the timid grin.

"Yah, we'll show 'em," said Murf. "See yah tomorrow."

"So lang den brothas," Ramona headed to the front door of her small house.

"You know what I saw Johnny?" spoke up Billy.

"So long Ramona. What's that Billy," said Johnny.

"Crummy Twins," interrupted Murf.

"Yah, stupid crummy Twins," agreed Johnny. The Airlords continued on. "Did you see that stupid grin on Charlene's face when we, well, when we couldn't get out?"

"I'd like to sock her noggin," said Murf as he dumped the broken glass and steering oar into the cradle of the ship.

"They couldn't make a ship if they tried."

"No way."

"Do you know what I think happened guys?" piped in Billy.

"What? I mean, that Charlene *must* have cheated?" said Johnny,

"Yah I think so Johnny," agreed Murf.

"I think so too," said Johnny.

"Me too," agreed Murf again.

"They probably cheated somehow," said Johnny. "Well, so long Murf."

"So long guys," Murf limped up to his gate, opened it, latched it, tried to toss his snowball over the house, but it only hit the top middle gable, sending more snow down on him. He brushed himself off and headed inside.

The snow had picked up; the dark clouds owned the sky. The Boone boys and Rudy took a left down Bridge Street. It was more tiring to push the ship in all the new snow falling down and the curved cradle legs made it an overall awkward task. The boy's conversation was left to strictly facilitating the best ways to get the broken ship home.

They came up on the Central Command, which nested in the palm of the big snow covered Oak. The two boys took a rest from their labor before heading the rest of the way home. Leaning on the big oak, they looked past the falling flakes, past the naked trees - who's branches stuck out like excited arms making the forest look as if it was dancing in a dark room with white confetti coming down – and looked past the junkyard to Pete's workshop. They could see the two men were still up from the candlelight and smoke coming from the makeshift shack.

The boys paused.

"Hey Johnny, let's go see the Scientist huh? Maybe he has some new pieces for us. That'll take our mind off things."

"Okay yah," said Johnny.

The Boone boys and Rudy started walking toward The Workshop.

"Know what I saw," said Billy.

"What's that Billy?"

"Well…I saw them Dunce Brothers hanging about the sleds when we were getting the talking to of the rules from Oliver. One of them was bent over even. Looked to be looking closely at the Earth Cruiser. If yah ask me, I think they must have cut the twine. I think they must have wrecked the ship. Mm hm. That's what I think."

"YOU DID? Well, well why didn't you say so?"

When the Boone boys got close to The Workshop, Johnny grabbed Billy's collar and pulled him back.

"Wait!" said Johnny.

"Hey, what's the big idea?"

"That Kringle fella's in there, I can see 'im through the window."

"So what?"

"Why don't we hang back, send Rudy in, take a crouch under that window there and do a little spying."

"You don't trust Kringle huh?"

"No."

"How come?"

Johnny didn't answer.

"Go on Rudy," said Johnny as he gave Rudy a little push for the door. Rudy gladly headed toward what he knew was his warm bed.

Pete heard a scratch at the door, put his rugged tea down, stood up from his bed and let a wet Rudy inside. "Oo no, no, boy please don't…" Rudy walked in a circle in the center of The Workshop and shook the fresh layer of snow off his bum, back and snout. Snow flew; everything got wet. "Awe. Well, welcome home." Rudy looked tired. He was exhausted from the day. He rubbed against Pete's leg, walked over to Kringle, who was sitting on his bed facing Pete's bed drinking his warm rugged tea, and rubbed against Kringle's leg as well before circling his blankets and lying down for the night. Pete grabbed a towel and started mopping up Rudy's slop and then Rudy himself.

Pete hung the wet towel over his workbench chair, took the hot pot that was half filled, topped Kringle's mug off, then his own and sat back down on his cot facing Kringle. The men were having an honorable discussion about "honesty" and where that fits into a man's legacy.

The Boone boys were couched under the window listening.

"How so Kringle? Water your logic, so I can see it grow."

"Well, one shouldn't cheat or lie, that's a given. But during these times, these days, when there are so many hurting, hungry, so many poor…well," Kringle took a cautious sip of his rugged tea. "No, I don't think it's right for a man to steal from a rich man, but what I am getting at is, stealing one loaf of bread from a man with six just isn't the same as stealing another man's only loaf."

"It's still stealing."

"Yes, it is. It's still stealing. But if we are talking about 'what is good' and 'what is bad', one could say that it's wrong for a man to have six loaves of bread knowing that there is a man on this here earth without one in the first place – let alone a child."

Outside the Boone boys listened.

"What are they talking about? Stealing? He *is* a bank robber Johnny."

"Shh!"

112

Inside The Workshop the men discussed further.

"Now us people, human people that is, the smart apes, we make up the words, we speak 'em, and we give them their definitions. But what is the soul itself supposed to feel if a man 'steals' a loaf of bread from a greedy man who has six just to give it to a dying, starving man, woman or child. Is that a good act, a heroic act, or a bad act?"

"You'd go to jail either way if you're caught. I'll tell you that much."

"Exactly. See that's what I'm saying. We made the words and we made the laws, and I don't think all the actions of us men fall simply in accordance with those words, definitions and laws. Now okay see…if you ask me…I think the Lord would think every man who has abundance and doesn't help is the one whose morality needs to be repaired. That man should be praying for forgiveness; greed's a sin too. It's number six."

"So you think it's okay to steal from *greedy rich* men, is that what you are saying?"

"No. I think it's wrong, very wrong. I'm a bit saddened that you and me are a part of this; that's why I'm bringing it up. It's just *easier* for me to turn a blind eye here, in this job, because the people buying the furniture we are making, well they're not even thinking rationally. They're too consumed in the pageantry of it all. See, they love what we make because they gloat that it is made somewhere far away where no one else can reach; they don't necessarily love the craftsmanship. Pete, you can't tell me some other fella a few towns over isn't making the same quality stuff."

"Well, we do disagree here, 'cause yes, I do say that ours *is* the best in the world Kringle." The two men laughed and cheered their hot mugs. "No, but yes, I understand your words Kringle; I can see the leaves of your logic. That's the truth, Walter down in Essex and Thomas's son Thomas Junior over in Ipswich, they do fine work."

"Exactly. What Mr. McManus is doing is wrong, we know this, but these people buying our work…they have so much more than everyone else these days. They're spending five times the amount of money, if not ten or twenty times, just because they can say it's from a foreign land. France 'n' such. They're buying a bragging right, that's all, it's shameful and, well, it'll cost them. And again, not to get all excited, but I feel that's much more wrong of a man, let alone a God serving man, 'cause in these times, these days, when there are so many dirt kicking poor, no one should be spending money on a bragging right."

Crouched under the window the boys whispered.

"Billy I ain't sure what they're talking about, but I think Kringle may just be a robber like you said. But I ain't sure; I can't quite hear."

"I don't know Johnny, it sounds more like Kringle's a good guy, not a bad guy."

"No I think I heard him saying something about how he robs poor *and* rich people. We should get out of here Billy. C'mon."

And with that Johnny and Billy ran home.

Pete heard a thud against The Workshop window, but dismissed the sound.

"But Pete, I just don't know if I can cover my eyes if it's now with toys and with little children. I don't know. I mean, sure I know it's their parents buying them them toys, but it's what Ellie told me today and I think she is - stand on a mountain and scream it to God - correct."

The men thought.

Pete walked over to the door and latched it good, wrapping a strip of leather around two bent nails as if he was tying up a boat. It was a murdering cold outside; that if caught too long in, it would make your skeleton scream and shake so wildly that it would lose faith with the brain and believe it had gone mad. The wind picked up to a scream and the snow began to blow in upward swirls. It whirled about begging to be noticed. Pete took some of his shirts and placed them at the bottom of the small windows to lessen the rattling of the frames and cut down on the drafts sneaking in with each mid-December gust because even the slightest crack in a window frame would still send a cutting cold slicing up your back.

Rudy watched Pete and when Pete sat back down, Rudy nuzzled into his blankets once again.

Then Pete switched on the radio. Slow blues took to The Workshop.

"Ellie? What'd Ellie say?"

"Well, it's very much like what you told me the first day we spoke. Okay," Kringle repositioned. "You said, 'We make things everyone wants.' Well, Ellie said today, 'Kringle if I could make these toys, I'd make one for every child on this dang earth.' Well, she didn't say 'dang' but, see, the poor kids of this town, like Ellie Boone's boys and like the lot they run about with, well they dream of *wants* as well; and we could be the answer to their little prayers. We could make toys for everyone. No price tags. Like gifts for the good. You and me. Pete and Kringle – toy makers to the world."

Pete laughed out with his joyous watery green eyes, took his stained hat off, placed it on Rudy's head for a second, smiled and then placed it on his pillow.

"That's a lot of toys Kringle; we could barely make ten today." Kringle stood up, walked over to the warming pot, checked the flame, stirred the hot pot with a wooden spoon - the pot sizzled – he topped Pete's mug off once again and then his own, set the pot back down and stood thinking at the window by the front door. Pete spoke from his cot, "I mean, I like what you are saying Kringle. Don't you understand that my soul hurts too with what we do? I like to entertain the idea that I'm fair. My chest caves that I'm making this cross here to just go give it to a church whose congregation would be ashamed that I made it for them. Some of 'em would even be ashamed if I walked in and prayed to it. I know they only like it 'cause of the lie that surrounds it - that better men made it from some better place. And that's a disease if you ask me Kringle. One that can wipe out a village. They only like it 'cause they think it's fancy, but it ain't fancy, it's just special. I mean Kringle, I like what you are sayin', I do, it's just that you have to know – that I know it. See here, when I sit and carve that cross, I like to think that I'm going to hand it to Mr. Thomson. And that I am gonna one day hang it up in his barn. That's nice isn't it? I see everyone there all loving it and smiling. I bet Mrs. Thomson and some of the other ladies would even do that happy tearing thing they do when they're extra glad and from just seeing it up there, looking so nice for us all. They wouldn't mind it was made from a tree that grew on junkyard land, or that it was struck by lighting and carved in a shack by a man who be black. No, not them people. They'd be proud to have her. They'd be proud it was made by me."

Kringle sat back down on his cot.

"I know Pete and you're right. You're right. I don't mean to make a moral line between us. You gave me everything I got and only after hearing just my name. You can always assume that I'm thinking that your inner thoughts are solid and sound."

"Well I do, I truly think about that Kringle, every time my knife cuts a sliver off that lightning wood. And secretly, and I know it could be crazy to say, but I'll say this with you; I think it's a holy thing. I like to think God himself struck that tree with his mighty lightnin' to give me that wood to carve, to shape, to sand, to show people a sign, and give them hope. I do."

"I believe it Pete. Like you said, maybe *we are* at the crossroads with this here job."

It was the type of talk where men feel raw, because there was something that wasn't right happening all around. That night wasn't fair, at least it wasn't for fair people. There was one thing, however, the two men did know and that was Mr. McManus was building to swindle children for his own wealthy gain. But it is the riddle of the loyalist to ask himself if a swindler swindles with joy or simply from the absence of empathy.

The men had said enough. There was much to ponder once lying down for the night or while working hard the next day. Pete picked up his guitar after a long stretch of silence, took two big sips from his mug and then strummed a slow open G chord. He then noodled along with playing the blues to the hanging radio. Rudy's eyes opened just a crack. Kringle tossed his jacket on, grabbed his red hat and red gloves, found a flashlight and two candles, pocketed a handful of nails and set his hammer in his black tool belt before he fastened it on.

"Where you off to?" asked Pete.

"I got one thing I can do for someone tonight. I'll be back."

Pete didn't need to know where or what Kringle was heading off to do, he knew the feeling well. Kringle just needed to go have a good "think" - a needed medicine for a restless pondering man.

Rudy now was watching the men with wider eyes. Pete clicked the radio off and started playing his own slow blues on his guitar while humming. Rudy was torn for whom to stay with, he looked back and forth for some direction, but got none. Rudy figured Pete was warm and getting cozy. The hot stove warmed the last bit of Pete's rugged tea and the song from his guitar would protect Pete inside The Workshop from the agitated heath outside. So Rudy decided to stand and stretch, then went with Kringle. Kringle looked like he needed a friend.

Kringle approached Central Command with snow battering his face. The flakes were small and attacking in all directions, as playing kittens do. Both Kringle and Rudy had to squint to see. Both Kringle and Rudy were quickly collecting a layer of snow. And both Kringle and Rudy's bodies were icing. It was dark –

much too cold for even the stars to be out.

Kringle approached Central Command. He would start his work with its ladder.

"Okay Rudy, you wanna help?"

Rudy gave out a quiet bark and sat down at attention. Kringle snapped on the flashlight and offered it to Rudy to hold in his jaw. With the flashlight now placed, Rudy began to growl at it and shake it all about, making the light dance among the snow and the naked trees whose branches looked to be reaching tall, inquisitively searching for the absent stars.

"Oo boy, eh-eh. Here-here." Kringle tapped the first board with his hammer. Rudy knew the two were now in work mode. Rudy shined the flashlight toward the board; he was always an enthusiastic helper. Kringle fished out a few nails from his coat pocket. His fingers were cold and nerveless; he warmed them with his breath. First, Kringle analyzed the nails that were already in the boards. It seemed that Johnny would get two good nails in out of about four in each board; the other two nails were bent, but were pounded into the wood sideways rather than pulled out. It wasn't necessarily bad carpentry; Kringle knew that Johnny was working with used and crooked nails, so there was little Johnny could do – a nail can only be pulled so many times and still function. Kringle decided he would sneak his new nails to the sides of Johnny's bent ones – *Maybe they could be camouflaged there*, Kringle thought.

Kringle worked slowly. Steady. Smart. He started on the first board, then the second and on up. The wood was beginning to freeze up, but Kringle knew how to get his nails in; he was used to working in the cold. Slow, steady and smart, slow, steady and smart and the cold wood *would* accept the nail.

As Kringle climbed higher on the ladder, Rudy pointed his snout to the clouds. The snow was hail now, which made Rudy have to shut his eyes and listen rather than see for the sound of Kringle's next tap to know where the light was to shine next.

Kringle kept a few nails in his mouth as he worked. They tasted like iron and dirt. They would stick to his tongue and lips if he didn't fish them around his mouth. The boards he stood on were now strong under him. No longer did they spin like a rickety propeller. Kringle would bounce a bit on each board he finished as he worked to check its durability.

Starting a nail - Kringle would give it seven quick taps and then pound it in with three mighty blows. Once the eleventh board was secured Kringle climbed down and brushed the collecting ice off Rudy. Rubbing and warming Rudy, Kringle decided he would carry him up the ladder over his shoulder to Central Command for the rest of his work because he knew that the loyal dog would wait for him outside even if it meant freezing to death.

"Okay Rudy, are you ready for an adventure?"

Pleased - Rudy stared into Kringle's eyes, with snowflakes and iced droplets stuck to his eyelashes. Kringle lifted Rudy up and held him over his right shoulder. The extra weight didn't bother the newly secured boards; they held strong. Rudy wasn't used to being held, so he just became limp and allowed Kringle to take control. While over Kringle's shoulder, Rudy got a grand view through the falling hail. He could see The Workshop, the train tracks, the Boone house and a blurry view of the Snowy Owl dogfighting with two spastic bats.

Once inside Central Command, Kringle lit the two candles he brought. Smelling the Airlords, Rudy put his nose to the floor and excitedly sniffed out every inch of the room. Kringle put one of the candles on an upside down wooden milk crate and investigated while holding the other. The two candles with the two visitors began to slightly warm the room. Or maybe the little fires just seemed to. Kringle first held the light to the chalk on the wall – *The Airlords* it read. The leather helmets, scarves and goggles hung like uniforms under it. Kringle walked over to the Lazy Susan. Rudy and his nose sniffed on. Opening the Lazy Susan, Kringle found the entire collection of *Buck Rogers* comic strips taken from *The Worcester Evening Gazette*. Grabbing another old wooden milk crate, Kringle sat down for a short read. Buck Rogers, Wilma, spaceships and amazing stories - Kringle flipped though the comics. He recognized some of the Airlords' jargon. Placing the comics back, Kringle looked to the left and noticed the rolled up blue prints on the floor. He walked over, got down on his hands and knees and unrolled the schematics. Satisfied with his lay of the room, Rudy sat by him.

Ship after ship, Kringle looked them over. Johnny's plans reminded Kringle of himself when he was younger, save Kringle wasn't making spaceships; he was carving horses. It wasn't a new respect necessarily that filled Kringle concerning Johnny Boone, more, it was an accidental connection he felt. Being from a family of seven sisters, Kringle couldn't help but wonder what his life could have been if he had had Johnny as a friend. Or brother. But there was work to be done. Kringle stood up, placed the candle on the floor, snapped on the flashlight and began feeling around the room for places that needed reinforcement.

✻

Ellie's Sunday dress dragged in the snow. It was frozen all along the bottom seam. The icy snow and hail hadn't collected too much yet, but enough to reach Ellie's ankles. As she walked down Bridge Street, almost home, she shivered violently, holding Miss Winkelplex's key against her chest with both hands – fearful of losing it. But her dread got the best of her, for Ellie was too cold and too tired to overpower it; she sang a song in her head, a song she wished to forget:

> *"Here comes the mighty giant,*
> *Run, run - here she comes*
> *Here comes the mighty giant*
> *Big 'n' huge - she'll step on You!"*

Ellie looked up from the ground and noticed light coming from inside Central Command.

"No!" she shivered out. It wasn't like her boys to disobey her. *Why would they still be out?* she thought. Then she got scared - scared that something was wrong and at the same time, she got angry – angry to now be scared. She approached the big oak and screamed against the unmerciful wind and hail. "Johnny!? Billy!?" she hollered out, but no one came to the window. Then a cruel gust of wind blew hard against Ellie's face, she tightened up every muscle; her babushka flapped off her head and twirled around her neck. She winced until the gust moved on east to attack someone else. Ellie screamed out again to the light, raising her voice even more. She pushed the threshold of her volume, straining her vocal chords in order to overpower the wicked wind. "JOHNNY!? BILLY!? ARE YOU UP THERE? ANSWER YOUR MOTHER!"

A very excited Rudy, with tongue out and eyes wide, came to the window. He was having fun in the Command Center. He barked from excitement.

Hearing Rudy bark, Kringle came around the outside of Central Command, maneuvering in the outside palm of the great oak with the flashlight in his mouth. He held on to one of the fingers of the mighty oak and squinted into the tundra. Then another cruel gust came making Kringle and Ellie both tighten up with their eyes closed until the torture had once again moved east.

Ellie couldn't see who the man was, but knew it was a man's figure and not her boys. Her fear and anger doubled. She stomped forward. She pointed her finger that was under a mitten. She began to yell with even greater amplitude, she began to prepare herself for a confrontation and she also, unknowingly, dropped Miss Winkelplex's key into the snow.

"WHO ARE YOU!? WHERE ARE MY BOYS!? YOU GET OUT OF THERE!? I'LL GET THE SHERIFF! I'LL GET THE SHERIFF ON YOU! MY HUSBAND HAS A GUN! JOHNNY!? BILLY!? BOYS!?," Ellie screamed like she'd never screamed before.

Kringle shined the flashlight on his face.

"Miss Boone, Miss Boone, no no, it's me Kringle. It's just Rudy and me. Your boys ain't here."

"WHAT!? KRRRINGLE!? What the devil are you doing up there Kringle!? You ain't to be up there!? You living up there, are ya? Get down from there right now, right this instant!" Ellie didn't have time to be glad her boys weren't up there; she was too cold. Instead, she just changed gears.

Kringle went back inside Central Command through a window, blew out the candles, tossed Rudy over his shoulder and headed down the ladder.

"Miss Boone, I didn't mean anything, I was just…"

Ellie jabbed two of her mittened fingers into Kringle's chest.

"Look-a-here Kringle, I'm too tired and too gosh dang freezing to be a part of another one of your nonsensical rants, so button it. I have to get home and get to my boys. I'm freezing *and* tired. You tell me quick, why you are in my boys' Space Station."

Ellie could see Kringle's face take on an honest and innocent shape. His eye were wide and nervous.

"I-I just saw how rickety the boys club house was earlier today, so I thought to come by and strength it."

Ellie's rage lessoned; she thought that a perplexing act. People didn't do things for others unless they were getting paid or got a hot meal out of it.

"You did huh," said Ellie sternly, but inside she just thought it was simply sweet of Kringle. "How long you been out here?"

"About an hour Miss."

Kringle had actually been out there longer than that. Ellie patted her coat pockets.

"W-uh. Where? Wait. Oh my. Wait. Lord where the devil…? Wait a minute. I just had it."

"Where is what?"

"The key! Miss Winkelplex's key. I just had it. Oh No!" Ellie started to frantically check her coat pockets and then looked to the ground. On her hands and knees she searched through the snow. "Oh no-no-no…where'd you go?"

"Keys?"

"YES! A KEY!" said Ellie continuing to look through the snow on the ground; Kringle followed her lead and shined the flashlight to where she was looking. Ellie's mittens tossed the light new icy snow all around. "No-no-no. Why-why-why-why-why? Where'd you go; I just had you. Oh Lord why? WHY?! DAMN IT! Come back to me, pleeease," Ellie pleaded.

Ellie's body gave up; she sat on her knees and looked down with her mittens over her face; the bottom of her Sunday dress settled in a circle around her – then she leaned forward to break down.

Kringle and Rudy stood motionless as Ellie cried into her mittens. Her body shook from being cold and from sobbing hard.

She cried, but all you could hear was the wind.

"A key, you dropped a key," Kringle shined his flashlight all about Ellie's footprints that were slowly disappearing. "I can help you find your keys. Absolutely. No problem. I can find them. Don't cry Miss Boone." Kringle sifted through the icy snow and hail. Rudy began sniffing around. For a moment Kringle thought he could quickly patch the problem, that moment passed and all you could hear was the wind with short breaks of Ellie catching her breath. All Kringle could look at was Ellie hunched over in the storm, shaking with her light blue and white dress settled around her and her long black hair whirling wild in the wicked wind.

Kringle shuffled all around on his knees beside Ellie, then he put his arm around her, rubbing her to keep her warm. Rudy stopped and sat for a moment, then slowly continued to sniff around for anything that smelled like either of them.

"It's okay Ellie, it's alright."

"It's not alright."

"I can find your keys; they're just here somewhere."

"It's your fault."

"I shouldn't have been up there. I…"

Another big gust screamed hard and sharp from the north and punished them both for longer than they deserved. They huddled. It was now hailing; you could hear it hit you and see it bounce off you. The hail no longer sizzled, because it had grown in size. Now, there was more of a thumping sound all around them.

"Why are you here? You're *always* around now. Why won't you just leave me alone; leave my boys alone? You stress me out so."

"I'm sorry Ellie, Miss Boone. I don't know, I…I was just fixing their tree house."

Ellie looked to Kringle; her eyes were big, beautiful, blue, wet, wondering and wonderful.

"Why would you do that? That's not normal."

"It seemed rickety and dangerous. I passed it earlier today. I-I thought I'd help, I thought I could help and secure…"

"What? What are you even talking about?"

"I don't know. I'm sorry; I shouldn't have, I shouldn't have."

"She's going to fire me."

"Who is?"

"Miss Winkelplex, my boss; I lost her key. Now what am I going to do? Oh Lord. It's so much, everything is so much."

"It's alright, okay a key. One key," Kringle stood up, took Ellie's mittens in his gloves and helped her to her feet, then held her close for comfort and warmth. Ellie allowed it; she was exhausted. "I can find your key Ellie. One key right? Ya I can find that!" Closer than they had ever been, their faces only inches from one another, Kringle began to lose track of his thoughts after noticing how red Ellie's nose and cheeks became when she was cold – he thought it newsworthy of an honest charm.

"I'm so tired," Ellie said sullenly.

"You head home Ellie. I'll find your key. I'll find it and bring it to you."

"No. That doesn't work, because what if you can't find it. I *must, must* find it."

"I have all the confidence in the world that I will find your key Ellie Boone. I will find it even if I have to melt all this lousy snow. Me and Rudy will make torches, it's not a problem."

Ellie smiled very subtly. Kringle was shocked.

"You might have to," she said. "Ya? You'll find the key? You promise?"

"Yes. I will not return empty handed."

"You promise?"

"I promise. I mean gosh, some men spend years searching for the right key to a woman's hea…" Ellie's subtle smile dropped.

"Cut it out Kringle, I'm too tried and fff-frozen."

"Yes right, sorry, okay, you head home. I'll be there shortly with your key."

Shaking, Ellie retied her babushka, "You find it; you get a warm dinner. Make sense?" She cupped her hands under her chin and headed home.

Johnny was stirring the mashed potatoes that he had gotten started on the front burner. He held ice, wrapped in a white dishrag with faded yellow flower print onto his blackened eye. The corned beef was heating nicely on the back burner and the biscuits were browning in the oven. The fire was healthy and strong; the blues played on the radio and it smelled of subtle pine from the logs Billy had brought in. Billy stood by his mother, holding out in front of him Johnny and his Sunday clothes, which were draped in his arms - Ellie was inspecting piece by piece the new tears she'd have to patch for next Sunday's service. Patching patches was a weekly chore. Ellie would shake her head back and forth, fold the torn garments neatly and place them in her new sewing pile; her tired Sunday dress started the pile. Ellie couldn't scold the boys for not changing out of their Sunday clothes and tearing them up, because she had done the same. So she just said they all did an unmindful job that day and that collectively they would be smarter than that next Sunday.

The boys were dressed in their full red and white-striped one-piece pajamas. Ellie would have slipped on her nightgown, but because she did feel that Kringle *would* find Miss Winkelplex's key from the determination in his tone, she was certain he would be joining them for dinner. So Ellie put on her long white skirt and green plaid button-up.

Ellie wasn't used to not doing a task herself, so knowing that Kringle was off doing something that would help her made her feel somewhat vulnerable…vulnerable in a way she did and did not like. It made her fidgety.

Billy was now setting the table, holding plates.

"But Momma, where's Kringle going to sit? We only got three sides."

"Just pull the kitchen table out from the window."

"Oh. Oh ya."

"I don't get why he's coming for dinner anyways," said Johnny suspiciously. "Don't him and Pete have their own dinners at their own house?"

"Johnny Boone, I told you already. How's the corned beef coming?"

"Light brown. Mostly."

"Let me see," Ellie took the ice from Johnny's eye and inspected the bruise. "You boys just bash your bodies right up." Ellie then placed the ice back on the wound, took the wooden spatula from Johnny, inspected the corned beef, checked the biscuits and turned the stove off.

"But *why* is Kringle coming by," asked Johnny. "You like him? You fancy him?"

"Hush no Johnny, Momma doesn't fancy strange hobos that come jumping off trains. Lord no. Silly boy. Psst. I told you, he just helped your Momma find a key. He's just bringing it by. Doing nice things...does what Billy?"

"What, oh, doing nice things gets nice things done for you in return."

"That's right; good boy."

"But why?"

"Why what Honey?"

"Why were you with him; why's he finding a key? Why don't you have it?"

"Jeepers Johnny, Momma was walking home and saw Kringle. I dropped the key in the snow and Mr. Kringle was nice enough to say he'd find it, so I could get home to you boys and start up dinner."

"And now he's gonna have dinner with us?"

"Yes, and because he helped your Momma out, he will have dinner with us."

"But why?"

"Hush boy."

Knock-knock-knock!

"Yay this is fun," said Billy as he did a little jump in his red and white-striped one-piece pajamas, ran over to the door, and slid on the floor with his soft covered feet. "I got it."

Ellie slowly placed the wooden spatula down, washed her hands in the basin, dried them with a matching faded flower hand towel, smoothed her bold black hair that was pulled back in a wrap, brushed her shirt and skirt off, pinched both her cheeks, then rolled her eyes at herself. She didn't know why she was anxious; Kringle was sure to be conversationally exhausting. Other than Flo, and occasionally Pete, Ellie and the boys just did not have guests over to the house.

Billy opened the door. Rudy came rushing in with his nose to the floor. When he realized he had rushed by Billy, he spun around, wiggled his butt and greeted him excitedly. Ellie approached Kringle. Johnny watched with a sideways glare from the stove.

Kringle had both of his hands behind his back. He was ice covered and crunchy. His cheeks and nose were red and his hat was off and his hair was crunchy as well.

"Well, you being here means you found it? Hm? Ya?" Ellie asked.

"Maybe. Guess which hand."

"Kringle," said Ellie subtly in her Papa voice, but she knew no matter which hand she chose, at least he had the key. "That one," she said testily while pointing. Kringle switched the key to the hand she had chosen and then presented the key.

"Ta-da!"

"Thank you Kringle; this truly helps me. Still your fault though, that's to be remembered," Ellie said as she took the key from him. Ellie brought the key two inches from her eyes to make sure. *He did a good job,* she thought, and then brushed the thought off. "And you stay outta that treehouse you odd-odd man. I won't hesitate to get the sheriff on you if I see you in there again."

"Yes ma'am. Don't tell the boys I was there. Johnny might not like it."

"No he wouldn't, and yes I won't."

At dinner, Billy and Kringle did most of the talking. Johnny was quiet. Ellie was quiet too, save correcting Billy's grammar and table manners as he spoke. The four sat at the small kitchen table. Rudy was sleeping centered under the table. The window was over Kringle's left shoulder. The frame of the window projected on his place setting and the shadows of the snow animated the inside of the reflected glass panels.

125

"My father taught me," said Kringle.

"And they really come if you sing it," asked Billy with a mouthful of mashed potatoes.

"Billy, what did I say?" asked Ellie.

"Sorry," said Billy still with his mouthful.

"Swallow," she corrected again.

"Sorry," said Billy again, but now with a clean mouth. "They really come if you sing?"

"Well no, not always. They have to be able to hear the song while at the same time they have to decide if they trust you."

"How do reindeer decide if they trust you?"

"They can tell. They're sharp. They're smart. See, if you are nice and good, and if they can hear your song, my Poppa told me that, *sure* they will show themselves. But if you're bad or naughty, if they don't trust you – they'll stay far, far away. Deer are extra cautious animals. Extra smart. Sometimes I'd sing and they wouldn't come, so I'd ask my Poppa, 'Is it because they don't trust me'? And he'd say, 'Were you good this year?' And if I had been I'd say, 'Yes Poppa', then he'd go, 'Well then, they just must be too-too far to hear you then. Or you know they might be visiting someone else.' See Billy, if you know in your heart that you've been good, then *you know* they should trust you. They call that - clarity."

"Clar-ity. Huh. Have they ever come to you?"

"Well sure."

"Wow. Imagine that."

"I don't believe it," interjected Johnny.

"Shush Johnny," Ellie said quietly.

"What's the song?" asked Billy.

"You wanna hear it?"

"Ya I do. Will you teach me?" said Billy.

"I wanna hear it too," said Ellie smiling.

"Okay, but remember you have to sing it softly."

"But-but then they won't hear it."

"That's the tricky thing. You can't sing it too loudly or you'll scare them, but you have to project it out into the forest enough so they *can* hear it. It's an art Billy." Kringle put his fork and knife down, wiped his mouth and cleared his throat, then sang:

"The reindeers are coming – trollop, trollop
The reindeers are coming – trollop, trollop
Spit-spot – with any luck
The reindeer will come - trollop, trollop

Deep in the forest – they lay, they lay
Deep in the forest – they lay
But if we ask and ask real nice
The reindeers will come - trollop, trollop"

Billy started to sing it back to Kringle; Kringle helped him with the words. Johnny watched his mother watch Billy and Kringle. She was smiling a child's smile. Johnny felt a bit on the outside of it all.

"Bah, I don't believe it," said Johnny.

"No?" asked Ellie, "I'm surprised."

"Nope. That's silly, wild animals don't come to people when they sing. No waaay, no hooow."

"Well, you *do* have to believe it for it to work. See Johnny, you always have to believe something is going to work if you're going to try and make it so."

"But I don't see any reindeer outside; *so*, there, *see*, it didn't work."

But it had worked. Billy's wide eyes were looking over Kringle's left shoulder – out the window. Billy could swear he saw three deer moving though the storm.

"Magic is a curious thing Johnny. We all have the ability to make it, but only a few of us know how to recognize it. While on my travels, making my way south, I've found there are two kinds of people in this world – those who make magic and those who wait to see magic. Magic comes from the same place joy and merriment come from. You'll find Johnny that joyless people blacken the joy that surrounds them. The people who create it, replace it. It's all a magnificent, curious thing."

"But there are no reindeer outside," said Johnny.

"Well, you are supposed to be outside, deep in the forest when you sing. I mean if it always worked, then you'd have reindeer in your bedroom and you can't have reindeer in your bedroom."

"That's true Johnny, I mean I can't have reindeer in here. You two are

127

messy enough," said Ellie as she smiled rubbing Billy's head as she gazed outside in the direction of his eyes.

"So Johnny, how did the race go; how'd the sled slide?" asked Kringle, changing the subject.

"We lost," Johnny said looking down.

"Ah that's too bad. Did she run well though…in your opinion I mean?"

"No she fell apart, stupid sled, stupid-crummy sled."

"Johnny, no moaning at the table," said Ellie.

"No way, it was a good sled. See what happened see, was it ah…um…it was…" thought out Billy. "What was the word you used Momma?"

"Sabotaged." Ellie helped.

"Yah it was sabotaged. I saw them Dunce Brothers there. They're two big ape like fellas in town," said Billy.

"Ya I know 'em," said Kringle.

"They were loosening the skis. And I swear by it." Billy crossed his heart with his finger.

"The boys say the two men loosened or cut the twine securing things. It made the entire sled crash," helped Ellie. "That's how Johnny split his lip and got that blackened eye. If it's true, then them dense boys are gonna get quite a tempered talk to by me," said Ellie, then murmured to herself before taking a sip of her water, "Mess with my boys? Eh-eh. Psst, I'll show 'em what that gets 'em."

Kringle smiled at Ellie's protective motherly display.

"That true Johnny?" asked Kringle. Johnny didn't say anything. It got quiet. Billy, Ellie and Kringle were all looking at Johnny who was still looking at his plate. "Well if you ever want some more parts for your sleds, sorry, ships I mean, you feel free to come by the yard. I know you don't need any help buildin' and all, but I'd sure like to see yer work sometime Johnny."

It was quiet. Everyone still stared at Johnny.

"We got a new sled to build Mr. Kringle, maybe you can help us build it and then we'll zip past them Twin's *Mongol Machine*. Yah Johnny?" said Billy.

"Like Ma said, Billy, we don't need any help from some strange hobo who come into town jumping off trains. I can make it just fine by myself," said Johnny.

Ellie put down her fork and knife calmly, wiped her mouth, took a deep breath up into her chest and put her hands on her hips.

"Johnny Boone!" she said softly but sternly. "You stop speaking foul muck and apologize to Mr. Kringle right now."

"No. Why?"

"Because he's our guest and you *are not* to speak that way to guests."

"You said it first. You said it just there, right before he come in the door."

"Johnny Boone! I am warning you. You stand up and go up to bed this instant."

"Why? You said it."

"JOHNNY!" Ellie stood. Johnny stood up, dragged his white and red-striped feet and went up the ladder to the loft.

From up in the loft Johnny spoke, "You did. You said it first."

"Well I best be going; it's getting late," said Kringle. He wiped his mouth, folded his napkin and stood. It *was* getting late. The boys had school the next day and Ellie had to be up early for work. And the room now had an awkward air. "Lovely meal Miss Boone. I'll see you gentlemen later on."

"Bye Mr. Kringle," said Billy. "I'll sing your song some day."

"You do that Billy. Bye Johnny."

Ellie walked Kringle to the door. Rudy followed.

"Will you be all set with them dishes?" asked Kringle.

"I will."

"Okay then, thanks again for the meal. It was delicious. It was just what I needed. Keep that key close."

"I will and, well, you earned it. Sorry about Johnny, I didn't say exactly what he said, see I just said…"

"Oh, it's okay. He's just protecting. I had seven sisters; I did a lot of protecting."

"Interesting. He probably was and that's probably true. Anyways…sorry you saw me so upset earlier as well, in the snow and all that; I usually am not a crier."

"S'okay. Crying is good for you, well not being sad is better for you, but crying is good for you I bet.

"Yes, I suppose so. Just forget about it, that it happened, is all I'm saying."

"*Neither of us* was there then. Good night Miss Boone."

"You can call me Ellie, Kringle. Good night. Walk wise; it's icy. Bye Rudy boy."

Ellie closed the door. When she turned, she saw Billy in his red and white-striped one-piece pajamas holding a stack of dishes clearing the table, but more, he was gazing out the window searching for reindeer.

TURNING DIALS OF MYSTERIOUS TOYS
BRINGS SMILES TO EVERY
GIRL AND EVERY BOY

WARM HANDS

COLD NOSES

SKATING AT NIGHT

STORY 3

✳

AS SILLY AS YOU THOUGHT

When we are different
As different can be
We worry and worry
But that's just silly
Different is what we look for
        when choosing a kitty
Different is what we love
        when I chose you and you me
The same is abundant
The same - always safe
The same is more comforting
A recognizable place

But different is different
A brave change in the norm
So feel glad you are different
And worry no more
But if you get nervous
More than you ought
Remember you're beautifully different
And as silly as you thought

✳

Story 3:

TURNING DIALS OF MYSTERIOUS TOYS BRINGS SMILES TO EVERY GIRL AND EVERY BOY

The little white fawn understood her mother's eyes; they were warm; they were soft; they were plump with love. But she did not understand her father's. He seldom looked upon her. He always stood ten feet ahead of her. When the white fawn was confident enough, she would walk over and sit by him, yet he would always then take ten steps forward again – ahead of her. She didn't understand this. It hurt her. She wondered if he loved her, as she did him. He was so distant and always focused on the horizon. Endlessly, he stood and stared into the trees, smelling the wind. It was a curious thing.

But he did love her. The little white fawn and her mother were the most important things to him now. And it was because of them that he was so focused on the horizon, so focused on looking deep into the trees - always aware of every sound and smell around the three of them. The father deer knew the world was hungry. He knew what canine teeth wanted. And he knew it was up to him and him alone to keep his family safe and together. If his white fawn were to enjoy all the magic of the world, he would have to protect her from all the violence it conjures as well. He *did* love her, but she did not know this. And he didn't ponder for even the shortest moment that she worried so. Sometimes love is scary. Sometimes love is confusing. And sometimes we fail at letting others know the grandeur of love we have for them. This time, however, when the little white fawn mustered enough confidence to walk over to her father, she did not sit once she reached him. Instead, she kept walking, past him and on forward into the unknown. She had discovered - her first curious scent.

A caramel colored fawn was already staring in her direction as she cautiously emerged from behind two bending birches. He was slightly older or maybe he was just a bit bigger. Muscular. White spots covered his back, and the inside of his tall ears were white like all of her. His most pronounced feature was the mark on his right hip. It was a patch of white fur that was in the shape of a heart and which seemed to have an arrow going through it. He stood by his parents grazing on a small patch of grass not covered by the recent icy snow. When his parents looked up to where he stared, they both took one step back, baffled by the white fawn's angelic overexposed color.

The white fawn's father and mother came along side her. Everyone stood. Everyone stared. It was quiet, slightly tense. A flock of geese honked above, flying south in a clumsy M formation. And a garter snake, which was being quite picky of where to hibernate that season, slithered into the scene - black with yellow stripes, with his tongue slapping in and out of his mouth - stopped frozen in his tracks. He too felt the tension in the air. The caramel fawn took the first step, but stopped when his mother let out an apprehensive breath. His mother was unsure of the white fawn; she was different and unknown to her.

The white fawn's mother picked up the emotion of the other mother's breath. She knew her baby was different. But she also knew her baby was special - beautifully special. She looked to her child. The white fawn's eyes were wide and her posture tight; her heart was pounding; she didn't know what to do. The white fawn's mother, however, knew that her baby wanted to investigate, so she nudged her forward.

After her first step forward, the caramel fawn walked to her. Both mothers watched and both fathers smelled the air and looked all around through the bowing frozen trees. Once close, the caramel fawn began to sniff her all over. She stood still. Frozen, save her heart. First he smelled under her jaw, then behind her left ear, then her shoulders and then again to her jaw. He was filled with excitement to be with a creature much like himself, but a thousand times more stunning. The white fawn was more scared than she had ever been, but she liked his scent enough to not flee from him. When he was done, he stood still and allowed her to smell him. Cautiously she smelled under his jaw, behind his left ear and then his strong shoulders. When she backed away - their eyes were locked and the mothers came in to smell one another as well. The geese had flown on, followed by a band of three, in a perfect V, that squawked loudly as they flew overhead catching up nicely. The garter snake took advantage of the moment and wiggled into a hollow log, where he would sleep for the rest of the winter.

The caramel deer bounced back and did a little twirl, pranced forward and then bounced back again. She thought that looked fun to do, so she did the same, and before the mothers had time to understand each other's scent – the two fawns dashed off together, deep into the white woods.

Both pairs of adults made chase. Everyone was fast. The trees blurred. The mothers ran while watching their babies, the fathers looked ahead scanning for undesirables. The mothers then took positions behind the fawns; the fathers came up fast and strong on both sides of them and ran a bit ahead - with their massive antlers ready. The white fawn ran with the caramel fawn and the caramel fawn ran along with her. They leaped over fallen trees and zigzagged through the standing ones. The caramel fawn had run only a few times before with his parents, when trouble had been scouted, but this was the white fawn's first dash. They ran. And they ran. It felt good to her. Her muscles all worked together and she felt strong. They ran. And they ran. It was awakening to her body. Shocked, two bunnies dashed into their hole. Alarmed, a flock of crows scattered and reassessed in a taller tree. The two young fawns ran and they ran. They dashed into their world together, without direction or any plan. It was nice for them both - to be side-by-side - even though they had just met. There was a bond between them. Connection.

Once the trees began to thin and the fawns began to head toward where the scent of man became more potent, the two fathers pushed ahead, turned sharply and ended the sprint.

Both families then stopped short. The mothers immediately began to graze on grass that was taller then the fallen snow, creating a sense of calm, as if the sprint had never taken place. The fathers scanned. And the caramel fawn took a small step closer to the white fawn, put his nose to the snow and began to graze as well. She followed suit. It was quiet again, much like before, but much different. The white fawn buzzed with happiness inside, her heart pounded still; it was her first juicy taste of – joy.

Low on her lap, with her eyes looking forward, waiting for the right moment for Miss Magnolia to look the other way, Ramona carefully read Johnny's note, then quietly folded it back up, and handed it slowly behind her to Amelia-Ann McDonald (the stealthiest note passer in Miss Magnolia's class, mind you), who then almost invisibly passed it to her left to Molly Madison (the second most stealthy note passer), who then placed it in Murf's back pocket on her left - to read. When Murf went to scratch his bum, he accidentally found the note.

Oliver stood at the head of the class giving his oral report on: '*How The Settlers Survived The First New England Winter*'. Miss Magnolia knew something was amiss because every child was looking forward and no one was dozing off. Sitting at her desk she put on her glasses and scanned the children, looking for the note she was sure was in motion.

"The settlers actually lived inside the Mayflower that first terrible winter," said Oliver clearly and confidently. "Inside was wet and cold, but the Mayflower did provide a place for them to live, sleep, and tend to the many, many sick people, until houses could be completed ashore."

Murf slowly brought the folded note to his lap, keeping one eye on Oliver and his other on Miss Magnolia. When the time seemed right, Murf looked down, but only with his eyes. It read – 'REVENGE' - in big red letters. Quietly Murf refolded the note while he continued to keep his eyes locked on Oliver. Miss Magnolia squinted her eyes as she scanned the oddly historically interested class.

But Murf is clumsy.

When Miss Magnolia's eyes locked with his, he flinched and dropped the note. It now lay on his shoe. Seeing the note fall in the corner of her eye, Ramona screamed and kicked back her chair.

"SPIDAH, SPIDAH!!!" she hollered, pointing to the floor. The class jumped from fright. "A BEG HAIRY SPIDAH!!!" she hollered again. "WID TEETH!"

Oliver stopped. All the boys looked under her desk. All the girls scattered to the front. Miss Magnolia leaped to her feet, grabbed her coffee mug and walked quickly over to Amelia-Ann.

"Simmer down class, Simmer down. Ramona my gosh, my gosh, my gosh, you're giving the class a heart attack. Now where-o-where is this spider of yours?"

"It vas dere."

"Well, where is it now?"

Murf reached down to his feet and picked the note back up and took a peak at what it said:

'CODE RED! *Airlords of Hamilton + After School + Snow Balls = Revenge On*

The Dunce Brothers'

Murf then sent the note two desks up to Terrance, as Molly Madison gave Amelia-Ann the nod that the note was secure.

"I-I I den't 'new Miss Megnoliah. It vas just dere, big 'n' hairy. And I dink I saw teeth even." said Ramona.

"Mm hm. Okay, I see, everyone back to your seats. Go on. Go on then. There's no spider. Girls – back to your seat. Boys – sit up, there's no spider down there. Ramona was seeing things, weren't you Ramona?"

"I swear I saw a spidah."

"Sure you did Miss Grey. Just remember young lady, Irish lies are still lies. Now if I see a note being passed around, I won't think twice about reading it to the class. Remember that. So I suggest you keep your hands to yourself and listen to Oliver. Go on Oliver. Continue."

Oliver went on detailing the grieving struggle that the passengers and crew of the Mayflower endured during the first winter in New England. Miss Magnolia knew her threat had ended the note passing because many of the children began to doze off to Oliver's monotonous tone.

At lunch, Ramona was commended for her now legendary note passing save. She felt good to be praised so positively from her peers. Amelia-Ann and Molly gave Ramona a few – 'well dones' as well. After lunch, once settled in their seats again, Miss. Magnolia addressed the class.

"Now class, Marlene and Charlene have a fun announcement if I'm not mistaken. Girls? Would you please come forward and address the class?"

Charlene stood and confidently headed to the front of the class with her head held high, holding tight to her chest a small stack of printed fliers. Shyly Marlene followed.

"Here, Marlene, you can hand them out," said Charlene as she handed Marlene the stack of fliers. Marlene handed a flier to Miss Magnolia first, then one to each of her peers. "As you all know, the annual *Ice Dance* and *Winter Auction* are coming up. And for those of you who haven't attended yet, like you Miss Magnolia, well, I will explain. My Daddy throws two grand parties every year so we can all have a fun time. Isn't that swell of him?" No one answered. "Well, at the Ice Dance, like every year, there will be games, and sweets, ice-skate dancing and of course - FIREWORKS!" All the kids begin to cheer and clap. Miss Magnolia smiled and softly clapped as well. Marlene looked up shyly when she handed Terrance a flier. He took the flier and handed her back a small

139

folded note in return. Charlene continued, "So the Ice Dance will be December 22nd, starting at 7:00PM. Don't be late. It's rude. And this year's Winter Auction will be Dec 24th at 7:00PM as well. But listen; this year we have something exciting and brand new at the auction. This year there won't just be stuff for grown ups to buy," Charlene was so excited she was bursting at the seams. "Ready? Okay here it comes. There will be...there will be, *toys* for auction too?"

"Toys?" the entire class said befuddled and curious.

"Yes toys! Toys from all around the world, toys from across the ocean. My Daddy told me that he met famous toy makers from far away exotic countries like Paris and France. And the toy maker men told my Daddy that they are going to make our town our very own toys. You will be able to see them today at my Daddy's store - *Bonne Affair*. So! Everyone! Tell your parents to come Dec. 24th to town hall at 7:00PM sharp and bid to buy toys for you. And Miss Magnolia, my father says he has a seat for you right up front."

"Well, thank you Marlene and Charlene for that announcement. You may return to your seats. And tell your father that that is too-too kind of him. Please do tell him I said so. Well now," Miss Magnolia took off her glasses. "Isn't this grand. I am very excited. From the sound of it all, it looks to be a lot of fun. And yes, Charlene, I *have* heard of your father's famous Winter Auction. It is very popular around town, and, yes, this *will* be my first time attending. I will just have to go and bid on something won't I? Now this Ice Dance...tell me class, is this the type of dance that you bring a date to?" asked Miss Magnolia, who was honestly curious if she needed to bring a date or not. Then, as if by clockwork, seven girls heads, longingly, looked at Johnny Boone. Johnny kept his eyes on Miss Magnolia – he didn't notice the girls' glances. But Miss Magnolia did and Charlene did.

"No! You don't need to bring a date," said Charlene a bit loudly. "Most people just come and dance with people there. I mean, if you're married, I guess you could bring a husband."

"So you do not need a date," said Miss Magnolia factually.

"You could if you wanted too. I think that's swell", said Molly Madison as she snuck peeks at Johnny. Miss Magnolia knew that Johnny was the choice of most of the girls in her class. She thought it sweet that he didn't know. "I think if a boy *wanted* to ask a girl that'd be a good idea and he should go ahead and ask her," continued Molly.

"No! People don't bring dates!" said Charlene as she began to get even more uncomfortable noticing the many sneaked peaks at Johnny.

"I'm just saying, if a boy *wanted* to - he could; not that you *have* to," said Molly.

"Yah, if a boy *wanted* to, he should. I bet any girl would love to be asked," said Amelia-Ann, also sneaking peeks at Johnny.

"Oh I see," said Miss Magnolia. "You don't have to, but you can if you want. Well then, some of you boys might want to think about asking some of the girls from class to go with you. That *would be* swell."

"No! No dates," said Charlene folding her arms.

"Why not?" spoke up Ramona.

Terrance took that opportunity to look behind himself at Marlene. She was folding his note back up.

"Marlene McManus! What do you have there? Is that a note? I'm sorry, but you must bring that up here to me this instant."

The class stopped their discussion and all turned to Marlene's desk.

With her head down low, Marlene stood. With her head down low, Marlene walked to the head of the class. And with her head down low, she handed Miss Magnolia the folded note and sat back down.

"I am very disappointed with you Marlene. Who gave you this note?"

Terrance's hand slowly rose.

Miss Magnolia unfolded the note.

"Let's see what was *so* red hot important that it couldn't wait until after class shall we?" The class hushed. With faces as red as circus balloons, Marlene and Terrance looked at one another, sunk in their chairs and then looked down at their laps. Miss Magnolia began to read the note to herself, but then realized she may have made a mistake and wasn't sure what to do next. The note read:

> *"I think you are very pretty Marlene. I like your hair. I like your hat that you wear sometimes. It's swell. Would you like to dance with me at the Ice Dance this Friday? Circle Yes or No. It would be my honor. With Best Regards Terrance."*

'*Yes*' was circled.

The class was silent. Waiting. Miss Magnolia pretended to keep reading, but she was really just trying to figure out what to do next. She had once had a note taken away from her in grade school, a note from a boy she thought was the best of them all, and her teacher read it to the class. It embarrassed her more then she, even to this day, had ever been embarrassed. Miss Magnolia folded the note back up and put it in her back pocket. She then sternly looked at Terrance.

"Terrance McKool if you need help on your oral report you can ask Miss McManus after class, there is no need to distract her during class. Miss McManus indicated, 'yes', she would be glad to help you. But next time Terrance, wait until after class or I will have to bring down your next report a full letter grade and inform your parents you are distracting classmates during school hours. And I'm sure your mother and father would not be happy with that would they?"

"No Ma'am."

"I thought not. Okay class let's get back to your reports. Miss Madison, please come to the front; your report on *'What The New England Settlers Ate'* is next.

Terrance was buzzing inside. He was sure Miss Magnolia was talking in code, like when Wilma talks to Buck Rogers in the comic strips. He wished he could see the note, so he could see - 'Yes' circled himself, but he understood Miss Magnolia, and Marlene and he both appreciated the secret being kept.

It was now after lunch. Kringle and Pete had washed their dishes in the soapy black basin and mixed their leftover beans into Rudy's chow. Pete laid the bowl of dog chow mixed with warm water down for him to slobber up. Rudy wiggled his bum. His tail slapped The Workshop floor. The men were energized. Sharp. Maybe their high spirit came from the crisp and sparkly day outside, or maybe it came from the fact that they heated a second kettle of strong coffee, different from their normal daily ration of just one. But more, it was because the two artists knew that their day was opened strictly to crafting their beloved art – carpentry.

Collaboration. Kringle rubbed his red scruff that was coming in, dragged his stool around to Pete's workbench and took a seat while sipping his second hot coffee. Before lunch Pete had finished the sketching for his first toy-box, which he was now ready to craft. Kringle looked over some of Pete's notes:

Story 3

Location: *The Junkyard. November.*
Characters: *Father, mother, me as a boy, Rudy as a pup.*

Animation: *Rudy and Pete playing tug of war with an old tire (black rubber band), Father and Mother twirling together inside the home (dancing).*

Kringle thought Pete's animation ideas for this toy-box was a fun and not too difficult place to start such a new craft: the twirling characters would be easy for Pete, while the challenge of carving the diminutive models of Rudy and Pete swaying back and forth pulling a rubber band were a good test for Pete's meticulousness. The two men had measured and cut the frame of the toy-box earlier that morning and placed it by the stove so that the glue would be set once the day had begun. Rudy sniffed the box frame every hour, thinking there were grubs warming inside, but he always found the box empty. The two men had also collected the needed wood pieces from the junkyard that they'd be carving and put aside the tools needed for the job: a fine saw, three fine files, three different grades of sandpaper, a crank drill with small drill bits, a small hammer, glue and cleaning towels. The tools now lay spread out on Pete's workbench holding the ends of his blueprints from curling in. You could hear the melting icicles dripping off The Workshop's roof outside. Quiet blues music played from Pete's hanging radio.

Centering himself at his workbench, Pete took a seat next to Kringle, stretched his arms up big and strong, took his hat off, scratched his hair, slapped his hat back on and placed the topside of the toy-box down in front of him. They would start with carving the small characters because they were the second most difficult piece to this puzzle - the mechanics to move the characters would prove to be the most challenging.

Pete had finished carving all the large characters he needed for his toy-box earlier that week. They were lined up in front of him next to the small ship he had begun. Kringle thought they looked marvelous. On the faces of his parents there was minute detail; their expressions of happiness were endearing. The task for Pete to carve Rudy as a pup and himself as a boy was even more difficult, because they were half the size of his parents' characters. Small carvings meant - eyes squinting, meant - eyebrows low, meant - wrinkled lips and a wrinkled nose. Pete's hands were big and calloused, but he used them with the same delicate care of a new mother combined with the certainty of an accomplished surgeon.

Pete pulled his red handkerchief from his back pocket and wiped his perspiring forehead. Even though it was a bit crisp in The Workshop, Pete's intense concentration was warming him.

"Okay, let's get these dowels inside," Pete said as he picked up his crank drill.

"Okay, the moment of truth," Kringle said with a smile.

This was the tricky part.

Kringle securely held the characters upside down so that Pete could drill inside them a small hole to place a dowel. Once the dowels were glued and secured, Kringle helped Pete connect the dowels to spring-loaded levers. Then both men cut the other needed mechanics: a crank for the outside (to crank the animation to life) and the needed camshafts.

As the Sun moved to a different window to sneak her mid-day peeks, the work had pressed on and the mechanics to Pete's first toy-box were almost complete. Pete and Kringle had a fulfilling afternoon. They liked measuring, cutting and tackling problems together. Pete was a natural and Kringle's designs were one of a kind.

Pete had finished. It was time to try his toy-box out. He took the frame that had been warming by the stove and placed it on his workbench. He and Kringle now stood in front of it. Pete then took the top off the toy-box, with his characters on one side and his mechanics on the other, he slowly placed it down inside. Pete carefully located the crank in through the hole on the side and secured it by the open bottom of the toy-box.

Both men stood in front of the toy-box. Rudy came along side and jumped up with his front paws on Pete's workbench to see what the interest was all about.

"Glue all dry you think?" checked Kringle.

"Should be sound."

"Well then. Go on."

"I'm a bit nervous."

"Go on, give her a whirl."

"Okay here we go."

Pete touched the crank and began to turn it. The magical toy-box moved in this way:

Once the crank turned, the beveled camshafts spun like horizontal pistons, moving each lever. Rudy's and Pete's character levers were being pulled back by loaded springs that were connected to the dowels that were secured in each of their characters that were placed on the top of the toy-box. Pete's mother and father characters spun freely in a circle without any loaded springs pulling them back. Everyone was in motion.

The figures of Pete's mother and father twirled in a romantic embrace while the young Pete and young Rudy characters pulled back and forth, playing tug-of-war with a yet to be seen tire. It had worked. The wood was now magical. Pete cranked on and all the pieces played out as they should. Rudy barked at the moving parts. Pete grinned. Kringle grinned. And Pete cranked on, mesmerized by his new skill and new art.

"She works. And on a first try no less. Nice job Pete."

"I can't believe it, they're all moving and everything."

"Hard part's done."

"Ugh sure is. Lord my eyes hurt from concentrating."

"Now you can just do the details – craft The Workshop, the yard piles, the tire, then paint it up all nice - paint the sides, paint the characters, all that fun stuff. 'S great when all the insides are done huh?"

Pete just kept cranking, grinning and saying, "They're all moving and everything."

Mr. McManus' Duisenberg was running much better now with gasoline in its tank. Driven by Lloyd with Elmer beside him, the Duisenberg bounced up and down on the narrow horse path of a road. The Duisenberg spun and spit up dirty snow into the air, working hard for traction. Mr. McManus sat in the back, dressed up more than usual. He had a big black top hat on, a grand grey and white rabbit fur coat, white pants and black shiny shoes; he held a cane, was smoking a pipe and was even wearing a spectacle.

Knock-Knock-Knock!

Kringle, Pete and Rudy heard the Duisenberg coming, but made no mention of it, for there is never anything to say when an offensive man approaches and will, undoubtedly, spoil the air of a room.

Knock-Knock-Knock!

Kringle opened the door to The Workshop. Mr. McManus entered the room with one arm extended with his cane like a medieval jouster followed by jesters. It was such a loud entrance that Rudy was unsure what to do, so he barked to be safe.

"Shh, it's okay boy, it's okay," Pete reassured Rudy.

Mr. McManus entered The Workshop yelling.

"Okay boys, here we go, here we go; we got a lot to talk about." Lloyd walked in with Mr. McManus and stood by him with his arms crossed in the center of The Workshop. Elmer hung back, standing in an intimidating fashion with his arms crossed at the door. "Now, Miss Winkelplex took the train to Boston and then the trolley to Cambridge concerning our *new, one of a kind, imported all the way from Europe'*..." Mr. McManus was sounding like a radio commercial, "...*'exquisite toys, seen nowhere else'* – the same toys I am about to sell hundreds of. No, thousands of. So listen up, Miss Winkelplex had dinner with many exquisite families, collecting buyers, generating demand and making us all future lettuce in our pockets. Now! She collected many orders of what the people *want*. Here they are." Mr. McManus first went to hand the list to Pete, but then changed his mind and handed the list to Kringle. "Can you make these?"

"Let's see here: toy cars, toy boats, wagons, trains, dollhouses. Sure thing this is easy stuff Mr. McManus, sir." Kringle read on - "boomerangs, sling-shots, hoops, fishing rods, um, sure. I never made a fishing rod, but it's not a problem. Okay um, building blocks, not a problem...but hm wait, I don't know about this here."

"What? What can't you make? This list is important Kringle; it's our start. Make their wish come true one time and you'll have them for life," said Mr. McManus sternly.

"Well it says here 'pistols' Mr. McManus."

"Yah, so what? You can make a pistol can't yah. Hell, *I* could make a pistol for a kid Kringle."

"Well, sure I could make a child a pistol, but Mr. McManus guns aren't toys. Guns kill; that's their purpose. Seems harsh. Violent. Guns are what's killing these kids' fathers. They don't understand that you see? They don't know what they're asking for - truly. I think we should skip pistols. I'm a toymaker; pistols aren't toys." Kringle handed Pete the note. "I can make everything else though." Kringle had lost his interest in the over romanticizing of guns after one of his sisters found his father's old war pistol in a tin box, wrapped in a flag, deep in their father's closet. Thinking it was harmless, she lifted that gun like it was a toy and shot Kringle's favorite sister down. Dead.

"Oh, you won't, will you?" challenged Mr. McManus.

"No sir, that ain't responsible of me. But I'll make the children anything else you got on any list you bring. Anything, sir. Just not pistols. It teaches murder. Let's stick with laughter. I'm sorry Mr. McManus, sir. You can respect that can't ya?"

"Oh now you're telling me, are you? You're telling me what you *are* and *are not* gonna make? So *you're* in charge? The boss huh? Hm. Well I didn't know. Didn't have the foggiest. Tell me Kringle how much are you paying me then? These orders don't come cheap you know?"

The Dunce Brothers snickered.

"No it ain't like that sir."

"No? 'It ain't like that?' Well Kringle, yes, I do believe it's exactly like that. See, I'm standing here, right here, and I'm listening to you, and you're right there, right-right there, telling me, me, *you're* boss, what you *will*, and *will not*, make for me. I find that precarious. Especially in these times, times when many men need a good paying job. Let me test your philosophy Kringle. Hm, now, does the policeman get to decide who he *does* and *does not* hold to the law? No. Do the firemen decide which houses they *will* or *will not* let burn? Noo. Or wait, do the teachers decide who they will or will not teach? Better still do the doctors decide who they *will* cure and who they *will let die*? No! They do their *job*! The job that's required of them to do. At least that's how *I* thought this great nation was run."

"It just ain't like that sir. I…"

"No, I heard you Kringle, no need to repeat yourself. I see through this as clear as fresh water. *You* say to *me*, me standing here, and you standing there, at precisely…" Mr. McManus patted himself down for his pocket watch, then realized it was sitting on Kringle's workbench to be fixed. "At about two o'clock that *you*, a toooymaker, *my* employee, will not make my good friend, our graciously loyal customer, Mr. Gilbert from the Harvard Music Association's son Alexander Jr. a silly little wooden pistol. A toy. I mean…that's what I heard." Mr. McManus turned to Lloyd to his left. "Is that what you heard?"

"That's exactly what I heard sir," said Lloyd deadpan, staring at Kringle.

"And I do believe the deal is that Miss Winkelplex finds buyers, makes a list of what they want, gives it to me, I give it to you, you make what's on the list and *I – PAY* YOU!" shouted Mr. McManus. Kringle and Pete jumped. "Now!" Mr. McManus snatched the list and pushed it into Elmer's chest. "Now I believe a stupid wooden 'pistol' is on that list; do you see the word 'pistol' on the list Elmer?" barked Mr. McManus staring aggressively into Kringle eyes.

"Sure thing Mr. M., right after building blocks," said Elmer.

Mr. McManus pulled out from under his jacket his billfold and pulled out a few notes. "See here boys," Mr. McManus brought his voice down to a more soothing tone. "No more tit for tat. Yah? Yah? I just simply cannot bear it. There's your cut from the sales Pete, there's your cut Kringle. Let's remember how everything works here. You make, I sell; we all get paid, we all stay happy. Now I have to get to *Bonne Affaire*, my new toys have been on display all day and I want to be there when school gets out. I had my girls make an announcement at their school today, you see. That's how you market, you get into their homes; you get into their lives; that's how you do it; that's smarts." Mr. McManus smiled and put back his billfold. "Fine? Are we all okay now? Tantrum over is it? Coup complete? Good. You boys make what's on that list there. *Everything* that is?"

Kringle wiped his face muscles loose starting with his eyes, took a breath and then let it out slowly.

"I understand Mr. McManus and I appreciate this job you've given me, I appreciate the money, the house, the bed, everything. Truly. And I understand how your system works here. I truly do. And I want you to know that I will make everything on that list here." Kringle took the list from Elmer, folded it and placed it in his breast pocket. Elmer and Lloyd smiled to one another. Mr. McManus took a seat on Pete's stool, sat back pleased and lit his pipe. "And I'll make them toys better than anyone in this whole entire world, no doubt to that sir, no doubt at all. But Mr. McManus sir…I will not be making a little, not knowing child, a pistol for his play. Pistols are weapons. Soul takers. Kids are special. They're learnin' when they're young and that's a negative lesson. It's the pistol, and pistol alone, that will be the death of them kids' family the more we glorify them. I'm an adult; I know this. Them are kids; they don't know this.

148

They'd eat rubber if I told 'em it was gum. Evil is evil. Wrong is wrong. And truth is truth. You can't borrow evil for something you want, like making a dollar or three and then after say you's a good man. A God man. No you can't borrow evil." Mr. McManus turned around on Pete's stool, now facing Pete's workbench. "See, Sir, there's two kinds of evil here on earth: Natural Evil – which is like a hurricane, a blizzard or a tornado. You can't control that evil. They're acts of nature. You can only prepare, take cover and pray. But Moral Evil – see, that's what man makes. Moral evil is murder, guns and war." Pete was staring at Kringle with wide watery green eyes; he was nervous and certain that this would be his last day he'd be working along side such a fine carpenter as this Kris Kringle was. Kringle went on with a clear tone of certainty, "See, I am a spiritual man Mr. McManus, so you'll understand how I can't bring myself to be a part of any evil, any at all, especially an evil that's - man made evil. Moral evil. No sir, I'm a man that stands as a deterrent to evil."

But Mr. McManus wasn't listening; he had turned his back from Kringle and was now staring down at Pete's toy-box slowly cranking it.

"Marvelous, simply a treasure," Mr. McManus said out loud. "You don't want to make the blasted pistol Kringle - fine. Just stop talking; you're making me tired. Moving on shall we?" Mr. McManus looked over his right shoulder smoking his pipe. "How long does it take to make one of these boxes here?"

Pete decided to take the floor in the rising hope that his work partner may have hung onto his job. He walked over to Mr. McManus intentionally blocking Mr. McManus' sight from Kringle for a moment.

"Oh well, sir, I'd say one full day and night for one; wood glue's gotta dry, paint's gotta dry. You understand," said Pete.

Mr. McManus began to mutter to himself, "One day, hm, too long for one. Well, with more workers we could fix that in the future, and definitely cut out so much of the detail in everything, make it simpler, maybe build them in stages, yes stages. Like those Lowell factories, yes, but for toys though. We could also cut down on the wait for this drying problem, get a work line going, sure, a strong work line that's it - we could make much, much more." Mr. McManus stood up and pointed to Kringle's pile of toys he made that day. "And Kringle what, you made all these toys today and Pete just made this one?"

"Well, yes, but what Pete is building is much more complex."

Mr. McManus grumbled to himself as he tried out all the push-toys. Lloyd and Elmer laughed at the silly sound the duck's rubber feet made as they

149

slapped on the wooden floor. They wanted to have a go at them, but knew to stay put. It saddened them.

"You're just being modest Kringle, that's why I like you. You're better, that's the correct answer. These are much better toys then those on the list there. They're more extravagant you see? Different. They're outside the box if you will. Exotic maybe. "Exotic" is a popular word with women these days; it makes the sale. Hm, okay, change of plans boys. Kringle I want you to write me down a list of *all* the toys you know how to make. Draw a picture too. The more original, the more different and never seen before, the better. See, the more "exotic" they are, the more people will think they are special, different, better and from a far away fantasy place. Meaning – they'll pay much more; much, much more." Mr. McManus stood and began to pace back and forth puffing on his pipe. "But I want you to make everything on that list as well. Three of everything. And scratch the "evil pistol" as you call it." Mr. McManus said sarcastically. "You really need a back bone Kringle or this world is just going to eat you alive. Tell me..." Mr. McManus then moved past Pete and got close to Kringle's face. "... are you going to be muttering to me about "moral evil" after a little bitsy birdie is shot down from one of the sling shots on that list or if a fish is caught with a fishing pole you made?" Mr. McManus didn't wait for an answer, the way many bullheaded men do when they feel they could be outwitted. "Nice work boys. Make what's on that list, times three, and Kringle you make me a new list. EXOTIC! Remember that word. Write it down, X-A-W-T-I-C-K. And think "money" boys. That's what we're doing here. Remember that. Exotic and money; exotic and money!"

"Yes sir."

"Yes, sir. Thank you Mr. McManus sir."

"Also, you fix my watch yet Kringle?"

"Not yet sir, it's next on my list."

"You do that, because if I'm late for anything it's your fault! Your head!"

With that Mr. McManus and the Dunce Brothers exited The Workshop.

Outside Kringle and Pete watched as Lloyd and Elmer worked at getting the Duisenberg out of the mud. After about fifteen minutes the three of them drove on to town.

Kringle closed the door and checked how many notes Mr. McManus had given him. There were three.

"How many notes did you get Pete?" asked Kringle.

Pete took out his folded paper.

"Two."

Kringle started to roll his right sleeve up and pull his stool around to face the small center table. Pete did the same thing, knowing there was no way to bicker about it. Arm wrestling over the difference of their pay was now the understood way the men handled the issue.

"I swear Kringle, you're the only fella who has ever been so bent on giving me his money."

Bonne Affaire was packed with shoppers. People from all over New England were elbow-to-elbow, huffing and puffing, irritated and claustrophobic. They had all shown up to see *Bonne Affaire's* new, "one of a kind, exotic toys," they had heard about and that were now on display.

"I will give you two dollars for these two here. That should be five times what they're worth," said a well-to-do woman, dressed in a folded plaid coat with a gaggle of other ladies dressed the same around her. The group had come up to Boston all the way from Hartford, Connecticut for some shopping. Upon hearing about the toys from Miss Winkelplex at a dinner party put on by *The Corporation* at *The Lobe House* in Harvard Yard, the ladies took the north train up to Hamilton the very next morning.

"I'm sorry Miss, but like I mentioned these toys are just for display, they are examples of the kinds of exquisite toys that will be up for auction at this year's annual Winter Auction. It will be held on December twenty-fourth at seven o'clock, please take a flier," said Ellie as she spun her head this way and that, trying to keep an eye on all the customers bustling about.

The women and her gaggle of hens became cross.

"I already have a flier," the woman said and waved it in Ellie's face. "I was given one on Friday, that's why I'm here now."

"We were all given fliers," said one of the other women and they all waved their fliers in Ellie's face.

"I want to see Linda Winkelplex. Is she here? She told us she'd be here. I want to see her."

"Yes ma'am, she's my boss."

"I'm sure she is. But what I said was - I want to see her. Now!"

"Yes ma'am. I can get her for you."

"Oh my lord ladies, this one just doesn't get it. YES! YES! That is what I said darling. Fetch me Linda. Go-go-get." With that, the gaggle of women turned their backs on Ellie and surrounded the table that displayed the miniature model ships of the Nina and the Santa Maria that Kringle and his father had made.

Ellie had to execute a series of clumsy *chaine turns* in *half-point* to maneuver through *Bonne Affaire*.

"Flo, Flo, there you are," said Ellie

"Hitch a saucer and kiss a martian, there *you* are Ellie. What is going on; who are all these people?" Flo looked stressed, her curls were coming out of her bun and her cheeks were rosé from being flustered.

The crowd knocked Ellie and Flo into one another; they were now face to face.

"I don't know. But," Ellie went to a whisper, "that wicked little woman over there told me that Miss Winkelplex handed her a flier about the toys on Friday."

"Ya, I saw 'em. That," Flo went to a whisper, "chew-spit fat-cat over there told me he got his Monday. Last Monday! She must'a been givin' em out all week. Could'a warned us."

"Psst you could say that again. You seen her?"

"Ya, she's over there, next to the woman with the silly peacock feathers in her head. Heard that's the Mayor's twin wife; the mayor's the one with the cigar."

"What'd you mean twin wife?"

"The twin."

"Well, what do you mean "the twin"? They ain't twins. Are they?! They're twins and they're married?!" Ellie cupped her mouth and snuck a peak at them.

"No, no. They ain't twins. Honey you gotta know the story of the twins. It's *old* paper news."

People began to shove one another because a woman intentionally flared her elbows out making everyone lose their footing. Ellie and Flo shuffled their feet, apologized to the people around them and then got their footing once again.

"No, I don't follow news anymore; it's always bad."

"Well 'bout four years ago, Mayor's wife died, see? Edith was her name. Well, a year later, he go and marry her twin sister. Boom-snap-clap; married again. Carrie's her name. I followed the story closely. *Daaancin'* scandalous huh?"

"Whoa. And that's the sister?"

"And that's the sister. The twin. Can you believe? I mean Ellie, I understand why he gone and done it. Men are men. But oo-wee Ellie, if my sister done that, you bet the Lord himself would have to come down and jump in-between Ghost-Flo and her. I'm getting angry just thinking about it and I ain't even got a man. Or a sister."

Both women smiled and looked at one another as they swayed with the crowded room.

"Well, I gotta interrupt or those hens over there will get me in more trouble with Miss Winkelplex than if I didn't interrupt. Dang it all."

"You want help? I wanna talk to the twin."

"No-no you got your own storm to row in."

With that Ellie headed over to Miss Winkelplex, Mayor Nichols and his wife Carrie Nichols. They all turned to her when Carrie Nichols' eyes widened.

"My apologies for interrupting Miss Winkelplex."

"Well, is this the Southerner or the Lone-Okie?" asked Mayor Nichols, smiling and smoking his cigar. All three turned to Ellie.

"The what?" Ellie asked befuddled.

"She's the Okie," Miss Winkelplex answered.

"Ah, the Okie. How are you getting along now?" asked the Major almost worried.

"Yes dear, how are you getting along?" repeated the Major's wife.

"Oh just fine, as you see we have a wonderful and exciting new shipment of beautiful toys all the way from Europe and it just pleases me so much to show them all to these interested and intelligent people from all around. But may I ask, what is an Okie?"

"Oh how darling," said the Major's wife.

"That doesn't matter Ellie. We were just talking about how you came to work for me and about your husband heading west," answered Miss Winkelplex.

"It's a farm hand. A laborer. A worker looking for work. Named after Oklahomans that migrated west to California for work." explained the Mayor with something kind and something missing in his eyes. "You see Miss?"

"Boone," Miss Winkelplex answered.

"You see Miss Boone, your husband himself is an Okie of sorts. As Miss Winkelplex has told us, he himself headed to California for work. Must have gotten one of those fliers that have been going around," said the Mayor.

"My husband?" asked Ellie a bit thrown off.

"Lovely how she took you and the other one…" the Mayor's wife turned to Miss Winkelplex.

"Florence," she answered.

"Yes, Florence. Linda took you two in and got you two girls up and working."

"Quite a wonderful little story Miss Boone," added the Mayor. "We need more people with your determination; with your heart," said the Mayor; stabbing his cigar in the air with every word he spoke. You keep this great country floating on the ocean.

"Well, I don't have a husband anymore," said Ellie as her entire body began to tingle a crescendoing burning sensation of pins and needles.

"We know dear," said the Mayor's wife as she touched Ellie's arm and squeezed. "And how is that?"

Miss Winkelplex stared at Ellie. Her eyes were trying to coach the right answer from her.

"Oh it's fine. I get by. This job helps tremendously. I owe a lot to Miss Winkelplex really," said Ellie. But it was a lie; Ellie worked for *Bonne Affaire* long before Mr. Boone left.

"Splendid. What a ripe apple," Mayor Nichols smiled, and the Mayor's wife and Miss Winkelplex smiled back. "I should hire you two to show New Englanders what…" Mayor Nichols closed his cigar hand into a fist and said with conviction, "…togetherness is truly about. '*We the people*', it has always said. Not 'I'. And it will have to be all of us working *together* for us to get us out of these damn, damn times."

"Oo do you know what darling Ellie needs?" smiled the Mayor's wife.

"What is that?" asked Miss Winkelplex with a high school girl's expression.

"A widower," she said flashing her husband a cheeky look.

"Oh my, you are right," said Mayor Nichols and then looked up in thought. "Well let me see, let me see. Who do I know that's widowed? Dr. Williams is widowed."

"Oo a Doctor, you could marry up Ellie," smiled the Mayor's wife and everyone had a chuckle. Mayor Nichols looked skyward and thought on.

"Hm, well, ah, Frank Moore was, but he remarried that woman, the one with the thin hair."

"Lisa-Anne," said the Mayor's wife. "You're more darling than she is," said the Mayor's wife to Ellie. "She, well…" The Mayor's wife pantomimed drinking.

"Jack Anderson doesn't care for his wife. You could be a mistress." said the Mayor and they all, save Ellie, exploded in laughter. "No, no Ellie, but it's true, it's true. A widowed man is a lonely man. He *needs* someone. He'll nearly take anyone. So I say, save up, get a nice dress, clean up in all those womanly ways, head into the city, find yourself a widower and…bring…your…self…up." Again the Mayor punctuated each of his words with his cigar. "And it wouldn't hurt, not mentioning your first marriage. Men don't like that. There! A good plan is set."

Ellie could feel the blood rushing though her fingers, arms, chest and face. She had only been this insulted one other time – when Mr. Boone left and she had only been this angry one other time – when Mr. Boone sent her the contract to "unmarry" for her to sign. But those times were behind her now. Forgotten, or trying to be forgotten. As the Mayor's wife rubbed one of Ellie's shoulders, Miss Winkelplex touched her other. Miss Winkelplex could tell Ellie was frozen in dark thoughts.

"Ellie, what did you want to ask me? We can't spend all day figuring out your life," Miss Winkelplex said with a chuckle.

Ellie took a deep breath, wiped her forehead and smoothed out the front of her dress. It was an almost obvious signal for the ladies to take their hands off her, but not obvious enough to be rude. Ellie spoke cheerfully with clear articulation.

"Well, there is a kind woman here with her lovely friends. I believe you had dinner with them at the Lobe House at Harvard University Friday night?"

"Ah yes the ladies from Connecticut," said Miss Winkelplex.

"Oh, the leaves there in the fall…" gushed the Mayor's wife. "…as lovely as a poem."

"Yes Ma'am. She would like to purchase the two small model ships."

"Well Ellie, tell her they will be up for auction December twenty-fourth."

"I did Ma'am. She said she would like to buy them today, as a gift. And that she – traveled too far to just gaze at them like an adoring orphan child. She said that last bit herself."

The conversation was becoming undesirable for Miss Winkelplex. The Mayor and his wife began to look off, bored by the fact they were not included in it.

"Ah I see. Well, let me accommodate her. Carrie, Mayor Nichols, would you excuse me?"

"Of course."

"Of course and good luck Ellie. Remember, you can only go up," said the Mayor's wife as she turned away.

Miss Winkleplex grabbed Ellie's arm, dug her fingernails in just slightly and pulled her down two inches so to reach her eye.

"Don't you ever interrupt or embarrass me like that again Ellie! I have the mind to throw you out with today's garbage. You should feel grateful that I don't. Ten women would walk in, in ten seconds flat if I posted a help wanted sign in the window. And you remember that!" she said. "Now where are they?"

Miss Winkelplex and Ellie approached the gaggle of women standing around Kringle's and his father's model ships of the Nina and the Santa Maria. The ladies were all fanning themselves with their fliers, looking bothered.

"Carol," Miss Winkelpex let out with a big smile as she opened her arms up for a hug.

"Linda, Linda," said the woman that was giving Ellie a hard time. The two women embraced and began gabbing. Ellie stood back waiting to be needed. She looked out over the shop. Flo was also doing her best *Saut de basque,* spinning to one customer; answering her question, spinning to another, answering hers and then spinning to the next. Ellie noticed that the only time Flo didn't look like she was dancing among the hungry wolves was when she would stop and talk in her normal posture and what looked to be her true tone, to the less-to-do customers from town. From a distance Ellie could see her talking to Ramona's parents – the McDonald's, Claire and Pete. Mrs. McDonald held Ramona's little sister Katherine in her arms. Mr. McDonald was holding one of Kringle's wooden dolls. The conversation looked to be having a disappointing outcome. Flo was shaking her head back and forth and Mr. McDonald was rubbing the back of his neck. Mrs. McDonald took the wooden doll out of her husband's hands and showed it to Katherine. Katherine looked hopeful. Then Flo said something that seemed to surprise the McDonalds. Mr. and Mrs. McDonald both shook their heads "no" and handed the wooden doll back to Flo, which she then placed back on display. Katherine reached for the doll and her mother placed her arms down and then rubbed her child's forehead and hair. Mrs. McDonald looked to be politely thanking Flo. Katherine looked saddened. Mrs. McDonald turned to leave the shop, but took a moment to whisper what looked to be soothing words to Katherine, and then she made her way through the crowd to the front door. Flo turned to the next impatient customer. Mr. McDonald stayed. He picked the doll up and began to analyze it. With his fingers he seemed to be taking measurements, his eyes would look to the doll and to the ceiling and his mouth seemed to be doing calculations. He then placed the doll back on the table, backed up a stepped, analyzed the doll one more time, stepped forward and picked it up for one last look. Ellie then noticed him stare off daydreaming. As he looked around the room he caught Ellie's eyes, smiled and waved to her. Then he made his way to the front door as well.

"Ellie," Miss Winkelplex turned to Ellie and waved her over. "This is Mrs. Caldwell, she will be buying these." Miss Winkelplex then turned back to the ladies. "Well what can I say Carol really? These heavenly made ships of the Nina and the Santa Maria are just; well, unlike anything I have ever seen. *And from Italy*. Just beautiful. You simply can't get this kind of craftsmanship anywhere around here I tell you. So we will keep these up for the remainder of the week for display, but they are *your* beautiful, beautiful ships."

"Oh thank you Linda," said Mrs. Moore. "And you believe the craftsman has already sent the Nina from Italy as well?"

"Oh yes, he sent it months ago. I do not know how they got separated," said Miss. Winkelplex.

"Wonderful. My husband will die, Linda, just die. He himself thinks he's some sort of captain after last summers sailing trip to Canada." All the ladies smiled and went on with their conversations. Ellie's eyes glossed over. She scanned the room of Fortunate people who were all slightly pushing each other, trying to spin Flo their way. She caught Flo's eyes only for a moment and then looked past her to the window, where the snow was starting to fall and where the McDonalds where bundled outside heading home.

When Mr. McManus came by *Bonne Affaire*, he danced the room like a true politician. There was boisterous laughter; firm handshakes and many of the Fortunate gayly kissed one another on their cheeks - each and every one caught up in the swirl of the stunning European toys all around them. Mr. McManus and Mayor Nichols smoked cigars, patted each other's shoulders and made big plans to make big plans. Mr. McManus talked about expanding his shop, by relocating *Bonne Affaire* to the Back Bay of Boston. And after Mr. McManus told Mayor Nichols he could get his son some of his most exquisite toys from Europe, and after Mr. McManus told the Mayor's wife that he could get her a *French art deco vanity dressing table* for no cost - just for her to speak kindly of it to her friends – well, Mayor Nichols began to holler, "Hear me now McManus, this country *needs* a man like you in our political system. I'll drag you down town kicking and screaming if I have to. Frankly, I say this, the United States of America, *needs* entrepreneurs just…like…you." That got Mr. McManus glowing, Miss Winkelplex as well. She just about looked at Mr. McManus like a proud First Lady.

When the bustle began to calm and the Fortunate people began to head home, there were only a few leftover town folk milling around *Bonne Affaire*. Mr. McManus and Miss Winkelplex knew they weren't *real* customers, so they headed to the back of the shop to discuss the improved details of their ever-expanding swindle.

"Ellie," Mr. McManus boomed, "Here are some fliers, hand them out to people as they head home," said Mr. McManus as he headed to the back room.

"Yes Mr. McManus," said Ellie as she made her way to the front door. Flo stayed inside to clean up from the day's heavy traffic.

Ellie stood out in the cold, handing people fliers as they walked by. Mostly Pacers took them. They'd take the flier, thank Ellie, look at the flier and then look back at her with a confused air. Not only did she know none of the Pacers would want expensive European toys, but she also knew they simply could not afford them. It was almost an insult. Each Pacer looked to her to see if it was a cruel joke she was playing on them. But they would quickly realize that, poor Ellie standing out in the cold was just doing her job, so they'd thank her, fold the flier, pocket it and walk on.

Inside Mr. McManus and Miss Winkelplex were grinning and giggling like hyenas. They sat across a small table in Miss Winkelplex's cramped office. Miss Winkelplex was meticulous: one wall of her office was devoted to different packaging supplies to wrap and secure the furniture to be delivered by the Dunce Brothers, one wall was strictly filing cabinets, one wall was for the safe and books on Europe and European furniture and the last wall was for the door and the two lamps on either side of its frame. A table stood in the middle of the room. There were no windows.

"I have written up and designed the new *Letter of Authenticity* for my toys," Mr. McManus said with his cigar in his mouth, opening his briefcase with both hands. "Take a look; they look perfectly legal." Mr. McManus pushed the stack of papers towards Miss Winkelplex and sat back. "I had my lawyer do all the wording. It's perfect. You see, each one for each land – Italy, Holland, France and Switzerland. All that stuff you can't understand is legitimate, my lawyer had some of his men re-translate what I wrote, they used 'word confusion' as they call it. "Miss Winkelplex looked through the letters. "All them French and Italian words help woo American buyers see. Buyers love that stuff. They eat it up. Frankly they love with a sickness reading things they don't understand – makes them feel scholarly." Miss Winkelplex looked up and the two exchanged hyena grins and giggles once again. "Do you have the seals?"

To make things look even more official, Miss Winkelplex had wax seals made in Boston. Each seal has different symbols representing different, non-existent, craftsman's coat of arms. She began doing this after a woman on Beacon Hill returned one of Pete's greatest *French Walnut Dining Table Desk* because it didn't have a wax seal from the craftsman.

Miss Winkelplex put the new *Letters of Authenticity* to the side. She then went to her safe, turned the big combination dial, opened the heavy door and took out a fancy small box. She placed the box in front of Mr. McManus and then stood behind him.

"I had four made last Saturday." Mr. McManus opened the box. The box opened like a jewelry box, having three tiers. Each level held wax seals. "They are the four on the top." Mr. McManus took the first one out. He looked at the top where the symbol of the seal was drawn. "Jean-Louis Lalor from Nancy, France will be the craftsman, so he has a J.L. and his symbol is a Bell. That one is Lukas Frankhauser, L.F. from Chur, Switzerland and, as you see, his symbol is a Pine Tree." Mr. McManus grumbled a pleased grumble and took out the next seal. "Salvatore DaVinci, S.D. from Sant'Antioco, Italy. It's one of the islands. The top one, we must mention that and really over dramatize that he is from an island. Say like, 'oh the beaches, oh the water, the boats, the cliffs, sunsets, warm

159

nights, blah blah blah'. All that. His symbol is a Star. And finally that one, that's Augustijn Maarschalkerweerd from Nijmegen, Netherlands. I wanted to find a very difficult name to pronounce. I think that's fun for the buyers and helps with that needed laughing moment when we discuss price. He's obviously A.M. as you see there and his symbol is simply a wrapped Gift with a bow. Get people in the mood to hold their own gift, you see. It's all psychology; it's all psychology."

"And you did all the back stories of these four men?"

Miss Winkelplex turned back to the safe and placed on the table a black leather button string envelope. "All of it is in there. That's for you to read up on. For each craftsman, I go as far back as their great-great grandparents. It's fabulous stuff; buyers will eat it up. It's all very emotional, but not too emotional, the stories will pull their heart strings as it pulls out their wallets."

The two grinned again.

"Fine. Good Linda. Good. Now sit-sit. It's time to discuss money."

And they did discuss money. Mr. McManus explained that with this new venture, he would be taking half of her share and his share as well, to put towards relocating *Bonne Affaire* to the Back Bay of Boston. "It's time to relocate. In the city, we will more than triple our sheep to shepherd into *Boone Affaire*. There are more people, richer families, but most important, more fortunate kids who will whine and whine for our toys. Money, Linda. Focus on money." Miss Winkelplex didn't like the idea of half her money being taken away. She believed he was up to something because she knew Mr. McManus well, and he was always up to something. But what could she do? No one said 'no' to Mr. McManus. "It's an investment," he told her. "These toys are going to make you double at this year's Winter Auction what you made last year," he kept telling her. She felt uneasy. He was using the same tone with her that he used when he swindled others. She felt like she was being double-crossed and her inner voice coming from her logical left shoulder, started to tell her she was right.

"If you think so," is all she could say.

When the school day had ended and Miss Magnolia dismissed the class, Johnny, Billy, Murf, Ramona, Terrance and Rudy (who was patiently waiting outside the schoolhouse) together sprinted down Commonwealth and then down Bridge

Street. The Airlords were fueled with fire to get to the old oak that cupped their clubhouse to discuss the matter of the new Code Red. The fresh day, filled with friends, found the Airlords talkative, with red noses and red cheeks, displaying pleased expressions with laughter while their run slowed down to a panting walk.

Most of the Airlords were already in the clubhouse taking off their layers, but Ramona held back with Murf, who had been running a bit slower than the rest of the Airlords.

"So oi Murf, um, arr'e rue g'nna go to da Vinter Ice Dahnce den?" asked Ramona slowly and quietly as she and the rest of the Airlords made their way up the ladder to have an important meeting in Central Command.

Murf and Ramona headed up the ladder. They were still a bit breathless from the dash.

"Well sure I am; we all are," answered Murf, bouncing a bit on the ladder, noticing it seemed a bit sturdier, then scurried into the clubhouse once he was at the top.

Rudy barked up to Ramona and spun in a circle three times, telling her he'd keep watch from below.

"Gid boy Rudy, gid boy. Well yeh duh. I know we're all goin', bat vhat d'ie mean is, 're rue goin' to ask…" Ramona looked up to notice that Murf was no longer there.

Inside the Central Command the Airlords were lined up sitting on crates listening to Murf as he paced back and forth in front of them. Murf was in character. Like always, he took the tone of Buck Rogers himself.

"Listen up space soldiers, our spies have informed me that the *Earth Cruiser To The Nine Moons Of Saturn* did not malfunction because of anything we overlooked. No! False! Not affirmative! No, our informants tell us it was… well it was - sabotaged."

"Sebetagg'?" questioned Ramona.

"Sabotaged?" corrected Terrance.

"Dats v'hat I seid, sebetagg'?" repeated Ramona.

Johnny took one of the pieces of straw out from his back pocket and tossed it in his mouth to chew on. Then he brought his newsboy cap low so to better listen.

"Hey that's what *I* said. It wasn't no spies. Unless you're saying I'm the spy. Can I be a spy?" interjected Billy.

Murf ignored everyone and continued.

"And who is our new enemy that's gone and done us in? Well see, it was no other than…the Dunce Brothers," said Murf and then raised his open hand and slowly made a fist as if showing how he was going to crush them.

"Da Dunnc Brre'ders?" questioned Ramona.

"The Dunce Brothers?" questioned Terrance.

Johnny nodded slowly, held his straw as he chewed it and squinted as he puckered. It felt good for Johnny to have a true scapegoat.

"That's what us spies saw," said Billy. He was hoping to now be considered the spy in the Airlords. But as he looked around he realized no one was listening to him.

"Vhet rr ve genna deu den?" questioned Ramona.

"Yah what's the plan?" asked Terrance.

"Well, if you ask me, I say we shave their heads and glue their hair back on their eyelids while they sleep," spoke Johnny.

"I say we put white paint in their milk bottles," said Terrance a little louder.

"Oi, I sey ve put vorms in der shoes, ya?," shouted Ramona.

"No, I say we put hungry raccoons in their closets," shouted Johnny, his suggestion raising the bar of swindling possibilities.

"Yah, I say we put hungry raccoons *and* rabid skunks in their closets," shouted Terrance even louder.

"Oi ye, I sey ve pit 'ungery rekkoons 'n' rabid sk'nnks 'n' poizonous speders, da kind wid hair on 'em 'n' dem big snakes, de kind that ve saw 'n schoo dat c'nn eat sheep…get all dem 'nd put 'em in deir closets dere." shouted Ramona even louder and a bit out of breath."

"Gun powder in their pepper and bug killer in their salt", shouted Johnny and the bar was now raised again.

"Gasoline in their kerosene lamps," shouted Terrance as he stood up on top of his crate.

"Ne-ne, I say ve hang 'em from a tree ye? In de center e' town, tar 'n' fea'der 'em 'n' beat 'em vith sticks yah? Until dey scream dey'd done it 'n' dey be sorry fer doin' it too," shouted Ramona as she and Johnny both got on their crates too and they all began to holler.

Billy jumped on his crate as well and tried screaming over his friends; "Ya…Ya…and let's throw snowballs at them too! Big ones."

The Airlords screamed on and Rudy, hearing the commotion, barked from below.

"OKAY EVERYONE, EVERYONE OKAY, OKAY…LISTEN UP, I GOT IT, I GOT IT, screamed Murf. "SPACE SOLDIERS, SIT DOWN, SIT DOWN."

Panting and sweating the Airlords returned to sitting position.

"Okay, those were all great ideas Airlords, but I have it," said Murf as he began to pace like a drill sergeant again.

"What is it Murf?" asked Johnny.

"In the center of town, where everyone can see, whenever we can figure out the exact time when Mr. McManus visits his shop, hopefully it can be high noon, we'll…"

"Ya," asked Terrance.

"Ve'll vhat?" asked Ramona.

"We'll attack them…with," Murf spoke slowly on purpose.

"With what?" asked Johnny.

"Oi brotha, spit it out den," pleated Ramona.

"With…with…big snowballs," Murf stood proud.

"Hey, wait a minute, I said that," chirped Billy, but again no one could hear him under the approving cheers. And just like every time Billy was ignored, he brushed the credit aside and began cheering along with everyone else.

After hours of going over the plan, after everyone understood the attack through and through, the Airlords headed down the ladder to head home for supper.

The horizon of the setting Sun was the color of a multitude of yellows, yet the sky held mostly beautiful blues. The Moon played it confident, handsomely gazing down at the blond Sun hoping she'd notice him, being so big, so bold and so blue that night. And as she took her last check around herself, to see if she had remembered everything she had brought with her that day before leaving for the night, the Sun glanced up to Moon and the two exchanged a special silent smile. Bashful flirting.

As the Airlords made their way down the ladder, Johnny did notice how sturdy it felt. As he slowly climbed down, he shook the boards and inspected them for new nails. But he didn't see any under the ice and snow, so he forgot the thought, deducing that the ice had frozen them more in place.

"ey Murf," Ramona said.

"Ya, what is it," Murf replied as he buttoned up for the walk home.

"So yer goin' ta da Dance den 'eh?"

"Well of course. You already asked me that yah crazy monkey. Are you not feeling all right Ramona?"

"Naw I feel fiiel foin. So 'eck, you bringin' anyone to it den er ya?"

"Well sure."

"Ye er?" said Ramona a bit sullen. "Who yah brinin'. Molly iz it?"

"Molly! Yuck! Heck no yah rabid oily monkey. You're sounding crazier and crazier. Well I'm goin' with you guys of course," said Murf.

"Oh rit, rit," said Ramona.

"You're daff Ramona, daff I tell yah. Don't become a Dumb Dora on us all of a sudden." said Murf as he jogged ahead, grabbed some snow from the ground and tossed a snowball at Ramona, hitting her right in the chest.

The act erupted a mini-war. *The Airlords* all took cover behind snowy rocks and snowy trees for a small, but swell, sun setting snowball fight.

The next week was cruel for most. Daylight was extremely brief so the people of Hamilton lived mostly in darkness. It was the time of year when New Englanders would be hit by their powerful – winter blues. Warmth and food were the most desirable during these dark times, that is, after family and laughter. It was hardest on the children of Hamilton. Miss Magnolia's final project and final exams for the term were on Friday. This meant that all the parents kept their children inside to prepare and there would not be any playing outside, like there had been when the snow first fell. Even though the children of Hamilton only had one week left until their winter vacation, they felt they had waited long enough, and with the winter blues gripped on everyone in town's back, the lack of sunlight and the final projects, with exams on the horizon, left the children pouting and dragging about.

The weather was cruel as well. One night there would be a hard blizzard; the next night the hail would fall - then the cold-cold rain. When the town thought the worst was over, a wicked winter wind came screaming down from the north and made its wicked way through Hamilton, freezing everything. Ice.

In the small town, mouths used glowing words to cheer acquaintances up, while eyes were regretfully used to display longing. To the people of Hamilton, everything seemed to be a struggle since the cold front came in. Life was frozen. The trees were frozen. Little Island Pond was frozen. The roads were frozen. And the people were frozen. Pacers pacing would slip, crash and curse. The working men and women walking to work would slip, crash and curse. The sheriff, slipped, crashed and cursed. Pastor John, slipped, crashed and prayed to the Lord for "deeper patience". Miss Magnolia slipped, crashed, cut her chin and teared. And Mr. Riggelsworth slipped, crashed and just sat there in the road with the snow slowly burying him until the pain in his left elbow subsided. Small children slipped, crashed and cried. Even Rudy and Periwinkle slipped, crashed and felt embarrassed when they dared an excursion outside to take a tinkle during that cruel, cruel week.

The spoiled wind pushed everyone out of his way that week: the elderly, sick and fragile; he had no regard for others. But each night, the stars agreed to shine extra bright to help those who gazed upward, a chance to see beauty in the world from their beds.

Kringle and Pete spent all of their days and nights making toys. Wisely they had gathered all the supplies they needed before the heavier snow and ice had taken over the junkyard. But there were many days that the two men would have to head out to the junkyard with a pick, crowbar and shovel to chip through ice to find certain imperative pieces for their projects. These days and nights were spent strictly on crafting and the two carpenters spoke strictly of their work. The two men would often make plans to craft extra toys for the children in town whose parents couldn't afford them, but Mr. McManus' list was so long and the tasks so mighty that the two men never had the chance. Time seemed to go by too fast to get their daily tasks done. It was as if God had widened the hour glass hole and the two men were drowning.

That week, Mr. McManus was always at The Workshop, bringing in orders, looking at what Kringle and Pete had made, while roaring about money, smoking his pipe and scratching his chest.

Kringle did fix Mr. McManus' pocket watch. There was nothing wrong with it. It just needed to be wound. Kringle got no thanks from Mr. McManus.

When The Workshop was quiet and the men concentrated in silence, Kringle often thought of Ellie. He hadn't seen her since the night he had brought her key to her. He wondered if she really did think he was a just a "strange hobo". The nights when Kringle had to work late and The Workshop's stove was unable to push the frigid cold front out Kringle had trouble blocking out the negative whispers coming from his left shoulder. He'd begun to believe that to Ellie, he *was* just a "strange hobo" with burned clothes and a scruffy keep. When Pete began to notice that his friend's spirit was beginning to look broken, he'd switch on his hanging radio and the two men would listen to music, or just sit back with a rugged tea and listen to amazing stories *of Buck Rogers*. And if that didn't work, Pete would take out his guitar and make Kringle take out his harmonica and the two men would play uppity blues as Rudy sat in between them hollering up a good one.

Ellie and Flo were low as well. They felt hollow in their chests when they had to stand outside in the cold and hand out Miss Winkelplex's new fliers to those walking by *Bonne Affaire*. It affected them greatly. All too often the people of town would turn and look back at Ellie and Flo with tired eyes. Ellie noticed herself thinking of Kringle more so than she felt sensible. She was surprised she hadn't seen him and wondered if he had moved on from the town. The thought of Kringle came to her often, but those thoughts distracted Ellie, so she did what she could to put them away and instead would think of whatever needed to get done. Flo was waist deep in her winter blues as well. She felt lonely. Overlooked. When couples came into the store together, laughing and having a swell time, she felt even lonelier and even more overlooked. Flo felt she had a lot of love inside her to give, it just seemed that no one was interested in receiving it. She didn't know why.

Most of the town felt down. But everyone in town focused on doing the only thing a New Englander knows is best when deep, deep in the winter blues; and that is to work hard to make it to their collective goal, their reward – The Ice Dance. This type of mentality shaped the people of Hamilton and the towns around. It made them strong and grateful. Winter blues is a time when people shift around their wants and needs. They squabble less with one another, for it is the cruel winter that punishes them all equally. They help each other more because they know they were just recently helped themselves. Even though their sky and their souls were dark and cold, people, more so than any time of year, understood one another. And that is the personal, emotional defiance and emotional freedom that New Englanders share with one another when they collectively push back the cruel winters that they all endure - together.

The Airlords were feeling it as well. After school, Johnny obsessed with the *Battle Cruiser's* blueprints. He was also quieter than normal. While Johnny's mind was distracted, Billy often sat with Rudy and the two of them would watch Johnny work and fetch him things as he needed them.

Some lucky ones found a bit of warmth that week. One snowy sunset Marlene came by the McKool's pharmacy with her mother and sister. She had told Mrs. McKool at the counter that someone had left Terrance a note under the pharmacy's doormat. It was she - of course. Since then, Terrance and Marlene began passing notes in this manner. Ramona spent a lot of her nights that week asking her mother questions about boys. Mrs. McDonald loved the bedside conversations, while Mr. McDonald worried about them from another room. "*Bet vhat de I de 'bout d'hat?*" was Ramona's constant cadence. Murf spent most of his time listening to *Buck Rogers* and practicing the tone and inflection for future Airlord meetings. He would try out his speeches on his folks and they would sit up straight, proud and impressed. At the end of Murf's speeches, his mother and father would stand up and clap and Murf would push his chest out and take different leadership stances as if he was being photographed for the *Worchester Evening Gazette*.

Mr. McManus was rarely home that dark week. He worked endlessly on plans for the coming Ice Dance and Winter Auction. Mr. McManus along with Miss Winkelplex and the Dunce Brothers made many business trips out to surrounding cities and towns, from Lawrence to Bedford, from Charlestown to Lowell, trying to reap as many buyers in as they could before the big Winter Auction. Mr. McManus had been putting in double time with triple the excuses with the Twins about where their father was. Charlene seemed to have it the worst, because, along with her father being absent, she felt her sister was making good with the enemy. Charlene spent most of her time stealing Marlene's notes from Terrance and reading them aloud to Marlene as Marlene chased her. Periwinkle did not like that game one bit.

It had been a cruel week for most - cold and icy, dark and gloomy. For some it was simply a week of being their sad self. But, the town of Hamilton pressed on and, while everyone climbed into bed and brought their heavy wool blankets up to their chins, they envisioned the coming Ice Dance and imagined themselves having a perfect night.

The schoolhouse doors exploded open, smashing back with a crash, sending colossal clumps of snow down from the rooftop covering the leaping children. Patches of ice were worth sliding on again. Smiles were worth exchanging again. Miss Magnolia stood at the door watching her students dash from her. They slipped and fell, they cheered and hollered. Miss Magnolia was pleased as well. She leaned on the doorframe, took her hair out of the braid, closed her eyes while raising a smile and let out a slow, slow breath.

Vacation was here.

The Airlords were at Code Red. They sprinted out of the schoolhouse faster than any of the other students. The gang had acquired information from Billy that he had retrieved the night before while listening to his mother at the dinner table telling him and his brother her schedule for the weekend. Ellie had said to her boys that Mr. McManus would be at *Bonne Affair* at 4:00PM to greet the early weekend shoppers and that she would be coming home late that night. Johnny didn't listen; he was distracted by the adventures of *Buck Rogers* playing on the radio in the background and by the new experience of dipping his biscuit into his mashed potatoes. But Billy did listen. Billy passed the information by note to Murf, by means through Oliver, to Marline, to Maggie, to Molly and then to Murf, in class the next day. The note stated the fact that Mr. McManus, most likely with The Dunce Brothers, would be at *Boone Affair* at 4:00PM. Later, Billy didn't get any verbal recognition of this imperative information, yet the *Airlords* were now referring to him as their 'spy', so Billy knew that his skills were noted one way or another.

It was 3:30PM. Bright. Painfully overexposed. Clear skies. Dirty snow. The ground was wet and melting. The Sun was high and stretching out. The Airlords jumped, splashed and slipped as they sprinted down Commonwealth Street. They had only a half an hour to get to *Bonne Affair*, make piles of snowballs, and be perched for attack before The Dunce Brothers arrived.

Murf lead the Airlords to the back of *Bonne Affair*.

"Okay Airlords, see here; this is the spot. We'll all boost ourselves up on the roof," Murf instructed.

"The roof?" questioned Johnny.

"Yah, ya-see the roof is flat up there, so there's enough snow collected that we can make all our Death Balls no problem. It'll be perfect." The Airlords had never heard of the term 'Death Balls' before, but they nodded that they all understood and liked the term just the same. "And yah, see the snow over here?" Murf showed a section of snow that the wicked wind had layered right up the side of *Bonne Affair*. "It's untouched, so when we have to eject, we can just jump and land here. Poof. Perfect landing. Then we make our way to the Central Command. 'S a cinch of an attack Airlords."

"Wew Murf, how'd ye know ta deu all dat?" Ramona asked.

"Heck Murf, that sure is thought out," added Terrance.

Murf puffed his chest out.

"Well, you know it's my job to know these things. 'S why I'm captain. Now let's get a move on, we don't have much time. I'll go first; someone give me a boost," said Murf as he put his hand on Terrance's and Johnny's shoulders. It wasn't easy getting Murf up on the roof, and it seemed that a pound of good snowball snow fell down on the rest of the Airlords as they worked getting Murf up onto the roof. Second up was Ramona. Then Terrance. Then Johnny and, lastly, the Airlords pulled Billy up by his hands, collar and belt.

Inside *Bonne Affair* Ellie and Flo looked to the roof each time an odd thump or bump was heard. But the shop was beginning to get busy with potential buyers and Miss Winkelplex had a stern eye on the girls so the two ladies ignored the peculiar sounds from above and tended to the customers.

The snow on top of *Bonne Affair* was as high as the Airlords knees. The Airlords pushed the snow forward and stacked it into a small wall at the front of *Bonne Affair*. Behind it they made their Death Balls.

"We sure are gonna get them back huh," said Johnny as he made his tenth Death Ball and stacked it on a pyramid by his knees.

"We'll show 'em," said Murf focused and confident.

"I'm gonna get them Dunce Brother square in the face, I tell yah. Boom! White wash!" said Johnny. He was excited for his revenge. "No one messes with our ships."

"Oi, I bet ve vould'a won teh race if it wasn't fer dem Piss-Ants," said Ramona, then she spat to the side.

"Sure we would'a," said Johnny back.

"And we're gonna fly by that Mongol Machine and win next time, I tell yah," said Terrance showing the Airlords that he still has allegiance and that his note passing with Marline changed nothing.

"You said it, we're gonna blast off and scream right by them Mongols.

We're gonna speed down Robin's Hill like nobody's ever seen and show 'em all," said Billy, as he noticed the size of his Death Balls were smaller than everyone else's.

"How do we look," asked Murf. "Everyone ready? Johnny?"

"Check. Ready"

"Terrance? Ramona?"

"Chauk. Reddy"

"Check. Ready"

"Billy?"

"Check. Ready"

"Okay Airlords, now we wait."

If you happened to be on Commonwealth Street at 3:55PM, if you happened to be looking up, and happened to have a hat on to block the sun's rays, then you might just have seen five little hats with dashing eyes popping up and down from under a snow-wall atop the rooftop of *Bonne Affair* in downtown Hamilton, Massachusetts.

Mr. McManus and the Dunce Brothers we're right on time. The black Duisenberg skidded up to *Bonne Affair*, spitting and spraying dirty snow everywhere. Mr. McManus leaped out, tossed on his black hat, brought his spectacle to his eye, checked his working pocket watch, made sure his jacket was straight and lint free; lit a cigar and headed inside. He was bursting with excitement to mentally examine and calculate his potential future profits.

The Dunce Brothers stayed in the Duisenberg.

When the Airlords heard the approaching car they ducked down behind their snow wall.

"Is that them?" asked Billy.

"Dat 'em brothas?" asked Ramona

"It's gotta be," answered Johnny.

"We gotta check to make sure," said Terrance.

"I'll check," said Billy.

"No, no, I'll check," said Murf.

They crouched down even lower and everyone grabbed a Death Ball for each hand. Slowly Murf crept out from behind the snow-wall. First, the fuzzy ball of the top of his green hat was visible, then the rest of his hat, then his eyes. Murf squinted and locked his sights on the Duisenberg.

"What do yah see," whispered Johnny.

"It's them alright, but they ain't getting outa the car," whispered Murf.

"Well, what are they doin'?" asked Johnny.

"Smokin' gaspers I think," whispered Murf back. Then he ducked back down.

"Wha' de wi de now Murf?" asked Ramona.

"Well, let me see here," Murf thought.

"I wanna look," said Billy and he began to stand.

"No wait!" said all the other Airlords as they all pulled him back down.

"You gotta be real careful Billy. We can't be found out. This is the real deal here; code red" said Murf.

"So what are we gonna do then? I wanna throw these?" said Billy as he showed the Airlords his stack of Death Balls.

"V'ell ve can't wait 'ere all day 'cause vhat if dey never git out?" questioned Ramona.

The Airlords hadn't thought of that and they all took expressions of deep thought. "We gotta flush them out, that's what we gotta do, like Buck Rogers did in last week's - *The Battle Inside The Land Under The Ocean*," stated Murf.

"Flush 'em out, yah," agreed Terrance. "But how?"

"Well, see here Airlords, I'm gonna toss this here Death Ball," Murf showed the Airlords his biggest and most well smoothed snowball. "I'm gonna toss it right at the center of their window there. After that, they'll come jumpin' outa that car ta see who gone and done it. See?"

"Then we attack," added Johnny.

"Yah, then we hit 'em with everything we got," said Murf.

"Okay," chorused the Airlords.

"Can I throw the first one Murf? I sure do wanna." asked Johnny, as he turned his newscap around and placed the straw he'd been chewing in his back pocket. Murf could tell Johnny was more sore than the rest of the Airlords about losing the race and having the *Earth Cruiser to the Nine Moons of Saturn* sabotaged.

"Sure thing Johnny. Just hit that front window, square in the middle.

Them Dunce Brothers will come scurrying out like barn mice in a hay fire," said Murf.

"Ye lick a bunnch a cackroaches scurryin' outa a burnin' log brothas," added Ramona. Then she nodded to Murf and then to Johnny.

"Yah ready?" asked Terrance.

"I'm ready. Okay, 1…2…3!" said Johnny, then he leaped up from behind the wall. Johnny's eyes gazed upon something different than he expected to see. His eyes relayed back to his brain that Sheriff Jones seemed to be kneeling down beside two older, well-to-do women, who seemed to have slipped on the icy sidewalk outside *Bonne Affair*. Johnny quickly lowered his Death Ball and ducked back down.

"What happened? Why didn't you fire?" asked Murf.

Johnny looked spooked.

"What'd yah see?" asked Billy.

"The sheriff," answered Johnny surprised and wide eyed.

"Da shah'riff Johnny-boy? Oi!" repeated Ramona.

"Is he coming?" asked Murf.

"Does he know we're up here with these Death Balls?" asked Billy.

"No I don't think so. Seems two old city ladies were plopped on the ground there, looked to have slipped or something. They don't look happy neither," said Johnny.

"What do we do?" asked Terrance.

"Well, let's keep our cool Airlords. We'll ah…we'll wait 'till them women are up and gone and the sheriff is done and left and then we, well, we stick to the plan. 'S good plan still."

The Airlords waited for about 2 minutes.

"Can we look yet?" asked Billy.

"Not yet," answered Murf.

The Airlords waited for a collective 3 minutes.

"Can we look now?" asked Terrance.

"No no, not yet, not yet," answered Murf.

And the Airlords waited for a collective 3.09 minutes.

"Ah c'mon, cnn wi lauk now Murf? Ve dant wanna miss eur chance ye?" asked Ramona.

"Okay, *now* we can look; it should be clear," said Murf surely. "Johnny you still tossin'?"

"Does a red rocket booster blast? Heck yah I'm still tossin'," said Johnny as he got into crouch position. "Okay ready…1…2…3!"

Johnny sprang up, squinted his eyes and hurled his Death Ball.

BAM!

POOF!

Johnny's Death Ball hit the Duisenberg dead center of the front windshield. Snow sprayed out covering it.

Johnny ducked back down.

"Did you get it," asked Murf a bit panicked.

"I got it good," said Johnny. He was over the top excited.

"Let's do it," said Terrance.

"Should we do it?" asked Billy.

"Let's deu it brothas, let's drown dem cackroaches," said Ramona and then she spat to the side again.

"GO!" screamed Murf.

All the Airlords leaped up with a Death Ball in each hand. But the Dunce Brothers were nowhere to be found. What they did see was the windshield wipers of the Duisenberg going back and forth. The lethargic Dunce Brother inside the car thought the snow simply fell from the roof or from a tree above and thought nothing of exiting the car for a scuffle.

The Airlords ducked back down.

"Well that didn't work," said Terrance.

"No it didn't, did it," said Murf a bit befuddled.

"I don't think they thought they were under attack," said Billy.

"Yaa, naw…I dink 'ey dought it fell frem a tree or a bird or somethin' Murf," added Ramona. "Vhat should ve do now den?"

"Just attack them all at once?" questioned Murf.

"Yah, with everything we got?" questionably agreed Johnny.

"Yah!" said Terrance.

"Yah!" solidified Billy.

"Absah'lutely brrrrothaaas!" riled up Ramona.

And together the Airlords counted…

173

…"1…2…3…!!!"

ATTACK!

BOOM! BOOM! BOOM! BOOM! BOOM!

BAM! BAM! BAM! BAM! BAM!

POOF! POOF! POOF! POOF! POOF!

From inside the Duisenberg it was a thunderous happening. Relentless Death Balls plummeted down onto the front windshield bending it in, each hit hard producing booming sounds that were so shocking that the cigarettes hanging from both Lloyd and Elmer fell from their mouths and onto their laps.

"AHHH!" chorused Lloyd and Elmer from the sound and from their now smoking trousers. The two men leaped from the car grabbing snow from the ground to put out their ember glowing knickers.

"THERE SHE BLOWS AIRLORDS!" screamed Murf. "ATTACK!!!!"

The Dunce Brothers only had seconds. They looked up to see ten Death Balls screaming toward them. Followed by ten more.

SWOOSH…

SLAM! SLAM! SLAM! SLAM! SLAM!
SLAM! SLAM! SLAM! SLAM! SLAM!

SWOOSH…

SLAM! SLAM! SLAM! SLAM! SLAM!
SLAM! SLAM! SLAM! SLAM! SLAM!

It seemed to never stop.

Death Balls hit Lloyd and Elmer square in the face - knocking their hats off, Death Balls hammered at their legs – knocking them over and Death Balls continued to rain down from above until there was nothing one could do but cover themselves as best they could with their hands and holler. After awhile Lloyd and Elmer tried to stand, but they'd slip and slide and get knocked off balance from the Airlords aggressive aerial assault.

The Airlords cheered.

"Keep them coming," Murf shouted.

Inside *Bonne Affair* everyone took a pause to stare out the front picture window to see two men being pummeled by the largest and heftiest slow flakes they had ever seen.

Everyone inside gasped.

The customers covered their mouths and looked at Ellie and Flo.

"Oh dear," one woman said allowed.

"Oh my," said another.

"Well break a plate and kiss a frog," said Flo as she loosened her posture, leaned her elbow against the window frame while cupping her cheek in her hand, smiling, enjoying the silly sight.

"What is happening to those two men?" asked Ellie.

"That's Lloyd and Elmer," said Miss. Winkelplex as she looked up to Mr. McManus.

"What the dang nab bit are those two wood brains doing now," said Mr. McManus as he headed for the door, angered that his business was being interrupted.

Outside, the Death Balls continued to rain down. The Dunce Brothers could only see the bright color of small hats through the whitewash of snow. From the roof the Airlords saw Mr. McManus followed by Miss Winkelplex, Ellie, Flo and all the customers scurry outside.

"EJECT AIRLORDS! EJECT!!!" screamed Murf. And all the Airlords turned around and leaped off the roof into the cushioning untouched snow. Behind the shops and restaurants the Airlords dashed down Commonwealth Street. They cheered and laughed, panted and coughed; they teared from giggles and slapped each other on the backs as they ran.

Revenge was served cold.

✳

The Airlords ran down Commonwealth Street, cheering and laughing, hidden from the town's people behind different shops and homes. One by one they would break off from the collective gang as their homes approached. As each Airlord headed into their home, the rest of them would whistle, clap and cheer their name aloud.

Murf thought it wise not to fall back to the Central Command even though everyone wanted to, but instead for everyone to head home in order to develop solid alibis.

The Airlords were in high sprits. They had won their Death Ball battle, avenged the death of the *Earth Cruiser To The Nine Moons Of Saturn*, just started a week's vacation from school and, most importantly, they had a new ship to build.

Once Johnny and Billy reached Bridge Street, they slowed down and walked the rest of the way. Both boys were grinning wide and shaking their heads back and forth repeating the words over and over again - "We sure did show 'em, didn't we?"

As the two boys came up on the Bump Track they could see Kringle down a ways sifting through the snow-covered piles of junk.

"Say, there's Mr. Kringle guy. See 'im?" said Billy.

"I see 'im."

Billy looked up at his brother because of his tone.

"You don't like him much huh?"

"We heard him; he's a bad guy Billy. A swindler."

"Well, I don't think so."

"You should think so and why should I like 'im anyways?"

"I don't know. I don't mean you *have to* like him, just saying that you *don't* like him. Like you got some sort of itch from 'im. That right Johnny? That fella make you itchy?"

"What you mean itchy? I don't like him 'cause Ma said for us to stay away from 'im. He's up to somethin' Billy, I know it. And he's a hobo. You saw 'im jump off that train."

"Yea, Momma did say that."

"I mean c'mon Billy, that Kringle guy he just…"

"But after Momma said stay away from him, then he came over for supper. Why would Momma allow that then? She don't allow *anyone* to supper. Don't that mean then that we don't need to stay away now. I like that man Mr. Kringle; I like his stories."

"I don't know why Ma had him over. She said she made a deal or somethin' with him. Never mind that. It don't change that he's a hobo Billy, probably up to somethin' bad and Ma knows it, she said, 'stay away from 'im'. Ma knows best."

"Ya, Momma does know best. But…"

"But nothin' Billy."

"I like his stories Johnny, that's all, you gotta admit he got some swell stories."

"What, that story about them dang reindeer? Well that ain't true Billy. I don't believe in it. I'd prove it to you and sing the crummy song right now, but that hobo man would hear us and he'd come a walkin' over."

"He looks to be walkin' over anyways Johnny."

Kringle had seen the boys and thought to walk over to say 'Hi'. He had a little gift for them and he also was hoping he could hear a little about what their mother had been up to. He thought of Ellie often.

"He helped us with that mean cat and with Terrance, Johnny. That means somethin' don't it?"

"He did what any adult would have to do. And besides, Terrance would have done fine on his own. And I did half the work too, don't you go and forget that."

"No I ain't forgotten that. Just sayin' he helped, that's all."

"Bah."

Kringle approached the two boys. His cheeks and nose we're red from the cold and he held a red bandana tied like a small sack in his right hand.

"Hey Boys," Kringle started.

"Hey Mr. Kringle," said Billy.

"What chah doin'?" asked Kringle.

"Ah just waitin' for the five-o'clock'er. Get some coal, that's all. It ain't stealin'," answered Billy.

Johnny just looked down, with his eyes pointed up at Kringle. Johnny was looking unimpressed, looking distant, and looking bothered while chewing on a straw.

"I see. 'S been a cold-cold week huh? Today's alright though. How you been getting along? Y'all alright? You're mother all right? How's she been?"

"Yah we're alright; we're on vacation," said Billy with a grin. "No school for a week."

"Well is that so?" said Kringle. "That must feel great. Heck I'd like a little vacation. You got any new ships you're buildin' there Johnny."

"We ain't supposed to be talkin' with you Mr. Don't you remember?" said Johnny. Billy nudged him to take it easy, which was seldom done. Johnny nudged him back harder. "Ma says to stay away from people like yourself 'member?"

"She did say that huh?" spoke Kringle.

"Ya remember, she went - 'you boys stay away from that man who be jumping off trains'. And so that be you Kringle. So we gotta stay away from you. See the deal?" said Johnny.

"Huh. Well yah, sure I see it boys. You best listen to your mother."

"Well I don't think so Mr. Kringle. You ain't a bad guy; I know it," said Billy. Then Johnny nudged him so hard he almost fell over.

"Clam it," said Johnny.

"Thanks Billy. But your brother's right, if that's what your Mother wishes. And you're Mother, she's a smart lady, so we all best do what she says." Kringle put the small sack into his red coat pocket.

"What's that there?" Billy asked.

"Ah just some...not-so-bad nails I pulled. They're for you Johnny if yah want 'em, for buildin'," said Kringle as he held out the small sack.

Just then Betsy Bound's whistle blew and far over the pines you could see her distant black smoke staining the purple sky.

"No thanks," said Johnny back, then he turned slightly, boxing his shoulders to the Bump Track.

"Right. Ok. Take care boys," said Kringle and he put the small sack in his pocket, turned around and headed back to the junkyard. "Wait 'till the train passes before you go grabbin' boys."

Billy watched Kringle walk away. Johnny watched the train approaching.

"Okay Billy, here it comes. Keep an eye on them fallin' coal or we'll be diggin'", said Johnny.

Betsy Bound came up fast and loud. And once its coal cars hit the

Bump Track, coal started to sprinkle down along with the snow that had collected on top of them. Through the spray of coal and snow, with the loud rumble of Betsy Bound, Johnny dashed this way and that pocketing as much coal as he could.

Billy reached down and grabbed a few himself, then looked to his left at Kringle who was watching the train pass. While Johnny was distracted, Billy took one of the pieces of coal and threw it at Kringle. The piece hit Kringle in the shoulder. When Kringle turned he saw Billy with his hands up ready for a catch. Confused, Kringle took out the small sack in his pocket and held it up? Billy nodded his head 'yes' and raised his hands higher. As the train rumbled by, as old Betsy Bound's whistle blasted, as Johnny was distracted dashing for coal, Kringle tossed Billy the small red sack.
And Billy caught it.

The warm day had allowed much of the snow to melt away, but there was still a slushy foot of it everywhere. Johnny and Billy walked home with a good bounty. The two boys had filled their pockets and socks to the tippy tops with coal. It was quite quiet as the two boys walked home, other than the occasional grunting about their frozen feet. Once home, the two boys hung their socks by the fireplace to dry and emptied their pockets into the coal pail. Ellie had fixed up a potato stew for the family the night before. Johnny took it out of the icebox and placed it on the big hunk of cold metal that was their stove.

"Seems extra cold in here don't it Billy? And look there's snow on the stove," said Johnny as he backed away from the stove.

"Look Johnny, look," said Billy as he pointed up.

There was a break in the roof. The small chimney tube of the stove had broken off and there were branches of a small pine tree poking through the roof.

"Well, I'll be, a tree's come down," said Johnny.

The Boone boys ran outside of the house. They couldn't see the damage from the front so they rushed along the left side of the make-shift home. There, they could see that a small pine tree had broken half way up its trunk. The top half of the tree now lay on the small home's roof.

"Whoa Johnny," said Billy. "What should we do?"

"Don't know. I guess wait for Ma," Johnny said.

The Boone boys decided to sit by the fire wrapped in a big tan blanket until their mother came home from work. The small radio played mostly commercials, but Jazz came on every now and then. Johnny and Billy were both still quite quiet. And quite cold.

Once home, Ellie inspected the roof the best she could from outside and inside the home. She put their biggest bowl under the break in the roof to collect the snow that the wind would send in. Without the stove to warm the potato stew, Ellie heated the stew by the fire in an iron pot while Johnny split logs out front and Billy brought them inside to her. Ellie and her boys sat on the floor by the fire eating their warm potato stew. The boys mentioned to Ellie that they had seen Kringle that day, but that they did as she instructed and told Kringle that they were to – "*stay away from him*". That made all three of them quite quiet. The boys knew the mood of their mother by how she moved though the house and tonight she moved slowly, mechanically, one foot in front of the other, with feeble efforts. At seven o'clock a new *Buck Rogers* adventure came on through the static of the small radio. Billy stopped as he brought the dirty bowls to the sink. Passing clouds strobed moonlight through the now ice covered windows allowing the reflection on the eating table to dance as boiling water does. Billy gazed down at it, lost in its beauty. Outside, Johnny split a few more logs. In their winter bundles, the boys began washing the dishes and pans from supper. They were trying hard not to clank the dishes together too much so to better hear the amazing stories on the radio. As they washed, they also watched their mother sitting by the fire wrapped in the big tan blanket thinking. They wondered why she had become quiet like them.

"We're done with the dishes Ma," said Johnny, but Ellie didn't respond. "Ma?".

Billy went over to his mother wrapped in the tan blanket by the fire.

"I think she's asleep Johnny," whispered Billy in a soft surprised tone.

"She is?"

Billy put his face an inch from his mother and whispered, "You awake Mamma?". There was no answer. Billy tip-toped to Johnny and whispered again, "Ya she's asleep. Say Johnny, I got an idea?"

"What's that?"

"Let's head over to Pete's and do some spying like we did under the window. I can prove to you Kringle's a good guy. I believe in him Johnny."

"You can't believe in him."

"How come?" whispered Billy back.

"'Cause he ain't family."

In the Boone family, saying 'I believe in you' was much like saying 'I love you', yet it meant more that one believes in everything that made up that person - their merit, their heart, their values, their strength and perseverance; they were someone to be recognized and celebrated.

"Well if he was, then we'd have another person; four people being one is even stronger than three people being one - well right?"

"I mean yah, but..."

Seldom did Johnny get stumped long enough for Billy to speak again.

"But nothin', let's go; I'll prove it."

"Fine, but we gotta hurry. If Ma wakes up and we ain't there, it'll be you who get's in trouble, not me!" said Johnny. Then the Boone boys bundled up and headed out into the cold.

The Workshop wasn't much different. Kringle sat at his workbench facing forward as if working on something, but there was nothing in front of him. He just sat with his hands clasped and his brow low in thought. Rudy sat next to him looking up. Pete was on the floor by Rudy's bed in between the two cots. He had the wooden cross on the floor and was shaping it with sand paper, a chisel, a rasp and his whittling knife.

"What are you harboring on Kringle? Lord you've been just sitting there like a frozen ice man. You're spooking Rudy. Look how worried he looks. He's just sittin' by you, gettin' all spooked. Kringle spooking you boy? Kringle's spooking me," said Pete looking up from his cross.

Kringle snapped out of his sad looped thoughts.

"Sorry, it's just that I saw them Boone boys earlier. They told me Ellie had instructed them two to stay away from me. I just feel like I've done something wrong. I feel like a bad man somehow Pete. Have I done somethin' so wrong that people need to stay away from me? Maybe this ain't the town for me. Maybe I was wrong. What did I do you think; I do something bad?"

"Grab some of the light grit sandpaper over there and help me with this part here," said Pete motioning to the sandpaper on his workbench. Pete had never invited Kringle to work on the cross with him before, so Kringle thought it a bit of a moment. Kringle stood, put the kettle on for some rugged cocoa, grabbed a small tear of sandpaper and sat by Pete. The talking and movement made Rudy feel relaxed. He walked over to where the two men sat and where his bed lay. Rudy circled his bed a few times and then lay down with his chin on his paws watching the two men work. Dogs don't purr, but Rudy seemed to be letting out some pleased low breaths.

"Now, if you don't mind, I have some, well, some advice," said Pete as he pointed to the section of the cross for Kringle to sand and shape. "And I know they say – 'advice should only be givin' if it's asked for or life threatening', so…" Pete stopped talking, but kept working.

There was a silent pause, and then Kringle smiled and understood.

"Oh, by all means. Please would you share your advice with me Pete?"

"Right. Well now, it seems you are thinking about Ellie in a way like you care for her. And that's good, that's good. But you're thinking about the Ellie *you* know. I'm seeing here that you're thinking about how *that* Ellie - the only one *you* see - how you two are getting along together.

"I am. I am," said Kringle as he ran his hand over the mighty cross feeling the difference in the finished, smooth, areas and the raw un-sanded parts.

"You gotta go and ask yourself who this woman is. Take you outta her story. Take you out entirely. Who is Ellie? Who is she? What's her situation? What's she got on her plate and hangin' on her back?"

"I understand Pete. Yah."

"Well, now wait. I'm askin' you. You tell me. Go ahead. Who is Ellie? Who is that girl? What's she got on her plate and on her back?"

"Oh, well, she's a very strong, smart and beautiful woman."

"Well, no, see you are telling me what *you* think about her. I already know what you think. You're smitten. You think she's hotsy-totsy. Ain't no reason for you to lay that down for me," said Pete as he laughed. "You're like a school boy Kringle; you're like a dizzy puppy dog." Pete laughed and made a whining puppy sound that made Rudy open his eyes slightly. "But no, sincerely, who is - *she*? I told you some things about her. You remember?"

"Sure I do."

"Okay, so you know some things. With some of them facts you know, go on, go on with - who…Ellie…is."

"Ellie…well Ellie…she's um…well…" Kringle thought for a spell as he sanded the cross down. "She's got a tough life here," said Kringle as he looked up for Pete to say something, but Pete's watery eyes were down at the cross meticulously shaping it. "She's nervous too. She has to run that house, bring up them boys, get food on the table, all by herself. And that makes Ellie nervous."

"Sure it does. What else? Poor girl."

"She doesn't let that change anything though, it seems from what you told me. She stands up to reality and raises them boys well. She works hard at the shop too. She brings home food for them boys every week. And, well, she's making things good for them. That's a noble thing. More than most can do these days."

The kettle began to rumble. Pete stood, stretched so long he touched The Workshop's ceiling, patted Kringle on the shoulder as he passed him and then grabbed two mugs from the small sink. He put two dollops of rugged mint in both mugs and two scoops of cocoa. As the kettle began to whistle, he took it off the stove and filled the mugs with hot water then swirled his hodgepodge with the butt end of a wooden spoon. Pete handed Kringle a mug and sipped his own carefully as he sat back down on the floor. Rudy let out a long deep breath through his nose and began to drift off into a dream.

"So now you tell me what this Ellie woman might think about *you*. And let's say she knows nothing about you. But let's go on and also pretend that she might like you a little bit. See, you may never know when a woman has a shine for you Kringle. They're good at keepin' that hidden if they choose to keep that hidden. Or even, she might not even know she has a shine for you herself, what…with all that's on her plate and on her back. I mean, you can't stop to smell the roses if you're on fire. So now how then is she supposed to show or know she likes you if she's on fire? Women *are* women Kringle. All of them. Women *are all* women. Detailed. A bit baffling, but always worth it," said Pete as he sat back down, felt the smoothness of the cross and then brought his hands around his mug for extra scalding warmth.

"Huh. Well, I guess she wouldn't trust me much. I guess she might not trust men in general too much. Maybe she just don't want me to mess up what she has going. Like ah, like she don't want to risk anything right now. That is, if she can help it. Like she went swimming and got bit by a water snake, so now she doesn't wanna go in the water any more."

"That's what I'm thinking too. You don't worry about yourself Kringle and don't you go worrying about if she likes you or if she don't. You're naturally nice. And all that 'hobo' talk neither; don't worry about that. Now I ain't sayin' she likes you. And I ain't sayin' she don't. And I ain't saying I'm a man to tell other men what to do when it comes to them…them…creatures that are always on your mind…but I do know one thing."

"What?"

"That you got to ask her to that Ice Dance there Kringle." Kringle looked up surprised. "Oh I know, I know. She'll say 'no', but you ask her anyway."

"Why? And what then would I do *when* she says no. What's the point?"

Smiling Pete says, "The point? Well you go and tell her the exact time you're gonna come by to bring her and tell her you're gonna look real fine when you do. *Real fine* - make sure you say that part. *Real fine.* Then you simply tell her that you two are gonna have a swell night and that you're really looking forward to spending time with her."

"What? You're a loon. You think? That sounds like the opposite of what I should do Pete. *The* opposite."

"I don't think, I know Kringle," said Pete. Then he smiled even bigger as he sanded the cross down.

"Wait a pan flashing minute, do you have a woman in town here Pete?" asked Kringle.

"Well, no."

"No, huh?"

"Well, I kinda write this one girl some songs, or I should say…I write my songs about this one girl. She don't know it, but she likes them tunes when I play them on Sundays. She dances right up on to 'em. She's a good stepper too."

"Yoooou gonna ask her then to the Ice Dance are yah then Pete?"

"Heck no Kringle; women make me nervous."

The two men laughed it out and continued shaping the wooden cross. Rudy had long since fallen asleep.

Outside the small window of The Workshop, both Boone boys crouched. They had been listening for some time. Billy whispered with a big smile to Johnny, "Kringle likes Momma Johnny."

ICE ON THE POND
FIRE IN THE SKY
DASH THROUGH THE DAY TO
DANCE UP THE NIGHT

STORY 4

✳

WHERE DO THE FISH GO, WHEN THE POND FREEZES OVER?

"Where do the fish go
    When the pond freezes over?"
Asked a small inquisitive girl
    To her wise strong father.

"Do they go on vacation?
    Do they head to California?
Or are they down there somewhere
    Trapped all through December?"

"Oh the fish are fine my dear
    Happier even still
They can't be reached by men's hooks
    Or diving loon's bills.

See, they love to look up
    And gaze at you and me
Skating atop the frozen pond
    Joy filled, laughing and carefree."

✳

Story 4:

ICE ON THE POND, FIRE IN THE SKY; DASH THOUGH THE DAY TO DANCE UP THE NIGHT

It was easy for the Dunce Brothers to follow the deer tracks in the snow. The night wind had brought in a puffy snowfall from the north and the tracks were deep and clear. It looked to be three sets of tracks - two grown deer and one fawn. And it looked as if the fawn was still fairly young as well, for the height of the snow seemed to reach all the way up its legs until its belly was scraping the top of the snow line.

The tracks headed south.

Lloyd and Elmer walked with their guns pointed out. Lloyd held a 12-gauge shotgun. Elmer held an over-under rifle. As payment one season, Mr. McManus gave both guns to the brothers. Neither worked too well. Mr. McManus just wanted to get rid of the old guns while also not wanting to pay the two dense men their promised salary. Instead, Mr. McManus bought himself a brand new Remington shotgun with all the money he saved cheating them.

The two hunters wore overalls, wool coats and boots. They wore red plaid hunting hats that had flaps to cover their ears. Lloyd and Elmer followed the tracks slowly. The hunt had no goal other than to - shoot something. Anything. Before they had found the deer tracks, the two brothers were shooting up at birds and down at rodents. Now with clear tracks, they had a clear hunt.

The tall pines and bending birches looked wet from the ice that covered them. The branches hung low with icicles dripping from them. The light layer of fresh snow looked as if someone had placed cotton balls atop everything. The forest sparkled. It dripped. Purples, blues and pinks inside of the icicles and inside of the droplets made everything look like it was heaven on earth. Everything except the two clumsy hunters.

"I said *stop* pointing it at me," said Lloyd as he pushed Elmer's 26" barrel

189

to the side.

"I ain't," said Elmer as he recoiled his over-under.

"You is. You is. See I'm leading us, so I can have my gun out like this. But you're behind me, so when yous do it, well, you be pointing your gun at me. My butt. See?" said Lloyd.

"But I ain't. I been pointing it to the sides."

"You start to point it to the sides, but then you forget and I can feel it pointing right at my dang buttocks. And I swear Elmer, if you shoot my buttocks again, I'm gonna shoot yours back. Yah hear me?" said Lloyd. "Keep it up to the sky or choose a side dang it."

Elmer didn't have much to say after that. Last season he had shot his brother in the buttocks after slipping on a frozen root. Now his brother's bum had small craters all over it. The two brothers walked on, still with *both* of their guns pointed forward.

The father deer was sure that something evil was in the forest that morning. The whole family was uneasy; they tried to walk quickly, but the snow was very deep for the white fawn. With each step the white fawn would have to struggle to get her thin legs over the tall snow. The father deer walked beside his young fawn. He was worried. The mother deer walked ahead trying to make a path for her baby. She was worried as well. Often the white fawn would fall into the snow exhausted from the hike. She would grunt quietly. And would look up to her mother and father for direction. Struggle after struggle the white fawn fought to get herself up and out of the deep snow. Her parents would wait for her and help her up with their noses. The mother deer could feel the extra uneasiness from her partner. She looked deep into the trees that her partner seemed focused on.

Earlier that morning all of the sounds in the forest were normal. Snow clumps falling from the trees, big and small branches snapping and cracking. But when the booming started, the father deer knew there was, in fact, an evil in the forest. Each time the booming came, it made the birds overhead fly in a panic. What first worried the father deer was that the booming always seemed to be the same distance from the family even though the family was moving. Yet, what made the father deer most nervous, was when the booming stopped. It was then that the father deer felt as if his family was being followed. Stalked. Hunted.

Lloyd and Elmer were now moving faster than the tired white fawn. They pushed through the snow rather than up and over it. Lloyd whispered to Elmer that they were close, so he began to follow the tracks a bit steadier and a bit keener. Believing they were gaining on the family of deer, the two brothers changed their mindsets from tracking to hunting. Their eyes scanned the trees, their ears searched for sounds.

Then Lloyd stopped. He turned around slowly to Elmer with his finger on his lips. Upon seeing Elmer's over-under pointed at his buttocks again, Lloyd pushed the barrel away and gave his brother a nasty look. Lloyd pointed to his own eyes and then far up ahead.

Elmer scanned the forest squinting. He searched the sparkling forest for any movement that was not icicles dripping. Finally he saw it. Two large deer were hunched over a small white fawn that looked to be stuck in the heavy snow.

Lloyd pointed to the far right and hooked his finger out and around, pantomiming to Elmer their attack plan.

"I don't get it," whispered Elmer.

"Shh," said Lloyd quietly. "You go up ahead to the right and I'll go up ahead to the left. We'll meet up ahead. This way they will walk to us. Don't move in unless they hear us and sprint in another direction."

"Okay," whispered Elmer.

"Shh," shushed Lloyd back.

"Okay," whispered Elmer a bit softer.

Then the two brothers moved out and around.

It became still. Droplets seem to have frozen in mid air. The father deer raised his head, turned his ears and sonically scanned the forest. The white fawn wiggled out of the snow just to fall back under her mother's belly for a rest and some warmth. The father deer knew his baby needed rest, so he sniffed and licked them both to let them know they were to stay there for a moment. Then the father deer stood tall, brought his chin high, squinted and searched the forest some more. The mother deer came down and lay around her baby. She licked her as she watched her partner search.

The father deer looked behind them to where he had heard the booming earlier. But now he felt trouble all around them. He bent down to lick his partner's and baby's heads one more time to instill more calm in them. And

191

to calm himself as well. The father deer's heart began to race. He felt trapped. He felt predators. Canines. He could feel the fact that they were in danger. The father deer turned west to a snapping branch. He turned east smelling an odd sent in the breeze. He looked south where they were headed. South didn't feel right anymore. But then again, no direction felt good to him anymore.

They would have to move he thought, even if his baby was tired. The father deer turned to his partner and baby and nudged them to stand. When they didn't he stomped his hoof down and nudged them some more. The white fawn had settled nicely from the rest and it was difficult for her to get back up. She wobbled, rose and looked up to her mother who was staring down at her.

That's when everything went white. That's when the white fawn saw her mother leap over her and that's when she heard the deafening sound.

BOOM!
BOOM!

The white fawn had fallen back from the loud sound. Her ears rang. When she opened her eyes she saw that her mother was standing in front of her now. She had leaped over her. There were red droplets and red spray in front of her mother. The mother deer staggered back. Then half sat. The white fawn looked even further ahead and saw her father sprinting forward with what looked to be half of his antlers. The mother deer had in fact jumped in front of her baby when she had heard the hunter's movement and smelled their stink, while in fact the father deer had jumped in front of her as well when he saw red hats and gun barrels through the trees. The father deer had taken the buckshot. It had shattered half of his mighty antlers and opened his forehead enough to spray blood back upon his partner. The mother deer was untouched; she checked her fawn as her ears rang something vicious.

It took three leaps to be upon the two men. Lloyd and Elmer fell back from fright. Their guns fell from their hands and plunged into the snow. Lost in the white; it was now a fair fight. The massive deer was upon them, with broken antlers, a red forehead and direct eyes. The two men rose and ran. The father deer slammed into Lloyd's buttocks throwing him back. Lloyd jumped up and ran for a half fallen frozen tree. He tried his best to climb it, but it was slippery to the touch. The angry father deer turned to Elmer and charged. Elmer got one in the buttocks as well. The father deer watched the two men clumsily jump and slip, trying to climb the frozen fallen tree. Stamping the ground, with air shooting out of his nostrils and blood streaming down both his ears and cheeks, the father deer charged again. He hit Elmer's buttocks with such a mighty force that it sent Elmer up the tree hitting Lloyds buttocks with his head. The two men grabbed the icy tree with all of their appendages. They looked down at the pacing, angry father deer, barely hanging on to their grips of the tree. The father deer stayed for three harsh breaths, circled the tree, butted it with what was left of his antlers and then leaped back to his family. Together again the father deer sniffed his partner and white fawn's bodies. The white fawn was scared. Motionless. Her parents helped her to get on her feet and find her wits again. Then they all leaped deep into the forest.

Ellie felt quite stupid. Humbled. Her cheeks felt hot red against the cold winter wind. Her hands felt sweaty under her mittens. And she could feel the blood rushing all around her body as she walked from her makeshift home to The Workshop. Ellie held a small crock of potato stew and had two small bandanas of coal in both her jacket pockets. These were peace offerings. It was difficult for Ellie to show up at The Workshop after it had been leaked that she had mentioned to her boys to not be spending time there. It was bad enough that her boy Johnny had told Kringle what she had said about him before he had graciously shown up at dinner with Miss Winkelplex's key. But if Kringle had told Pete Ellie's off-the-cuff words, well, she just wouldn't have the words for explaining them. Ellie had known Pete for a long, long time. He'd take it hard to hear that she told her boys to never come by anymore. Ellie felt just rotten. Silly. Young. She walked quickly, hot under the collar and breathed shallowly and fast. She didn't like the feeling. Ellie felt quite stupid.

Pete and Kringle sat at their workbenches working on toys. Many different length lists were nailed in front of them. The two carpenters referenced the lists after finishing each toy. They would then cross out the toy they had finished, circle the next one on the list and then get right back to working. President Hoover spoke through the static of Pete's radio. He spoke of jobs, America and the strength of its people.

Kringle

A timid mitten-muffled-knock came from their door.

Both toy makers looked up at the door and then to one another. The only visitors they ever got were Mr. McManus and that was not his knock. Rudy's head looked up as well, then turned left and right to both men. When they didn't react, Rudy stood, walked to the door, began to smell under the bottom crack and then proceeded to slap his tail hard on the floorboards while he wiggled his bum back and forth. Rudy then whined a bit and proceeded to wiggle about, sniffing frantically.

Pete stood up slowly, and then nudged Rudy back.

"Hello?" said Pete to the door.

"Hiya Pete, just me Ellie."

Pete's and Kringle's eyes widened. Quickly they grabbed the toys that were piling up around their workbenches and tossed them into their trunks and under their beds. Kringle motioned to Pete to take down all the lists that were nailed to the wall as well.

"Just one second Ellie, just one second," said Pete, as he hurried the last of the toys into his trunk. The two men scanned the room. Kringle sat back down. Pete opened the door as Kringle spotted a wooden doll and quickly stuffed it under his shirt. "Well Ellie, how-how you doing, come in, come in," said Pete calmly as he took off his hat. Kringle's eyes widened and his heart took to an uppity beat. "Let me get this for you. Oo-oo what do we have in here?" Pete took the crock-pot from Ellie and set it on the small table between the two men's workbenches. "Rudy, no-no, sit-sit." After circling Ellie and smelling up and down her coat Rudy wanted at the crock-pot. "Siiit. Let me take your jacket there Ellie. Not too bad out today huh? The Sun is doing her job nicely."

"Thanks, no-no, not too cold. Hello there Kringle."

Kringle stood, rubbed-quick his red bearding face and adjusted his hair and shirt hiding the doll.

"Hello Ellie. All well?"

"Well, Miss Winkelplex's got Flo and myself workin' like squirrels. The shop has been all the bustle these days. Boston women mostly, some men, all coming in and on weekdays even. And each one of them is all worried and frantic. Those toys are like honey to bears with these city people." Ellie untied her babushka and checked her hair for snow and bumps. "That there is just a little potato stew I made the boys." Ellie then went over to her jacket hanging on the wall and pulled out the two bandanas of coal and offered them to Kringle. "And here is a bit of coal the boys collected the other day. They mentioned they saw you Kringle."

Kringle took the coal, unwrapped the bandanas, placed the coal in a pail, then brushed off the bandanas, folded them nicely and handed them back to Ellie.

Pete turned down President Hoover.

"I did see your cubs. They looked focused." Kringle leaned over the crock-pot and breathed in. "Thank you for this. We sure do need a little something different, something with flavor. Pete here was jealous of the dinner you made me last week. Here you are," Kringle handed Ellie the folded bandanas. Pete nodded that - truth was truth.

"Well, thank you. I can't say it's a turkey dinner with stuffing inside, but the boys and you did like it and that's the test."

"Ahh pardon us." Pete turned his workbench chair to face the small table. Ellie sat down. Kringle turned his chair around as well and sat down. Pete took a seat on his cot holding Rudy back from the crock-pot. "What brings you by and with gifts even?" asked Pete.

"Well, Pete, yesterday's wind brought a small pine down on the house. Smashed the roof and the stove's chimney tube. From the side it looks like it's fully lying on the house. Hard to see though with all the pine needles and snow. Looks to be a fairly big one. Not one of the massive ones. But now there is an openings in the roof where the chimney tube was. Snow's coming in a bit. I thought I might ask you if you could come take a look at it. Maybe today even, that is, if ya could."

"Lord Ellie! That's terrible. Dangerous too. You were all freezing last night then huh?"

"A bit cold ya, but like you said, last night and today aren't so bad."

"Sure I can take a...well no...hm...wait, I can't Ellie."

"No? Oh okay. That's fine. I can try and see if I can fix it."

Ellie was now certain Kringle must have told Pete what she had said to her boys and now Pete must be sore from it. But in fact Kringle hadn't mentioned anything specific to Pete; Pete just had other plans in mind.

"Well you see Ellie, I'm sorry, but Mr. McManus has me working around the clock."

"Oh Pete you don't have to be sorry, I understand. He's got us girls' dance-cards filled as well."

"But you know, Kringle here, he knows a thing or two. Don't ya Kringle?"

"Well, um," muttered Kringle.

"Sure, Kringle why don't you go have a look. Yah I'm sorry Ellie, I just can't today."

"Oh no, no problem Pete." Ellie was still quite embarrassed to be asking and anxious that the men were sore with her, so she became very agreeable. "Sure it's not too much trouble Kringle?"

"Oh no trouble at all. I'm sure Pete's better though, if you want to wait until he's free," said Kringle. He didn't know why Pete was volunteering him, when Pete knew Ellie didn't want Kringle around her boys.

"Oh no, Kringle, I'm sure to be busy all week. Just head over there, take a look. If you can't figure how to get that tube back up, just come back and tell me what you figure and I'll be sure to tell you what needs doin'."

Pete was being odd, unlike himself and his plan was odd as well. But both Ellie and Kringle, being thrown off, agreed to the plan and quickly found themselves walking back to Ellie's.

The walk was silent.

Kringle was in his head wondering why, when he left The Workshop, Pete was smirking and spinning around like he was dancing with a woman. Then it hit him. Pete wanted him to ask Ellie to the Ice Dance. It was a set up.

Both Kringle and Ellie looked down as they walked silently in the puddle mudding ground, until Ellie softly spoke.

"Hunters were out today."

"Oh ya, I heard them. Quite a lot of shots."

"The boys counted eight."

"Hm. That's bad shootin'"

Ellie smiled to herself.

"Sure is. Haven't seen you around these days. Thought you might have jumped on a train again and rolled onto another woman's porch."

Kringle smiled to himself.

Ellie was nervous that her comment might have been too close to calling Kringle *a train-riding hobo* like she had said. Her worried thoughts looped telling her that she was *dumb* and *rude*.

"No, no…just been working hard for Mr. McManus that's all."

The two became silent, both searching their minds for simple topics.

"Say, are those your boys there? What'er they doing there, making a snowman?"

Johnny and Billy stood beside a half finished snowman and behind a half rolled ball of snow. They faced their mother and Kringle standing dumbfounded.

Why would she be bringing Kringle back to the house to fix the stove and roof? She said she was getting Pete, the Boone boys thought.

Johnny and Billy looked up to where Kringle was on his hands and knees sawing different pieces off the fallen pine and tossing them to the ground, where Ellie collected them and placed them in a pile.

"He's just helpin'. He's just fixin' the roof," said Billy.

"I know what he's doin', Billy, I'm just saying why's it him doin' it?" said Johnny.

"'Cause he knows how."

"Pete knows how."

"That's true. Maybe Pete's busy."

"Mm," said Johnny unimpressed.

"Why Kringle make you so itchy Johnny?"

Johnny looked down at his brother, who was packing snow around while smoothing out the circumference of the big snowball they were rolling.

"I told you he don't. I'm just sayin' Ma said not to hang with this fella. Then she brings him over for dinner again. Right? And-and now he's on the roof with a saw."

"So?"

"That's odd Billy? I mean none of that makes sense?"

"So what?"

"What do you mean so what?"

"Well, she can change her mind; I d'know. Maybe she likes him."

"She don't like him."

"How do you know?"

"'Cause I know."

"Ya, but *how* do you know."

"'Cause I just know, Billy."

"Mm," said Billy, unimpressed. "I like him."

"I know you do."

"I don't know why you so itchy over it all Johnny."

Johnny turned to his brother and pushed him enough to make Billy fall over. "I AIN'T ICHY!"

"Fine. You ain't," said Billy as he stood up, brushed himself off and scowled a bit at his brother, because he felt that that push was not like their normal roughing.

Up on the roof, by the broken iron tube of the stove, Kringle had sawed off most of the small and medium branches and was starting on the bigger ones. The iron tube of the stove wasn't too damaged; it would just have to be reset. Then the roof holes would have to be patched up around it. The most difficult and time-consuming part of the job would be sawing through the thicker frozen branches of the pine and pushing the bigger pieces off the roof without damaging the roof or getting damaged himself. Kringle worked hard.

The boys continued to stand, now in silence, beside their half finished snowman watching Kringle on their roof.

Ellie finished putting all of the small and medium sized branches in a pile along the side of their makeshift home. Then she took off her babushka and mittens, stuffed them in her jacket pocket, flipped all her black hair behind her shoulders and approached her boys.

"You boys alright?"

Billy snapped out of his stare.

"Yup. Look Momma," Billy pointed to the big ball of snow that was to be the base of their snowman.

"Sure looking good. It's gonna be a big one huh? Make sure you can lift the other pieces on top of it. Don't make them as big as the Moon now."

"Ya," said Billy in agreement and then looked down, puzzled, wondering about whether or not he and his brother could lift the top piece he was smoothing out.

"Why is Kringle up there helping us Ma? You said..." started Johnny.

"Well, forget what I said okay?" Ellie knelt down and brought her voice to a whisper. "Momma was wrong to say those mean words. You hearing Momma?"

Both boys were looking past her and up to where Kringle was sawing.

"Boys. Eyes here," Ellie snapped her cold fingertips. "Now put yourselves on memory record okay. Momma was wrong to say them things about Mr. Kringle. He's now done two good things to help this family."

"You said he was a bum," said Johnny.

"Johnny Boone, what did I just say? Momma was wrong. I want you to be nice to Mr. Kringle when he comes down from there. Also, don't be going over to that side of the house, Mr. Kringle's throwing big tree limbs down. Stay out here and where you are until I say otherwise. We can't have one of them limbs falling and bopping you on your heads now can we?" Ellie took her hand and tapped it on both Billy's and Johnny's heads. Billy smiled a bit to his mother. Johnny readjusted. Ellie went inside to inspect the hole from inside.

Kringle continued to work diligently sawing through the big frozen pine while the boys continued working on their snowman. Billy was fixated on the crafting of the snowman while Johnny became a bit distracted – looking up at Kringle every few seconds. Ellie danced between them all, checking in. Eventually Johnny and Billy, with the help of Ellie, got the snowman's head up on top of the middle piece. They began securing it with snow and smoothed it out nicely.

"This sure is a good one, huh," said Billy.

"It sure is," said Ellie. "What do ya say Johnny?"

"It's strong," said Johnny working and not looking up.

"Well, it's not a true snowman until it has a face, right men?" Ellie pulled out a handful of coal and they all packed them into the snowy face of the snowman – two eyes, a nose and a smiling mouth. "There we go. All done. That's fine boys, truly fine."

"Wait-wait," Johnny said as he pulled out a straw and placed it in the snowman's mouth. "There."

The three of them backed up for a better view just as Kringle approached.

"Now that's a perfect snowman there," said Kringle as he took off his hat and scratched his hair and bearding face.

"Ooh Kringle," Ellie was a bit startled. "I didn't hear you. How is it up there?"

"Well, I got all the fallen branches down. Now that was something. You can burn all that once it gets less fresh. I was able to set the tube back up; it wasn't too damaged, just a few dents and was pulled from a few bolts. I can come by and fix that up later. It's sturdyish though. For now I'll try patching around the tube, that way you can get the heat going again. I don't have my tools with me though. Johnny can I borrow your hammer?"

"Huh?" said Johnny.

"Can Mr. Kringle borrow your hammer?" Ellie repeated. "It's actually my hammer, he just steals it," Ellie said to Kringle. "Go get the hammer Johnny and some small wood pieces to patch around the hole."

"I have nails!" said Billy, smiling to Kringle. Billy ran off. Johnny walked in Billy's direction.

"Well, you know Kringle, thanks again for all this," said Ellie as she slightly touched the snowman.

"Just happy to help."

"Sure was a lot of work up there though huh? And cold."

"Wasn't so bad. That is one prize-winning snowman though. But it needs a hat."

Billy returned walking alongside Johnny, they were murmuring and slightly pushing one another. Billy handed Kringle the nails; Johnny handed him the hammer and held on to the wood pieces.

"Say boys you wanna help?" asked Kringle.

"Ya!" said Billy.

"Oh no, I don't want the boys up there on that ladder," said Ellie.

"No, I mean from the inside. Someone's gotta let me know if I've covered all the light-holes."

"Oh sure, you boys wanna help Mr. Kringle? Help him with light-holes?" asked Ellie.

"Yes!" Billy said.

"I could do that," said Johnny.

For the next hour Ellie watched as her boys stood on chairs around the stove and listened with low brows and puckered lips to Kringle's questions:

"How's she look?" – "Is there still a crack of light?" – "What do ya think I should do?" yelled an unseen Kringle from the rooftop.

Her boys buzzed. They shouted out instructions and got excited as each light crack was covered.

"More to the left."
"Yah to the left."
"No too far, too far."
"Now to the right just a bit"
"You got it."

"You got it," the Boone boys yelled skyward.

Ellie liked how the day had turned out. She was happy when her boys were happy. And they both seemed happy. Ellie liked seeing them buzz with the excitement as they worked together. They also talked to Kringle differently than they did with her; Ellie thought that an interesting one. She liked seeing a hidden side of them.

Once Kringle came inside and it was official that all the light-holes were covered, Ellie sent the boys outside to fill the coal hod. Together they all got the stove going again. There was no back draft; the stove and the dented tube worked just fine.

"You boys were a great help ya know? I couldn't a finished it without you," said Kringle and both boys nodded in agreement with him.

"Ooh, it's warming already. Do you feel that boys?" said Ellie with her palms out facing the stove.

"See boys, if we didn't get all them light-holes, it sure wouldn't have warmed up this quickly. Nice work."

"It was fun," said Billy as he began taking his jacket and boots off.

"Ya know, I got a new sled going," said Johnny, as he too began to take his boots off.

"You don't say; how's it coming along?"

"Pretty good. Got it all plotted out, blueprints - you know."

"Sure, blueprints, that's wise - know what you're doing *before* you do it. Smart Johnny."

"You could come by and see it once we're done with it," invited Johnny. He was feeling more as an equal to Kringle after helping with the roof.

"Sure, and feel free to come by if you need anything," said Kringle.

Kringle and Johnny then slightly looked to Ellie.

"That'd be fine boys. Okay Johnny help your brother with his boots," Billy was on the floor going in circles trying to get his left boot off.

"Well, see ya," said Johnny to Kringle with a low wave and no eye contact.

Kringle then got a shot of nervous adrenaline. He knew it was time for him to make his exit, but didn't know if he would, could, or should ask Ellie to the Ice Dance that was going on the next night.

"Well, I should be heading back now," said Kringle. It was 3:45PM and the Sun was setting. "Still got a lot to hammer out for Mr. McManus and all."

"Boys, say bye to Mr. Kringle," said Ellie.

"Nice work boys," said Kringle one last time.

"Err, ehh, n-nice w-work Mr. Kringle," grunted Billy, while his brother pulled at his left boot, dragging him.

"Bye," grunted Johnny back.

Kringle and Ellie headed to the door.

"Well, you sure been a help. Let me know if I can do anything for you and Pete, maybe I'll make you a second stew if you liked the first."

Kringle's heart was pounding. He was quiet and looking to the floor as he bundled back up.

Ellie thought the silence odd.

"Really, thank you. Even seems to be warming up faster than it did before that big old tree came down," Ellie chuckled.

"W-well Ellie," said Kringle as he turned to face her standing in the doorway. Ellie stepped out a bit and closed the door some, to keep the heat in. "There *is* something you can do for me."

"Oh ya, now what's that and don't go saying to go to that dance tomorrow night, because well I don't dance," Ellie laughed thinking it a fine joke. Ellie's laugh decrescendoed.

Kringle's mind sank, but then he thought about what Pete had said to him and decided Pete's advice was the only possible choice for him. He stood straighter and looked Ellie in her - bluer than most blue eyes - eyes.

"Well, that is what I wanted to talk to you about. I'm thinking I'll come by around five-o'clock. They say it don't start until six. That'll give us a fair amount of time to walk there. You know at a calm pace, not hurrying or anything."

Ellie let out one short laugh.

"W-what? Are you serious Kringle?" Ellie looked behind her and closed the door a bit more.

Kringle shuffled a bit into an even straighter posture.

"I sure am Miss Boone. Ellie. That there was a lot of work. And like you said, you owe me. And I found your key for you too – that's two for one. See?"

Ellie stood a bit straighter as well, took a big breath into her chest, put her hands on her hips and said, "No-no, I made you dinner, that was the deal."

"Well, that's true, that's true. But this here, you owe me for one then - for the roof. And being my dance partner tomorrow night should settle that even."

"Oh it would, would it?"

"Yes Ma'am," Kringle said quietly.

202

"Kringle, I can not go to the Ice Dance with you. I don't think you even know what you are asking. First off I don't want to go. Second I don't dance. And thirdly, this…this town here, you can't just, we couldn't just *go* to the Ice Dance. Mm-mm. *I* couldn't just hop up to the dance with you like it was…" Ellie brought her voice quieter. "Kringle no-no-no, that's not an idea to have – people talk. It's bigger than you're thinking."

"Well, the way I figure it Ellie is you owe me – one. And I'd like to have a dance partner for tomorrow's dance. It'd look very odd me dancin' alone. It's my first Ice Dance here in town and it'd be nice to be a part of it."

"Well, ask someone then," Ellie interrupted.

"I am."

"No, not me Kringle, err, another girl."

"I'm gonna go with you Ellie."

"Oh you are, are you?" Ellie squinted her eyes and puckered her lips a bit. Kringle still felt her lips very kissable lips.

"I'll come by at five-o'clock, that should give us enough extra time, so not to hurry."

"Look-a-here Kringle. I cannot. So-so stop this. Stop what you're saying already. Button this up. You're going on again like you do and I don't know what you're doing when you go on like this. No. No dance. Think of something else. Stew I can do; I'll do a stew. There. Done. I'll bring another stew for you tomorrow. That's a great deal. Okay."

"Well, were gonna go, you and I. I'll be here at five-o'clock tomorrow."

Kringle began to leave.

"Kringle stop, come back here. You don't understand. Please. You ain't… you…err…look Kringle…I have boys. I was married you see. People will talk. It's not simple. It's not fun. It's complex. I can't be doing things like that, you just don't know. You don't. Lord, can you imagine? Ugh. Err, I can't be just…oh." Ellie stopped, closed her eye and said quietly, "Kringle. No. Please? People talk."

"We'll go as just friends Ellie. If anyone asks, we'll both just tell 'em - 'Oh we're just friends,'" said Kringle as he turned and began his walk home. "See you tomorrow at five-o'clock Ellie," said Kringle as he walked past the snowman, plopping his red hat down on its head.

That night Ellie went up to the loft earlier than she usually would. Ellie didn't know how one finally decides on a thought that will represent their next action, when their logic and emotion battle ever so loudly. The Boone boys stayed downstairs listening to *Buck Rogers*, wrapped in a blanket by the stove, while occasionally looking up and talking about how well the tube was sealed. Ellie sat cross-legged under the covers. In front of her was her Sunday dress spread out; it still had a tear in it. In Ellie's hands was Kringle's red hat; she poked her fingers through its burned holes. Ellie wasn't listening to her boys talking anymore, she wasn't listening to the *Buck Rogers* show either, she wasn't even listening to her own thoughts anymore. She just sat there - melancholy. Her eyes were glazed over.

The conceited winter brought a sharp gust in and one of the birch's frozen limbs slapped the window to her right. For a moment Ellie snapped out of her daze. She noticed the Moon's light had once again cast a frame of the window upon her hands. Ellie looked down at her hands holding the red hat, both of them glowed angelically from the moonlight. Her eyes then went up to the window and to the stars; she stared out the window for some time. Ellie centered on one star, it wiggled and blinked. The lone star let its long lines of light spread out and then retracted them in an almost slow heart beating pulse. Ellie took a deep breath, closed her eyes, reached under the bed and pulled out a small tin box. For so long Ellie wanted her life to be grounded. Stable. She wanted every decision presented to her to be answered with simple yes's and no's. She tired of feeling unbalanced. Ellie didn't like change any longer, like a tear in a sweater, that at first you resent, yet later absorb as a recognizable friend, Ellie was used to being a woman without a man. She believed factually that she preferred it. Pulling her Sunday dress up on to her lap, Ellie opened the tin box, threaded a spool of light blue thread, began to patch her tear, and then made a faint smile with a hint of sadness.

It was fifteen minutes to five-o'clock. The Sun smiled with envy, watching everyone in Hamilton getting dressed up for the big Ice Dance that night. She was saddened to set.

"Tell me how their dance goes?" she asked the Moon.

"With details," he answered back.

Rudy enjoyed his meal more that night than other nights, not because the food was taster, but because he liked watching Pete and Kringle bustling about putting on their nice clothes and fixing their hair. Rudy walked in many excited circles and was panting from the buzz in The Workshop. Pete and Kringle took turns bathing in the outside tub as it lightly snowed. They took turns running in and out of The Workshop shivering for more pans of hot water.

Ellie sat by the stove in her small chair, diligently inspecting her Sunday dress. After she had fixed the new tears from the night before, she added a nice islet white trim to the bottom of the dress, shoulders and neckline. Once Ellie's inspection was complete, she went to the sink to scrub the stains out of her white gloves. She didn't want to think about how much she disliked being bullied into going to the Ice Dance with Kringle. Instead she centered on the steps she must take to look presentable there, and there was no time but to race through those steps and get it all done before five-o'clock. Pressure moves Ellie. And all the while Ellie shouted to her boys her instructions and reasons why they were to put their pajamas on under their Sunday clothes. With limited time, it was the only way she could think of to keep the boys dressed warmly for the night's activities outside. Ellie thickly layered her boys' winter bundles as if she believed that an inch of clothes could cushion the teeth of the biting cold from reaching their skin.

Ramona and her mother stood in Ramona's closet of a bedroom bickering with salty words about whether Ramona did or did not need to wear a dress that night. Her father watched from the doorway smoking his pipe, smiling at his saucy princess. Murf and his father stood with their hands by their side as Mrs. McCullough stood on three books combing their hair down and inspecting their waistlines. Terrance sat on the couch by his father, who was reading the *Worchester Evening Gazette*; Terrance had been dressed and ready since half past three.

Miss Winkelplex had begun drinking early that day in celebration of all the hard work she had been putting in lately. She sat in her faux French bergere arm chair playing Lawrence Welk records, twirling her fingers in a drunken conductor fashion.

Over at the McManus' home, Periwinkle had turned her nose to her dinner and her back to the family. She felt that no one in the house was giving her her normal attention – especially Marlene. Periwinkle settled on her pillow near the living room's west window; she'd sleep then and on until lunch the next day. That would be punishment enough. The ladies of the McManus family were all upstairs getting ready while Mr. McManus tried out the speech he was to make that night on the Dunce Brothers who sat half asleep on the McManus' French provincial carved sofa settee.

The Moon was now at the height of the sky; he watched the last of his love hue away and then did as she had asked. He settled big and bright over Little Island Pond and made sure to ask the birds to tell the approaching clouds to pass around and not under him. He was prepared to have a full glow cast down for the good people of Hamilton had earned their perfect night.

Ellie wasn't fully done with her sewing tasks when she heard Kringle's knock at her door at precisely five-o'clock. She had become stressed with her boys running around her being difficult as she tried to get ready for a dance she didn't particularly want to go to.

KNOCK KNOCK KNOCK!

"Mr. Kringle's here Momma," said Billy looking down from the loft.
"Yup," said Ellie as she hid something quickly and stuffed her needle and thread into the pocket of her jacket that was hanging on a nail.
"But Ma, it's hard to move with my pajamas on," said Johnny.
"They'll keep you warm," said Ellie as she let out a stress breath. "And that's what's most important."
"But I ain't cold," corrected Johnny.
"You aren't now, but you will be later."
"I don't think I'm gonna wear them," said Johnny as he began to take his clothes off.
"Johnny Boone, don't you take those clothes off. You hear me?" said Ellie as she checked her hair, pinched her cheeks, smoothed out her dress, took a deep breath and rolled her eyes at herself.
In the middle of the small makeshift home, both Johnny and Billy stood in front of their mother, staring at her, blocking her from the front door.
"*You* don't have your pajamas on," mumbled Johnny as he began to put back on his clothes.
"Stop," she said as she shooed her boys from staring at her and approached the door.
"Coming," she said.

"Good! Finally we can go!" whined Johnny.

The Boone boys were antsy to get to the Ice Dance, not just because at seven-o'clock the fireworks began, but because of a recent plan Johnny and Billy had come up with the night before while listening to a perilous *Buck Rogers* adventure.

Ellie turned to correct Johnny's whining as she opened the door. Billy ran in front of his mother.

A freshly shaven Kringle stood at the door holding a tiny wooden flower. He wore his best shirt and borrowed a red tie from Pete. His pants were washed and ironed and he was wearing nice loafers that he had pulled out of Pete's shoe barrel. They were a half size too small, but they looked nice and shiny. Kringle didn't have a nice jacket, nor did Pete, so he still had on his burned red coat, but he had washed it as best he could.

"Hey, Mr. Kringle. Cool, what's that; did ya make it?"

"Scoot, scoot Billy," Ellie moved her littlest one to the side. "Kringle," she started. Ellie noticed Kringle's effort. To her, Ellie *could* entertain the thought that Kringle was probably handsome to other girls, but she showed no signs of being impressed by his subtle clean up. Ellie stood with her arms crossed, looking cross.

Kringle's eyes watered slightly, the way Pete's do, at the sight of Ellie. He thought her to just pop out from all of the other sights of the world. She glowed to him, even if she did look unhappy to see him. And he was more than pleased to see her in her Sunday dress again.

"I was nervous you weren't going to go with me," smiled Kringle as he raised his tiny wooden flower. "But you're all dressed. That means you are." Kringle handed Ellie the flower. It had a tiny green stem with three small leaves and a red tulip top.

Ellie took the small wooden flower without looking at it.

"Well, as I remember from our last conversation – I didn't really have a choice. Remember Kringle this makes us even Steven. What's this?"

"It's a corsage."

"Well, that's *not* a corsage."

"Well, sure it is. See?"

Kringle took Ellie's hand that held the wooden flower and turned it over. It had a pin connected to the back.

"I see. Well a corsage Kringle is actually made of actual flowers," Ellie

207

wasn't sure why she was giving Kringle the run-about; it looked to be a nice little flower. She was just stressed out and hadn't a clue of what they should be talking about.

"Oh no, ya, right. I know. But there aren't any flowers about this time of year, so I made one. I wasn't sure if this was the type of dance where ladies would have corsages on. Pete said 'maybe', so I figured…best have one, 'cause that'd be better than if you didn't have one, when you should have one. So I made one and brought it. And that's it."

"But we are going as friends, Kringle, remember? Friend's don't need corsages."

"So we *are* officially friends now? You said it," said Kringle with a smile.

"Don't start with me Kringle; I'm getting cold."

"Let's go Ma!" yelled Johnny now sitting at the table with his chin in his hands.

"He got her a flower, I mean he made one," whispered Billy to Johnny from the door.

"He did?" said Johnny confused and then shook the thought off. Johnny didn't want to get to thinking about something new; he had bigger plans to ponder.

"So you don't want it?" asked Kringle. "It's nice'ish though, see?"

"No, I'll take it. Thank you Kringle." Ellie took the flower and inspected it. "Where did you buy this?"

"No, I made it, I didn't buy it."

"Did you find the flower out in the…um, the piles and put this pin on it?"

"No, no, I made it. I made it from wood."

"You made this?" said Ellie impressed. She twirled it in her fingers inspecting all the sides.

"Yes, do you like her?"

"Well, it is quite something. So small. The detail. I didn't know you knew how to do this. It really is quite something." Ellie pinned it on the left side of her dress. Then turned and knelt down to show Billy who was leaning in to see.

"Look inside the leaves," said Kringle.

Ellie looked down and saw her name written diminutively in nice cursive inside one of the small petals. "And the other one," suggested Kringle.

There was his name as well.

"Kringle. Wow. I'm impressed. But Kringle don't be crossing the line here, this is all nice, but…"

"I know, I know, look there." In the third petal it simply said – "Friends". "We're just going as friends. That there is just a friendship corsage, I just put my name there in case you forgot it. You know, you'll probably be dancing with all these other fellas and then say to yourself - 'didn't I come with someone, what was his name again. Freckle?' - then you could just look down and, boom, there you go – 'Kringle, ah right, Kringle.'"

Ellie looked up at Kringle and gave him a smirk.

Johnny swung the door fully open and said, "Okay, c'mon you two. Let's go! Let's go! Can't you two talk and walk or what?"

And with that, the four of them headed down Bridge Street.

✳

The Boone boys walked a bit ahead to keep the pace moving quicker and to discuss privately the details of their most recent idea.

"Okay, you're going to have to look to the side for a while," said Ellie.

"To the side?" asked Kringle.

"Ya, look that way as we walk; over there. I have to finish something."

Kringle looked to where Ellie had pointed.

"Did you get me a corsage too?"

Ellie rolled her eyes and smirked to herself.

"Noo, I didn't get you a corsage. Hey, no looking. Over there. C'mon, eyes that way. I have no problem not giving you this back."

"Back? Okay. Um, well, there was a nice sunset today. Did you, ah, happen to see it? Orange."

"Mm. No."

"So you're not a dancer, huh?"

"Nope."

"I'm a pretty good dancer. Just follow what I do."

"Mm."

"Is it that you don't like uppity music? Don't like fast dancing? Or is it that you don't like slow dancing? What I mean is which are you better at?"

"Neither. Almost done. Keep your eyes over there."

"Okay. Well, we can start with slow dancing and then move to a quicker step if we feel that's fun."

"Mm. I don't know if I'll find either 'fun'. Okay all done. It ain't much, but it's, well, it's done. You can look."

In Ellie's mittens was Kringle's red hat. And all the burn holes had been patched up nicely. No longer would Kringle's hair spring out of the many holes it once had. Ellie had also added white fur around the border of the hat and a white ball to the tip of it.

"Well, I'll be. Thanks, Ellie. This is fine." Kringle took off his red gloves and with his bare hands touched the soft fur. He then inspected all around the hat and showed Ellie each patch she made. Ellie would smirk slightly and nod her head slightly at each. She pointed to one he missed. Then Kringle put it on. "It fits great Ellie. I think it's even warmer now."

Ellie rolled her eyes.

"Well, no need to overdue it. The holes just annoyed me; I had to patch them."

"How do I look?"

Kringle stopped walking. He put his fists on his hips and looked to the sky presidentially.

"Well, it matches your tie. And jacket," Ellie said.

"I look handsome you say, why thank you.

Ellie rolled her eyes again.

"Ho-ho-ho, look at me. The fanciest lost fireman to ever…"

"HEY! C'MON!" screamed Johnny, who was up ahead. He pointed to the glow that was above Little Island Pond's tree line. "LET'S GO! IT'S STARTING!"

"No, really, thanks Ellie, I appreciate it. My ears feel incredibly soft. I like the white fluffy stuff," said Kringle. And the two began to walk again.

"It's nothing."

"Ya, well, *thank you.*"

"You're welcome."

Upon reaching Little Island Pond, one would have thought they had fallen asleep and awakened inside a storybook. All around white lights were hung on snowy pine trees that circled the modest pond. Little merchant shacks selling hot chocolate, hot cider, fried dough, warm cookies, warm pretzels and more were set up. Along side these shacks were carnival games that were a penny to play. Streamers of pine boughs and popcorn were strung all around. The smaller pine trees were decorated with little bulbs and some even had hidden candy canes hanging deep inside them - a traditional game for a few lucky children to find.

There was a stage set up for the night's announcements and a raffle just before the fireworks display. The Uppity Boy's instruments were set up to provide the music for the dance - for now a Polka record was playing. There were four bonfires blazing around the Little Island Pond. Each bonfire was for a different age group to huddle around: Adults, young adults, teenagers and children (with or without their parents). Everyone in town knew which bonfire was theirs.

There was a small booth where you could rent skates that already had a line forming in front it, and, of course, there was Little Island Pond itself, iced over, cleared of snow and ready to be skated on.

The Ice Dance looked bright and welcoming. The bonfires and food huts kept everyone toasty inside and out. The entrance to the Ice Dance had a grand banner that read:

Welcome To Little Island Pond's Annual Ice Dance 1929

Mrs. Robin came walking up rather quickly to the front entrance of the Ice Dance with Sheriff Jones trying to catch up behind her.

"I tell you Sheriff, it was four young trouble-makers," said Mrs. Robin.

"What were they doing?" said the sheriff.

"Well they were starting all kinds of trouble."

"What kinds of trouble?" asked the sheriff.

"Well, they were standing together and laughing and just looking like a whole heap of trouble."

Mrs. Robin and the sheriff looked all around the entranceway.

"Where are they now?" asked the sheriff.

"Well, I'm, I'm not sure. They were just here," said Mrs. Robin. "Oh no maybe they went inside."

"Hi ya Sheriff," said Riggels as he puffed on a pipe.

"Evening Riggels. Say, you seen any teenagers here, starting trouble?"

"Sure," said Riggels.

"See, he'd seen 'em. Where'd they go?" asked an excited Mrs. Robin.

"Anything to mention Riggels?" asked the sheriff.

"Oh no not much. They started a little teenage tantrum," said Riggels.

"See?" said Mrs. Robin nodding.

"What kind of tantrum?" asked Sheriff Jones.

"Oh, one boy, Mack, I think they were calling him, was waiting for a smaller boy. He was looking to fight the smaller boy. Tim I think they were calling him. Timmy maybe. I think it's Frank Donnally's boy. But I'm not certain. Looked a bit like Frank. Anyways, I come up the road, see them shuffling and barking a bit, figure it isn't a barking type night, so I made conference with this Mack boy - Mack and his buddies," said Riggles as he took out his pipe and poked at it's contents with a small toothpick.

"A fight. See that's no-no good. Teenagers coming here to fight. We never had a thing like that when I was a girl," added Mrs. Robin.

"Anything else to mention Riggels?" asked Sheriff Jones.

"No, not really. I told that Mack boy about how I used to box in the army and that if he felt himself to want a boxing match with this Timmy kid, then I'd feel fine with taking Timmy's place and giving him a better fight. He didn't think that too much of a good idea. He was quick to promise to behave Sheriff," said Riggels and then continued to have a go at his pipe with his toothpick.

"I think we should go in there and get him out of tonight's affairs just to be sure," said Mrs. Robin.

"Well, I'll go find them boys myself and have a good talk with them. Why don't you get back to the music, Mrs. Robins? The record's gone and stopped. I'll take care of everything. Thanks for your tip though. You're a very keen lady."

"Keeping things safe and clean that's what we're doing here. Thank you Sheriff. Riggels," Mrs. Robin gave them both a small nod, then re-entered the Ice Dance proudly.

"Is it anything to worry about?" asked Sheriff Jones.

"Naw, those boys won't be pushing their chests out anymore tonight."

"Well, thanks for breaking it up."

"Ma always said I was good in a fight," said Riggels and both men re-entered the affair laughing.

Once Ellie, Kringle and the Boone boys passed under the banner, Johnny and Billy sprinted off to their designated bonfire. Everyone in town was filtering in behind Ellie and Kringle as the two of them continued to stand under the sign. They were one step from entering.

"Wow this sure is something," said Kringle.

"Sure is. If you ask me, I think it's nicer than the summer's - *Annual Pond Swim-In*. The pond in the summer can get a bit rowdy," said Ellie.

"So what does one do here? Firstly, I mean?" Kringle asked.

"Well, honestly I don't know. This is the first year I'm not workin'. I usually work the cider booth with Flo, but Miss Winkelplex didn't want to"... Ellie began her impression of Mrs. Winkelplex..."pay two girls for a job one can do'. So technically this is my first time coming socially since I was a teenager."

"What did you used to do?"

"Oh talk with the other girls over there at that bonfire."

Kringle smiled from the image.

The two began to walk around the bustling happening. Families, couples and hope-filled gaggles of singles all walked about red cheeked and bundled.

"Everyone seems to be cupping hot drinks. Let's get hot drinks," said Kringle.

"Sure. Flo's booth should be the last one by the bonfire that has older people standing around it. You know Kringle; she may give us a drink-e-drink. And no charge even." Then Ellie puckered her lips, nodded her head up and down giving her best pirate wink. "Giggle-juice."

"You don't say? Giggle-juice?"

"A drink-e-drink."

"I get ya Ellie," Kringle smiled. "But how's that?" said Kringle a bit shocked.

"Well, Flo's booth is for hot cider see, but Miss Winkelplex likes to warm herself up with a few dollops of smarts. So she always keeps two bottles back there, with Flo and me, to serve up her and anyone else she may have shared her password with. We usually dip into it as well. I bet Flo is feeling pretty warm already," Ellie laughed.

"Password, huh? Is it all very secret-secret?"

"Yes and no, I mean I don't know what the password is, but we know Flo. And don't worry about it; the sheriff knows; he sips on one himself once the fireworks start. It ain't fully illegal."

As Kringle and Ellie approached, Sheriff Jones and Mr. Riggelsworth were waving goodbye to Flo holding special steaming cider.

"Hey there Lost-Fireman and hey there my Ellie girl, you gorgeous sheba," said Flo from behind the small cider stand.

"Told you she was warm," whispered Ellie to Kringle.

"Evening Flo," said Kringle.

"Oo wonderful trim. Ellie!" said Flo, then leaned over, touched the new lace work Ellie added to her Sunday dress that was peaking out from under her jacket, then whispered in Ellie's ear, "You look cuter than two bunnies nappin' on my lap."

"Thank you," Ellie said calmly. "That was Riggels, Kringle. He was walking away just now."

"Ya, I just gave Riggels a Miss Winkelplex special. Sheriff came by with 'im and gave me his 'he can have one' nod. Something about helpin' him." Flo then pulled back and slapped her mitten hands down. "So, two *Parisians* for you two as well?" Flo said, while winking the word "Parisian".

"I swear she uses the same password each season; everyone's gotta know that password by now," said Ellie. "Yes please."

Flo ducked down and began making their Parisians.

"I told Riggels he could have another Parisian if he told Pastor Finn to visit me 'n' ask me to dance," said Flo from under the cider stand. "I'm such a confession huh?"

"You did?" said Ellie, a bit surprised.

"Ya, well, I ain't working a dance and not dancing at least once. Psst," said Flo, as she came up with the drinks.

"Flo likes to dance?" asked Kringle.

"Flo likes a lot of things," said Ellie as she took the drinks from Flo and handed one to Kringle.

"Wait, a humming bird flap. Did you two come in together? Are you tooogeeether?" asked Flo with her mittens in the air.

"No, no," said Ellie.

"No, no," said Kringle.

"I mean, yes we did, but no we aren't," added Ellie.

"Just friends," said Kringle.

"Just friends," said Ellie.

Flo just stood there smirking and silent.

"No, Flo. It's ain't like that. I'll tell you later. Kringle did me a favor, so I said I'd show him around the Ice Dance. That's all. We're just here as friends," said Ellie matter-of-factly.

"Got her to say it, huh Kringle?" winked Flo to Kringle. "Okay, well that there is your business and it won't be my business 'til later," winked Flo to Ellie. "She didn't tell you she was scared of dancin' did she?" asked Flo as she gave Ellie a disappointed look.

"She did," said Kringle.

"Ellie?!" Flo burst out.

"I didn't say those exact words, I said…"

"She's good, Kringle, get her out there for one of them fast drummin' ones," interrupted Flo and then she began to do a bit of the Charleston. "She usually dances all night with a mess a different fellas, so keep her close."

Kringle smiled and nodded.

"No. No I don't. Don't-don't-don't say that, don't listen to her. She's teasin' me. Flo!" said Ellie making wide eyes at Flo. "Let's move on, Kringle, you wanna see everything don't ya?"

"Sure do."

"Well, if you see any cute men out there," Flo cleared her throat, "Pastor Finn! You tell them, him, that Ellie's dance-card is filled, then tell them, him, the word Parisian and to come see me. I mean *Lord be bashful* a lady sometimes just has to ask herself to dance with these timid men of today," said Flo as she cleaned up her station.

Ellie turned to the pond to sort where she would bring Kringle next. Kringle took out a few coins and handed it to Flo for the drinks.

"No charge, you patient cat you. Oh, and hey, Kringle, you know sometimes it takes a few Parisians to warm up a hardworking gal like you have there. But bein' a pleasant man like yourself sure helps too," said Flo shooting Kringle with a finger gun and then turning to help a few new customers approaching.

Just about everyone in Miss Magnolia's class was huddled in small groups around their designated bonfire. Riggels stood by Miss Magnolia.

"All of them?" asked Riggels.

"Sure, all of them. And more, this isn't even the whole tribe of Indians you see out here," smiled Miss Magnolia. She was bundled well under many layers, but you could still tell she was petite, even for a petite woman. She looked darling, mind you.

"So will you be watching over your little Indians all night?" asked Riggels.

"Oh no. I can go; I'm not officially watching them. I'll probably just stick around until I feel sound that all these Indians know not to keep their mittens so close to the flames," said Miss Magnolia, then she turned from Riggels, took off her mitten, snapped her finger impressively and said a bit louder - "Eh-eh Oliver mittens off if you're gonna do that."

"Are you with a date tonight? Is a fella getting you some cocoa? I don't mean to bother..."

"Oh, well. Um. It's no bother, no, no I don't. I didn't know people were supposed to bring a date," Irish lied Miss Magnolia.

"Well would you like to dance later, when the band starts up?" asked Riggels.

"That'd be lovely."

"Would you like a hot cocoa now, while you're watchin' the little Indians? It's warming."

"That would be lovely as well. Yes thank you...Mr.?"

Riggels took off his hat and a glove.

"Oh, pardon me, James Thomas Riggelsworth. People just call me Riggels for some reason."

"Lorelei Elizabeth Magnolia, nice to make your acquaintance James," smiled Miss Magnolia as they shook hands.

"I'll go get you that cocoa."

"Lovely."

BOOM!

A snowball hit Riggels square in the chest. Both Riggels and Miss Magnolia turned. Miss Magnolia had her free hand in the air; her finger was up authoritatively and her eyes spoke discontent. Madison and Maggie were both pointing to two distant Indian silhouettes running into the crowd.

"They threw it," they both said.

"Rockets? I don't know, Johnny, you think that's a good idea? I mean if the sheriff catches us we'll get slaaaam-clicked for sure," said Terrance.

The Airlords stood in a circle by the bonfire warming their hands. Johnny had just finished explaining to the Airlords his new plan that would assure the Airlords a win over the Twins the next time they raced down Patton's Hill.

"Ain't no way he'll catch us." Johnny pointed to Lloyd and Elmer who were laying out the boxes of fireworks under a small tent, a fair distance from Little Island Pond. "We'll sneak real good, like we had the cloaking device on and everything, see? Anyways the sheriff loves the fireworks show; he'll be staring up at the sky like everyone else. And I'm tellin' yah gang, if we can get our hands on two rockets, just two rockets, well then we'll blast right by their Mongol Machine. Just like the real rockets on Buck Rogers' ship. Just like it!" pleaded Johnny.

The Airlords started to nod slowly in agreement.

"Roikets sh'rre vould blast us by dem twinz," muffled out Ramona. She was completely wrapped up in jackets and scarves - save her eyes.

"Hm. Ya, we could really show 'em." said Murf.

"Sure would," said Johnny.

"Sure would," said Billy.

"How you wanna do it though Johnny? I mean, the Dunce Brothers handle them fireworks and if they catch us stealing some, they'll do worse than slam-click us. So, how we ain't gonna get caught?" asked Terrance.

"We need Rudy," said Johnny as he pointed to Rudy sitting by the stage beside Pete and the Uppity Boys.

"Let's play this game here," said Kringle. Ellie and he had been walking around The Ice Dance observing but had yet to participate.

"Ooh I don't know Kringle. I can be pretty competitive and can get a dash sulky if I fail at something. I don't think I should. But you can," said Ellie. "I'll watch."

"Oh well eh-eh, see now that sounds like something I wanna see. Excuse me, sir, may we have a go?" said Kringle.

A thin gamekeeper smoking a short cigar grabbed three Raggedy Ann

217

dolls and set them down.

"Okay, see, now you gotta get all three dollies in the hole see? These three dollies here gotta fully go inside the clown's mouth there." The hole that participants had to sink the dolls in was a bright painted clown's mouth opened wide. "You get one dolly in – nothing, see? You get two dollys in – still nothing see? But three dollies, three, one-two-three? HOTDOGS! HOTDOGS! BOOM-SMACK-CLAP – fanfare and champagne – And this lovely lady here gets the big prize." Then the Thin Gamekeeper with the short cigar pointed to a large white teddy bear hanging from the ceiling. "Who will it be, who will it be?" asked the Thin Gamekeeper with the short cigar.

"You go," said Kringle as he handed Ellie a doll.

Ellie set her hot cider down, shuffled her shoulders and stretched her neck from side to side.

"Okay, Kringle, but like I said, I can get a bit bothered if I don't do well. Just warning you," said Ellie as she took the doll in her hand, threw it two inches up and caught it again, then squinted at the hole in the clown's mouth.

"Okay darling, one-two-three, BOOM-SNAP-CLAP, we want a winner," said the Thin Gamekeeper with the short cigar as a shorter Plump Gamekeeper with a long cigar came to the side of his game hut to watch Ellie toss.

"You can do it lady," said the Plump Gamekeeper in a low ashtray grumbling voice.

Ellie took a deep breath, jiggled her throwing arm, then straightened her arm out to aim, brought her arm back, stretched it out to aim again, brought it back and tossed.

THROW!

BLAM!

The first Raggedy Ann doll hit the hole, but didn't go all the way through, the dolly lay half in and half out of the hole of the clown's mouth.

"Ooh," said Kringle.

Ellie looked up to the Thin Gamekeeper in question.

"No matter, lovely lady, no matter. See, if any of your next two tosses drops that little pesky dolly in, it's still one-two-three, see? You're still in the game. Now c'mon. Big winner, big winner!" yelled the Thin Gamekeeper in hope of drawing a crowd.

"You're still in it Ellie. You can do it," said Kringle.

"Oh, I'm getting all hot now. Kringle would you hold my scarf?" said Ellie, as she handed Kringle her yellow scarf.

"Here we go, here we go; gather round, gather round. See the lovely lady win a prize," said the Thin Gamekeeper.

"Here we go lady, here we go. Send the dolly on home," encouraged the Plump Gamekeeper.

A few people stopped to watch.

"See, now my heart's going. Now I'm nervous," Ellie said.

"You got it, just think if you get it in, it would dunk Miss Winkelplex in one of those dunking tanks," smiled Kringle.

Ellie stretched her arm out, took aim, brought her arm back, stretched it again and then…

THROW!

SWOOSH!

…The second Raggedy Ann went right on through.

"Well done, well done. Miss Lovely Lady has one and a half dollies in. Must be three, must be three! One-two-three!" yelled the Thin Gamekeeper.

"Ooh darn it, I didn't knock the other one in," said Ellie and then she stomped the ground lightly with her foot. "Sir, can you not call me Lovely Lady, it's distracting me."

"Yes Ma-am, yes ma-am. How's Lucky Lady?"

"No, not that either."

"What's wrong with Lovely Lady Ellie?" said Kringle.

"I don't want to be called it, let alone shouted it."

"How about I don't yell at all for this throw?" said the Thin Gamekeeper.

"That'd be swell. Thank you," said a focused Ellie.

"I won't yell after this. STEP RIGHT UP, STEP RIGHT UP, see the Shy Lady win a prize!" said the Thin Gamekeeper as he rang a hanging bell. Then the Thin Gamekeeper and the Plump Gamekeeper turned to each other and secretly looked to be making bets on the last toss.

"You got it Ellie," said Kringle. "Pretend it's a rotten apple going right into Miss Winkelplex's mouth. Worms and all."

Ellie stretched her arm out, aimed, brought it back, stretched it out again, aimed, pulled it back and tossed.

THROW!

SMACK!

The third Raggedy Ann lay right on top of the other hanging dolly – half the dollys' arms hung out and their feet dangled inside.

"Ooh, tough luck, tough luck," said the Thin Gamekeeper as the Plump Gamekeeper handed him a dollar.

"Grrr," said Ellie, then stamped her foot down a bit harder into the frozen ground.

The few people who had stopped to watch turned and walked on.

"Another try for the Love…, the um, Luck…, the Lady?" asked the Thin Gamekeeper.

"Yes Sir, one more try," said Kringle as he put his coin down.

"Ah no, Kringle, save your money. Like I said, games just make me mad," said Ellie as she went to take her scarf from Kringle.

"Well no, Lucky Lady, I have an idea. Let me see your jacket. Give it here," said Kringle as a new set of three dolls were set down in front of Ellie.

"My jacket?"

"Ya, give it here, I think it's limiting your toss," said Kringle; then he folded the jacket with the scarf and laid them both down on the booth.

"Awe the Lady has a manager, I like it; I like it. See that's good, that's good," grumbled the Plump Gamekeeper.

Kringle then picked up one of the dollies and tied its arms and legs to one another.

Both gamekeepers nodded in approval to one another.

"Good manger," said the Thin Gamekeeper as he cheered his cigar to Kringle.

"See it ain't your aim Lucky Lady. It's these dang flailing legs and arms."

Kringle handed Ellie the balled up doll. "Try this."

"Okay, but after this - next game - you play - I'll watch," said Ellie as she took the balled up doll, stretched her shoulders and neck again and even dug her feet into the snowy ground like a baseball pitcher.

The two gamekeepers whispered a new bet to one another and then shook hands on it. The Thin Gamekeeper didn't shout a word.

Ellie took aim, pulled her arm back and...

THROW!

SWOOSH!

...The balled doll went right on through the clown's mouth hole without touching its edges.

"Hotdogs, that's it. That's one. One-two-three," grumbled and smiled the Plump Gamekeeper. The Thin Gamekeeper looked down at him unimpressed.

Kringle handed Ellie a tied up doll.

Ellie stretched her neck again, took aim again, squinted her eyes and puckered her lips, then pulled her arm back and...

THROW!

SWOOSH!

...Another balled doll went right on through the hole.

"Wow," said Ellie. She looked over at Kringle with a smile and then punched him lightly in the arm. "Wow Kringle, good idea."

Kringle winked at Ellie.

"That's two," said the Plump Gamekeeper. "Nice throw Darling. Did you see that one Ralph?"

"I saw it, I saw it. But it takes three, see? One-two-three, to be a big winner, see?" said the Thin Gamekeeper.

"Okay Annie Oakley, last one. You got it. One-two-three," said the

Plump Gamekeeper.

"I'm nervous," said Ellie to Kringle.

"You got it," said Kringle.

"STEP RIGHT UP, SEE THE..." started the Thin Gamekeeper.

"Shh," said Kringle and the Plump Gamekeeper to the thin one.

"Just doing my job," he grumbled back.

Ellie dug her feet into the brown snowy ground, she squinted, puckered, reached her arm out to take aim, brought it back, reached it out again, brought it back, then stood back straight and shook her whole body a bit, then took aim again, brought her arm back...waited...waited...and then...

THROW!

SWOOSH!

One-two-three!

"I GOT IT!" screamed Ellie as she jumped up with her fists in the air.

"YOU GOT IT!" said Kringle with a big smile.

The two looked at one another smiling and shuffling about from the win.

DING – DING – DING, went the winning bell.

"AND WE HAVE A BIG WINNER! BIG WINNER HERE. SEE THE BIG WINNER GET THE BIG PRIZE. EASY-EASY ONE-TWO-THREE! BOOM-SNAP-CLAP!" yelled the Thin Gamekeeper as he handed the Plump Gamekeeper a dollar.

"Nice work Annie." said the Plump Gamekeeper as he stuffed the dollar in his pocket.

The Thin Gamekeeper handed over the big white bear with a red bow to Ellie.

"Nice shootin' Annie," he said.

Kringle helped Ellie back into her jacket.

"You got it!" exclaimed Kringle.

"*We* got it," exclaimed Ellie; then she squeezed the bear tight. "I've never won before; I always just come close. Billy will love this."

✳

The night moved on, announcements were made about the big raffle, thank yous were given to the people who had made the whole night possible, the Uppity Boys took to the stage, and just about everyone in Hamilton was skating, skate-dancing, playing games or just gabbing at bonfires cupping warm drinks.

"Ooh nice bear," said a young lady to her date in arm as she passed by Ellie and Kringle.

"Thank you," said Ellie proudly.

"I want a bear like she has; will you win me one?" the young lady said to her date as they walked off.

"That's four compliments. Aren't you the popular one?" said Kringle.

"Well, the bear is the popular one, but you know what - I do like it," said Ellie. "I admit it. I just have never been the girl with the big bear before. It's fun. I mean I know I should be embarrassed, but I ain't."

"You don't have to feel embarrassed, why would you…"

"Kringle," said Mr. Thomson with Mrs. Thomson from the Barn-Church. "Hey-hey I better see you up there later. I better, you hear me. Hello Ellie. Nice Polar bear." He then held his skates up. "Once I put these on, I ain't taking 'em off 'till I hear you play that harmonica again."

"I think I will a bit later," said Kringle.

"Wonderful bear," said Mrs. Thomson to Ellie.

"Thank you, Mrs. Thomson. It wasn't easy to get," said Ellie with a smile. The Thomsons chuckled and moved on. Their ciders smelled like they knew the password. "Do what?" asked Ellie to Kringle.

"Oh, Pete may want me to…"

"Well, if it ain't Crackle," said one of the men from Mr. Thomson's Barn-Church.

"Kringle," said Kringle.

"Krengle, that's it - the man from up north. You be playing tonight as well Krengle?" asked the man.

"I do believe I will."

"Oo, that's fine, that's fine. Well, I'll be watching and dancin'. Not skate-dancing. Oh heck no, break my butt I would. But I'll be on the side dancing

223

just the same. Well, look at that, that's a very nice bear Miss," said the man as he walked off.

"I'm the popular one? More like you're the popular one," said Ellie. "Oo-oo, let's go visit Flo, she's waving at us, see?"

"Alright."

"What is it that all those people are asking you if you're gonna do?" asked Ellie.

"Oh well, I play a bit of the harmonica and last Sunday I played at Mr. Thomson's...."

"At his barn; the church there. Ya-ya, Pete goes there."

"Ya there. So I played a few tunes with Pete and his boys."

"The Uppity Boys," said Ellie smirking. "Well, well, well, you're gonna go up on the stage tonight?"

"I believe so, later on."

"Well, this sure is turning into something interesting of a night."

"Well, hello you two. Heck, fly a donkey and pluck a pig, tell me you did not win her that bear," said Flo as she set down two new Parisians.

"Oh no, Ellie won it," said Kringle.

"*We* won it," corrected Ellie.

Kringle and Flo were now a pretty good teasing team when it came to Ellie. They had guilted her into agreeing to join in the festivities and skate-dancing. The second Parisian helped a bit too.

Young and old, single or smitten - the people of Hamilton skated around Little Island Pond as a wonderful one. The hung lights sparkled, the air smelled of cinnamon fried dough and the Uppity Boys were tuning up to play.

The inner circle of the pond skated young girls who held hands. They would skate five girls across, as young boys practiced their skills of speed and their agility to skate under the young girls locked arms.

The outer circle skated older couples that glided at a slower pace. They skated hand in hand, talking, laughing and occasionally cold kissing.

Kringle and Ellie sat on a bench lacing up their skates. They had left Ellie's big white bear with Flo to gab to."

"Do you know how to skate Kringle?" asked Ellie.

"Mm, hm. I can go backwards and everything. How about you?"

"Course, I'm a New England girl. We gotta know. I can go backwards too."

But once Ellie and Kringle took to the ice it was clear that they had different ideas of what good skating was. Ellie glided onto Little Island Pond like a ballerina, while Kringle more chopped down onto the ice like a chef chopping at a head of lettuces.

"Whoa," Kringle said. "Whoop I got it, wait-wait, whoop. Wait, nope... yup, I got it."

"I thought you said you knew how to skate," laughed Ellie, while she skated backwards watching Kringle stabilize himself.

"I am. I'm skating." Kringle found his groove. It was choppy and uncertain, but he was moving forward just the same.

"If you say so."

Kringle skated up to Ellie and grabbed her arm for support. Ellie almost toppled over; she began to laugh.

"Why are you laughing? You're laughing at me aren't you? I'm a good skater; I just got to get comfortable."

"I'm not sure I believe you. Here, let me," Ellie took Kringle's arm and stabilized him as they coasted off together. They were slower than the other couples. The young boys zipped by them almost knocking Kringle to the ice.

"So, where are you from anyways Kringle?" asked Ellie.

"Oh, up north."

"Maine?"

"More north. It's a small town." Kringle was skating better. His face read deep concentration. Kringle could now look up and not at his feet.

"Oh, Canada? Are you from up there in Canada?"

"Oh, no. More north."

"You can't go anymore north Kringle. 'More north' are those ice territories. I hear people live there, but I hear those people are like ice Indians. Free from the world. You aren't an ice Indian are you Kringle?

Kringle laughed.

"Oh no. I'm not an ice Indian."

"Well, where then? Are you embarrassed to tell me?"

"No, no, I'm not embarrassed. I just stopped telling people because no one's ever heard of it and no one's ever been there. Most people don't think it's real. I'm from a small town up north thats sits in between two rivers - the um, whoa." Kringle wobbled and pulled a bit at Ellie's arm, but then stabilized again. "The um, Chena River and the Tanana River. It's called…"

Four young boys slipped by both sides of Ellie and Kringle. This startled Kringle. He slipped, did an awkward three-sixty and fell down on his butt.

"Ouch," Kringle let out.

"Ooh, are you okay? HEY! Slow down! You're gonna get someone killed," snipped Ellie in her papa stance.

"Sorry lady."

"Sorry Mister."

"Sorry."

The young boys shouted as they skated off.

Looking up to Ellie, Kringle said, "It's called North Pole."

"The North Pole?" Ellie repeated.

"No, just North Pole. But not many people live there."

"North Pole, huh? Wow, I've never met anyone from that far away. It's just so far. You know, I heard once that the sun leaves there for months. And so it's dark all the time. Even at lunch time. That true?"

"That is true. Night and day become the same."

"Wow. Imagine that."

Ellie helped Kringle up.

"Thank you Miss Boone."

Kringle brushed himself off; Ellie helped. The two started skating again.

"What's nice is, you can have bonfires like those ones…" Kringle pointed to all the bonfires circled around Little Island Pond. "…in the day time."

"Doesn't it get so, so cold there though?"

"Sure. But you get used to it."

"I can't even imagine a place colder than here. Does your family live there?"

"They do, ya."

"You think you'll ever go back there?"

"Oh sure. It's wonderful up there. It's full of nature – huge moose, deer, little foxes, and seals, even whales. And it's very beautiful. My heart does like to live in places where the place speaks directly to my heart. I also like how the sun plays by its own rules up at North Pole. It allows you to break out of the everyday hustle and bustle that people seem to be living in these days."

"Mm, that sounds nice. But I wonder if I could take not seeing the sun for so long."

"You do start to miss her. But a magical thing happens up there and I think it happens there because someone somewhere feels bad for us," Kringle was beginning to skate with a more realized ease. "Us not having the sun as much and all."

"What's that?"

"It's called the aurora borealis."

"Whoa, how the heck do you spell that?"

"I don't know actually. A-roar-ah."

"Bor-ee-al-is. Did I say it right? It sounds like a giant big foot polar bear or a giant seal monster squid. Watch out, here comes the AURORRAHH BORRRR-EALIS RUN!" joked Ellie.

Kringle and Ellie both laughed.

"No, that's the Yetti and he's a whole other story. The aurora borealis are rivers of green, purple, and pink lights in the sky. They show up and flash and waver and move all around. They just light up the darkness."

"Like a rainbow?"

"Like if a rainbow was washing down a river. But the river was in the sky."

"I wanna see that. How far is your home; how far is North Pole and these rivers of color in the sky?"

"Far, far away, but not far enough for an ocean to get in the way. Maybe I'll take you and the boys there some day."

Ellie looked at Kringle and gave him a small smile.

"Ya well, that would be quite impossible," said Ellie.

TAP, TAP, TAP.

Everyone stopped skating to look towards the stage. Pete and the Uppity Boys stood ready to perform as Mr. McManus and Miss Winkelplex stood at the center microphone. Mrs. McManus with the Twins stood on the side of the stage, with straight posture, smiling.

"Can they hear me?" asked Mr. McManus to Miss Winkelplex.

The microphone began to slightly feed back.

She nodded, "Yes."

"Can you hear me?" Mr. McManus then asked all of Little Island Pond. Everyone shouted, "Yes."

"Fine, fine. Well okay everyone. How are we all tonight?"

Everyone cheered and clapped.

"Well, thank you all for coming down. Tonight looks grand." Mr. McManus opened a note handed to him by Miss Winkelplex and put his spectacle over his right eye. "Right then, let's see here. Thank you to the Notre Dame Sisters, Sister Barbara and Sister Susan for their lovely decorations, to Mrs. Donnally's seventh grade class for the wonderful banner and to all the volunteers of course. Thank you, thank you. What else here?" Mr. McManus read as if he was completely disinterested in what he was saying. "A big thanks to the Topsfield Fair for bringing over these wonderful gaming booths. Thanks Tom. Thanks Fred. Thanks um…" Miss Winkelplex whispered something to Mr. McManus. "Thanks Howe. Thank you to Sheriff Jones, Pastor Finn and, of course, all of you for coming…here…tonight. Okay then. Done. Now, moving on. I just have a few announcements."

Mr. McManus took off his spectacle and squared his shoulders to the crowd.

"I have magnificent, outstanding news, actually the most sensational news that could be. On December twenty-fourth, at our yearly Winter Auction, which will be held in Town Hall at seven o'clock sharp - for those of you who don't know and will be your first time. Oh, and do try and not be late. It's rude. We will be blessed with gifts from far over the ocean. Far, far away. Distant lands. Toy makers from the European court sides have agreed to make our town of Hamilton, Massachusetts - original, absolutely special and most of all very *exotic* TOYS!"

A few people clapped, but not many. Many people at the Ice Dance didn't attend the yearly Winter Auction. It was much too expensive. The Winter Auction was more for fortunate city folk to come to and spend their money.

Mr. McManus went to a booming voice.

"TOYS FOR BABIES, TOYS FOR SMALL CHILDREN, TOYS FOR LARGE CHILDREN. EVEN TOYS FOR ADULTS. THESE TOYS WILL BE FOUND NOWHERE ELSE. MAKE SURE YOU ARE THE ENVY OF ALL. DON'T BE THE ONLY ONE WITHOUT THIS SPECIAL, SPECIAL OPPORTUNITY TO HAVE WHAT EVERY CHILD HOPES TO HAVE. TOYS!"

The microphone began to feed back more from Mr. McManus' loud display.

"A-hem. So make sure you save up your money and come down and bid. You can see some of these toys on display at *Bonne Affaire* down town. Okay, that seems good. I think that's everything. Oh, and don't forget to stick around at seven o'clock for the *Bonne Affaire*, Ice Dance fireworks show! Um, thank you. Good bye."

With that said, the Uppity Boys began to play. Everyone clapped. Mr. McManus thought the clapping was for him, but it was more because he had finished speaking and the music had swelled up.

The Uppity Boys started with a shuffling uppity blues. The teenagers rushed to get their skates on; they liked the fast blues. At Mr. Thomson's barn they had started calling it Rocking Blues because of how much it made the barn move and shake about.

"There that man goes on again about his dang toys. I swear I could recite every daft word he says in that speech. I've only heard it about five times a day for the last week," snipped Ellie as the two began skating again.

"How has the reaction *been* with the new toys?"

"Just like I said it would be. Rich elitist type people come in and complain and complain and then complain some more. I swear all these grown men and women coming in...their parents just *did not* do a good job. And like I told you would happen, I have to, daily mind you, explain to normal folk that there is no way in high heaven they will be able to buy them toys. But this one little hen comes in with all her hen friends following behind and she just throws a tantrum. A tantrum like a little child does. So Miss Winkelplex goes and allows her to buy one that wasn't to be sold."

"Buy which ones?"

"Oh, these little ships."

Kringle stopped skating.

"You sold those? They're gone? They-they were for display only."

"Ya I know that's what I'm getting at. But she just whined her way into getting her way. You know that type?"

"So they're gone?"

"No, we still got 'em. I think we ship them to her next Friday. But let's not talk about this stuff Kringle. Everything to do with that place makes me tight these days. Especially those toys and all the poor children drooling over them."

"Sure, okay. But just to be clear those ships are still in the store then?"

"Ya, they're still there. Why do you ask?"

Kringle began skating again.

"Oh, I just liked them that's all."

"Ya. They're expensive though Kringle. You can't afford 'em. I'm just saying."

"Ya."

The Uppity Boys were going into a slower number. Everyone stopped circling the pond and instead embraced to the love song like a normal dancehall dance.

Kringle stopped skating and bowed to Ellie like a proper English gentlemen.

"Care for a dance milady?" he said.

"Sure, why not," said Ellie and the two modestly embraced.

"So what about you, Ellie?"

"What about what?"

"What's your story, if you don't mind me asking?"

"Not much, really. You mean about my old husband and all?"

"Well, no I just meant..."

"Well, I might as well tell ya, because around here someone probably already has, so I guess I'll just be getting your facts straight. Around here I'm known as the woman who couldn't keep her husband around. The divorcee."

"I've never heard anyone say that."

"Ya, well you're new. I know what people say about me; they're not as clever hiding their hearsay as much as they think they are. Simple humans gossip; that's a simple human fact. Anyways, here goes. I'm from around here, met my husband – Jesse – the male hussy, in the fourth grade. We got married, we had the boys, he got bored, he left, and he never came back. It was very embarrassing. Still is. Then there was the gossip and well, well, I can't believe I'm telling a lost hobo-fireman all this."

Ellie and Kringle locked eyes and laughed a bit.

"So, he's remarried a rich land owner's daughter. I don't know her name. I don't wanna know her name. I'd probably punish every woman I met that shared it. I just refer to her as 'The Bluenose'. He'll be all set with money and a happy family and all that good stuff. But I don't mind him leaving me really, I don't wanna be with a man that don't wanna be with me. That's like choosing to eat food you hate, but worse. No, but what really makes me pray is – what about the boys? How'd he just leave them?"

"Don't know. But Ellie you do a great job raising those two fine boys on your own while working a job and getting three meals on the table like you do and all."

"Well, thanks, Kringle, but I'm not doing anything that special. Or looking for praise."

"Oh, I think you are doing something very special. And do deserve praise. It's hard these days, like you said."

"Mm," said Ellie, not really agreeing with Kringle.

The slow song ended, Ellie and Kringle dropped their embrace. Pete, seeing Kringle and Ellie from the small stage, turned to the Uppity Boys and cued another slow to begin. More of a slow jazz blues; it started with a soft trumpet.

"One more dance, then we visit Flo?" asked Kringle.

"Okay. Sure."

The two embraced again and slightly skated.

"So anyways, he's gone, I'm here and that's my story. I'm like a nun, but not by choice," laughed Ellie.

"Well frankly I wasn't asking you about him. I wanted to ask you about you. I wanna know you better. I wanna know more about you than I can just see myself. So okay, I'm gonna fire you off some questions, ya?"

"What do you mean?"

"Do you like dogs or cats better?"

"Um, dogs, they're helpful. Cat's are smart though. I love how they're convinced they're tough and not cute. So I say both. I won't choose."

"Chicken, beef or fish."

"Beef," Ellie smiled; she liked this game.

"Can you fish?"

"Can you? You can barely skate."

"What are you scared of?"

"Men," said Ellie with a bashful laugh. "But only between the ages of twenty and forty."

"Well, okay um, do you like the pictures?"

"I've only seen a few. I like Mary Pickford. She's darling. I'd like to be her."

"Where would you live if you couldn't live here?"

"Where the rainbows flow like rivers in the sky," said Ellie and then she laughed again. Ellie seemed to be enjoying herself. She seemed to be living life – not fighting it. "I don't know. Where would you?"

"Well, I came here, so, so far it's here. So is Ellie your real name or is it short for something?"

"Ugh, yes, it's short for Eleanor, but I hate that name."

"That's a nice name."

"No, it isn't. You don't have to be polite Kringle. Have an opinion."

"I'm not buttering your toast. I like it."

"No, it, it has just such a gloom to it. El-ean-or. Mm-mm, I don't like it."

"How do you mean gloom?"

"Well for instance, what it rhymes with, okay ready, um…" Ellie looked up in thought. "Snore and bore, and chore and poor. Then there's floor, gore, and of course - war. All those are bad things. It's just gloomy that's all. I wish I had a name like Mary."

"But it also rhythms with other words like…soar, adore, more and yours."

Ellie looked up, but said nothing. She liked that; she had never heard anything like that before. And she had never heard such words come from a man when speaking about her. It was nice. It was romantic. And Ellie didn't know romantic.

"Well, that's polite of you to say Kringle."

It was slight or maybe not even true, but Kringle felt that Ellie touched him a little tighter and brought him in a tiny bit closer. He thought he could feel her fall into him just a tiny bit.

The slow number ended and one of those Rocking Blues picked up. Without skates on, Flo slid right into Kringle and Ellie.

BLAM!

"Ellie, be a Momma bird and help her chick fly," said Flo pleading.

"Whatever do you mean?" said Ellie.

"Cover the booth for me huh? Just for a tune or four?" pleaded Flo with her best pleading face.

232

"Hello, Ellie."

Ellie turned and saw Pastor Finn skating up.

"Pastor Finn. Hello," said Ellie.

"He's my dance partner," whispered Flo into Ellie's ear as she pulled Ellie down to reach.

"And you are?" inquired Pastor Finn.

"Kringle," said Kringle.

"Ah yes, the man who saved the child from the train," said Pastor Finn.

"And the cat," added Flo.

"And a cat," added Pastor Finn.

"Pastor Finn! Nice to finally meet you. Yes, sir, yes. What a day that was. Oh-a, Pete and I have been working hard on your…" Kringle forgot for a moment that Pastor Finn couldn't know that Pete and he were crafting his cross and not some special ministry in Italy. "…Oh wait never mind, never mind. Sorry I was thinking of something else."

"Ah well, it'd be nice to see you some Sunday Kringle. Come by the church; consider yourself invited. An open door to the one that saves children," said Pastor Finn.

"And the cat," said Flo.

"And a cat. Sorry," said Pastor Finn.

"Could ya Ellie," pleaded Flo.

"Sure."

"Thanks, you Indian goddess you. Okay lets get me some feet-swords," said Flo as she took Pastor Finn's hand and began pulling him in a slippery sprint to the skate booth.

The Airlords laid on their stomachs behind Sheriff Jones' police car. Even Rudy. The Airlords were spying on Lloyd and Elmer, who were setting up fireworks away from all the festivities.

"Okay Airlords, we gotta get those Rocket Boosters," instructed Murf.

"Affirmative," said Johnny.

"You see that tent there?" said Murf.

"Ye I de," said Ramona.

"It's kinda blurry," said Terrence, "But, ya, I think I see it."

"Sure Murf, ya," said Billy.

"Rrr-Woof," barked Rudy.

"Okay. See, that's where the Rocket Boosters we need are stashed. Tell them Johnny," instructed Murf.

The Airlords pulled back and crouched in a circle.

"Okay Airlords here's the plan. We tell Rudy here…"

All the Airlords looked at Rudy and with confused excitement Rudy stomped his paw in the snow and made a low – *Woof*.

"…that's right Rudy. Well, we'll tell Rudy to go fetch two of them rocket boosters, he'll sneak over and bring them back to us. Easy as eatin' pudding."

"You mean, like the same Rocket Booster's that Buck Rogers got strapped to *The Observation Ship*, when Buck and Wilma…" Terrance made quotation signs with his fingers, "…set out to find and destroy the terrible Mongol Machine? Or do you mean more like the Torpedo Tubes or maybe the Rocket Tubes?" Again Terrance made quotation signs with his hand. "Strapped to the first of the American big Rocket Cruisers?" asked Terrence.

"How do you remember all that?" asked Murf.

"I got bad eyes, but a good brain," said Terrance.

"Like the Rocket Tubes," replied Johnny. "But on land."

"But the Rocket Cruiser is much bigger than our Battle Cruiser. That much power might launch it…." Terrance was interrupted.

"To fantastic speeds," blurted Murf.

"Whoa!" said all of the Airlords at once.

"Ya. Fantastic speeds. That's the *only* way we'll beat the Mongol Machine and teach them Twins," said Murf. Then he pantomimed a ship blasting through space with his hand.

"Bet, how ve genna get Rudy ta jest go 'n' get 'em den?" asked Ramona.

"Rudy does it all the time with Pete at the yard. He gets Pete all sorts of stuff. I've seen 'em," said Johnny.

"I've seem 'em too," added Billy.

"E'ell. V'ell, all rrigheet den," said Ramona then she spat in the snow.

"Rudy," Johnny said to Rudy.

"Woof," Rudy responded back to Johnny, then stomped his paw on the ground again.

"We're gonna fetch…fetch Rudy…we're gonna fetch this," Johnny smoothed out some snow and with his finger drew a rocket. "This here Rudy.

Rocket, Rudy, rocket. Fetch rocket." Then Johnny showed how big the rocket was with his hands. He then pointed to where Lloyd and Elmer stood with their backs to the Airlords. "Ya boy? Ya?"

Rudy did a twirl and stomped both his paws down showing he understood and was ready for his mission.

"Okay boy. Go fetch. Go fetch," said Johnny.

Rudy crouched low and began to make his way to the Dunce Brothers. The Airlords crouched back down to watch under the sheriff's car.

Lloyd and Elmer lit the annual Ice Dance fireworks every season. They made sure to always have a comfortable, yet not exactly safe, set up. All the fireworks were placed inside a tent behind them. In front of them was a small campfire. Lloyd and Elmer sat on milk crates warming cans of beans over the campfire. They laughed with snorts and spits. In front of them was an area where the snow had been shoveled clear. It had tubes set up to launch the fireworks from.

Rudy was low; he crawled cautiously. Rudy looked as if he was an Army dog from WWI bringing imperative information back to his battalion. The Airlords watched from fifteen feet away.

"He's almost there," said Johnny.

"What if he gets caught?" asked Terrance.

"Geet ca'oight doin' vhat?" asked Ramona. "A dahg can't get ca'oight valkin' roun'. D'ell dink he's jast lookin' fer food."

"Looks like he's got something," said Billy.

"You guys can really see that far?" asked Terrance.

"Ya, he's right behind them Dunce Brothers now. Right behind them. They don't even see or hear him," said Murf. "I think he's got something. Wait! He's coming back, he's coming back!"

All the Airlords crouched in a circle ready for Rudy's return.

Rudy rounded the police car. He had a full baloney sandwich in his mouth. He looked proud and placed it in front of Johnny. Then Rudy stomped his paw onto the ground.

"Wait, is that it?" asked Murf.

"Oi a sandvich?" perplexed Ramona.

"Aw Rudy. Um, no boy, no no," said Johnny kindly.

Rudys tilted his head.

Johnny picked up the sandwich.

"Okay boy, bring back, bring back. Fetch…" Johnny tried to draw a better rocket in the snow. "…fetch rocket, fetch rocket. Bring back sandwich, fetch rocket."

Rudy tilted his head the opposite way. He stomped his paw on the ground showing he understood. He took the sandwich in his mouth, crouched low and proceeded back toward the Dunce Brothers.

Lloyd and Elmer were bickering around their campfire.

"Don't spill yer beans again Elmer? Ya gotta watch 'em," said Lloyd.

"I am watchin' 'em," said Elmer.

"Naw you're watchin' the fire not your beans."

"Worry about your own beans."

"I am worrying about my own beans, 'cause if you spill your beans in the fire, you're gonna be askin' me to share my beans."

"No I ain't gonna."

"Ya-huh."

"Nu-uh."

Elmer repositioned himself on his milk crate and almost lost the can he had balancing on his spatula.

Rudy was low and quiet. He was just upon the Dunce Brothers. He placed the sandwich down where he had taken it and began to back up. The sandwich was now a little wet with drool. The campfire spit. Sparks and smoke took to the air. Rudy sniffed, blinked, closed his eyes, sniffed again, shook his head, then let out a big – sneeze.

Lloyd and Elmer spun around.

"Hey look," said Elmer.

"A dog."

"Ya, a dog. Well hey. You cold boy? You hungry dog?"

"That dog looks familiar."

"All dogs look like that."

"Suppose so. Get-get dog."

"AW DANG IT!" Elmer's can of beans fell into the fire. "I can save it, I

236

can save it."

"I told you!"

"Wait no, I got it. I got it." Using his spatula, Elmer scooped the spilled beans back into his can, along with red-hot coals and ash. "See I got it." He put his spatula under the can and brought it out of the fire. Using his hat as an oven mitt, Elmer brought the can up to his eyes, mixed the beans, coal and ash around and tasted it. "S'perfect. Ooh, but it's burning my mouth."

Lloyd rolled his eyes and looked behind himself.

"Huh, the dog's gone," he said.

Back behind the police car the Airlords were crouched and huddled ready for Rudy's return.

"Oh no," said Terrance.

"Naw offense bit I don't dink you're drawin' dem rockets good enough for Rudy. Ya?", said Ramona as Rudy placed down Lloyd's thermos of coffee in front of Johnny.

"Huh?" said Johnny.

"Huh?" said Murf.

"Let me," said Billy.

Billy drew a rocket in the snow with fire coming out of its boosters.

"Least he's gettin' closer ye know? I mean he could'a brought v'ne of dem Dunce Brathahs back," said Ramona then she spit behind herself again. And smirked at the boys.

Back on the beat, Rudy approached the Dunce Brothers. He placed the thermos down and backed up a few steps. Lloyd stood, stretched, took out a flashlight from his pocket, switched it on and put it on the ground, pointing it inside the firework tent. He then turned and saw Rudy crouched low a few feet back.

"That dog is back," Lloyd said.

Elmer turned.

"Hey dog. Guess what? Soon your big sensitive ears are gonna be a ringin' like you dropped a church bell," said Elmer as he stood up and, along with Lloyd, crawled inside the fireworks tent. Both men came out carrying boxes. They walked past the small fire and over to the tubes set up in the snow cleared area. They then hunched over and began to unpack the boxes.

Rudy approached the flashlight. Standing over it he stared down at it.

The flashlight looked like the picture Johnny and Billy had been drawing. And it did have fire coming out of one end. Rudy looked over at the Dunce Brothers, then he looked over at the police car and at ten little eyes glistening in the bold moonlight. Rudy thought some more. He tilted his head left to right. He even made a quiet whiney sound from all his confusion. Rudy had decided - *This must be the item his friends wanted.* Rudy leaned over it and opened his jaw to pick it up. But Rudy stopped. Slowly, Rudy looked to where the flashlight shined. Inside the small tent were rockets on top of rockets on top of rockets. Rudy's eyes widened. He rose from the flashlight, turned to the tent and crawled inside. *Bingo*, he thought.

"Wait, where did Rudy go?" said Terrance squinting. "I don't see his blur anymore."

"He's in that small tent," said Murf.

"That's where the rockets are," said Johnny.

"Ah, wet-sheep-turd, dis is making me fidgety," said Ramona. Then she pulled her scarf down and spit one last time.

"Oh no, look, the Dunce Brothers are heading toward the tent," said Billy.

Inside the tent Rudy had two rockets in his jaw. His eyes gazed out of the tent. And his ears turned toward crunching sounds in the snow. *Those big dumb ones are approaching*, Rudy thought.

"What do you want to get next, Lloyd?" asked Elmer.

"Let's get those big rockets," said Lloyd.

"Okay," said Elmer as he entered the small tent.

The Airlords' eyes were wide; they all had mittens over their mouths. Ramona's mouth was already covered with a scarf, so she covered her eyes.

Rudy hid behind boxes and rockets.

Elmer crawled inside and grabbed a few of the biggest rockets, then handed them back to Lloyd outside the tent. Then Elmer saw it. Something odd. Something out of place. Something small. Something furry.

Rudy's tail.

It was sticking out from behind Rudy's hiding spot.

"Psst, hey is that you doggy dog?" asked Elmer.

Rudy's tail disappeared from sight.

Elmer looked over his shoulder, handing Lloyd a few more rockets, "Lloyd that dog is in here."

"What are you laying down?"

"The dog. He's in here!"

"Is he peeing on the fireworks?"

"I don't think so."

"Well, get him out of there. If he eats one, he could explode. I've seen it happen."

"Wow that's something. Hey doggy dog. Hey you get outta here." There was silence. "I said hey dog. Dog. I know you're there."

Rudy peeked at Elmer from behind a few boxes.

"I see you…c'mon out of there. And don't eat any fireworks or pee on 'em. Ya hear me? He ain't comin' Lloyd."

"We'll drag 'im out. It's just a dog," said Lloyd.

With that Elmer crawled deeper into the tent.

The Airlords gasped.

"What? What happened?" asked Terrance.

"He's caught," said Johnny.

The Airlords watched as Elmer disappeared into the tent. Lloyd watched from the outside. The Airlords could see Lloyd shouting, but they couldn't make out what he was saying.

The tent wiggled. Then it wiggled some more.

"C'mon Rudy, you can do it," whispered Billy.

"Oi, if he goes 'n' bites one of dem, I bet de'll go get the dogcatcher to slam-click 'im," whispered Ramona.

The tent jolted. Then it jolted some more.

"Look," said Murf.

Lloyd bent down. He looked to be hollering up a good one. He too crawled inside the small tent.

The tent bounced. It bounced some more.

All the Airlords gasped. Then gasped some more.

The small tent started moving all about as if it was having a fit. It moved forward - then stopped. It moved back - then stopped. It moved to the left, right by where the fire pit still burned – then it spun in a circle and began to go crazy.

239

The Airlords were flabbergasted.

"Would you look at that?" said Johnny.

"What? What's going on?" asked Terrance squinting.

"C'mon Rudy, you can do it," said Billy.

"Ya c'mon Rudy-boy. C'mon," added Ramona.

"He'll show 'em," encouraged Murf.

It jiggled, it wiggled and then all of a sudden – it stopped.

There was silence, other than the faint sound of the Uppity Boys playing back at the Ice Dance.

Rudy dashed out with two big rockets in his mouth. The tent continued to move sporadically. Rudy sprinted. Rudy dashed. Rudy came around the side of the police car sliding in the snow. He dropped the two rockets in front of Billy.

"Good boy Rudy," said Johnny as he petted Rudy's head and then stuffed the two big rockets down the back of his pants.

"Oh, there he is," said Terrance. "Hey Rudy, how'd it go?"

"Look," said Billy pointing at the tent.

Lloyd and Elmer ripped out of the tent, both with their guns out. They frantically pointed them to the west, then to the east, south and finally north. The Airlords ducked and peeked. They could see the Dunce Brothers quickly put their guns down and straighten their clothes and hair, as Mr. McManus approached them.

"And what do we have here?" said a low booming voice.

The Airlords turned to see Sheriff Jones standing behind them. The Airlords quickly stood. Johnny did his best to hide the tails of the rockets poking out from behind his pants.

"Now tell me children, you weren't about to take *my* car out for a joy ride like you did Mr. McManus' were you children?" said Sheriff Jones sternly.

"No, Sir," they all cadenced.

"Well, then, what the devil are you doing over here then?"

"We-we-we wanted to see them set up the fireworks," Billy let out cautiously.

"Well, this is too close. Too dangerous. Why don't you all head back to the pond?" said Sheriff Jones.

"Yes, Sir," they cadenced again.

"And Johnny…you're Murf right…in fact all of you…no more driving

240

cars. You got me? Just stay away from them until you're taller," said Sheriff Jones once again sternly, leaning forward, pointing his finger at each of them. He then leaned back and let out a little smile. "Now get before I arrest you all and you miss the show."

"Yes, Sir," said the Airlords as they ran off.

✳

Miss Magnolia's class had packed snow all around Mr. Riggelsworth, all the way up to his trousers. He couldn't move an inch.

"He's a real snowman, Miss Magnolia," said Maggie as she patted down the snow around Mr. Riggelsworth's feet.

"Aren't you freezing?" Miss Magnolia said with an endearing smile.

"Oh heavens no, the cocoa's warming my insides," said Mr. Riggelsworth. "May I have another sip?"

Miss Magnolia held both their cups and gave Mr. Riggelsworth a warm sip.

"You don't have to do that, you know?" added Miss Magnolia.

"As long as you stay put, I'll stay put," said Mr. Riggelsworth.

"Stop talking Mister, you're breaking things up," said Oliver as he patched the breaking snow around Mr. Riggelsworth's stomach.

"Sorry little Indian," Mr. Riggelsworth said back.

✳

"We'll all be like, Ameeeerican royalty. You and me. Me...and...you. I can be a queen and you can be a queen too. No. No. We'll be princesses, yes, yes princesses. I always wanted to be a princess," said Miss Winkelplex as she swayed this way and that. Drunk.

Both Miss Winkelplex and Mrs. McManus stood on the side of the stage waiting for the Uppity Boys to finish their number so they could pick the winning ticket in the raffle.

"Honey, don't you think you should stop drinking?" asked Mrs. McManus as she tried to take Miss Winkelplex's Parisian from her.

"What?" Miss Winkelplex pulled her drink back from Mrs. McManus spilling some of it in the snow. "Oh you spilled it. Bah. You can't be a princess now. Only me."

The Uppity Boys finished their song; the skaters turned to the stage and applauded. Pete took a few steps back from the microphone to allow Mrs. McManus and Miss Winkelplex to announce the raffle.

Mrs. McManus held the bucket of tickets. Miss Winkelplex reached for the microphone, but hit the microphone stand off balance. When it teetered back it hit her in the forehead.

BLAM!

"OUCH! STUPID THING," Miss Winkelplex said through the microphone. "Hit me will you? I'll hit you. You, you, stupid thing." Miss Winkelplex swatted at the microphone, but missed.

Mrs. McManus put a hand on Miss Winkelplex's shoulder and whispered into her ear.

"Let's do the raffle my princess," she said.

Miss Winkelplex looked annoyed at Mrs. McManus.

"I know what to do, don't tell me what to…oh wait you called me princess, I love you," responded a three-sheets-to-the-wind Miss Winkelplex.

Everyone at the Ice Dance watched with disbelief at the performance. Back at the cider booth, Ellie gripped Kringle's arm with both her hands. Neither of them could believe Miss Winkelplex's display.

"Hello, everyone, it's time for the Ice Raffle," whispered Mrs. McManus into Miss Winkelplex's ear.

"*I know, I know,* I know what to say," said Miss Winkelplex. Then she tried to stand up straighter, trying to stand to what she believed was a more royal stance. "Llllisten up my devoted subjects. It is time for the rrr-rrr-rrr," Miss Winkelplex stopped.

"Raffle, Dear," whispered Mrs. McManus.

"RRRAFFLE!" shouted out Miss Winkelplex, then she began to giggle on Mrs. McManus' shoulder.

"Well this night has taken a fun turn. Does this happen every year?" asked Kringle to Ellie.

"Lord no. But it sure is interesting," said Ellie.

With their skates still on, Flo and Pastor Finn tiptoed up to the cider booth.

"Someone plug Jesus' ears before He starts sendin' lightening down," said Flo. Pastor Finn tilted his head like Rudy at Flo's comment. He had trouble understanding Flo.

"I know," said Ellie. "This is rich."

The crowd watched as Mrs. McManus helped Miss Winkelplex find the birdcage that had all the raffle names inside with her wandering hand.

"Well, I know someone who will be visiting me in the confession booth next Sunday," said Pastor Finn.

"Don't get cocky," said Flo, then winked and shot Pastor Finn with her finger-gun.

"Fifteen, no wait, sixteen. Is that a five or a six?" said Miss Winkelplex.

"That's eighteen," corrected Mrs. McManus.

"I know, I know. I can read. Okay, ready, eighteen, four, twenty-three," slurred Miss Winkelplex.

"That's twenty-eight."

"Okay, wait, let's start over. Eighteen, four, twenty-eight…um," continued Miss Winkelplex.

"She's wet," said Kringle.
"Soaked," said Ellie.

Miss Winkelplex had finally gotten all the numbers out – with the continued help of Mrs McManus. Ramona's mother Mrs. Grey was the winner. The prize was a small canoe that Mr. McManus had Pete fix last summer when it was dumped at the dump. However Mr. and Mrs. Grey had no use for a canoe, especially during the winter. And they had no means to bring it home. Awkwardly they both took a side and waddled it off the stage.

The Uppity Boys came back to the stage.

"Excuse me, pardon me," said Pete modestly into the microphone.

"Yay, Honest Pete!" screamed someone from the ice.

"Well, for this next song we would like to ask a new member of this here town to come up. He's gonna play his harmonica for us all. Mr. Kringle, I see you there. Come on up."

"Well, slap my bum and call me a race horse," blurted out Flo as she looked at Kringle grinning.

"Well, go up," said Ellie pushing Kringle. She was warm from the Parisians.

"Alright then," said Kringle as a few people applauded him to the stage.

The Uppity Boys started up the tune. The beat had an upbeat shuffle, much like the sound of a train. It almost sounded as if *Betsy Bound* was rolling past town. Kringle modestly walked onto the stage and pulled his harmonica out of his breast pocket. He exchanged nods with the Uppity Boys and Pete.

The song was in full swing.

Pete sang…

*"Lynn, Lynn the city of sin
You never come out the way you went in*

*Lynn, Lynn the city of sin
It's the worst damn town that you've ever been in."*

The townspeople skating on the pond tried to execute their best *Flea Hop, Varsity Drag, Balboa* and *Collegiate Shag* on the ice, while the more experienced skaters did the *Partner Charleston* with one person skating forward and one backwards. The tune was so fun and energetic that even the people not on the ice were dancing.

Kringle approached Pete's microphone and proceeded to solo. The townspeople cheered and danced, smiled and laughed.

"He's good Ellie," said Flo. "Like real good."

Pastor Finn was bobbing his head and smiling.

"Seems like it," said Ellie with a smile.

The drums were banging, the crowd was jumping and Kringle was thrilling them all.

Miss Winkelplex was also cutting a sloppy *Charleston*. She jumped back on stage and began to dance all around. Each time Kringle soloed, Miss Winkelplex stood to his side, pretending that she was the one with the harmonica. The Uppity Boys exchanged looks about Miss Winkelplex, but not one of them had the authority to tell her to stop. The tune played on and Miss Winkelplex danced on. Ellie also watched with worry every time Miss Winkelplex approached Kringle.

The shuffling number had a big finish and as the song crescendoed, Miss Winkelplex raised her arms and eyes to the sky grinning, drooling and laughing out loud. On the last hit, Miss Winkelplex did a little hop in the air, spun around, saw Kringle in front of her, grabbed his head and laid a big kiss on him.

Kringle looked dumbfounded. Ellie saw the kiss from the cider booth; her happy expression dropped. Kringle took a few steps back. Ellie took a few steps back. Kringle looked over at Ellie. Ellie was staring at Kringle. Miss Winkelplex staggered off stage laughing. A perplexed Pete started up the next number.

"Ellie girl, that wasn't his fault you know," said Flo leaning on the front of the cider booth.

"I'm gonna head home Flo," said Ellie.

"Ellie dear, that wasn't his fault there. You know this."

"I'm heading home Flo," said Ellie as she walked over to the fire pit where Miss Magnolia and an almost fully snow covered Mr. Riggelsworth were standing. "Miss Magnolia, have you seen my boys?" said Ellie with controlled anxiousness.

"Yes, Miss Boone, absolutely. They just showed up over there," said Miss Magnolia detecting a problem inside Ellie's soul.

Ellie's insides were on fire and she didn't fully know why. Her stomach felt as if she had drunk spoiled milk. It twisted and turned. Ellie approached the Airlords who were talking a few feet away from the bonfire.

"Boys, come with me," said Ellie sternly.

"Where?" said Johnny.

"Just come with me now. NOW boys. I'm not fooling around!" said Ellie sharply. She took Billy's hand and started walking toward the entrance of the Ice Dance. Johnny followed.

"What's going on?" asked Johnny.

"Ya Momma what's going on?" repeated Billy.

"We're leaving!" said Ellie.

"We can't leave!" pleaded the Boone boys. "The fireworks are about to start!"

"We're leaving," said Ellie.

They were coming up on the entrance way.

"Why?" pleaded the Boone boys once again.

"Don't boys! Don't! I can't be tested right now," said Ellie as they passed under the welcome sign.

"But I don't wanna. I wanna see the fireworks," pouted Billy.

"This is crummy Ma. Why are you dragging us out?" said a sulking Johnny.

Ellie stayed quiet.

Behind them they heard it…

SWOOSH…BOOM

Red lights sprayed the sky.

SWOOSH…BOOM

Green lights sprayed the sky.

Ellie, Johnny and Billy were now heading down Bridge Street to home. Quietly Billy began to cry. Upon hearing Billy's whimper Johnny put his arm around Billy's shoulder. Ellie could hear Billy's quiet sniffles, but was trying to ignore them. She was red hot with anger and was walking fast.

SWOOSH - SWOOSH

BOOM - BOOM

Red and green lights sprayed the sky.

Billy's quiet cry continued. Then Ellie stopped abruptly. She turned to Billy, crouched down and hugged him.

"Okay, listen boys, eyes here. Put your brains on memory record. Okay, you can go watch the firework show if you promise to walk home with Pete or Flo. But by no means, and I mean it…" Ellie raised her finger. "…by no means are you to walk home with that Kringle fella. You hear your Mother?"

246

"We don't like him again?" sniffled Billy.

"No, we don't," said Ellie as she stood back up and looked toward Little Island Pond. "You boys better get running back."

"You okay Momma?" asked Billy.

SWOOSH – SWOOSH - SWOOSH

BOOM – BOOM - BOOM

"What's wrong, ma?" asked Johnny.

Ellie looked wistfully to the fireworks.

"Yes, boys, I'm fine. Momma's fine. Momma just ate some bad food and is feeling sick. Run along back, you don't wanna miss the fireworks. Go on. Go on. I'll see you at home. Who are we not walking home with?"

"Kringle," said Billy softly.

"Johnny?"

"Not Kringle," said Johnny trying to look inside of his mother's eyes.

Ellie then turned her boys around and patted their bottoms for them to run back.

Both boys did run back…

SWOOSH – SWOOSH - SWOOSH

BOOM! – BOOM! – BOOM!

…but often looking over their shoulder to see their mother with her head hung low, jogging home alone.

SWOOSH – BOOM!

By the time the Boone boys got back to the entrance of the Ice Dance, Kringle approached holding the big white bear. They were running in opposite directions.

SWOOSH – BOOM!

SWOOSH – BOOM!

Passing one another they spoke quickly.

"Your Mother go this way boys?" asked Kringle while they passed.

"Maybe," said Johnny

"Yup," said Billy.

No one had time for chatter.

When Kringle reached the Boone home all the lights were out except one candle in the small off-centered loft window. When Kringle knocked on the front door, the small flame went out. Ellie was upstairs in bed, under the covers. The Moon shown in through the quirky window illuminating the frame on her dress that hung on a small chair. Ellie didn't feel like talking to Kringle. She felt that she didn't know what was going on with anything at that moment, especially what was happening inside her. Her emotions were a whirlwind of facts and doubt. She was having a nice night with this man, whom she didn't want to have a nice night with. She enjoyed talking to him for once. She enjoyed dancing with him as well. She knew it was a bad idea for her to show up with Kringle. She knew how the town talked. And she was happy to have finally been forgotten by the town's hearsay. But for her to then show up with Kringle, walk around with him all night, and with the big white bear even, to just have that wicked Miss Winkelplex kiss him, kiss him right up on stage for everyone to see…well, that was something she just couldn't bear. She knew the town would say the next day – "There's another man that woman couldn't keep." Ellie didn't want to talk to Kringle. She just wanted him to go away. She just wanted to sleep. So Ellie just sat quietly staring at her dress, with tears falling with every one of Kringle's knocks. When the softest part of the chest is mutated to fill with someone's love, to which that love is then lost, we are left with a hollow hole. Ellie stroked her heart as if she believed the act would reconstruct it.

Kringle stopped rapping at the door. He instead turned around and sat on the steps of the small home. He wanted to tell Ellie he was sorry. He wanted to go back in time and not let that woman kiss him. He wanted to be back at the Ice Dance having a fun night with Ellie. But instead he placed the bear beside him, took his hat off and scratched his head for wisdom. All that was heard was the distant finale of the fireworks and the cheers from the town's people. After a few minutes Kringle stood to leave, but thought he'd knock quietly one last time.

Inside Ellie still felt torn. She was happy that Kringle was still there, but she also wanted him to go away.

A few minutes later Kringle stood to leave. He noticed the Boone boys approaching. The fireworks were over.

"Oh hey boys," said Kringle.

"Hey Mr. Kringle," said Billy. He was looking sleepy.

"Well, look at that," said Johnny a bit surprised to see Kringle. "I can't follow this anymore."

"The dance over? The fireworks over?" asked Kringle.

Johnny could tell Kringle looked defeated. He had heard about what had happened from different people gabbing as they walked by Billy and him. Billy didn't notice anything because he was becoming sleepier by the second.

"Ya. Just ended. It sure was something swell," said Johnny as he repositioned the hidden rockets stuffed into his trousers.

"Sure was swell," said an almost asleep Billy.

"Go on in Billy. Here's the key. I'll see you in bed," said Johnny.

"'Kay. Goodnight Mr. Kringle," said Billy, as he hugged him, then trudged inside."

"Night Billy," Kringle said.

"Heard my Ma's boss kissed you. That's why she left huh?" started Johnny. "She told us she was sick, but that's not truth."

Kringle sat back down on the steps. Johnny was now standing in front of him.

"I believe she left because of that. Yes. That woman was wet with drunk though - you know that right?"

"That's what they say."

"They?"

"People, the people walking by."

"Oh I see."

"You know, you make my Ma mad Kringle...and you also make her act weird. Maybe a good weird. But it's a weird like I haven't seen..." Johnny looked down and played with some snow with his toe. ..."like I haven't seen in a while. I guess it's a good weird." Johnny looked up with his brow down squinting. "You like my Ma, huh Kringle?"

"Like her? Sure I like her," said Kringle.

"No, *liiike* her," repeated Johnny. "Like you wouldn't mind being handcuffed to her. Tiiiied to her."

Kringle laughed some.

"I do Johnny, I mean yes I wouldn't mind that at all."

"Ya, I figured. You always coming around and all. My Ma gets mad at you, so I figured she didn't like you, but now I'm thinking 'cause she's mad at you that that might mean she does likes you." Johnny sat by Kringle on the steps. "'Cause see, sometimes when Ma's mad at Billy and me for doing things, things she calls foolish - 'don't become a foolish man!' she'd say after we explain what we did that got us in the trouble. Then after being upset with us she'd says it's because she loves us and cares for us and don't want us hurt. And that makes her get cross. It's like how she gets mad at you. She only gets that way with me and Billy, see? Maybe it's the same."

"You think?"

"I don't know. Maybe not. Maybe. Hey don't tell my Ma we spoke. She wouldn't like it."

"Yes, she wouldn't and yes, I won't," said Kringle.

"You a good guy or a bad guy Kringle?"

"What do you mean?"

"Well, like my Ma says, *are you naughty or nice*?"

"Nice Johnny; I'm a good guy."

"Ya. Hm. I'm starting to see that. Well okay, night Kringle."

"Night Johnny."

Johnny headed inside.

For most people of Hamilton, Massachusetts, the Ice Dance was a welcomed change from their winter blues. But for others, it just added to them.

The Dunce Brothers carried Miss Winkelplex home. She lay in her bed passed out in her clothes. Mrs. McManus put her twins to bed. Mr. McManus slept in his big chair by the smoldering fireplace with a glass of old scotch about to fall from his hand. Charlene didn't have a fun night. No one had asked her to ice-dance. Marlene lay in bed dreaming of wedding plans because Terrance had sat with her during the fireworks. Terrance himself lay in bed thinking of Marlene. He replayed his heroic train saving of Periwinkle in his mind, but instead envisioned he was saving Marlene from crazed pirates. Ramona thought about the ice-dance she had with Murf. And Murf wondered why Ramona had asked him to ice-dance. Flo thought about the note she gave Johnny to give to Ellie, it read:

> *It's not important Ellie my darling dear. Forgive him; it wasn't his fault. And don't fuss yourself, remember - where gossip thrives, there's always a doctor praying to an angel – "why do we even try?"*

Pete thought about the walk he had, walking the girl he thought was something special home. Billy dreamed of fireworks. Johnny thought of his mother and of Kringle. Ellie silently cried, soaking herself in sadness. And Kringle was busy building a late night snowlady beside the snowman the Boone boys had made.

When Ellie awoke the house was empty. Ellie felt fine that morning but only because during her morning thoughts about the Ice Dance she *decided* she would be fine. Flo's note helped a little too. Ellie stood up with her chin held high, brushed her long black hair with a confident facial expression, inspected her face in the mirror, dressed, left her hair down and started breakfast. She felt good. Solidarity. This was the Ellie, Ellie liked to be. As she placed three plates down, she looked up and out the window. What she saw punctured Ellie and made her perfect posture deflate.

"Whoa," she whispered.

The snowman that her boys had made once again had Kringle's hat upon it. And beside him, holding hands was the snowlady holding the big white bear Ellie had won.

Ellie sat down. She paused. Then sharply she stood back up to look at what she had seen outside. And just as sharply, she sat back down. The many emotions returned. Again she felt angry, embarrassed; she felt smothered, but with a slight sense of feeling lucky. She was beginning to feel again – noticed.

Two little Ellies standing on Ellie's shoulders began to whisper in her ears:

"He could change your world," one whispered – "*But the people of the town would talk again,*" answered the other – "He could take you and the boys to where the rainbows flow like rivers in the sky." – "*That would never happen, what are you even talking about?*" – "He's a bit magical." – "*He is, isn't he? But*

251

you thought that once before remember? And look what happened." – "Kringle's a different magical." – *"Ya, I can see that, but it's just too complicated. You have a good thing going right now. Without him."* – "Do I?" – *"I don't know. Do we?"* – "I don't know."

The two little Ellies sat down on her shoulders and they all sat and thought.

Kringle and Pete sat facing one another mulling over all the lists of toys Mr. McManus had been bringing them. They were in stacks on every surface and were tacked to every inch of the walls. They were even bursting out of both men's pockets. Kringle and Pete decided it was too much work for the two of them. Pete suggested he ask Riggels to help. Riggels was a fine painter. And Riggels knew Mr. McManus was a cheat, so there was no worry about him being a part of building the toys and keeping the secret. Kringle suggested asking Ellie to come by to make all of the orders of soft-dolls and teddy bears. Neither Kringle nor Pete knew a thing about sewing. But that would mean telling Ellie about Mr. McManus' scam and Kringle and Pete weren't sure that was a good idea. Kringle even suggested asking the Airlords to help with the easy tasks, but that also meant telling them about Mr. McManus' scam. Kids can keep secrets better than adults, but it was still too high a risk. There was a lot on Kringle and Pete's plate. The two men stood at the crossroads of a life-shaping predicament. Each time they got to talking about how impossible it was to get Mr. McManus' orders finished, unveiling Mr. McManus' scam all together would come up. This kind of talk made Pete nervous.

Things got less stressful when Pete returned to The Workshop with Riggels. Kringle sat on his cot. Riggels sat on his old stool facing Pete.

"I thought that might be where these mysterious *toys* were coming from," said Riggels as he poked at his pipe with a tooth pick. "Sure I can help out."

"We'd pay of course," said Pete.

"I'll take whatever you can spare," said Riggels. Riggels took the list on the top of a stack that sat on the table in front of him. "I just don't know how we're gonna make all these."

"We can do it," said Kringle

"It'd be a miracle," said Riggels as he looked over the list and set it back down.

The men worked all day and into the evening. They only stopped to fry up some sliced potatoes with a few small slices of ham. The three men worked well together. The conversation was natural. It flowed. Kringle and Pete would craft different toys and then hand them off to Riggels to paint. Rudy helped the men by fetching a multitude of different items he felt they might need. And Rudy was often correct.

"Good boy Rudy, exactly," said Pete as he took a broom handle from Rudy and began to fasten it to a wooden horse head he had carved.

"Kringle, you're sayin' that we should make all these toys and then *not* give them to the people? I don't understand," said Riggels as he painted the eyes of a wooden horse.

"Well, you know Ellie Boone, right?" asked Kringle as he finished up on a toy-box of a train scene with *Betsy Bound* as his muse.

"Course," said Riggels factually.

"He likes Ellie," smiled Pete to Riggels.

"You don't say," smiled Riggels as he took a break to smoke his pipe. "She's a tough lady. Smart. But wait, I heard from Miss Magnolia, who heard from Miss Robins, that you gave old bird face Winkelplex a kiss last night. I didn't see because a bunch of little ones made me into a snowman and I wasn't positioned the right way. But I heard, I heard."

"No-no, that woman kissed *me*. It was a mistake," said Kringle also factually.

"A mistake huh. Well she was fairly wet with drunk as I recall," said Riggels.

"What's Ellie think?" asked Pete. "I know she saw. I saw her saw, I mean saw her see," said Pete as he took a table-leg from Rudy and handed it off to Riggels to paint like a fireman standing at attention.

"Not good I think. Haven't spoken to her. I was thinking of visiting her when we're done," said Kringle.

"Good luck," said Riggels sarcastically.

"Good luck," said Pete honestly.

"Anyways, my point is, she told me last week when I brought toys into her shop, that no normal kid would be able to have any of them. Play with them I mean. That all these toys will be too expensive and that only the fortunate kids will be able to have 'em and play with 'em," explained Kringle.

"That's most likely true," said Riggels.

"Doesn't that bother you a bit?" asked Kringle.

"Sure. But these days what doesn't bother me a bit?" said Riggels. "These are unfair times. I expect unfair things," said Riggels.

"Well, Ellie said, and I'm quotin' her - '*If I could make these toys, I'd make one for every child in the world.*' And then she said something like - '*to make them feel fortunate, even if it's just for one day.*' Don't you like that?" asked Kringle?

"Well sure, I ain't no grinch. It's a nice slice of kind pie. But what are you driving at? We can't possibly make toys for every kid in the world Kringle," said Riggels as he took a break to stand and stretch.

"Well, no. But maybe we could if we had more people making the toys with us. It's what she said that's all. I just don't think happiness for a child should be based off luck. Luck that they get parents that can afford a three dollar doll," said Kringle.

"Is that how much he's marking these up for? Jeesh. We aren't using gold paint are we?" joked Riggels. "Lord, a three dollar doll. Would you have ever thought?"

"Exactly. See what Ellie said, well it just haunts me. She said, 'It's like color costs money, but grey is for free,'" said Kringle. "Those kids are gonna pray and wish for these toys we're making."

"Kringle wants us to be the answer to their little prayers," added Pete. "It's a nice thought, but some of this worries me. One word why – McManus. And one reason why, he can get people locked up as fast as sayin' – Slam-Click!"

"I get it Kringle. And I like it. If you got a plan Kringle, I'll help you with that plan. My Ma always said I could tell when something important was about to happen," said Riggels. "But Kringle, we just can't go to jail over it. If I can help it, I like being on the other side of steel bars."

The men continued to make the toys on the lists. They talked about Kringle's plan. And they talked about the likelihood of how disrupting Mr. McManus would not only get them all fired, but possibly get them all behind steel bars. Each time they came to the conclusion that the plan was impossible, Kringle would say again and again, "I believe that *we can be* the answer to all the little prayers."

Pete and Riggels liked what they heard, they were inspired, but they couldn't help but worry, for Mr. McManus owned that town and he had become too big for truth and justice.

Miss Magnolia's class was once again gathered atop Patton's Hill. This was the last race before the official Red Robin Race that was to take place later that week at Robin's Hill – a much windier hill. It took Johnny and the Airlords four days after the Ice Dance to build their new ship, that they called the - *Lone Flyer*. It was a simple design of the canoe that Ramona's mother had won at the Ice Dance with the rockets Rudy had stolen from the Dunce Brothers. The rockets were roped down on either side of the canoe.

Oliver stood at the starting rope holding his blue hat high in the air. Marlene and Charlene were positioned on the *Flexible Flier*, focused and ready. Johnny and Murf sat in the *Lone Flyer*.

"Goggles on Murf!" said Johnny.

"Ay-ay caption," said Murf.

Terrance and Ramona stood ready with boxes of matches on either side of the *Lone Flyer*, ready to light the wicks of the rockets.

"That shouldn't be legal," said Charlene. "The Red Robin Race would *never* let you use fireworks."

"Ya they would. It's part of our ship. And they're rockets not fireworks," said Murf.

"First off," started Charlene getting angrier by the minute, "it's not a spaceship race you wet socks, it's a sled race. Second, those are fireworks, not rockets or whatever. And, what, are you seriously calling that canoe a spaceship, let alone a sled?"

"The Red Robin Race handbook states," said Oliver as he pulled out the *Red Robin Race Rule Book* from his back pocket. "That any self made sled can be a part of the race as long at it holds two people."

"Ya, but they didn't mean a canoe with fireworks strapped to it," said Charlene.

"Well, it didn't say you couldn't have a canoe with rockets strapped to it. Does it Oliver?" asked Murf.

"Let's see, hm, um, no, no, err, no it does not," said Oliver.

"Whatever," mumbled Charlene

"Okay! On your marks," Oliver started.

The Twins dug their mittens into the snow.

"...get set..."

Terrance and Ramona struck their matches.

"GO!" said Oliver and threw his blue hat into the air.

The Twins dashed down Patton's Hill. Terrance and Ramona lit their wicks. Terrance's rocket rumbled, then shot off the canoe and launched down Patton's Hill. It hit a tree and exploded in red sparkles. The second rocket, Ramona's rocket, stayed attached. But without the other rocket to balance the force, it began to turn the canoe counter clockwise. Johnny and Murf held on. The canoe began to spin faster and faster, around and around. None of the other kids could even see Johnny and Murf anymore; the canoe was just a blur of color twirling and whirling. Then the rocket stopped spitting sparks. The canoe came to a slow spinning stop. There was silence. Then the rocket exploded into green sparkles. All the kids of Miss Magnolia's class, save the Airlords, erupted in cheer.

It was once again - a lost race.

News traveled fast in the McManus home of where the missing rockets had gone. Mr. McManus had had enough of the Airlords. He screamed at Lloyd and Elmer to, "find them kids and scare them out of their boots." The Dunce Brothers were happy to oblige because news had also traveled fast through Miss Magnolias class and up to the Twins that it was the Airlords who had punished the Dunce Brothers with never ending Death Balls. The Dunce Brothers knew the Airlords were racing the Twins that morning, so they got started early with prepping their revenge.

Defeated, the Airlords pushed the canoe back to the Central Command. Both Johnny and Murf had singed hair and singed noses.

Following close behind, but hidden behind the different houses and shops that line Commonwealth Street, stalked the Dunce Brothers. They both held sacks. Elmer pulled out a snowball that glistened like glass in the sunlight.

"You sure it was them Lloyd?" asked Elmer inspecting his shiny snowball as his brother and he followed the Airlords.

"That's what the boss says," said Lloyd as he walked with a scowl.

"These iceballs will sure show 'em not to mess with us again. Huh?"

asked Elmer again.

The Dunce Brothers had made two-dozen snowballs. Lloyd dipped each one in ice water making the snowballs – iceballs.

"They'll sure crack some little noses. That's for sure," said Lloyd with malice, as his wet grin reflected in the iceball he was holding.

The Airlords turned down Bridge Street. The Dunce Brothers wouldn't have any more houses to hide behind, so they crept quietly twenty-five feet behind the Airlords. Stealthily, the Dunce Brothers advanced.

The Airlords were too busy chatting about the new ship to hear the Dunce Brothers' feet crunching in the snow behind them.

"HEY YOU!" Lloyd hollered. "PIP-SQUEEKS!"

The Airlords turned around to see Lloyd and Elmer holding what they thought was a snowball in their hands.

"Oh no," said Terrance as he squinted.

"WE'LL TEACH YOU TO STEAL OUR ROCKETS," screamed Loyld.

"AND MR. MCMANUS' CAR," added Elmer.

The Airlords were shocked with fright.

"CODE RED!" Murf screamed. "AIRLORDS RETREAT. I MEAN IT, RUUUUUUUN!" screamed Murf, and the Airlords left the canoe and dashed into the woods.

The Dunce Brothers made chase.

Lloyd threw the first iceball. It hit a tree by Johnny's head and shattered into pieces of ice.

"Those aren't snowballs, Airlords," screamed Johnny. "THEY'RE ICEBALLS!"

Elmer threw his iceball. It shattered against a tree by Ramona's head.

"CRAP-OLA! DEM *ARE* GOD FEARIN' ICEBALLS BROTHAS!" screamed Ramona.

The Airlords dashed while the Dunce Brothers made chase, hurling their iceballs.

Fearing for his life, Billy began to sing aloud as an iceball passed over his left shoulder – shattering against a tree in front of him.

> *"The reindeers are coming – trollop, trollop*
> *The reindeers are coming – trollop, trollop*
> *Spit-spot – with any luck*

The reindeers will come - trollop, trollop

Deep in the forest – they lay, they lay
Deep in the forest – they lay
But if we ask & ask real nice
The reindeers will come - trollop, trollop"

"WHAT ARE YOU DOING?!" screamed Murf as an iceball whipped over his left shoulder exploding in front of him. "SINGING?"

"I'M RADIOING FOR HELP," screamed Billy, then he kept on singing his song.

"THAT WON'T WORK BILLY!" hollered Johnny as an iceball hit him in the back of his knee. Johnny fell to the snow. "AHH!"

"I got one!" said Lloyd to Elmer as they chased on.

The Airlords stopped and quickly got Johnny back on his feet. Then they continued running.

Billy kept singing.

"HEAD TO CHEBACCO LAKE," screamed Murf.

Close to the town's end, where the next town, Essex, began, was a big lake called Chebacco Lake.

Billy sang on...

"The reindeers are coming – trollop, trollop
The reindeers are coming – trollop, trollop
Spit-spot – with any luck
The reindeers will come - trollop, trollop

Deep in the forest – they lay, they lay
Deep in the forest – they lay
But if we ask & ask real nice
The reindeers will come - trollop, trollop"

"VHAT DA HECK ARE YA SINGING BILLY-BOY?" screamed Ramona?

"IF WE SING IT RIGHT - IT SHOULD BRING REINFORCEMENTS!"

said Billy then he kept singing.

"IT WON'T WORK!" screamed Johnny, now running with a limp.

"HELL, I'LL TRY IT!" said Terrance and then joined in with Billy. Murf and Ramona joined in as well.

"Not too loud Airlords," said Billy. "Sing it like this."

"The reindeers are coming – trollop, trollop
The reindeers are coming – trollop, trollop
Spit-spot – with any luck
The reindeers will come - trollop, trollop

All the Airlords, save Johnny sang.

Deep in the forest – they lay, they lay
Deep in the forest – they lay
But if we ask & ask real nice
The reindeers will come - trollop, trollop"

The Dunce Brothers began to gain on the Airlords.

"C'mon Elmer, let's take 'em."

Both men laughed with wet spitting lips.

Up ahead the small white fawn heard the distant song. Her ears turned to calculate where exactly it was coming from. Becoming more curious and acute, she dashed to the sound. Her surprised grazing mother and father looked up to see their little white fawn take off like a comet into the woods. They were shocked. Darting after their fawn, they looked all around for the sound.

The white fawn leaped over a fallen snow covered tree, zigzagged through some bending birches and suddenly found herself running along side the Airlords.

The Airlords' eyes widened and mouths dropped. They all looked at the little white fawn running beside them and then back at Billy with astonishment.

It had worked.

The father and mother deer sprinted and leaped and also found themselves running beside the Airlords. The mother deer increased her speed and came up beside the white fawn that was running beside Billy.

"LLOYD LOOK!" screamed Elmer pointing to the deer family running with the Airlords. "IT'S THE MOOSE THAT ATTACKED US! THINK THESE ICEBALLS CAN FINISH THE JOB?"

"LET'S FIND OUT. TWO FOR ONE! LET'S GET 'EM ALL."

The Dunce Brother's unloaded their iceballs. One zipped by the father deer and fell into the snow below. The father deer did not know what had flown by him. He looked left and right, up and down. Another iceball zipped by his head and exploded onto a tree, spraying Billy, the mother deer and his white fawn with ice chunks. Frightened, the mother deer and her white fawn took a sharp right down a small hill heading straight for Chebacco Lake.

Murf looked to his right where the father deer ran beside him. Murf could tell he had become enraged. Cold air blew out of the father deer's nostrils like the smoke out of *Betsy Bound's* smoke stack. The father deer looked behind him as another iceball zipped past him striking a tree spraying ice on Ramona and Terrance. With a direct line of vision, the father deer looked over his shoulder and found the eyes of the Dunce Brothers.

"That's right, Mr. Moose, you're mine," said Lloyd as he threw another iceball.

The Airlords and deer family had made it down the small hill and stopped suddenly at Chebacco Lake's ice edge. The father deer turned to the approaching Dunce Brothers. Their panting and laughing made them drool and spit. The Airlords and the mother deer with her white fawn stood behind the father deer.

The Dunce Brothers approached.

"Well, lookie what we have here," said Lloyd.

"Ya," laughed Elmer, then wiped his red wet face. "Lookie what we have here."

"Thought you could just steal our rockets do ya? Thought we wouldn't find out it was you huh? Well, we know it was you. And you're gonna pay," said Lloyd.

"Leave us alone!" said Terrance.

"Ya leave us alone," said the rest of the Airlords.

"Or what?" laughed Lloyd. "Two for one. This is gonna be fun."

Lloyd tossed up an iceball in his hand, caught it, then wound up like a Red Sox pitcher and hurled an iceball at Billy.

BOOM!

Using his damaged antlers, the father deer leaped in front of the iceball, exploding it into pieces.

The Dunce Brothers paused. Then Elmer threw an iceball at Murf.

The father deer leaped and smashed that one as well.

BOOM!

"Huh," said Elmer.

"Unload them all!" ordered Lloyd. The Dunce Brothers took the last of their iceballs out of their sack. "One…two…three…FIRE!"

BOOM – BOOM – BOOM – BOOM!

BOOM – BOOM – BOOM – BOOM!

The father deer leaped and turned, turned and leaped smashing iceball after iceball. A few of the iceballs even broke off small sections of the father deer's injured antlers. Ice and antlers sprayed in the air showering down on the Airlords and the deer family, as if thunderclouds were colliding.

With their empty hands at their sides, the Dunce Brothers stood dumbfounded.

The father deer stomped the ground and blew cold air out of his nostrils.

"Uh-oh," said Billy.

"Uh-oh," said Elmer.

"Oi, I dink you lot 'r' in fer it," said Ramona.

The father deer slowly walked toward the Dunce Brothers while slightly turning to the right, making the Dunce Brothers slowly back up and turn around.

"Easy boy," said Lloyd. "Easy boy. We were just playin.'"

The Airlords and deer family followed behind the father deer. He was turning the group so that the Dunce Brothers were now standing at the ice edge of Chebacco Lake.

"Call that animal off," said Lloyd to the Airlords.

"Ya call that moose off," said Elmer.

"He ain't ours Mister," said Johnny.

"But he is on our side," said Billy.

"I guess he sure is," said Johnny.

The father deer stomped the ground and then took a step forward. The Dunce Brothers shook and took a step back onto the ice. The father deer stomped the ground again and took another step forward. Again the Dunce Brothers jumped from fright and took another step back. This continued until the Dunce Brothers were out ten feet on the ice of Chebaco Lake. The father deer stood strong at the ice edge.

"C'mon kids, this is crazy. Call that thing off," pleaded Lloyd.

"Like I said Mister, he ain't ours," said Johnny.

"I don't think he likes you though," said Billy.

"IF YOU DON'T CALL THAT MONSTER OFF THEN I'LL, I'LL..." The father deer turned around and looked at each of the Airlords, the mother deer and his white fawn to make sure they were all safe. Then he turned around, raised his front hooves up high in the air and pounced down onto the ice.

The ice rumbled. Then it rumbled some more. The Dunce Brothers looked all around the ice. A small crack opened at the ice edge. Its sound echoed and reverberated against the woods around. The crack got bigger - it spider webbed and started toward the feet of the Dunce Brothers. Lloyd and Elmer turned to each other looking glum. The ice then shattered. And Lloyd and Elmer fell into the ice-cold water up to their waists.

"AHHHH! THIS IS FREEEZING," screamed Elmer. Both Dunce Brothers held each other shivering.

The father deer came over to the mother deer and white fawn and rubbed his head on theirs.

"Wow! Thanks for saving our lives Mr. Big Deer. That was swell," said Billy. The rest of the Airlords thanked the father deer.

"Danks."

"Fantastic."

"W-w-well I'll be."

"Incredible."

The deer family walked off a few feet, turned to look at the Airlords one last time, then leaped - disappearing east into the woods. The Airlords waved good-bye to the deer family.

"Wow," was all a stupefied Billy could say.

Inside Central Command the Airlords sat in a circle huddled in blankets to keep warm. Rudy waited patiently outside beside the canoe.

"Ya, but I don't know if we will ever win," said Johnny quietly and surprisingly.

The Airlord's eyes and mouths dropped open.

"What do you mean Johnny?" said Terrance as he went to grab the blueprints for the *Battle Cruiser*. He laid them down in the middle of their circle. Each Airlord, save Johnny, put a hand down to flatten the blueprints. "The *Battle Cruise* is all plotted out, we just have to build it."

"It'll probably fall apart like everything I design," said Johnny looking at the floor. Johnny stood up and went to the window. He looked out over the junkyard and at The Workshop that had smoke puffing out from its chimney. As Johnny placed his hand on the window frame he looked down and noticed a nail that he was sure he didn't hammer in. He ran his finger over it. Then Johnny looked back up to The Workshop.

"Awe Johnny don't get down just 'cause that rocket shot off," encouraged Murf. "I mean I think I tied that stray rocket on. Sorry Airlords it was me. It wasn't your fault Johnny."

Johnny began to run his hand over the entire Central Command slowly noticing different nails hammered in beside his nails.

"Ya Johnny mate, ya make da best ships brotha. Everybody knaws that," helped Ramona.

"The *Battle Cruiser* will be top shelf. Top shelf I tell ya," said Murf.

Johnny continued to run his hand over the Central Command finding new nails. He stopped, looked out onto the junkyard at Pete and Kringle's workshop and thought about how Kringle had fixed their furnace chimney, patched their roof up and all the while included Billy and him. It also dawned on Johnny, *How would his mother pass Kringle on her way home. He must have been in the Central Command, securing things.* Johnny came around the Airlords and sat back down in his spot.

"Don't be down Johnny," said Billy.

As Johnny took a straw out of his back pocket and put it in his mouth, he turned his newsy cap around.

"Look-a-here Airlords. We wanna win right?" said Johnny.

"Mere den enyding," rallied Ramona.

"Right. And we all know that our ships have had a little trouble these past years," said Johnny.

The Airlords grumbled.

"I say before we make the *Battle Cruiser*, we go ask Kringle to look over the blueprints," said Johnny looking up with a stoic face.

The Airlords were surprised, but as they let the suggestion simmer, they all seemed to agree.

"We could go down to The Workshop, show Kringle the blueprints and see if we missed anything. *Then* we'll build it. Then…" Johnny paused. "…we'll, we'll build it *with* Kringle. I mean we gotta win, Airlords; we don't wanna be left in the snow any more. And if we need a little help, well, bowl full of dead fleas, that's fine by me," said Johnny with one of his hands lightly touching the floor board in front of him that had one of Kringle's nails hidden on the side of one of his own nails.

"Well sure Johnny?" said Terrance.

"Ain't nothing wrong with that," said Murf.

"Steell 'r design brothas. Steell 'r shep. Pete's da Airlord's scientist ain't he den? Kringle can be a scientist too, ya?" said Ramona.

"Ya-ya *Kringle* can be a scientist," agreed Billy.

"Ya," Johnny said. "Smart; he can be a scientist too. It's alright by me."

"Okay. Airlords, let's make it official. Hands in," said Murf.

All the Airlords put their hand in the center of their circle.

"From here forward, we the Airlords of Hamilton make Kringle a designated scientist - friend and helper of the Airlords, keeper of all that's good and just on this world and beyond, from this day forward," Murf said in his best official voice.

"Ay-ay," cadenced the Airlords.

The Airlords marched down to The Workshop. They held the *Battle Cruiser's* blue prints with them.

KNOCK – KNOCK – KNOCK!

Kringle, Pete and Riggels all looked up from making toys. They looked at one another inquisitively.

"You expecting anyone?" asked Riggels.

"Oh no not again," said Kringle.

"Who's there?" shouted Pete.

"Hey scientist, it's us, the Airlords. We've come to pay Kringle a visit," said Murf in his leadership tone.

Kringle and Pete looked shocked.

"We gotta cover up these toys," said Pete.

"All of them?" asked Riggels.

"All of them," said Pete.

"We'll be right there. Just a second," said Kringle, as Pete, Riggels and he dashed about putting bed sheets over all the toys. "Just one more moment," Kringle said. The three men started stuffing all the lists of toys in Kringle's and Pete's trunks at the end of their beds. Kringle even stuffed a bunch in his shirt, making it look like he had a big belly.

Pete unlocked the door. The Airlords came in very officially. They didn't seem interested in all the sheets covering up different parts of The Workshop. They had more important issues. The Airlords told Pete that they were going to make Kringle an Airlords' scientist - just happy to see Mr. Riggels, the Airlords told him he could be one too. The Airlords unrolled the blueprints to the *Battle Cruiser* on the small table. Johnny told Kringle how he'd like to know what he thought of the new ship's "schematics". He told Kringle he'd leave the blueprints with him and that they could meet the next day to go over his notes. Kringle agreed. The Airlords all shook Kringle's and Riggel's hands saying - 'Welcome to the Airlords'. The Airlords marched out confident. Pete closed and locked the door behind them.

It was a close call for the toymakers.

Ellie opened the front door to her makeshift home with her hands on her hips and walked down her porch steps with her head up squinting defiantly at the snowman and snowlady. She was bare foot. She wore a blanket like a shawl over her shoulders. Her feet crunched in the snow. Ellie puckered, brushed a lock of hair from in font of her face and grumbled at the snowcouple holding hands. The Sun was bright; it painfully brightened the snow all around. Ellie told herself she was just coming out to retrieve the bear so she could give it to Billy. She had heard it was supposed to snow that night so she didn't want the big white bear to get sloppy. But really Ellie just wanted a closer look at the snowcouple and her younger mind didn't want the bear she had won to catch a cold.

Ellie took small steps as if the snowcouple was booby-trapped. Coal was pressed in the snowman, as if he was staring, with a big smile, at the snowlady. Ellie took the big white bear from the arms of the snowlady, brushed the new layer of snow off it and held it in the same fashion as the snowlady.

Ellie then noticed something in the hand of the snowman. It was a folded piece of paper. She took the note from the snowman's hand. Ellie let out a labored breath and unfolded the note. Written in coal, written in clumsy letters it read:

"This is what it would look like."

"This is what it would look like?" Ellie repeated quietly. "This is what, what would look like?" Ellie wondered. Ellie then folded the note back up and looked up. Healthy snowflakes were beginning to fall. She followed one with her eyes. It turned slightly as it fell, then connected to another smaller flake falling beside it. They both plopped down on the head of the snowlady.

Ellie's feet were cold and numbing, but she didn't move. She just stayed standing, bare foot, in the light snow, holding the big white bear under her right arm while holding the folded note in her left hand. She watched for some time. More and more snowflakes fell and plopped down on Kringle's snowcouple.

Ellie wished she could do the night at the Ice Dance all over again. She thought, and the little Ellies on her shoulders spoke again: "I would have ripped that witch Winkelplex right off of Kringle" – *"But she's your boss, you can't do that"* – "But she embarrassed me in front of everyone; I *came* with Kringle, not her" – *"You would have been fired if you crossed her, let alone in front of the whole town"* – "Why would Kringle do that, he likes me" – *"You think he likes you?"* – "Well yes, I do." – *"What do you think of him?"* – "I think he should have run after me, that's what I think" – *"He did"* – "Ya well, he was too late" – *"You could have let him in the house"* – "I was too mad" – *"That's not his fault"* – "Mm" – *"Maybe he's embarrassed too"* – "Or maybe he's a bad man and makes women feel special, but really he doesn't care. Maybe Miss Winkelplex and Kringle are a couple now, men are all no good. *You* know this." – "*You don't really think that*" – "Men are no good" – "*He's sweet, you can see it in his eyes*" – "Men are no good" – "*That 'Adore, more' thing he said was nice*" – "Men are no good" – "*Oh Ellie*" – "Oh nothing."

Ellie then noticed how cold her feet were. She hopped on her toes back to the stairs and ran up them almost slipping. She headed inside where it was warm, closed the door and placed her feet by the fire. Ellie then looked at the note; the big white bear still under her arm. Looking over her left shoulder, out the kitchen window, she saw Kringle's snowcouple. Ellie unfolded the note.

"*This is what it would look like.*"

"I think it's wonderfully romantic," said the older woman in the blue chair.

"Romantic. Bah. It's a sin I tell you. A sin," said the older woman in the red chair, who was having her hair brushed by Flo.

When Flo had the time, she headed over to the Hamilton Tea House and spent time with the elderly women who met there. Flo talks with them, brushes their hair and brings them colored sugar cookies that she bakes in different fun shapes.

"All we did was ice-dance for a few songs," said Flo in her defense.

"Oh, we saw you," said the older woman in the red chair. "We saw you. Pastors aren't allowed to dance."

"Sure they are," said the older woman in the yellow chair as she carefully brought her teacup to her mouth and took a careful sip. "Everyone can dance if they *want* to."

"Not a pastor," said the older woman in the red chair.

"Well, why not?" said the older woman in the blue chair as she brought up the light blanket on the knees of the older woman sleeping in the green chair.

"Yeah why not?" said Flo, still brushing her hair.

"Because it's written," said the older woman in the red chair.

"Where?" said the older woman in the blue chair.

"The Bible of course," said the older woman in the red chair.

"No it isn't," said the rest of the women.

"Do you like him?" asked the woman in the blue chair.

"As much as a Sunday morning," said Flo.

"Do you love him?" asked the older woman in the yellow chair as she dipped her sugar cookie in her tea.

"Oh well, I don't know. I'd have to see if he loves me first. My Momma always said, never love a man that don't love you."

All the women nodded in agreement.

"Then, what if he does love you?" asked the older woman in the blue chair as she carefully chose a green pine tree cookie. "Then do you think you'd love him?"

"Pastor Finn can't love," said the older woman in the red chair.

"Oh that's a terrible sentence to say, 'can't love'. Oh it makes me sad hearing it and saying it. Oh that's just dreadful," said the older woman in the yellow chair as she set down her teacup with a shaky hand.

"Well, I'll sing like this, if Mr. Pastor Finn ever needed a life partner to play a never ending game of chess with, and he didn't have one – well I sure would be his partner," said Flo as she finished brushing and went to check on the fire.

"Oh I like that. I like that Flo. 'Partner'. That's lovely," said the older woman in the blue chair. "It's true you *are* partners when you are in love. Life partners."

"You are just a doll Flo, just a doll," said the older woman in the yellow chair. "You go tell him. You go tell Pastor Finn what you just said to us just now. Lovely. Oh to be young."

"She's right darling Flo, you go tell him. There is never a second to waste with love Deary," said the older woman in the blue chair as she dabbed her mouth with a napkin.

"They'll both go to hell," said the older woman in the red chair.

"Oh shut it Marjorie," said the older woman, who was thought to be asleep, in the green chair.

A deep day filling up with building a new ship, looking for needed parts, friendships becoming stronger and Rudy chasing Billy all around the junkyard.

Kringle and the Airlords labored in the junkyard collecting parts they would need for the new *Battle Cruiser*.

It was warm enough to work gloveless and hatless. Without their winter hats on, Kringle and the Airlords shared the same sprongy hair. The Airlords dashed about looking for needed parts. They all shouted excited suggestions.

"We'll need a grappling hook," yelled Billy as he tossed a massive metal hook used to hook lobster traps into the pile that everyone was adding to.

"Ye Billy-boy; dat's fer real. And ve'll need diss 'ere to pick up any of dem bloody Mongols radio communications," said Ramona as she tossed a broken radio antenna in the pile.

"We'll need these too," said Terrance as he came running over with the blades of a ceiling fan and one shabby snowshoe.

Confused, Kringle stood by the pile looking over the collecting junk.

"You sure we need all this Johnny?" he said with uncertainty.

"Wow! Would ya look at this! It's perfect!" stated Murf trying to properly hold a broken accordion. "We can use it for sure," Murf said as the accordion made awkward tones much like the calling of a loon. He tossed it down and ran back for more imperative parts.

"What do you mean?" asked Johnny, with a straw in his mouth and his arms crossed, sorting the pile into groups by moving things around with his foot.

"Well, I was thinking," said Kringle, as he crossed his arms as well. "We're making this ship for speed right?"

"Ya that's right the - *Battle Cruiser*."

Rudy came bopping up, dropped a perfect size nine shoe in the pile and ran back off to look for more needed things. Kringle picked up the shoe, checked the size, smiled and pocketed it.

"Well, okay, see now right there, that's where I'm getting a little lost. We're calling it a *Battle Cruiser*, but what I think we really should be designing is a *Speed Cruiser*. Ya-no?"

Johnny scratched his chin as if he had whiskers.

"You thinking all this stuff may weigh down the ship?"

"I do. I do."

"I can see that. Huh." Johnny thought. He circled the pile of old and odd, bashed and broken things, flipping each one over with his foot as if he was inspecting them for flaws. "Too much weight; too much weight." Johnny finished circling the pile and was now standing on the other side of Kringle. He looked up at Kringle. "Okay. Ya. I get ya the - *Speed Cruiser*. I like it." Johnny cupped his hands over his mouth. "AIRLORDS, AIRLORDS GATHER BACK, THERE'S BEEN A CHANGE OF PLANS!"

From all sides the Airlords came running back holding more old and odd, bashed and broken things in their hands.

"Okay, listen up Airlords we have a change in plans. We ain't making the *Battle Cruiser* no more," said Johnny confidently.

The Airlords were dumbfounded.

"Ain't making the *Battle Cruiser*?" said Murf turning his head back and forth to each Airlord looking for an answer.

"Oi, Johnny-boy. I ain't gettin' ya brotha," said Ramona as she scratched her hair with both hands making it all stick up straight.

"We're making a *Speed Cruiser*," said Johnny. "Tell 'em." Johnny kicked his head in the direction of Kringle.

"Okay Airlords now all this stuff you collected is great. Perfect even. And you should..."

Billy interrupted Kringle.

"We!" he corrected.

"Sorry *we*...we should keep all of it for a future mission, but maybe not this mission. See Airlords this mission is about speed. The *Battle Cruiser* is about battling. So I propose we make..."

Billy interrupted Kringle again. He said in awe, "The *Speed Cruiser*".

"Exactly," said Kringle as he gave Billy a smile, wink and patted him on the head.

"So what do we need?" asked Terrance as he scratched his head.

"Well, I saw this and I think its swell," said Kringle as he turned and picked something up.

"Vhat da heck is dat?" ask Ramona and then spat to her side.

"It's a cobbler's bench," said Kringle.

"Well wut dat?" asked Ramona as they all approached it.

With only three of its legs, the cobbler's bench stood at an angle. It had a small round leather seat for the cobbler to sit, then a narrow curved middle and a square work area at its front.

"This is where shoe makers make their shoes. See the cobbler sits here and makes the shoes there. These little nooks are where his tools go. We can knock off the sideboard and give it a smooth pointed nose. Johnny you could sit here where the cobbler would usually sit and Murf you could crouch up front. We could smooth it down and make it slick, make it fast. We just…" Kringle stopped and looked around. All the Airlords looked to each direction Kringle gazed a wonder toward. "We just need the right thing to put it on. Like the bottom of skates but bigger; metal that's curved at the tip, oh-oh like those candy canes that were hidden in the trees at the Ice Dance. See Airlords, we need something to glide on."

Everyone thought in silence.

"Well, I know," said Billy hugging Rudy's head. "The school Johnny…"

"Ya-ya Billy," said Johnny, he knew where his brother was going with his thought.

Billy continued. "Well, see Kringle, our school's got a staircase out front. And that staircase, well it has railings. Railings shaped like candy canes. They curve and everything."

Johnny went to his knees, smoothed out some snow and drew the dimensions of the schoolhouse's front step railings.

"They're about this long and they curve just like this," Johnny said, then he looked up at Kringle.

"You got a screwdriver Johnny?" asked Kringle.

"Yup," Johnny said as he stood and smiled.

"Well, take me to it," said Kringle and they all set out.

It was dark and smokey in Mr. McManus' study. The curtains were drawn. The fire burned big, casting vicious shadows on the cherry stained wooden walls. Mr. McManus sat at his desk, cigar in mouth, finishing up the last of his fake Letters of Authenticity. You could hear the faint sound of Mrs. McManus calling him for dinner, but Mr. McManus ignored her.

He ran his hand over the stack of false papers as he took a healthy gulp of scotch. With wet lips and greedy hands, Mr. McManus placed the documents in a leather envelope and tied it closed. He stood and walked over to a painting on the wall. It was of him standing proudly in his study by an equally healthy fire. With his plump fingers he felt behind the painting holding a small key. On the side of the painting's frame, Mr. McManus turned the key. He then opened the painting like a door. Inside were stacks of money. Mr. McManus smiled. With a grunt, he placed the sealed leather envelope inside the hidden safe, closed the painting door and locked it back up.

Mr. McManus then walked to his armchair by the fire to finish his drink. Sitting back down, staring at the flames he thought…

I'll open a store in Boston, then Cambridge, next Salem, Beacon Hill, maybe even in New York City. One day I will be Mayor. The trick is keeping some money on the side, so if things ever get heated, I'll be able to skip out. You have to cover yourself, that's the trick to life.

Mr. McManus took a long puff of his cigar and another healthy gulp of his scotch, which sent dribbles down his chin. Mrs. McManus didn't know about the hidden money behind the painting. No one knew how much Mr. McManus had stashed away.

Mr. McManus thought on…

Life is simply a totem pole and us top heads get to see the furthest. The only way you get to the top is to stand on the rest. That's the only way. And I am going to see the furthest.

Mr. McManus coughed, smoked and drank some more. It felt good for him to believe he was smarter than everyone else.

Dinner was quiet again at the McManus house. It was always quiet when their father didn't join them. Mrs. McManus thought as she watched her girls eat in silence - *The Twins characters are changing from their father pulling away.* Marlene had become more like her mother. She had become quieter each year. While Charlene seemed to emulate her father more, becoming more bold, direct and assertive.

The girls didn't ask their mother if their father was coming to dinner this evening or what he was doing. That ended. They knew he was in the house, but part of a different world. He had changed so much since Mrs. McManus had first met him after a concert at The College Club of Boston, many years back. She was an artist then; he was a confident charmer. Mrs. McManus resented the new him. He used to be so imaginative, so full of life and ideas. Mrs. McManus didn't know how he had changed or how she had allowed him to change. It just happened so gradually over the years. But the fear of the times and his always increasing lust for money was all she could figure that fueled the change within him. *It was so dishonest what he was doing,* she thought, as she stared at her girls. Mrs. McManus took a small bite of her now cold peas and prayed in her head for the good Lord to forgive her husband. But wrong is wrong and she knew that. Mrs. McManus just didn't know what to do in the house any longer. She didn't know how to keep things happy for the Twins any longer.

There was a sound of a distant cough and both girls looked toward the sound, then went back to quietly eating. Mrs. McManus sometimes thought of leaving him, taking the Twins and going back to Boxford where her family's house was. *I mean*, she thought as she pushed her plate away from her, *he's already left us.*

Rudy could tell that great things had happened that afternoon. Kringle and the Airlords were smiling big as they displayed to Pete and Riggels their day's work outside The Workshop. The *Speed Cruiser* was finished. It shined with a wet sparkle.

The *Speed Cruiser* looked fast. It seemed to have come straight out of a *Buck Rogers* comic strip. The front of the cobbler's bench was no longer square. Kringle and Johnny had made it a point much like a loon's bill, with a chipped boomerang secured at its bow. Under the cobbler's bench was the vertical fin, (the rowing oar from many of the Airlords' past ships) that Kringle and Johnny had sawed away from its staff. It would steer the *Speed Cruiser*. By means of two ropes tied to the wing tips of the boomerang, one could pull the boomerang left or right, turning the vertical fin. Holding the cobbler's bench up were the two handrails from the schoolhouse. The backsides of the cobbler's bench also had vertical fins to simply and cosmetically match the look of *Buck Rogers'* ships, while the sides had stabilizer wings protruding horizontally. It was to be painted with red and white stripes to match the Airlords crest in Central Command. It was perfect.

Everyone was proud of the *Speed Cruiser* and wanted to keep talking about her until the Sun was fully down. But it was getting late, dinnertime, so Kringle pulled whoever could wrestle their way onto *The Speed Cruiser* back to Bridge Street. Murf, Ramona and Terrance headed down Bridge Street for home while Kringle, Johnny and Billy kept the new ship at the Boone home.

Kringle hadn't seen Ellie since the Ice Dance, so he was on the fence as to what her reaction would be to seeing him.

Kringle

Ellie was preparing dinner: mashed potatoes with ground beef gravy and baked apples. She looked out of the window to see Kringle pulling Johnny and Billy on the new ship, a sharp release of adrenaline made her freeze and her eyes widen. She ducked away from the window. Quickly, she redid her hair bun. Then she took off her apron and walked to the front door to look out the window panes.

Ellie had thought long about what had happened at the Ice Dance and had decided that it was something that was best forgotten. Flo's note had helped and when Flo came by to check up on Ellie, she had told her – "There's no need for you to walk around each other like you both got glass in your shoes. And you two best just be getting on with what you were getting on with and leave that stinky sour night behind you both. It's too easy to be grumpy Ellie; it's much more difficult to be cheery, so don't be a lazy Sheba. Smack those little shoulders back and be cheery." Ellie had agreed mostly because she didn't know what else to do; she was out of ideas.

Ellie opened the front door.

"Ma, check out our new *Speed Cruiser* Ma," shouted Johnny from the bottom of the stairs sitting in the leather seat of the cobbler's bench.

"We are gonna blast by the Twins' Mongol Machine, no doubt Momma," said Billy gripping the two ropes at the bow of the ship and making sounds as if he was flying.

Kringle and the Boone boys walked up the steps; Kringle held the *Speed Cruiser* in front of him. He set the ship down on the porch and the Boone boys spoke with bursting excitement to their mother all about it. But Ellie and Kringle were eye-to-eye apologizing with eye contact and bashful smiles. Humble flirting.

"You know, I'm a lot taller than that," said Ellie kicking her head toward the snowcouple. Kringle quickly looked over his shoulder toward his art piece.

"Oh ya. You sure?" said Kringle back, straightening his stance. "I think I got it right."

. "What do you mean, I am way taller than that and you know it. And *you* are not that much taller than me," Ellie said as she brought a chatty Billy close to her side.

Kringle was relieved Ellie was friendly to him and glad that she liked his snowcouple. A woman can break daily, but always put herself together; when a man breaks he is often baffled of where the pieces once were. So, Kringle followed Ellie's lead, said nothing and agreed to stay for dinner.

Ellie laid down dinner for Kringle and her boys. The conversation was all over the place. The Boone boys talked fast about the crafting of the *Speed Cruiser*, often needing to be corrected to not talk with food in their mouths.

At the end of dinner, the Boone boys asked their mother if it was okay for Kringle to stay and listen to the seven o'clock *Buck Rogers* radio show, but Kringle explained that he had a lot of work still to do that night. Kringle even asked if Ellie would come back with him to The Workshop. Pete and he had something to tell her, something to ask her and something to show her.

Ellie agreed. She wrapped up some baked apples for Pete and Riggels, turned the *Buck Rogers* show up on the radio, wrapped her boys in a blanket by the fire, and walked with Kringle back to The Workshop.

The skeleton trees crackled in the wind.

"So what is it you want to show me?" interrupted Ellie as the two came up on The Workshop.

The small chimney poofed out smoke in puffy bunches. And its windows glowed from the firelight. From the outside, one could tell it was warm inside - magical and warm. It looked as if one had built a small house around a small flame.

"Well, I wanted to show you this…" Kringle opened The Workshop door.

Warmth, color, sparkles and all that makes up joy came to Ellie's eyes. Her mouth dropped and her hands came up to cover it. She was breathless.

Pete and Riggels sat at their workbenches. Pete was working on a toy-box and Riggels was painting one. Pete put down his small hammer and smiled. Riggels set his paintbrush down and smiled as well. They turned to Ellie and Kringle and lifted their rugged teas up to "cheers" them both.

"Welcome to our little toy shop Ellie," said Pete with his watery green eyes sparkling.

Kringle brought Ellie inside. He closed the door with his foot. Rudy greeted Ellie by her side. Kringle then took Ellie's jacket and gave it to Pete, who gave his seat to Ellie. Then both Kringle and Pete sat down on their cots.

"What-what is this? You? You Pete, you Riggels, Kringle…*you all* make the toys?" asked Ellie shocked.

"Well, I just joined," said Riggels with a smile.

"I don't understand," said Ellie.

"Well, Ellie, this might be a lot to take in," said Pete. "Can you keep a lock and key secret?"

"I can," said Ellie as she untied her babushka.

"See over there Ellie," Kringle pointed to the north wall, which had a pile of toys that reached the ceiling of The Workshop. "Those are for the auction. Those are orders we get from Mr. McManus. But over there, the rest is…" Kringle pointed to the south wall that had a much smaller pile of toys lining it. "…that will be a toy for every child in town."

The Workshop was filled with toy-boxes, riding horses, dollhouses, climbers, and more. The sight was magnificent. It was a child's fantasy come to life. The colors of the toys: bright reds, golds, greens and blues brightened the small workshop. To be there made you smile; to be there made your worries disappear.

Ellie stood and walked over to the piles. She picked up a moving seesaw piece of a boy riding a goose. It swayed back and forth.

"You? You made all of these?" said Ellie.

"That's what I do Ellie. I make toys," said Kringle.

"He taught me," said Pete.

"I paint them," said Riggels proudly.

All the men felt elated to tell Ellie. They could feel her glowing admiration toward them.

"Riggels got a list of names of the kids and what toys they dream of having from Miss Magnolia. Thing is Ellie, some things on the list we can't make," said Kringle as he picked up the list from Miss Magnolia that were separated from the many lists from Mr. McManus. He walked over to Ellie and showed her. "See, it says, 'a doll with long hair to brush' and here's another one, 'a doll with red hair like mine'. And there's more like, 'a soft teddy bear to hold', 'a piggy' and here 'I'd love to squeeze an elephant with a big trunk at night'. We can't make those Ellie," said Kringle. "I mean we could out of wood, but that's not nice to hug at night."

"We were wondering if *you* would?" said Pete as he brought Rudy close to him.

Then there was a silence as the men watched Ellie walk around the room looking at all the different toys. She stopped at a toy-box on Pete's workbench. She held it up and turned the crank: two people began to twirl inside a diminutive model of The Workshop as miniature models of Pete and Rudy played tug-of-war with a tiny tire.

"That's my mother and father there, they are the two dancing. That was my first toy-box I made, said Pete with a quiet proud tone. "I've made about nine now."

Ellie turned to Kringle's workbench and lifted another toy-box. She held it up and turned the crank: The toy-box was of the carnival game Kringle and she played at the Ice Dance. Small models of Kringle and Ellie moved. Ellie's little arm turned as if she was throwing a doll. Kringle's arms went up cheering as a small model of a doll came up and went through the circle of the clown's mouth. One of the two gamekeeper's arms went up like Kringle's cheering and the other gamekeeper's arms went out handing Ellie a small white bear.

"No! Kringle? These, these are wonderful," said Ellie. And as she turned to face the men, her eyes watered. "You really made one for every boy and girl in town?" asked Ellie. And then she walked on touching and testing each toy.

"Not enough for everyone. And with new orders coming in, well it's looking really hard to finish," said Pete.

"That's why we wanted to ask you for some help," said Kringle.

"Suuure I'll help. Where do I start?" said Ellie as she turned with her hands out and her fingers wiggling to get started.

"You sure about this Johnny?" said Billy as they closed the door of their home. Both boys were bundled up - boots, jackets, hats and gloves - yet they were still wearing their pajamas underneath. The Boone boys were curious of what Kringle wanted to show their mother so late at night, and they were still very awake from the excitement of finishing the *Speed Cruiser*. So the two headed out to see what was happening at The Workshop.

"I just wanna see," said Johnny. "I have a feeling it's top secret stuff."

"It's just that Momma will be red hot if she finds out we're outta bed, let alone outta the house this late."

The walk consisted of Billy saying they should head back and Johnny saying he needed to see what was conspiring.

"Okay shh-shh, I can see them in the window. See? Now let's crouch low and move in real quiet. Let's go to that window there," said Johnny already moving in.

Inside Kringle and Pete hunched over their workbenches as Riggels painted on the floor and Ellie sewed sitting on Kringle's cot. Rudy lay in his blankets staring up at Ellie.

"But no, it's wrong boys," said Ellie, as she cut the outline of a doll through an old plaid shirt.

"Which is?" asked Riggels.

"All of it. Lying to the people," replied Ellie with wide eyes.

The Boone boys had been listening outside the window for awhile. They huddled close for warmth and whispers.

"Mr. McManus is cheating people Johnny," whispered Billy.

"Shh," said Johnny. "Billy. Listen."

They listened intently to their mother's words.

Ellie continued with the men.

"Well, I don't know. You need proof. What if you got those fake "Letters of Authenticity" you were saying he counterfeits. If you got those, then I guess you could find the blank ones Mr. McManus fills out and then show them to Sheriff Jones as proof," said Ellie.

"How would we get those though?" said Riggels.

"I know one thing. We'd get locked up if we tried to steal 'em," added Pete.

"Well I bet they're in that elephant of a house he's got - in an office - in a fancy safe. Isn't that where people like him stash their soul's naughty secrets?" said Ellie as she let Rudy outside, set down her mug and began pinning her next doll.

"We gotta get those letters," whispered Johnny to Billy.

"And how," whispered Billy back.

"Let's gather the Airlords and find that safe," said Johnny with a puckered mouth and squinting eyes.

"Okie-dokie," said Billy as the two boys dashed off with Rudy.

7:50PM. Johnny, Billy, Murf and Terrance stood outside Ramona's house. Each one of them took turns hurling snowballs the size of crab apples at Ramona's bedroom window.

SPAT, SPAT, SPAT!

Ramona's window rose.
"Oi-Oi-Oi, brothas vhat's dis bushwa all ebout; I'm 'n bed ya thorny-weeds. And cripes, the last ten minutes of *Buck* iz on teu," assertively whispered a sleepy Ramona from her bedroom window.
"Code red," Murf whispered up. "Code red."
"Bloody hell. Bloody-bloody hell. Right, I'll be right dewn," said Ramona as she disappeared back into her room. "Every Goid dang time I..." muttered Ramona.
"So what's the plan?" asked Murf to Johnny.
"We're breaking into Mr. McManus' house," said Johnny chewing on a straw. "We're settin' to help out Mr. Kringle and Pete. They're under the gun see?"
"Oi. Brothas move back; I'm coming dewn," whispered Ramona as she reappeared with her winter bundle on. She crawled outside her window and sat down on her roof.
The boys stepped back.
Ramona dug her mittens into the snow and launched off as if she was on a sled heading down Robin's Hill. She slid down fast, flew off the roof and landed on a pile of snow.

POOF!

"Whoa," said the boys.
"Ye, I stacked de snow dere de other day. Ye know, just 'n case a moment like dis came up. Giraffes 're smart, you know?" said Ramona as she brushed the snow off herself.

"You made that for a code red? Wow!" said Murf.

Ramona gave him a wink, a nod and shot him with a finger gun. CRUNCH – CRUNCH – CRUNCH!

The Airlords stomped down an empty Commonwealth Street. The lights were out in all the shops and all the homes. The Moon seemed to follow the Airlords as they made their way to Mr. McManus' home. Johnny and Billy caught the rest of the Airlords up about the happenings of the swindle going on at *Bonne Affaire* and how they needed to find fake Letters of Authenticity to help Kringle and Pete blow the whistle on Mr. McManus. The Airlords agreed the mission must take place.

The Airlords came up on Mr. McManus' house. They hid behind a snowy bush by the mailbox. Mr. McManus' house was the biggest in all of Hamilton - by far. It had ten gables, a widow's peak the size of some people's homes, a long driveway for Mr. McManus' Duisenberg and an enormous chimney. All of the lights inside were off except for Mr. McManus' office; it had one candle flickering.

"Sounds dangerous, but I'm in," said Terrance. "And what if there's a fire burning in the chimney? We'll all be as burned as a cheater in Hell."

"No, see, there'd be smoke coming outta that chimney if it was still burning. No smoke - no fire," said Johnny holding the lobster hook that the Airlords had found in the junkyard that day in one hand and the battered snowshoe in the other.

"So what then?" asked Murf.

"Well see, look over there. See that?" said Johnny pointing to a lattice flower arbor. "Well, I'll climb that see? Then from there I'll be able to get on the roof. Then I'll climb the roof using this snowshoe. That way I won't slip. Once I'm at the chimney I'll toss the rope down. Then each one of you climb that flower gate, grab the rope and pull yourself up. You know, like burglars do."

"Bet den wha?" asked Ramona, pulling her scarf from her mouth.

"Then we throw the rope of the grappling hook down the chimney see, and climb down it," whispered Johnny.

"Whoa," said Murf. "Just like when *Buck Rogers* and *Wilma* climbed into the volcano on that alien planet that had too many volcanos."

"Exactly," said Johnny. "That's where I got it from."

"Vhat I mean is, but vhat do ve do, once ve're inside dat bloody castle?" asked Ramona, again pulling her scarf from her mouth again.

"Right, see then we'll look for Mr. McManus' fake Letters of Authenticity, they must be in a pile of fancy papers, with fancy words on 'em," said Johnny.

"I bet they're in a safe or something," said Billy. "Like the bank."

"What if we get caught?" asked Terrance. "We'll absolutely be slam-clicked."

"We won't get caught Airlords," said Murf in his commanding voice. "We are the Airlords of Hamilton, no one can defeat us. No one! We'll show 'em."

The Airlords all put their mittened hands in and then cheered quietly one time.

"Airlords unite!" they all said.

Johnny crouched and crawled toward the lattice flower arbor. He had the rope around his neck, the lobster hook in his left hand, and in his right hand he held the snowshoe. The rest of the Airlords watched from behind the snowy bush.

Johnny reached the lattice flower arbor; he turned and gave the Airlords "thumbs-up". They returned the message.

Carefully, Johnny began to climb the lattice flower arbor. It was icy, snowy and rickety. Johnny ascended. Once Johnny got to the top, he reached for the roof that the top of the lattice flower arbor was nailed to. With big snow clumps from the roof falling to the ground, Johnny now gingerly patted the battered snowshoe onto the snow in front of him and pushed it down to make sure it wouldn't slip. Johnny hopped onto the roof. He crouched with his knees in the snow and his hands on the battered snowshoe in front of him. He was still. He was secure. With two hands on the snowshoe Johnny lifted it and patted it down into the snow in front of him; he then crawled on his knees until his knees touched his wrists. Like an inchworm, Johnny made his way up the roof.

The Airlords held their breath as they watched from behind the snowy bush. Johnny did look like a burglar because in this moment, Johnny was a burglar.

Knees to wrists, inch by inch, Johnny made his way up. He was now only a few feet from the top of the pointed rooftop where the massive chimney was set. Johnny's mitten touched the top of the roof, he pulled himself up a bit, made sure his mitten grip was strong, then, with his left hand, he took the lobster hook, unwrapped the rope from around his neck and reached up to secure the hook into the roof.

The rest of the Airlords got in queue by the lattice flower arbor to begin their accent. One by one the Airlords climbed the lattice flower arbor - reached for the roof - grabbed the rope, and climbed their way up like little burglars in the night.

Murf and Terrance stood, balancing on the roof's point on either side of the chimney while Ramona and Billy sat on the edge of it with their legs dangling inside. They all helped Johnny get into position.

"Is the grappling hook secure?" asked Murf.

Billy tested it.

"Affirmative," Billy answered.

Lying on his stomach with his feet dangling inside the chimney, Johnny lowered himself, gripping the secured rope. Down he went. Johnny was now all the way inside the chimney. He looked over his right shoulder. A few red, but dying, coals still steaming at the bottom.

"The fire's out and dead. It-it..." Johnny grunted as he held his own weight. "...it looks to be just a few stubborn coals. Okay Airlords I'm heading down. Once I'm down I'll make the owl call. When you hear that, send someone else down."

"Vight brotha. Careful now Johnny-boy," said Ramona as she watched Johnny head down.

Johnny made his way down the chimney with care. The lower he descended, the smaller his friends' heads looked gazing down on him. By the square light of the Moon, Johnny looked at the burned bricks all around him. They were black and filthy, cobwebbed and stinky.

Left hand, right hand; left hand, right hand...

...Johnny climbed down. His body would touch and tap the sides of the chimney making ash and soot fall to the fireplace. Even the rope, secure over the chimney's mouth, would slide slightly making ash and soot fall on Johnny's face and hair.

Johnny's boots touched down on the smoldering coals. He crouched. Looked around. He was five feet from a snoring, sleeping Mr. McManus. Johnny looked back up the chimney. He could see four small heads looking down at him.

Johnny made the owl call...

"Hoo-Hoo--Hoo-Hoooo, Hoo-Hoo--Hoo-Hoooo,"

...one by one the Airlords dropped down. Once they were all safely down, they crouched together by the fireplace staring at a sleeping, snoring Mr. McManus, passed out in his armchair.

With ash and soot smeared on all their faces, the Airlords now looked like a group of young chimney sweeps.

"What's that sound?" whispered Billy.

"It's dere," whispered Ramon, pointing to a spinning record atop a turntable. The record was finished; warm static crackled.

"Should we fix it?" asked Terrance.

"No, let it spin. It'll be a sonic shield in case we make too much noise," said Murf.

"Okay Airlords spread out, we're looking for fancy papers that look like that big paper Miss Magnolia showed us. The old one.

"The Bible?" whispered Ramona.

"No, the other one," whispered Johnny.

"The Constitution?" whispered.

"That's it."

The Airlords spread out. They began searching around Mr. McManus' office.

"How will we know we have what we came to get, if we even do find it?" asked Murf. "What if we get the wrong stuff, like bills or taxes?"

"We'll worry about that once we find something at all," said Johnny as he opened one of Mr. McManus' desk drawers.

"Chripes Billy-boy, vat are ya doin'?" whispered Ramona and all the Airlords looked Billy's way.

Billy was standing inches from a sleeping and snoring Mr. McManus.

"Look," Billy whispered back.

All the Airlords looked to where Billy gazed.

"What?" said Murf.

"His hand."

"What, it's empty. You mean the glass," asked Terrance.

Under McManus' left hand was a fallen scotch glass. A bit of scotch pooled on the rug beside it.

"No, the other hand," said Billy pointing.

And there it was, trapped in Mr. McManus' sausage fingers – a key.

The Airlords circled around Billy.

"It's a key," Murf said.

"That's got to be it gang," said Johnny as he crawled toward Mr. McManus.

"Careful mate," Ramona whispered.

Johnny looked over his shoulder to the other Airlords. "I'm gonna try and take it," he said.

"Cripes be careful Johnny-boy, be careful," said Ramona again as she took her hat off and pushed her sprongy hair back.

Mr. McManus' chest rose with big breaths and then rumbled as he exhaled. His snores were of low tones and his lips smacked.

Johnny carefully reached forward. Half of the key was submerged in Mr. McManus' roley-poley fingers. Johnny touched the teeth of the key. He pulled slightly but nothing happened. Neither the key nor Mr. McManus' fingers budged.

Johnny looked back at the other Airlords.

"Try pulling harder Johnny," whispered Murf.

Johnny nodded and turned back. Mr. McManus took a deep breath and as he let it out Johnny gripped the teeth of the key, but this time Mr. McManus' sausage fingers gripped tighter on the handle of the key.

"Let me help," said Murf and he grabbed one of Johnny's wrists.

"Sure has a grip, don't he?" said Terrance as he stepped forward and grabbed Johnny's right wrist with both hands.

The three Airlords braced themselves as Mr. McManus took in another deep breath. As he let out his lip-slapping snore, the three Airlords pulled. But Mr. McManus' finger gripped even tighter and the key stayed stuck.

"Oi Billy-boy, let's help," said Ramona as she put her arms around Murf's waist, which made Murf's eye widen. Billy put his arms around Terrance's waist and the Airlords waited for Mr. McManus' next breath.

284

"SSNNUUCCKK…SHHOOOO!" snored Mr. McManus and all the Airlords pulled with everything they had.

POP!

The Airlords tumbled back like small rolling apples. The key was freed. Johnny held it in his hand. But the rolling of the Airlords had agitated Mr. McManus slumber. He began to mumble and toss about in his chair. He was waking up. The Airlords froze. Then all of their attention turned sharply, but silently toward the door. Its doorknob was turning. Someone had heard them. Someone was there.

The door squeaked as it opened. This too agitated Mr. McManus. He grumbled and turned this way and that.

The Airlords, still frozen in fear, stared as the door slowly opened.

A confident Periwinkle made herself known. She walked in with a chirp, smelled the air, walked in a circle, did a fancy roll on the carpet, then stood up, stretched, reached long, and sat down with her tail elegantly wrapped over her front paws. She then gave the Airlords a dignified look. Behind her, Marlene came into frame. She put her finger to her lips and then placed her hand out telling the Airlords to stay put. Then Marlene carefully closed the door behind her. All the commotion had stirred up Mr. McManus. He grumbled and tossed, he even brought his left hand up to his mouth, pantomiming taking a sip of scotch. He straightened a bit, brought his big hands to his face and began rubbing his eyes.

They slowly opened.

Confused Mr. McManus straightened himself a bit, looked left, yawned and looked right. The Airlords were all huddled in a bunch in front of him, but with Mr. McManus' sleepy eyes, and because all of the Airlords had streaks of ash across their faces, Mr. McManus didn't see anything out of sorts.

The Airlords huddled, frozen in fright. They closed their eyes making them even more invisible to the groggy Mr. McManus. Plump palms to his face, Mr. McManus began rubbing. He looked to be completely waking up.

But something happened. Something made Mr. McManus stop, slouch back into his seat and made his eyelids became heavy again.

The Airlords looked past Mr. McManus at Marlene beside the record player. She was hunched over it; she had rested the needle down at the start of the record. A soft trumpet played its lullaby and Mr. McManus went back to his snoring.

Marlene crawled over to the Airlords.

"Hi Terrance," she said with a slow blink. "What'ch ya doing here?"

"Oh, u-u-um, w-w-well…w-we," got out Terrance.

Marlene began to wipe Terrance face, cleaning him, with her hand.

"You're filthy. Did you all come down the chimney?" Marlene asked.

"Y-yes we did," admitted Terrance.

"Don't be nervous; I'm glad you're here. All of you. Really," said Marlene with a smile.

"You won't tell? You won't tell the sheriff?" asked Terrance.

"Heavens no. But I must say, you are an odd bunch," Marlene said again with a pleased smile. "But why are you in my father's office? As nice as it is to see you Terrance, it's rather peculiar."

Johnny caught Marlene up on the Airlord's mission. Marlene looked surprised, but not too surprised. Marlene, her mother and twin sister didn't know exactly how their father was making such a large quilt of money, but they knew there were lies sewing it all together. He never spoke about knowing anyone from across the seas to them, but he spoke about it constantly to others outside of their home. Mrs. McManus and her twins slowly learned to simply not ask any questions.

"You ain't mad at us?" asked Murf.

"No. I'm not mad. In fact I think it's a good thing what you're doing. My mother would say so I think. She taught my sister and me to tell the truth, so I bet that goes for adults too. I don't know. But I do know where that key goes," said Marlene with life in her eyes.

"Where?" said Johnny.

"There," said Marlene pointing to a large portrait high up on the wall. The portrait was of Mr. McManus sitting royally in his armchair. "The lock is on the side. At the top of the side."

The Airlords gathered under the portrait.

"How are we gonna reach it," asked Billy. "It'd take all of us standing on top of each other like them circus clowns to reach that."

"That's it Billy. I know what we should do," whispered Murf as he turned to Ramona.

"V'hat," whispered Ramona back.

"Don't you see?" said Murf, "We need you. Just get on my shoulders; you'll be able to reach it."

"Oi Murf, I dink yer bloody right. I can tiptoe up 'n' everyting."

Everyone helped Ramona get up on Murf's shoulders. Murf and Ramona stretched long and both went on their tiptoes.

"'kay I see it," said Ramona as she placed the key inside the lock and turned. The front of the portrait opened. "Oi brothas, it's full of money," said a shocked Ramona.

"Money?" cadenced the rest of the Airlords and Marlene as well.

"Ya. Hundreds," said Ramona as she lightly touched the notes.

"Well forget that. Do yah see them letters?" asked Murf tittering a bit.

"Um," Ramona took out a leather envelope and opened it. Inside were the filled out fake Letters of Authenticity and the blank ones as well. "Bingo brothas."

"You get 'em?" grunted Murf.

"Ya 've got 'em. Dis is it Airlords. Now let'z get out da 'ere," Ramona whispered down.

"Swell Ramona. What a bullseye," grunted Murf.

The Airlords helped Ramona down. Holding the letters under the dying candlelight, Ramona said "Chripes, I dink ve really got it brothas. See dis one iz the letter all filled out 'n' all, 'n' de'z onez 'ere 'r' da blank v'onez. I mean...I dink."

"I think you're right," said Johnny. "Take them all."

"Nice work Airlords, now let's get the heck outta here," said Murf as he rubbed his sore shoulders.

CLIP – CLANK!

CLAP – CLINK!

"What was that?" whispered Billy.

"Someone's awake," whispered Johnny.

"It came from over there," whispered Terrance, pointing to the west side of the ceiling.

"That's my room. It must be," whispered Marlene.

"Oi yah daun't dink?" whispered Ramona.

"I do. *Charlene* is coming," whispered Marlene with panic in her voice.

"What do we do?" asked Murf.

"Come with me, I can let you out the front door," whispered Marlene and all the Airlords tip-toed following her out of the office door.

The Airlords, Marlene and Periwinkle were now in a long hallway that had grand portraits lining the walls, all of Mr. McManus. Different dark door frames were visible, but what was inside the rooms was hidden in the darkness. The front door was to their immediate left and to their right was a grand staircase.

STOMP, STOMP, STOMP!

"'urry brothas," whispered Ramona.

"Come, this way, just go out here. This will lead you outside. Come on, hurry," said Marlene as she slowly opened the front door.

The cold air rushed in sending Periwinkle dashing down the hall and up the staircase. The Airlords and Marlene looked in Johnny's direction towards the staircase.

Standing on the top step with her arms crossed was a callous Charlene. She began to walk down the staircase, unsympathetic of her foot stomping volume.

"Well, what a bunch of wet-socks. Look at you all, just a bunch of dirt faced, wet-socks. Marlene did *you* let these garbage rats in? How could you?" said Charlene as she walked toward the Airlords and Marlene.

"Charlene. Shh. Let me explain," whispered Marlene.

The door was open. Light gusts of small snowflakes sprinkled in.

Most of the Airlords were in the door frame. Marlene and Johnny were just in front of it.

"Don't any of you garbage rats take another step. Thieves. Beggars. Burglars," spoke Charlene with a nasty look on her face.

"It's not like that Charlene," said Marlene. "Let me explain."

"Uh-uh. I'm telling father. All I have to do is scream and all of you thieves will get slam-click," said Charlene.

"Please Charlene don't," begged Marlene.

"Give me one good reason not to," said Charlene as she dipped her left hip.

"Let's run for it," whispered Terrance.

Then Marlene whispered something in Johnny's ear.

"What?" Johnny whispered back.

Again, Marlene whispered something in his ear. Then she nodded to him directly. Sternly.

"Do it," she said.

"No," whispered Johnny again.

"Hey, what did you just tell him?" demanded Charlene, with a bit of nervousness in her voice.

"Do it," Marlene said again.

"Bu-but, why?" whispered Johnny back.

"I said, what did you just whisper to him Maaarrlene. Marleeeene, answer me or I swear," said Charlene getting a bit aggravated and louder. "That's it, I'm gonna scream. I'm gonna do it. One, two…"

Charlene took a big breath of air.

"Johnny-boy do it, v'hat eva it iz," said Ramona.

Charlene's mouth opened to scream as Marlene pushed Johnny forward.

"Three," said Charlene.

Charlene's eyes widened; Johnny was just inches from her, she exhaled her breath.

"W-what?" Charlene stuttered. "W-what?"

That's when Johnny grabbed Charlene's shoulders, wrenched her forward and gave her a big kiss.

"*Thaaat's* what you told him?" whispered Billy to Marlene. "But *why*?"

"Oh Charlene has a big crush on Johnny. Ever since the second grade. He sends her," Marlene said as she watched with glee as Johnny and her sister kissed. "You can't tell?"

When Johnny pulled away the two were both flush red in their cheeks. Charlene took a step back - a bit dazed. She raised her wrist to her forehead.

"Woosh. Golly," she said tingling.

"Quick go," said Marlene with a smile, as she watched her confused sister collect herself.

Outside, Rudy jump straight up like a startled cat as the Airlords exploded out the front door.

They all dashed down Commonwealth Street.

Kringle

✳

Back at The Workshop Ellie was fixing to leave. The four toy makers had done a fine job that night, but it was time to retire and begin work again in the early daylight.

"I'll walk you home Ellie," said Kringle as he helped her into her jacket.

Riggels had already headed home and Pete was cleaning up their night's work. Together they had made great progress: toy-boxes, dolls, push toys, teddy bears, climbers and more. The Workshop was now looking more like a Toyshop.

"Oh you don't have to, but thanks just the same," said Ellie as she tied her babushka.

"I insist," said Kringle as he too put on his winter bundle.

"Good night Ellie," said Pete while holding one of Ellie's dolls. "Wonderful work you did here. Magical."

"Oh thank you Pete. Good night. I'll try and come by again tomorrow night to finish up. Good night," said Ellie and she and Kringle headed out to the moonlit world.

Johnny, Billy and Rudy rounded Commonwealth onto Bridge Street, as all the other Airlords were sneaking back into their homes.

"We gotta beat Ma home Billy," said Johnny in labored breath.

"You said it," said Billy also panting. "If she's home already we're done for."

"And how. Let's just hope she ain't."

The Boone boys were running in the hope of beating their mother back home. They could see a figure of a man walking down Bridge Street.

"Look…Johnny," panted Billy.

"I…I I see…him," panted Johnny back as Rudy dashed along side them both.

Walking down Bridge Street was a bundled Riggels. His pipe glowed and puffed out little clouds as if he was a miniature *Betsy Bound.*

"Must be…Mr.…Kringle…or…Pete," panted Billy.

"Naw…it's Mr. Riggelsworth…see the pipe?" panted Johnny back.

"Oh. Ya…ya…"

Johnny, Billy and Rudy came upon Riggels fast. They had no time to talk.

"Mr. Riggelsworth," shouted Johnny as they approached. "Our Ma at The

Workshop?" Johnny got out as he passed Riggels.

Rudy stopped and rubbed up against Riggels.

"Good boy. Okay-okay, go catch up. Don't mind me. Good boy," said Riggels as he scratched Rudy and gave him a tap on his bum, a signal to catch up with the Boone boys. Rudy took off. "Yup. But heading home now. You boys BETTER HURRY!" yelled Riggels back to the Boone boys crescendoing his voice as they ran further toward home.

"Thanks," screamed Johnny and Billy.

The cold birch trees held each other's branches tight, pleased with the romantic sight of Ellie and Kringle walking home in the moonlight. Kringle and Ellie walked close and slowly. Their shoulders rubbed as they walked.

"You'll have to teach me," said Kringle breathing warm air onto his gloved hands.

"Well, the first lesson is threading that finger biting needle. That can be tricky enough. Especially when it's cold like this," said Ellie, as she too breathed warm air on her mittened hands. "You have to teach me how to do all that you do. It looks so complicated."

"It's really just about honing in and taking the time with measuring. Everything is measuring. Once you get the proper focus for that, then comes the cutting. But the cutting is not a problem if your measurements are exact," said Kringle.

"I see."

Then Ellie shivered.

And Kringle rubbed her back.

Johnny, Billy and Rudy came up to the house. They slowed their run to a timid walk. Kringle and Ellie were walking up the front steps of the porch.

"Oh...no," said Billy, still panting.

"C'mon...let's head...to the back. The window. The back window," said Johnny and the two crept to the back of the small house, hidden in the shadows of the watchful trees.

Kringle and Ellie stood on the porch.

"I just think you should think about it. Tell me you'll think about it," said Ellie with her back to the front door. She pulled out her key from her jacket pocket and held it with both of her mittened hands against her chest.

"It's really up to Pete in a lot of ways. I'm still the new guy here," said Kringle.

"You could have your own shop. All of you - Riggels, Pete and you. You're all so talented Kringle, just open your own store."

Kringle leaned on the porch beam.

"That would be something swell. I just don't know if people who have extra lettuce would want to buy things knowing they were made by Pete and me. We're not exactly social models."

"Well, to the pig's trough with those types. Other people, normal people would. I would," said Ellie now leaning back on her front door. "I could work there too. I could sew. We could all make toys."

Johnny was already in the house. The back window was propped open with a birch branch. Billy stood on Rudy's back as Johnny reached down to pull him up.

"I got ya Billy," whispered Johnny holding both of Billy's arms. "Just walk up a bit, or better yet swing your leg over.

Billy swung his left leg up and hooked it on the window frame. Johnny pulled Billy inside.

"Good boy Rudy," whispered Billy down to Rudy. "Thanks a ton-ton-ton. Now head home to Pete's and Mr. Kringle's, I'll see ya tomorrow."

"C'mon Billy, c'mon," whispered Johnny as he was climbing up the loft ladder.

Kringle was shuffling his feet. His heart pounded. A little Kringle emerged on his left shoulder and spoke – "*Kiss her. Don't be nervous. Kiss her*", but another little Kringle emerged sitting on Kringle's right shoulder and answered – "That's a terrible idea. She'd smack your face right up." – "*No it isn't; no she would not. Don't listen to him. She wants you to kiss her. Just look at that face.*"

Ellie was leaning back against the front door, still holding her key to her chest with both of her mittened hands. Her eyes were locked on Kringle. They went to Kringle's eyes when she spoke and to his mouth when he spoke.

"You're a loon," said the little Kringle sitting on Kringle's right shoulder. The little Kringle on his left shoulder stood – "*Don't listen to him. Block him out. Just look at her lips. They're very kissable lips,*" he whispered – "I'll give you that," said the little Kringle, standing on Kringle's right shoulder.

"You're a good man Kringle. You shouldn't be wrapped up in this wickedness," said Ellie. "Well, I best get up to the boys," said Ellie as she slowly turned, slowly placed the key in the lock and slowly opened the door.

"W-wait," said Kringle.

Johnny and Billy were now in bed looking down from the loft as the front door opened. They could now see their mother standing in the doorway - she faced outward. The cold air whirled in the small home; Johnny and Billy pulled the blankets up to their noses. Their eyes peeked out.

"What's she doing?" whispered Billy.

"Don't know. But we made it. I can't believe we made it," whispered Johnny back as he tucked the fake Letters of Authenticity under the bed.

Kringle took a step closer; he now stood two inches from Ellie in the doorframe.

"I think Mr. Kringle's gonna kiss Momma. Hey wait a minute, you kissed Charlene. Why would you do that?" asked Billy.

"Ah forget about it. Marlene told me to that's all. She said it'd be the only way to shut her trap. She said it was the only way to get us outta there. So I did it. It had to be done. Forget about it."

"I thought you said she was a double spoonful of scum."

"Shh Billy. Look," said Johnny.

"Oh no not again," said Billy.

Kringle took off his hat, placed his hand on Ellie's waist and was moving in to kiss her.

The Boone boys gasped.

Ellie lifted her chin and closed her eyes. Kringle slowly got closer.

CRICK!

SNAP!

WHAMP!

The birch branch that was holding the window up snapped and slammed shut. Shocked, Ellie jumped back and hollered. Kringle also jumped.

And Rudy waddled in the front door, excited by all the sounds. He sniffed and sniffed, wiggling and jiggling. Rudy kept going through Kringle's and Ellie's legs knocking them off balance.

"Rudy boy come here. Sit-sit. Okay. Slow down boy. Sit-sit. Okay there you go," said Kringle trying to relax Rudy. Ellie collected herself.

"Oh Rudy. Where did you come from huh? Well, Kringle I best be heading to bed. I'll see you tomorrow," said Ellie. The moment had been lost and Ellie felt it smart to put the bookmark in for the night.

"Oh, right, yes. Course," said Kringle, also understanding the moment had been lost. "Good night Ellie." Kringle turned. "Come on Rudy boy. Let's head home."

And with that Ellie closed the door, leaned back on it and exhaled.

'DON'T CARES' BECOME TOYS,
CRAFTED BY LOW CANDLE LIGHT,
IN THE HOPE FOR ALL
TO FEEL FORTUNATE,
FOR EVEN JUST ONE NIGHT

STORY 5

*

THERE IS MAGIC ALL AROUND

It's okay to be worried
It's okay to feel down
As long as you know
There is magic to be found

And when you have discovered
All the magic in this world
Then it's your turn to share it
With every boy and girl

How wonderfully hard
*   it is to be brave*
Providers share joy
*   for those who need aid*

While children embrace the magic
*   that we hold out to share*
Grown ups learn that they are
*   the answers to little prayers*

So it's okay to be worried
It's okay to feel down
As long as you know
There is magic all around

*

Story 5:

'DON'T CARES' BECOME TOYS, CRAFTED BY LOW CANDLE LIGHT, IN THE HOPE FOR ALL TO FEEL FORTUNATE, FOR EVEN JUST ONE NIGHT

6:00AM. The Junkyard sparkled. A thin fog hovered low to the ground. Light gusts of wind whirled the fog mixed with light sparkling snow upward into the air. Magically floating whirlpools danced all around. It was cold, but the Sun was solidifying her position in the sky and her early morning rays were warm and yellow. As the Sun rose she reflected on everything around, making the dewdrops seem as if they were now filled with lemonade. 6:01AM.

That night, the deer family had stepped onto the Junkyard. The father deer had noticed the heaps of trash and how the blankets and tarps draped over some of the piles providing a nice place for his family to huddle for the night. They had chosen the pile of sinks, bathtubs and other plumbing parts sitting close to The Workshop. Its tarp was held in such a way that it acted like a camping tent, perfect for the three tired deer to settle into. The white fawn rose first. She was becoming spirited. Her nose peeked out of the snowy flap of their shanty tent. Looking left and then right, she thought her world a fascinating place and she was absolutely correct. With her long thin legs, the white fawn crawled out of the tent of plumbing parts. She stood quietly gazing at the sparkling wonderland. The whirls whirled around her. She squinted. Her color blended into her snowy world almost perfectly, save her eyes and cold red nose.

The white fawn looked back to see her mother slowly rising and her father stirring. The mother deer rubbed her nose on her partner's forehead, rose slowly and joined her fawn outside the tent. The white fawn circled her mother, brushing up against her to communicate her love for her. Then the two stood close and quiet.

Kringle had awoken and was brewing a small kettle for coffee. Pete and Rudy slept. Kringle turned on the radio. A violin player was trying to be heard through the radio's soft static. The warm water in the kitchen basin steamed.

Kringle soaped up his hands and washed them, then his scruffy face. He wet his hair sloppily, ran his soapy hands deep into his scalp, washed well, then rinsed his hair and dried it with a small hand towel. Rudy began to rise. Sleepy, but happy, Rudy walked over to Kringle and leaned his body against Kringle's legs.

"Morning Rudy boy," Kringle whispered as he filled his small bowl with chow. Rudy lay down as he ate.

Kringle then picked up a small mirror that had twine attached to either side of its frame and hooked it on the latch of the window over the kitchen sink. In one of the drawers of the sink, Kringle pulled out lather, a brush and a straight razor. The water had come to a boil. Kringle poured it in the kettle and coffee began to brew. Its awakening smell filled the small Workshop. The violin player was now playing with a cello player and hard-to-hear pianist. Kringle applied his lather, sharpened his razor on a leather strap and started shaving under his chin. Pete stirred. He pulled his pillow out from under his head and placed it over his face, as he always does when he knows he will have to rise soon. Looking in the small mirror hanging from the kitchen window latch, Kringle noticed how the lather made him look as if he had a full white beard - like his father had. Kringle took a minute to imagine a beard like that on himself. He smiled. That's when he looked past the mirror and noticed the two female deer looking out over the morning stillness. Kringle watched them as he continued his shave. Calmness.

When Kringle next looked up from the basin, he noticed that the two female deer were now facing the plumbing pile and looking anxious. Kringle rubbed his eyes, dried his face with the hand towel and squinted for a better look. He could see that the plumbing pile was shaking. It was a peculiar sight. It would shake, stop and then shake again.

Kringle went to the door and opened it a crack. He peeked out. The two female deer hopped back from the sound of the door opening and took a more bracing stance. But they did not run. They stayed by the shaking plumbing pile. That's when Kringle saw it – the nose of another deer was poking out from the pile. Kringle could see that some of this deer's antlers were broken. Kringle closed the door. He stood in The Workshop and thought to himself - *This is odd. One of them seems stuck inside that pile. Well, it's either stuck under something heavy or caught in something.* Kringle put on his winter bundle, grabbed a small crowbar from The Workshop's toolbox, put his straight razor in his jacket's breast pocket and slowly opened the door.

When the two female deer caught sight of Kringle for the second time, they again jumped back and took a fearful stance. Kringle stood still and set his eyes in the opposite direction of the two female deer. The two deer stared at Kringle with a direct line of vision.

The pile shook again. The father deer looked to be struggling to stand; something was holding him back. The father deer moaned and the mother deer moaned back to him. The pile shook violently this time.

Kringle took a few steps forward. The two female deer did not notice for they were focused on the father deer. He was getting tired from his struggles. Exhaustion.

Kringle spoke sweetly, "Okay now…what do we have here?"

With their heads still down, the two female deer looked up at Kringle with big, beautiful eyes.

"It's safe. It's safe. I know. I know this *is* a bit scary. I can help him. Ya. Yup, I can, I can help him. Suuure. Sure thing. No problem," said Kringle as he took small steps forward, yet always looking away.

When Kringle got close, the mother deer and white fawn jumped back. The white fawn spun around in a circle, confused whether she should stay or flee.

The pile shook, but not too much. The father deer was worn out from his efforts.

Kringle came up along side the opening of the plumbing pile. The father deer's chin rested on the snow and his eyelids were low from weariness.

"Hello big fella. Hello. Safe, you *are* safe. That's right - safe. You're fine," said Kringle as he pulled the left side of the tarp back to get a closer look on what was keeping the massive deer caught.

The back legs of the father deer were wrapped in an old discarded Gloucester fishing net. The tangle was messy and the legs were positioned in what looked to be painful.

The father deer looked up at Kringle with his tired eyes. He tried one more time to pull his legs out, but they were just two tangled in the fishing net.

"Calm, calm, let's stay calm. I'm a good man. No need to worry yourself," Kringle's voice was soothing. With his chin still resting on the ground, the father deer watched Kringle with his eyes. His breaths were labored. His muscles were tight. But the father deer allowed Kringle's help. With a dawning sense of calm, the mother deer and white fawn took a step forward.

Kringle

Kringle touched the neck of the father deer and rubbed him.

Kringle crawled inside the plumbing pile, all the while keeping one hand on the father deer soothingly touching him and speaking softly. "I like your family. They seem nervous though, so let's you and me not be. You're little one looks like a little comet from the sky. How is she so white and pretty?" Kringle looked to the fishing net to best plot his cuts. "You need a name Mr. Deer. Hm now. I got it. I'm gonna call you Basher. Is that okay with you? Why you ask? Well, because of your bashed up antlers there. You bash a lot. So Basher came to mind." Kringle looked the father deer in his right eye. "I'll fix this, you know?"

The fishing net was thick and frozen. It was wrapped all around the back legs of Basher. Some parts of Basher's ankles were raw and tender from trying to free himself. Speaking softly, Kringle took out his straight razor and began cutting. "That must be your wife. She's very pretty Basher. What shall I name her? Hm, what's another word for gorgeous – there's radiant and beautiful. What else. Hm. Dazzling. Ahh that's it there, let's try Dazzler. We'll see how she likes it." Because the fishing net was frozen it took time to cut through it. As Kringle spoke and occasionally rubbed the back of Basher, he would look up to see Dazzler and Comet peeking their heads inside the plumbing pile. They seemed to understand that Kringle was of help. Kind. Comet even took one step inside and stretched long to smell Kringle's boot.

"Well, hello there little Comet. It's a pleasure to meet you," Kringle said sweetly.

Square after square Kringle cut.

"Looks like a whole bit of smarts Basher. Your ankle looks pretty painful. Brave fella, brave fella. Okay, we're almost done here."

Kringle began to sing quietly as he cut:

> *"The reindeer are coming – trollop, trollop*
> *The reindeer are coming – trollop, trollop*
> *Spit-spot – with any luck*
> *The reindeer will come - trollop, trollop*
>
> *Deep in the forest – they lay, they lay*
> *Deep in the forest – they lay*

302

But if we ask and ask real nice
The reindeer will come - trollop, trollop"

"And there. Well, okay now, you look to be all set," said Kringle. Then he tapped the back of Basher signaling him to stand.

Basher mustered up his strength. He struggled a bit, then pulled his now freed legs up to his belly. Understanding now that he was in fact freed, Basher launched out of the plumbing pile. He bucked his back legs a few times, then turned to smell his Dazzler and Comet.

Kringle closed his razor, stuffed it in the breast pocket of his jacket and crawled out backwards. When he looked up, he saw all three deer standing in front of him, again with direct lines of vision.

Silence, save the light wind that whirled the loose snow into the air like wild whirlpools wayward from water.

Basher exhaled powerfully from his nostrils. He extended his right leg and lightly tapped his hoof to the ground in front of Kringle. Basher then turned and leaped away, Dazzler followed him, while Comet took a moment to stare at Kringle one last time until she too leaped away into the woods.

Kringle took a deep breath. He rubbed his face muscles loose. And when he brought his hands down he noticed lather on them from his face. He wiped the lather on his pants, let out his deep breath as well, smiled and headed back inside The Workshop.

Inside Pete was shaving at the kitchen sink, looking into the mirror that hung on the window latch.

"They seemed to like you," he said, then turned and smiled at Kringle with his sleepy watery green eyes.

If you are to race in the Red Robin Race there are three things you must have:

You must wear the Red Robin helmets that are decorated to resemble a
robin's head, made by Mr. Robin's wife - Mrs. Robin.
You must have a sled built for two.
And both racers must wear red clothing.

The top of Robin's Hill was a grand pageantry. Racing streamers were strung from the white birches and adolescent pines. Cider and hot cocoa stands were up. Racers, friends and family were all bundled and joking. Even Suds, the photographer for the *Worcester Evening Gazette,* was there and in top cheer. The race down Robin's Hill was much different than Patton's Hill. The races at Patton's Hill are straight down. The Red Robin Race down Robin's Hill was made from the old windy lumber path. Years back, trees were lumbered all over Robin's Hill and horses would bring down cut trees along this path. Robin's Hill had long since been lumbered off, but the annual Red Robin Race down the old horse path seems to be a well-substituted trade for the hill's purpose.

The old horse path had sharp turns at the top and wider turns near the bottom. To look down on it from the eyes of a bird high in the sky, the old horse path of Robin's Hill would look much like a great white snake wiggling its way up to the clouds. It took skill to ride down Robin's Hill. When taking a turn, it took smarts to keep from sliding off into the woods. The only two people to ever get hurt during the annual Red Robin Race was Phil Dunkin and his brother Sam. But Sheriff Jones said they had "a light spray of whiskey perfume coming off them", so everyone just chalked it up as their own fault.

The Hopkins sisters, Bridget and Meghan, were in Lane 1. The sisters were tough like their parents. Hardworking. But also, like their parents, they knew how to fake being proper when they needed to. And they did it seamlessly. They had a fast looking sled. It looked to be a promising candidate to win the Red Robin trophy and they knew it.

The Gardeners were in Lane 2. Claire and her father Patrick were ready, sitting down on their sled. Their sled was slender. Long. Handsome. And had a very nice shellac finish. They were contenders as well.

The McQueen's kids, Angus and Lorna, were as silly as always getting positioned in Lane 3. They joked and laughed knowing they wouldn't win, as they manned their beat up sled in Lane 3. They just liked to race for the razz of it all.

The Horwitzes were in Lane 4. Brian Junior and his brother Benjamin were just wiping down the rails to make sure there was no snow clumps collecting. They were good boys. Their sled looked fair. Not the best. But fair.

The Kluszewskis, Fredrick and Otto, were in Lane 5. Even though they seldom won the Red Robin Race, each year they got second. They were bad boys. Knaves. Many young ladies thought them something robust. The two brothers spit and swore and were reminded by Miss Magnolia that – "there are children around". They prepared for the race in Lane 5. Their sled was definitely a contender.

The McManus twins sat comfortably and confidently in Lane 6. Charlene kept her head forward and her mind centered. She did wonder deep in her hidden thoughts what their next conversation would be like. *Were they an item now?* - she wondered. Marlene had already waved to all of the Airlords and to Terrance three times. She was still jazzed from the sneaky late night at her home.

The Lorenzano's, Joey and Anthony, stood by their younger brothers Nicky and Mikey in Lane 7. Seldom did the Lorenzano boys take anything too seriously. Their mother Mary went back and fourth straightening her boys' and husband's hats, jackets and boots. Her boys were all big, but she was a tiny woman. They were a loving family, who would cut you a deal if they knew you needed it. But you had to show you appreciated the deal or the deal was off. Their sled looked good, but, because Joey and Anthony were big boys, their weight made other contenders feel confident that they weren't a dominant threat. Also, the Lorenzano boys were all displaying red cheeks and what seemed to smell like rugged ciders in their hands.

In Lane 8, were the Boone boys. Ellie and the Airlords stood a few steps back as Johnny and Murf positioned the new *Speed Racer*. They were upbeat, a bit nervous, but excited to see what kind of power their new ship had. Johnny and Murf were puffed up, talking about their strategy.

Kringle, Pete and Riggels were back at The Workshop making toys. They planned to be at the race, but had to squeeze in as much toy making time as they could. They were soon putting down their tools and quickly tossing on their winter bundles to rush to Robin's Hill.

Mr. McManus was yet to know that his office safe had been cracked and his Letters of Authenticity stolen. He stood near Miss Winkelplex and Mr. Robin discussing who would make this year's announcements. Every season Mr. Robin would announce the racers' names, announce the rules, make a few silly jokes and always shoot the firing gun. And he did this because it was his hill and his race. But each year Mr. McManus tried to debate with Mr. Robin that he should be the announcer and the one to fire the starter gun.

The Red Robin Race trophy stood glowing on a small card table beside the soapbox that Mr. Robin stood on each year. The soapbox had a small red bunting around it, sewn on by Mrs. Robin. The Red Robin trophy was three feet tall. It depicted a Robin flying like a World War I fighter plane. The Robin wore bomber goggles, a pilot's jacket, had a flowing scarf and was depicted in a diving pose.

The proud Hamilton Fire Department provided music. Along side them were firemen from the towns close by. They had marching drums, trumpets, trombones and bagpipes and they all laughed boisterously with booming cheer.

Ellie looked around the gathering with squinting eyes looking for the Dunce Brothers. That morning Ellie's boys had told her about how Kringle's deer song had worked and about the iceballs hurled at them by the Dunce Brothers. Ellie found them. They were sipping hot cocoa, standing near Miss Winkelplex, who was by Mr. McManus who was still trying to convince Mr. Robin that he should give that season's announcements.

The small fireman band kicked up a marching tune.

"Good luck boys. I'll see you at the finish line," said Ellie to Johnny and Billy.

"Is Kringle still coming?" asked Billy.

Johnny looked at his mother.

"He said he will be. We'll both be at the finish," Ellie said and then kissed the top of Billy's head.

"He said he will be," Billy repeated quietly.

As Ellie made her way to Miss Winkelplex, Flo stopped her. Flo was standing with Pastor Finn.

"There you are my bold beauty. Say where you heading with that look all over your pretty face? Come with us, we're heading down to the finish line," said Flo as she pointed to the six-horse-drawn sleigh that brought spectators up and down Robin's Hill.

"Well, hello Pastor Finn," smiled Ellie. "Hey Flo. Sure thing. Just let me do something real quick," said Ellie as she reapplied her serious face.

Ellie excused herself and headed toward Miss Winkelplex.

"She looks awfully angry. What is it you think she's about to do?" asked Pastor Finn.

"Oh Sweetie you're cute. Well, let's just say, mother hen just needs to go protect her coop."

"Oh," said Pastor Finn. He was beginning to understand Flo's riddle-speak much better. He turned and got up on his tippy toes for a better view.

The Airlords where ready for launch. Ramona put her hands on Murf's shoulders and loosened him up like a boxer's ring man.

"Oi Murf-boy you ready brotha? You straight? Don't worry 'bout no phonus balonus. You'll show 'em," she said as Murf put on his Robin helmet and goggles.

"You reckon Momma's right Johnny? You think Mr. Kringle's gonna come see us race. Think he wants to see the *Speed Racer* in action?" asked Billy as he handed his brother his Robin helmet and goggles.

"You never know Billy you never know. Best not think about it, I reckon," said Johnny as he suited up. "But maybe."

"What about those letters we got from Mr. McManus' house? Do we tell Momma or what?" asked Billy.

"I've been thinking all round and back again about that. I think after the race, we bring them to Mr. Kringle. We best leave Ma outta it. Her knowing we burglared Mr. McManus ain't the wisest," said Johnny.

"Ya, smarts," said Billy.

"After *this* mission we'll take on *that* mission. Like Buck Rogers says, 'Best focus on the mission at hand...'"

Billy finished his brother, "'...if you're gonna save the world.'"

Mr. Robin had finally pulled the microphone out of Mr. McManus' hand and was stepping up onto the soapbox to officially open the Ninth Annual Red Robin Race. Mr. Robin's voice amplified through the small-coned speakers.

"Attention, attention everyone...welcome to the Ninth Annual Red... Robin...Race!"

All the racers and spectators cheered.

The firemen ended a driving cadence and set down their instruments to listen.

The Dunce Brothers were four steps behind Mr. Robin standing on the soapbox, Mrs. Robin beside him, Mr. and Mrs. McManus with Miss Winkelplex beside Mrs. Robin.

Mr. Robin spoke, welcoming everyone, announcing the annual auction that was to happen that night and going over the rules for the race.

Ellie walked behind Mr. Robin as she approached the Dunce Brothers

still sipping their hot cocoa. She was in plain sight of all the people. She was just
a bit behind and to the side of Mr. Robin. Because of the determination in Ellie's
walk, everyone at the race looked past Mr. Robin and at Ellie behind him.

Mr. Robin spoke on with his happy voice booming out of the coned
speaker. He was overjoyed. This was his favorite time of year.

Ellie approached. She took a deep breath into her chest, put her hands
on her hips, puckered and squinted. The first thing Ellie did was slap the hot
cocoa out of both of the Dunce Brothers' hands. Then she pointed a finger in
both of their chests.

"What's my name?" she said.

"Excuse me Ma'am," Lloyd said in a nervous tone.

All of the racers and all of the spectators' eyes widened as they looked
past Mr. Robin and at the display behind him. No one could hear what Ellie was
saying, because of Mr. Robin's speech, but it was undoubtedly clear to them that
Ellie had a wrinkle to iron out.

"You know me don't ya *Lloyd*?" Ellie said "I know you." She turned to
Elmer. "You know me too, don't ya *Elmer*."

"Yes, Ma-am," said Elmer with a shaken voice.

"Then what is my name?" Ellie straightened to look as big and as bold
as her frame would allow.

"Well, you're Ellie Boone of course," said Lloyd factually.

Ellie looked right at Elmer.

"You're Ellie Boone Ma-am," said Elmer and his posture sank.

"That's right you sacks of bushwa. Now let me be clear with both of you
upright monkeys. Let me perfectly get this through to those hog brains of yours.
Those..."

Ellie turned and pointed strongly at her boys and the other Airlords.

All of the racers and all of the spectators stared at Ellie's display, save
the Airlords, and quickly diverted their eyes up at Mr. Robin, pretending to be
listening to his speech.

"...those are *my* boys Johnny and Billy Boone and their friends. You see
them? You see them all right there?" Ellie said, then turned around to face the
Dunce Brothers again.

"Yes Ma-am," said Lloyd.

"And you?" asked Ellie.

"Yes Ma-am. I see 'em there," said Elmer.

"Now if I ever catch word that you two have chased, hurled *iceballs*, approached, spoken to, or even looked at my two boys and their friends again, well..." Ellie moved in. All of the racers and all of the spectators watching Ellie leaned a bit in as well. Ellie snapped her fingers in front of the Dunce Brothers' eyes.

SNAP!

"...eyes here you blubbery monsters. Now put your brains on memory record. I will not hesitate to bite your disgusting, and I do mean disgusting, boogery little noses off and replace them with a rotten carrot. That way everyone will know what kind of twisted little witches you boys really are. Now have I made myself furiously clear?"

Ellie leaned back. All of the racers and all of the spectators watching Ellie leaned back as well. Mr. Robin spoke on as Ellie put her hands on her hips and puffed her chest out one last time.

"Yes, Ma-am," Lloyd said.

"And you?" asked Ellie.

"Yes, Ma-am," said Elmer.

Hearing Ellie's threats, Miss Winkelplex looked over her left shoulder. She looked astonished.

"Good! Don't tempt me boys or I'll be back for your noses," said Ellie as she tucked her thumb under two fingers, as if she had snatched the nose off Lloyd's face, then slowly turned around, never loosing eye contact with the frightened Dunce Brothers.

The people wanted to look away, but they noticed the fiery Ellie next catch the eyes of Miss Winkelplex who was standing a few feet to the right of the Dunce Brothers.

"Break a plate and kiss a frog, she's gonna go and do it, ain't ya flower?" said Flo as she grabbed the arm of Pastor Finn.

"Do what?" asked Pastor Finn.

"Oh, just change the weight on the seesaw that's all," said Flo. "Take her down Ellie girl; sink that dead fish stinkin' ship. Best pray for her would ya, Jim?"

Ellie leaned into Miss Winkelplex's ear. Mrs. Robin and Mrs. McManus had now noticed that everyone in front of them was looking past Mr. Robin and at Miss Winkelplex next to Ellie.

Ellie's finger came back up.

"Hello Linda. And do *you* have *your* brain on memory record?" Ellie didn't wait for an answer. "Kringle is hands off. Hear me? Hands off. You keep your sloppy mitts and lips off him. Or I tell you Linda, I'll bite that crooked nose off of you and replace it with a carrot. A rotten carrot."

Miss Winkelplex looked at Ellie, then at the people staring at them both and then back at Ellie.

"How dare you speak to me like that," said Miss Winkelplex with very little confidence.

"If he's anyone's, he's mine. You got that Lllllinda?" said Ellie more aggressively.

"What makes you think you can..." Miss Winkelplex stopped. Ellie exhaled through her nose the same way Basher did.

"You got that?" Ellie repeated in a lower register.

Afraid now, Miss Winkelplex looked down. "Fine. I got it," she said.

"Say it."

Miss Winkelplex looked up.

"He is yours," she said. "Sorry about that Ellie."

"Accepted."

Ellie turned. The people staring looked back up to Mr. Robin as he continued on. The Dunce Brothers and Miss Winkelplex looked down with a red face. Ellie walked over to Flo and Pastor Finn.

"I'm all set if you wanna head down the hill," Ellie said with a smile.

"Flower, you sure bring a new talent to being a mother hen," said Flo, and the three of them walked to the six-horse sleigh.

From the bottom of Robin's Hill spectators gathered to watch the race. From below, the tight turns at the top looked even tighter. And the wider turns near the bottom looked even wider. Spectators at both the top and base of Robin's Hill watched the race and cheered for their choice racer. Some spectators brought binoculars. Mr. Thomson was famous for bringing his telescope and shouting to those who were squinting which racer was in the lead. He screamed like an old Gloucester fisherman, catching sight of the distant Kraken.

Like the top of Robin's Hill, at the bottom, booths were set up with warm drinks, a warm pretzel, popcorn balls and red and green streamers were strung all around. A few horse carts were filled with hay for families to sit in and keep warm as they watched. Everyone's mittened hands steamed holding close a cider, cocoa, or pretzel. Everyone's cheeks were rosy. Everyone's nose was red.

The six-horse sleigh was just making its way to the finish line when Kringle, Pete and Riggels approached. The three toymakers' eyes looked tired. Bloodshot. But when the three men caught sight of Ellie, Flo and Pastor Finn they lit up with honest smiles.

Back at the top of Robin's Hill things were a bit more serious. The racers were all lined up. Each one of them had their Red Robin helmets on. The helmets had red feathers, silly googly eyes and yellow beaks. Mr. Robin stood on the soapbox with the starting pistol in his hand. He was bursting with excitement.

"The tight turns usually knock a bunch of racers off," Johnny said to Muff with his boots positioned on the boomerang and his mittened hands clenching the steering ropes.

"Ay-ay captain," said Murf sitting close behind Johnny, pulling down his goggles and gripping the sides of the *Speed Racer*.

Billy's, Ramona's and Terrance's hearts pounded as they stood a bit back with the other spectators.

"Then, when we get to the lower part of the hill, with those wider turns – that's gotta be all speed for us. We have to really pick up as much as we can for the last long slide in to the finish line," said Johnny while he ignored his heart pounding.

"Ay-ay. We'll stay as inside as much as we can, while staying stable. We don't wanna flip over the edge and into the trees," said Murf.

Mr. Robin brought his starting pistol up above his head.

"Are all the Robins ready to race?" yelled Mr. Robin through the cracking cone speaker.

Everyone cheered; the racers took on a more deadpan readiness.

The fireman drum Line went to press rolls on their snare drums that were slung over their shoulders. The bagpipe players played.

"On your marks!" shouted Mr. Robin.

Billy's, Ramona's and Terrance's eyes squinted and they slung their arms around each other.

"Get set…"

All the front racers gripped their ropes and pressed their boots into their steering boards. All the back racers dug their mittened hands into the snow, so as to launch at the starting gun.

"GO!" screamed Mr. Robin. Then he shot his starter pistol, jumped down from the soapbox and hugged his wife out of adrenaline excitement.

BANG!

The racers launched over the edge of Robin's Hill. And the spectators and supporters at the top and bottom of Robin's Hill cheered.

Fredrick and Otto Kluszewski took the lead, followed close behind by Bridget and Megan Hopkins and the Twins. The first four turns down Robin's Hill were the tightest. Racers were hunched forward like horse jockeys. When the sleds took the turns, their runners dug in, making snow spray in the air. When the snow sprayed its highest, all one could see was Mrs. Robin's Red Robin Helmets – it truly did look like massive robins racing down a white covered hill.

Behind the first three sleds were Johnny and Murf neck and neck with Claire and her father, Patrick Gardener. Tied in last place were Brian Junior and Benjamin Horwitz, Angus and Lorna McQueen and Joey and Anthony Loranzano. Even though Brian Junior and Benjamin Horwitz's sled had a slow start it was coasting strong and picking up speed. Angus and Lorna McQueen's and Joey and Anthony Loranzano's sleds were riding a bit squirrellier. Wobbly. Spectators laughed knowing neither the Loranzanos nor the McQueens took the race too seriously.

The four tight turns were approaching. The first two turns were more treacherous because all of the racers were packed close together. Fredrick and Otto intentionally slammed their sled into the Twins on the first turn.

"Hey, what's the big idea?!" screamed Charlene through the whitewash.

"Move it sister," barked Otto back.

This gave Bridget and Megan Hopkins a chance to pull forward into a more competitive first place.

Johnny and Murf, parallel with Claire and her father, approached the first turn.

"Lean right, lean right!" screamed Johnny as he dug his left boot into the broken boomerang and pulled with his right arm that gripped the steering rope toward his chest. The *Speed Racer* took the turn well. For a second, the left runners lifted off the ground.

"Ya!" screamed Murf. "She flies like a wonder! Faaantaaastic speeeeds!"

Close behind were Brian Junior and Benjamin Horwitz - Angus and Lorna McQueen - and Joey and Anthony Lorenzano. The Horwitzes began pulling away from the back line. Losing a bit of speed were the McQueens. Lorna, sitting behind her brother Angus was having a laughing fit watching her brother, turned around and standing up on their sled, waving at the Loranzano boys behind them, like he was a flirting flame.

Joey and Anthony Loranzano simply looked confused still holding onto their steaming rugged ciders. They tried to sip them as they steered and bounced about. Their cheeks were red and their mouths were wet.

At the second turn Charlene in retaliation, knocked her Flexible Flyer into Fredrick and Otto Kluszewski's sled.

"Hey, back off Half Portion," screamed Otto.

"Bah, go chase yourself. You started it," yelled Charlene back.

Then Fredrick pushed the back runners of the Twin's Flexible Flyer, spinning their tail out.

"Marlene lean right!" screamed Charlene as she tried to steer them straight again. This cost the Twins their top three position. Johnny and Murf, beside Claire and her father, Patrick, advanced past the Twins.

"Ahh upchuck," screamed Charlene. "C'mon Marlene we gotta pick up some speed." Marlene dug her mittens into the snow and started digging in.

"Hellooo boys, hellooo. Try and catch us if you can," teased Angus at the Loranzano boys as his sister laughed hysterically behind him.

"Joey, that Irish boy seems to be tryin' to tickle us," yelled Anthony, as he put his empty cup of rugged cider in his coat pocket and brought his Robin helmet down over his brow, getting focused on the race.

"Well, let's teach 'em a lesson shall we?" yelled Joey back to his brother, also bringing his Robin helmet down.

At the third turn, Bridget and Megan Hopkins were neck and neck with the Kluszewski brothers. It was now a tie for first place: The Kluszewski brothers on the left and the Hopkins sisters on the right. They all took the third turn hard

313

and approached the final tight turn before the track widened.

Johnny and Murf were pulling ahead of Claire and her father, while the Twins were pulling up alongside them.

The Twins pulled up parallel to the *Speed Racer*, passing the Gardeners. "What happened?" screamed Johnny to Charlene. "I saw ya spin out."

"Those wet socks knocked our sled," screamed Charlene.

"That's against the rules," screamed Johnny back as the white wash sprayed and they all took the third tight turn.

"Ya telling me something I don't know," screamed Charlene back as she straightened her sled out coming out of the turn.

The Gardeners, followed by the Horwitz brothers, took the third turn. Brian Junior pulled at his steering ropes. The sled took the turn nicely. But Brian Junior was strong and just before pulling out of the third turn, his steering rope snapped.

Brian Junior flew back knocking him and his brother off their sled. The two brothers somersaulted in the snow as the Gardeners watched the Horwitz's now empty sled come toward them fast.

BLAM!

The Horwitz's unmanned sled slammed into the Gardener's sled. The sled runners had hooked and were now causing the Gardener's sled to veer left toward the tree line.

Claire screamed.

Her father reached down and began working at pulling the sleds apart. "I can get it!" he screamed. "I can get it!"

The McQueens passed the Horwitzs who were sadly sitting in the snow, followed by the angered Loranzano boys.

Patrick Gardener was still reaching forward trying to free their sled from the unmanned Horwitz sled. Patrick handed his daughter the steering ropes. From behind, Claire kept the sled as straight as she could. But the fourth tight turn was approaching.

"I almost have it!" screamed Patrick Gardener.

Angus McQueen was now attempting to surf on his sled.

"Look Lorna, look, I'm surfin' like one of them surfer-Joes," screamed Angus, "I'm-a-waterskiing."

"Dah-ha-ha," erupted Lorna; she thought her brother the funniest thing to ever walk the world.

"Now I'm a race horse," said Angus as he slapped his own bum and waved at the Loranzano boys. The brothers did not find it as much of a razz.

"Oh that's it, they're toast," said Joey, as he steered and as his brother Anthony dug his mittens in like a charging grizzly bear.

Before the Loranzanos could reach the McQueens, a branch from a bending birch caught the collar of Angus's jacket. It hooked him like a railway bag. Angus hung in the air dumbfounded and bouncing.

Surprised, Lorna turned back, saw her brother hanging and erupted in an even bigger giggle fit. When she turned back around she saw that her unmanned sled was about to fly off a small drop on the edge of the track. She covered her eyes with her mittens and took the plunge.

"Wheee!" she screamed.

SWOOSH!

PLOP!

Lorna landed in thick snow on her back. She sat up quickly. Smiling, she looked back at her brother hanging from the bending birch. He waved to her. Lorna waved back. Then she fell back laughing as she made a snow-angel in the snow.

The Loranzano boys were coming up on Angus McQueen who was hanging from the bending birch. Joey grabbed Angus' boot, pulled, then let go. Like a slingshot, Angus was launched into the air. He plopped down head first into thick snow. Anthony fired two big snowballs at Angus' bum that was sticking up in the air.

BLAP! BLAP!

Angus turned himself around and shook his head to clear away the snow. But once he wiped his face with his mittens, two more snowballs coming from the woods white washed his face again. He could hear Lorna's far away laughter.

The Loranzano boys coasted ahead, passing the struggling Gardeners.

315

They advanced strongly trying to catch up with his racing pals.

Patrick Gardener pulled with both hands and with all his might at the locked sleds.

"Rawww!" he screamed as he pulled, and the Horwitz's sled runner detached from the Gardener's sled. "I got it!" The Horwitz's sled flew off the track, hit a tree and smashed.

The tail of the Gardeners' sled spun out left, then right. But the Gardeners were focused. Patrick Gardener put his mittened hands over the side of the sled to stabilize it while Claire pulled at the steering ropes from behind.

"Nice work Pop," Claire yelled as she handed her father back the steering ropes.

They had done it and were back in the race.

Up ahead, the forth and final tight turn approached.

The Kluszewski brothers took the turn, followed closely by the Hopkins sisters. Both sleds' runners dug in. Both sleds sprayed snow. Both sleds now had just three final wide turns to pick up as much speed as they could before the last long coast to the finish line.

Mr. Thomson was using his telescope to keep the people updated.

"The Robin's sure are flying. It seems the Horwitzes and McQueens are out of the race. It stands: The Kluszewskis and Hopkins have taken the front line."

Johnny and Murf took the fourth and final tight turn beside the Twins. Both sleds dug in. Both sleds sprayed snow. And both sleds came out of the turn with a bit more speed.

"Johnny!" screamed Charlene.

"What?" screamed Johnny back, as he gripped the *Speed Racer's* steering ropes as snow sprayed all over his goggles.

"We can't let those creeps win this!" Charlene screamed back.

Johnny thought. He looked over at Charlene who was also gripping her sled's steering ropes as snow sprayed all around her.

"You're right! Okay listen up - Murf, Marlene it's gotta be one of us that wins this. Got me?" screamed Johnny. And everyone nodded their heads in agreement as their sleds flew into the first wide turn. "You gotta really dig your paws in! We both really need a kick here."

Murf and Marlene both began to dig their mittens in for maximum speed.

"But wait," Mr. Thomson checked his racing program. "It seems the Airlords, as it says they're called here, and the McManus Twins are catching up fast. They seem to have some reserve vigor."

Standing together – Kringle, Ellie, Pete, Flo, Pastor Finn and Riggels cheered.

Mr. Thomson continued, "Behind them, now rounding the fourth tight turn are the Gardeners followed by the Loranzano brothers.

"That's it, that's it, we're gaining!" yelled Charlene.

Johnny, Murf and the Twin's sleds were now just behind the leading sleds.

"Oh no you don't. We're not getting second this year," said Fredrick Kluszewski as he grabbed the back left runner of the Hopkin's sled and yanked it back, moving their own sled back to the lead position.

"HEY!" screamed the Hopkins sisters.

The Kluszewski brothers laughed.

Johnny and Murf and the Twins' sleds advanced to the front.

All the sleds took the second wide turn.

"Hey you wet socks! Ya you," screamed Charlene as her sled came alongside the Kluszewski brothers' sled. "You're cheats!"

"Ah, find a cliff and take a jump Half Portion," yelled Otto back.

Charlene growled; only her sister could hear it. She turned to Johnny and Murf, "C'mon fellas, let's take these wet socks off the line." Again Murf and Marlene dug their mittens in. The sleds took the final wide turn.

Johnny screamed over the spraying snow to Murf and the Twins, "This is it. Robin's Hill straightens out after this turn. Pick up as much speed as you can and keep digging in 'till the finish line."

"Oh no you don't," said Fredrick again. And he grabbed onto the back of Marlene's jacket and began to pull the Twins' sled back.

"He's got me," screamed Marlene.

Johnny grabbed the front runner of the Twins' sled and tried to pull them back. It was now a tug of war with the Twins.

"Keep digging," screamed Johnny.

"Think your boyfriend's gonna save ya, do ya Half Portion?" said Otto to Charlene.

"Eat a triple scoop of rotten scum!" shouted Charlene back.

"Well, let's just see if he can drag you to the finish after this," said Otto.

"Fredrick, take their left runner."

"With pleasure," said Fredrick and he kicked at the Twins' left runner. Marlene screamed.

"I'll knock you," screamed Charlene.

"Well, let me help free your hands for you," said Otto, as he took out a small jackknife and made a swipe at Charlene's steering rope.

SNAP!

Charlene's steering rope snapped.

The Twins no longer had control of their Flexible Flyer. Johnny turned, saw what Otto had done and held tighter to the front runner of the Twins' sled. He pulled them closer to the *Speed Cruiser*.

"I got ya," Johnny screamed. Charlene looked at Johnny and gave him a nod, then turned to Otto with lightening in her eyes.

"You won't get away with this you cheats!" she screamed.

Fredrick once again kicked the Twins' left runner, loosening the screws from the base. The Flexible Flyer wobbled. Murf grabbed the Twins sled as well.

"Marlene, keep digging in. We'll show 'em," screamed Murf.

Marlene gave Murf a nod.

Mr. Thomson had been describing the happenings to all the spectators.

"And now, and now it seems the Airlords have the McManus Twins' sled stable. They're, they're towing them in to the finish. But wait, no wait. Yes!" laughed Mr. Thomson. "The Hopkins sisters are also helping," Mr. Thomson erupted in laughter. "They're pelting the Kluszewski brothers with snowballs from the back. Oh lord, right in the face. Yes, yes Fredrick has let go of one of the Twins. I can't tell which one. OH MY, AGAIN IN THE FACE! The Hopkins girls are really letting the Kluszewskis have it. Okay the Kluszewskis can't see a thing. Their faces are being assaulted with snowballs. Otto is no longer steering. They're, they're starting to fall behind. Oh and here comes the Gardeners." Mr. Thomson again erupted in laughter. "OH WOULD YOU LOOK AT THIS? The Gardeners are pelting the Kluszewski brothers with snowballs as they pass them too. The Kluszewski brothers are just covered in snow. They're so covered they look like abominable snowmen." Mr. Thomson took a break from his telescope to lean over in a laughing fit.

The spectators were all leaning forward. It was the most exciting Red Robin Race to ever take place.

Even though everyone could now clearly see the racers, Mr. Thomson kept commenting. He loved to announce the winner. "Coming in now are the Hopkins sisters neck and neck with the Airlords pulling the McManus Twins. Here they come ladies and gentlemen. Here they come. This is it. Suds, get that camera ready."

Suds from the *Worcester Evening Gazette* positioned himself for the photo finish shot.

Charlene and Marlene dug their left mittens in as Johnny dug in with his right mitten and steered with his left mitten, while Murf held onto the Twin's Flexible Flier with his left mitten and dug in the snow with his right mitten. The Hopkins sisters were also digging in for extra speed. The Gardeners had caught up as well from all the antics brought on by the Kluszewskis.

It was anyone's race.

"Murf?" screamed Johnny as he tried to keep the Twins' sled straight. "Slingshot, slingshot."

"What?" screamed Murf back.

"Slingshot, like Buck Rogers did for Wilma when they escaped the aliens from the nine moons of Saturn."

"Right. Slingshot. Ay-ay. Ready and waiting," screamed Murf back doing his best to keep the Twin's sled straight while keeping a competitive speed.

"It's a photo finish everyone!" yelled Mr. Thomson. "Here they come!"

The Gardeners had made it to the front. The finish line was only a few yards away.

"BLAST THEM OFF MURF! BLAST THEM OFF!" screamed Johnny and with all their might Johnny and Murf pulled as hard as they could to whip the Twins forward.

Charlene and Marlene looked to their side at Johnny and Murf as they passed them.

"OH MY," screamed Mr. Thomson. And all the spectators cheered as they watched Johnny and Murf slingshot the Twins toward the finish line.

Without Johnny and Murf holding their runners still, the Flexible Flyer's right runner quickly came loose and broke off. The Twin's sled slid over the finish line with only one runner.

Suds of the *Worcester Evening Gazette* snapped his camera.

SNAP!

"AND IT'S THE MCMANUS TWINS IN FIRST, HOPKIN GIRLS IN SECOND AND THE AIRLORDS BRINGING IN A NOBLE THIRD!" announced Mr. Thomson and all of the spectators cheered.

It truly was the most exciting Red Robin Race ever.

A crowd had formed around the racers. Everyone laughed and socialized while recapping the race and sipping on steaming hot ciders and cocoa and munching on warm popcorn balls and pretzels.

But, instead of congratulating his daughters, Mr. McManus stood on one of the trailers of hay with Miss Winkelplex and announced that evening's auction that was to take place at the Town Hall.

"Don't forget ladies and gentlemen, tonight at seven o'clock sharp - the greatest toys in the world will be up for auction for you and you alone."

Only fortunate people from out of town gathered to listen to Mr. McManus. All of the other spectators cheered the racers as they gathered around Mr. Robin, who was positioning his soapbox in preparation for the official presentation of the Red Robin Trophy.

Over the commotion, Riggles caught sight of Fredrick and Otto Kluszewski heading home. He tapped Sheriff Jones on his shoulder.

"Think we should have a talk with these boys Sheriff?" he asked.

"That's a good idea. Let's," said Sheriff Jones, and the two men called out to the Kluszewski brothers.

"Gather 'round, Red Robin Racers, gather 'round," said Mr. Robin from his soapbox. The racers, save the Kluszewski brothers, stood in front of Mr. and Mrs. Robin.

Ellie went to her knees and gave Johnny a big hug. Kringle stood beside her.

"You did so well Johnny my boy. So well. I'm so proud of you two," said Ellie.

"Thanks Ma," said Johnny.

Billy, Ramona, and Terrance approached.

"That was incredible!" said Billy as he hugged his brother as well.

Ramona punched Murf in his arm, but rubbed it after.

"Oi, nice v'ork Murf," Ramona said

"Thanks. It sure was somethin'," said Murf back. "Hey Mr. Kringle the *Speed Cruiser* was fantastic."

"Ya it sure was. It handled swell," said Johnny to Kringle.

Kringle smiled.

"Well, it's all in how you command the ship and you two looked to have been commanding," Kringle said back.

Ellie smiled at Kringle. She felt solid and strong that day.

"Awe thanks Mr. Kringle," said Murf.

"Ya thanks. But hey, there's something, something important that us Airlords got you Mr. Kringle. It's real important and I mean real top secret important that you have it."

Ellie and Kringle smiled; they believed that the Airlords had gotten Kringle a gift for helping them with the *Speed Cruiser*. And in a way they had.

"Okay Red Robin Racers, this year's winners of the Ninth Annual Red Robin Race are..."

The Firemen's Drum Line went to snare drum press rolls.

"...Charlene and Marlene McManus," said Mr. Robin, as he handed Charlene the Red Robin trophy.

Everyone applauded. Mrs. McManus smiled. The Firemen's bagpipes began to join in with the drum line.

"No way, you guys should have it," said Charlene as she pushed the trophy in Johnny's arms.

"No way, you two deserve it; you came in first," said Johnny as he pushed it into Marlene's hands.

"No way, we wouldn't have won if you guys hadn't helped our broken sled," said Marlene as she put the trophy in Murf's hands.

"Well, we wouldn't have been able to get those creeps off you if it wasn't for the help of you two," said Murf as he put another trophy in Bridget Hopkin's hands.

When Suds of the *Worchester Evening Gazette* snapped the photo of who had won the Ninth Annual Red Robin Race for next week's cover story, all one could see was a bunch of small children all trying to push the big trophy away from themselves and Billy Boone smack-dab in the middle smiling to the camera.

Back at the Central Command, the Airlords stood with their arms crossed staring up at the Red Robin Trophy centered on their shelf.

"We did it," said Murf.

"We sure did," said Johnny.

"Wow," was all Billy could say.

"Sure was nice of them," said Terrance.

"Sure was," said Johnny.

"The *Speed Cruiser* was fantastic," said Murf.

"Sure looked so," said Billy.

"Kringle's a great scientist," said Johnny.

"What's that?" asked Murf.

"I don't know," said Ramona, holding a red ribbon. "Marlene gave me two of 'em." Ramona took out another red ribbon from her overall's center pocket. "She said they match my hair and freckles."

"I think it's actually for your hair," said Terrance. "She wears 'em. I've seen it."

"Oh," said Ramona a bit confused.

"Alright Airlords, I sure would like to do this all night, but like Buck Rogers says…" Johnny turned his newsy cap around and put a straw in his mouth…"*Once an adventure ends, a new one begins.*"

Murf walked in front of the line of Airlords and in his best Captain tone said, "We gotta get them letters to the Auction. And quick!"

Hamilton, like all of America in 1929, was a place where beauty took the form of one's love for family and friends, respect for others, devotion in charity, and strength in personal will to create a piece of Providence for everyone. But it goes without saying that there were still those who dolled themselves up in fabrics and stones to boast of their beauty, because they seldom saw the true beauty of their time.

The Town Hall was filled with fortunate people. They came from all around: Boxford, Newton, Quincy, Boston, Cambridge, Manchester, even the Hamptons. Hearsay had it that there were swanky people all the way from

Philadelphia, Albany, New York City, Providence and even farther. In the social circle of the fortunate, it was *the* place to be seen.

Red and green streamers were strung. There were seats lined up from the back of the room all the way to the front of the stage. And all the seats were filled. Bidders were dressed up and socializing as tea and sugar cookies were being passed around. Cinnamon candles made the room smell nice. It was warm inside the Town Hall. People wore big smiles and laughed heartily. Even Major Nicols and his twin wife had come. They sat centered in the front row. Miss Magnolia sat beside them. She had a bit of trouble following Mrs. Nicols' conversational topics. Noticing this, Mrs. McManus, sitting with the Twins, helped Miss Magnolia by engaging her in some less flamboyant dialog. Suds from the *Worchester Evening Gazette* snapped photos. Miss Winkeplex schmoozed. And classical music played from a decorative phonograph.

Stepping into the Winter Auction, Ellie and Flo couldn't help but make note of the gaudy coats, dresses, hats, jewelry and perfumes. The two friends entered the lobby of the Town Hall where Sheriff Jones stood. He was instructed by Mr. McManus to – "Keep the riff-raff out." Standing at the doorway of the lobby to the main room were the Dunce Brothers. They were dressed up, handing out programs. Elmer handed Ellie and Flo a program, yet he kept his eyes to the floor. Ellie slightly squinted at him anyway – just to make sure he still knew who was boss.

Ellie and Flo entered the main auction room.

"And what are you two doing here?" asked Miss Winkelplex.

"We're here for the Auction," said Ellie.

"Well, non-bidders are to be seated upstairs," said Miss Winkelplex as she pointed to the rafters. "You should have known that."

"A better view for us then. I mean, I wouldn't want to be crowded down in this pigpen anyhow," said Flo, inspired by the way Ellie had stuck up for herself earlier that day. The two friends began to head up the stairs.

Miss Winkelplex made a face of disgust.

"Mind your words Flo. This pigpen, as you say, wouldn't have you beggars anyway. Well, off with you two, I have much more important matters to address. Come to think of it girls, I'm not too sure I'll need your assistance at the shop any longer. Consider yourselves free to find new employment. You know, free to pace Commonwealth Street with the rest of the down and outs," said Miss Winkelplex.

Kringle

"Look-a-here Linda," Ellie no longer called her, now old boss, Miss Winkelplex. "I know more about the difference between European wood and craftsmanship and our New England wood and craftsmanship, so don't you get too confident. Best mind *your* words, you slattern of a woman. Truth is truth and you never know when a fable will end."

"Well I..wha-what is it you're implying? If you are suggesting that…" Miss Winkelplex started.

"Come on Ellie, we don't have to listen to this ankle biter any more. Have a worrisome evening ya slice of tar," said Flo. And with that the two friends headed up the stairs to the rafters.

It took Kringle and Pete four trips pulling enormous red sacks filled with toys on their sleighs from The Workshop to the Town Hall. The two men were now positioning the first toy on the podium that was placed center stage. It was a three-foot tall dollhouse, fully furnished, with three levels and a shingled roof with a chimney. When they placed it on the Auction podium, the fortunates pointed and whispered from the exciting sight, while the fortunates' children pointed and demanded.

Kringle and Pete had mixed feelings preparing the toys they had crafted to be auctioned off. The two men and Riggels had decided to keep things quiet about where these toys actually came from. They had deduced from long and late night discussions at The Workshop that the times were too tough for them and most Americans to speak the truth, especially when the truth could swiftly lead you to unemployment, hunger or even slam-click. Instead, Kringle and Pete decided to do whatever Mr. McManus instructed them to do. They worked silently. Their postures sagged and their faces were melancholy. They looked empty.

After the dollhouse was perfectly positioned, Kringle and Pete went back stage where the rest of the toys were lined up. Kringle reached into his back pocket to grab his handkerchief, he was sweating from the harsh stage lights. But when he reached into his pocket he discovered a note.

A note from Ellie:

Kringle - my new friend,

I know you, Pete and Riggels have made your decision, but please reconsider. Honesty is the best legacy a man can achieve. You are a skilled man Kringle. A thoughtful man. And just like how you kept your sisters back home happy in their darkest times, you, Kringle, are a man who will one day make hundreds of people joyful in their darkest times. I just see little children all over this world sending you letters of what they can only dream to have. And you will be able to craft their little dreams to make them all feel fortunate, even if it's just for one day.

Think about it,

Ellie

Kringle handed Pete the note as Mr. McManus passed them and took to the stage. Applause thundered. Everyone took his or her seats. Pete handed Kringle back the note. The two men briefly exchanged a look, but said nothing. Kringle and Pete stood in silence as they listened to Mr. McManus' introduction. Their silence meant their decision had not changed. Yet their hearts ached more heavily from Ellie's words.

The Airlords were suited up wearing their goggles and helmets. Johnny and Murf pulled Ramona, Terrance and Billy in the *Speed Cruiser*; they knew the three of them wanted to feel how it flew. Rudy walked beside them. The Airlords were focused. Determined. This mission alone was more important to them than any other. Ramona gripped the stack of fake Letters of Authenticity in her mittened hand. The gang had *Buck Rogers* in their hearts and all of the Airlords looked strong. Fearless.

That night there was to be an eclipse with the Sun and the Moon. Hamilton's sky was already beginning to look different than it normally did. Pinks battled purples for the dominant hue of the sky. Anywhere you were in Hamilton that night, you could hear the applause from the Town Hall.

The Airlords walked down Commonwealth Street. They looked as if they were flying through an uncharted galaxy. They were living their dream of protecting the good of mankind.

The Auction was in full swing. Mr. McManus danced the stage as Miss Winkelplex assisted him. There were cheers, applause, *"Ooh's and Aah's"*; Mr. McManus and Miss Winkelplex were in their version of Heaven.

"Do I hear ten dollars, ten dollars for this one of a kind toy-box all the way from a small village in Italy? And I'll tell you, I still can't believe people actually lived in this teeny-tiny village. It was smaller than a bunch of huddled Indians," said Mr. McManus, and everyone laughed. "There we go, ten dollars to the gentleman in the third row. Do I hear twelve dollars? Twelve to the lovely lady right here. Fifteen, fifteen dollars? Remember folks, this was made by an old-world toymaker, barely could stand, with a face like the bottom of your shoes, living in a meager home that took me days to hike to. Fifteen dollars is a steal. You just can't get craftsmanship like this in America. Well, *here* you can. One of a kind. No one else will have its double. Only you! Only you! I mean ladies and gentleman, what is life if you can't enjoy the very best?"

"Twenty!" screamed a man in the far back.

"Twenty to the wise man in the back. He knows about the good things in life. He values the valuable. Do I hear twenty-five? Going once, going twice – sold to the scholar in the back row. Now, as we wait for the next marvelous, one of a kind toy to make its presence known, let me just remind everyone that once one wins a bid on a toy it will be wrapped up with a bow by our own Linda Winkelplex here and ready for you to take home. Also, there are Letters of Authenticity for each item. Now this is important, Linda will be mailing to you these documents, so don't forget to talk to Linda once the Auction closes. And yes, that is right, not only do you get a one of a kind hand crafted toy that all your friends and family will flutter over, but you will have a letter of proof, signed and stamped from the toymaker himself. These letters are so you can learn about the toymaker, read about where he comes from and feel closer to these beautiful toys while not having to actually go to these primitive villages like I did." Once again the bidders erupted in laughter. "These documents are also to squash any jealous naysayer that may want to challenge your authenticity from, frankly, just being a sore looser that they weren't here tonight," said Mr. McManus, and all of the Town Hall applauded.

Kringle brought out the next item as Pete took the toy-box to the back to be wrapped with a bow.

Pastor Finn was just sitting down next to Flo when Kringle caught sight of Ellie up in the rafters. He smiled a guilty smile to her. Ellie waved back.

Mr. McManus snatched from Kringle the card that came with the next toy to be auctioned.

"Ah lovely, lovely. This here is one of my favorites. I actually wanted to buy it for my lovely daughters. But instead I made it available to you because that's the type of man I am." The fortunate were awed at Mr. McManus' kind heart. "This toy comes from…" Mr. McManus read the card. "An old toymaker in Lille, France. How exotic. How exotic."

Toy after toy sold: toy-boxes, dollhouses, push-toys, climbers and more. Children tugged their mothers' dresses. Wives tugged their husbands' arms. The fortunates bought up every last toy like it was the last kiss on Earth.

Back stage, Kringle and Pete stood beside each other as they listened to Mr. McManus' deception. Kringle and Pete were both sweating from the hot lights of the stage. Their sadness to being part of such deceit was visible on their faces. Both men clenched their fists with every lie that was spoken. Both men couldn't help but close their eyes when Mr. McManus would laugh out loud. Yet both men did nothing.

The Airlords burst into the lobby of the Town Hall. Sheriff Jones was quick to stop them.

"Woah now gang. Where do you think you are going?" said Sheriff Jones.

The Airlords all spoke at once.

"We have to stop them," said Billy.

"It's code red Sheriff," said Murf.

"Ve have ta get dem da secret papers," said Ramona.

"It's the only way. Code red Sheriff, code red," repeated Terrance.

"We gotta save Kringle and Pete, Sheriff," said Johnny more directly.

Rudy barked, turned in a circle, sat down and barked again.

"Okay shoosh-shoosh now," said Sheriff Jones.

The Airlords were dressed oddly and talking what seemed to be imaginative nonsense. Sheriff Jones shooed them out saying, "Okay children, well there's important adult stuff happening here tonight, so best play somewhere else."

Sheriff Jones herded the Airlords out the front door of the Town Hall.

When he shut the door, the door tapped Murf's bum. Murf bumped into Billy, who bumped into Johnny, who bumped into Terrance, who bumped into Rudy, who bumped into Ramona, sending the stack of Letters of Authenticity up into the air.

A strong gust of wind took the pages up and whirled them down Commonwealth Street. The Airlord's made chase.

For Mr. McManus, the Auction could not have been going any better. He could calculate his new fortune in his head with ease. Major Nicols bought a full wooden train set for his son. He also bought a dollhouse made from a bureau that had a working light and doorbell. A man from New York bought a wooden model of the Empire State Building. A woman from Providence bought three horse-heads on wheels. And a philanthropist from the Hamptons bought the most expensive toy auctioned thus far. He bought a toy-box of a baseball scene taking place at Boston's Fenway Park. The small toy ball that was on a round swivel even flew over the green wall when the toy-box was cranked.

Kringle and Pete watched as their hard work was distributed to the wealthiest in the land. They watched their boss became richer and richer from their work and his own crookedness.

The Airlords had retrieved all of the loose fake Letters of Authenticity. Standing outside the Town Hall they tried to think of their next plan of action.

"J'sst den't understand vhy da sheriff den't believe us. It's a dang code red 'n' everyting," said Ramona trying to get the letters back into a neat stack.

"He thinks we're just being silly kids or somethin'," said Murf.

"Well, we're gonna have to get in some other way," said Johnny.

"We could try and run past him," said Terrance.

That's when they heard a toilet flush.

"There," said Billy, pointing to the window. "We can go through that window just there."

The window to the ladies' room was opened just an inch.

"Okay Airlords, let's crouch and crawl," said Johnny. The Airlords got on their hands and knees. Even Rudy got down a little lower. They crawled over to the window to the ladies' bathroom and huddled under it.

"We gotta see if there's anyone in there before we touch down," said Murf. "Ramona you look."

"Oi, vhy me? You look," said Ramona.

"Well, 'cause you're a girl. And if someone's in there, well it's better a girl is looking in the ladies' bathroom, than a boy. Just figurin'," said Murf.

"And besides, you're the tallest," added Johnny.

"Ah bushwa," said Ramona as she spit and handed Murf the letters. Ramona mumbled to herself as she prepared to look in. "Oi I'm nervous brothas," she said.

"You can do it," said Billy.

"There's probably no one in there anyway," added Murf.

"Okay, ready," said Johnny.

"I dink," said Ramona.

"Okay, One...two...three," said Johnny.

Ramona peeked her nose up to the cracked window and lifted it up a few more inches. Mrs. Robin was sitting on the toilet.

"AHHH!" screamed Mrs. Robin.

"AHHH!" screamed Ramona.

Mrs. Robin leaped up and off the toilet, flushed, then ran out of the stall of the ladies' room.

Ramona ducked down with the other Airlords.

"'Probably no ones dere huh? Phonus balonus. I dink I scared the leggings off of Mrs. Robin," said Ramona, as she snatched the fake Letters of Authenticity back from Murf.

"Well, we better go for it now," said Johnny. "Quick everyone inside." The Airlords climbed up and invaded the ladies' room.

"Rudy, stand guard, we'll be right back," said Billy from inside the ladies' room.

"Okay Airlords, here's the plan. Once we exit this room, we gotta find the main room where Kringle and Pete are," explained Murf.

"Then what?" asked Terrance.

"Well, then we just make a run for it," said Murf.

"Run fer it', what ya mean, 'run fer it'?" asked Ramona.

"I mean we gotta just get these papers in the hands of Kringle and Pete and not let anyone stop us," said Murf.

"Ya, and once Kringle and Pete have the papers then…," started Johnny, but was interrupted by a loud sound.

BOOM!

The door to the ladies' room busted open. The Dunce Brothers stood in the doorway. Startled, the Airlords huddled in the bathroom stall.

"Shh," whispered Johnny to the Airlords. "Don't make a sound."

"There ain't nobody here," said Elmer. "I bet that old bag was just chasing shadows."

The Dunce Brothers walked inside the ladies' room.

"Maybe," said Lloyd as he scanned the room. "Wait, there," Lloyd said as he pointed to all the little boots clustered in the stall.

"Well, what do you know," said Lloyd. "Looks like we either got a ten legged spider in there or a bunch a peeping Toms."

"We're found out," whispered Terrance.

"Shh," said Johnny.

"Hey you kids in there," hollered Lloyd. "I see your little boots."

"Okay on three let's make a run for it," said Johnny.

"One…," said Murf.

"Tew," said Ramona.

"Three," said Terrance.

And the Airlords busted open the bathroom stall door and made a run for the door.

"AHHH," screamed the Airlords.

"Get 'em," screamed Lloyd.

Johnny went for the door, but Elmer put his foot in front of it. The Dunce Brothers grabbed the collars of all of the Airlords.

Outside, Rudy began to bark. He backed up and tried to jump through the ladies' room window - but missed. Rudy tried again - but missed again. The Dunce Brothers opened the door to the ladies' room and brought the Airlords out into the lobby. The Auction was still going on in the main room. Rudy tried for the window again and this time he made it through. Barking up a good one, Rudy entered the lobby where Sheriff Jones was.

"Hey, what's going on here?" said Sheriff Jones.

"Mrs. Robin said there was someone peeping through the bathroom window," said Lloyd, holding on to Johnny's, Ramona's and Terrance's collars. Rudy growled. "When we went to check it out, we found these little rug rats all hiding in the stall."

"Is this true?" asked Sheriff Jones.

"Well yes, but…," started Johnny, but then all the Airlords spoke at once.

"It's code red, Sheriff," said Murf.

"Ve gotta get dez secret papers to Kringle and Pete," said Ramona.

"It's all a scam sheriff," said Terrance.

"Ya gotta let us see Kringle," said Johnny.

"We gotta get him these secret documents," said Billy.

Lloyd motioned to Elmer that Ramona was holding a stack of papers against her chest.

"Okay c'mon," said Sheriff Jones as he walked to the front and opened it. "What did I say about playing? C'mon kids, I won't tell you again. Off with you. You have to play your games outside."

Lloyd and Elmer brought the Airlords to the door. Rudy was still barking.

"Okay out you go Rudy," said Sheriff Jones. "You kids too, out ya go."

The Airlords were pushed outside the Town Hall.

"Now I don't want to see you again tonight. Is that clear?" said Sheriff Jones.

"But, but," said Murf.

And as the front door was being closed to the Town Hall, Lloyd said, "I'll take these," he said and ever so quickly snatched the papers out from Ramona's hands. Then the doors closed and the Airlords where back outside in the cold.

Inside the Town Hall, the sheriff shook his head smiling, thinking the Airlords were just playing a game. He headed into the Auction room.

"What are those?" asked Elmer.

"I don't know, but I bet the boss would want 'em. We'll hold on to them until after the show. Then we'll show Mr. McManus. See if he knows what they are," said Lloyd.

Outside, the Airlords stood in a circle.

"Sorry brothas, he-he just snatched 'em," pleaded Ramona.

"It's okay," said Murf as he put his arm around Ramona. She looked devastated. "There was nothing you could do."

"What now?" asked Billy.

"We gotta get back in there and get those letters from them Dunces," said Johnny. "We're not done yet!"

Back in the Auction room, Mr. McManus was finishing with the last toy up for bid. The last and final item to showcase was the cross that Pete had crafted. It wasn't to be auctioned, but rather presented to Pastor Finn as the closing event for the night. Pete knew the cross was next. His stomach felt like worms. He could feel his heart beat in his palms. His heart felt open.

From the rafters Ellie could see Kringle and Pete off stage and a bit to the side. She'd been watching them all night, hoping they would change their minds and unveil the deceit. Ellie saw Pete whisper something into Kringle's ear. Kringle then nodded and Pete walked off.

Pete headed to the back door of the Town Hall. Feeling ashamed to be a part of Mr. McManus' swindle, he needed to go outside for some air and to collect himself.

Outside, Pete's breath steamed and floated to the stars. Pete looked up to where his breath lifted. He gazed on the eclipse that was beginning. Pete's watery green eyes wavered in the night-light. Then he began to pray out loud.

"Lord, please forgive me for lacking the strength to let these people know that them toys are made by us. Please forgive me for being a part of this all. I wanna say something. I truly do. You just gotta know that, which I figure you do. It's just, this life here, I guess I mean society these days, well it's a bit against people like me. Even if I say the truth, Lord, I don't think anyone will believe me. It's them powerful men Lord. Them crooked powerful men. They, they just make the rules these days and if people like me don't follow them rules…even if them rules are wrong…well we, me and Kringle, we'll lose our jobs. We'll lose our home. We'll be outside in the cold. And all that just for saying what's right. So I say nothing. And I feel more than rotten about that. So forgive me, Lord, I don't mean to help these lousy men. Please give me a sign so I can know what to do. I'm confused."

Pete watched as his words lifted up into the sky. Then he closed his watery green eyes and went back inside to see his cross presented to Pastor Finn. But, Pete's mind was distracted; he didn't fully close the back door to the Town Hall.

✳

The Airlords were now aggravated. They had lost the fake Letters of Authenticity that they had tried so hard to get. Things seemed hopeless. The mission was failing.

"No, no, we can't do that, the sheriff will stop us right away," said Johnny.

"Nat if ve run real fast. I mean jest slam dem doors open 'n' make a cat dash," said Ramona.

"I get ya, but what else?" asked Johnny.

"We could check the back door," said Billy.

"Let's see if the window is still open," said Murf.

"What about a chimney? Does this place have one? We could go down that. It worked last time," said Terrance as he squinted upward.

"Let's just check the back door," said Billy.

"I say ve just blast through da front door 'n' make a cat dash fer it," repeated Ramona. "Vhat de you say Murf, ya?"

"I just ain't sure," Murf said as he scratched his chin.

Billy and Rudy began to walk off.

"Hey, where ya going Billy?" asked Johnny.

"You guys ain't listening to me," said Billy as he kept walking. "Me and Rudy are gonna check the back door."

"Ya sure, that's a good idea," said Johnny. And the Airlords followed Billy to the back of the Town Hall.

The Airlords took the turn around the Town Hall and saw the back door was ajar just an inch.

"Well, what do you know," said Johnny. Then he patted his brother on the back. "Nice Billy."

The Airlords huddled at the back door. After some code red discussion, the Airlords decided it would be suicide for them to all go in through the back door. Sheriff Jones or the Dunce Brothers were sure to see them.

"So den what?" asked Ramona.

"Well, we send Rudy in to fetch the Letters from the Dunce Brothers, like he did with the rockets. Rudy will then bring the Letters to Pete and Papa, oops, I mean Kringle," said Billy, as he began to draw the papers in the snow for Rudy to see. "See this Rudy. Fetch. Bring to Pete. Bring to Kringle. You got that boy? This here. Fetch. Bring to Pete. Bring to Kringle."

Rudy pounced his front paws on the snow; spun in a circle, then pounced his front paws down again.

"Good luck Rudy boy, good luck," said all of the Airlords as they watched Rudy crouch low and enter the back door of the Town Hall.

The Airlords ran to a window to watch Rudy. They all climbed up and balanced, standing on three garbage cans lined up under the window. Only their eyes and noses peeked over the window's ledge.

Kringle and Pete wheeled out the cross that they had mounted on a dolly. A white sheet covered the cross.

The crowd "Ooh'ed" and "Aah'ed".

"And here it is all the way from Italy. Where is Pastor Finn? Where is the Pastor of the hour?" said Mr. McManus. "Oh look, he's up there with the non-bidders." Mr. McManus erupted in laughter. "What are you doing up there Pastor Finn? Come on down here to us. Take the stage. Please everyone give a hand for Hamilton's own Pastor Finn," Mr. McManus announced.

Pastor Finn made his way down from the rafters and to the stage. Everyone stood and applauded.

Kringle and Pete stood on either side of the covered cross. Kringle looked up at Ellie. Ellie was already looking down at Kringle. But then Ellie noticed something behind Kringle. Something was peeking out from the side of the stage. It was Rudy. The thunderous applause made Rudy draw back, but he reemerged and while staying low to the ground he made his way to the aisle opposite the one Pastor Finn was walking down. Everyone was too busy celebrating Pastor Finn and the cross to notice Rudy sneaking his way up the aisle toward the Dunce Brothers, who were standing in the back by the lobby doors.

Pastor Finn took the stage and Mr. McManus gave him a big bear hug.

As Mr. McManus told the lie to Pastor Finn and the crowd about where the covered cross had come from, Kringle looked to his left at Pete. Pete's head was down. He looked ashamed to hear the lies coming from Mr. McManus. As Kringle looked at Pete, he noticed one single tear fall from Pete's watery green eyes and splash down on the stage floor.

From outside the Town Hall, the Airlords, standing on rickety trash cans, cheered Rudy on as they watched him sneak by everyone as if he alone had a cloaking device. Rudy caught sight of Lloyd with the fake Letters of Authenticity in his hands. He approached cautiously - inch by inch. The crowd listened to Mr. McManus tell about how he had met with the Vatican, told them of the loyal, faithful hearts New Englanders were blessed with and how he alone worked out the gift of this cross for Pastor Finn's church.

Pete looked down. Kringle stared at Pete. Ellie motioned to Flo that Rudy was sneaking up the aisle. Flo motioned to Ellie the five pairs of eyes looking through the Town Hall window.

"And now, here it is in all of it's true glory," said Mr. McManus, as he motioned to Kringle and Pete to take the white sheet off the cross.

The crowd became silent. Kringle and Pete lifted the white sheet off the cross. Town Hall erupted into a standing ovation. The cross was grand. Beautiful. Bold. And strong. It was seven feet tall, made of strong dark wood; it set forth a pleasing spiritual presence.

Then it happened. In all of the commotion, Rudy made his move. He sprung into action, leaped up, snatched the fake Letters of Authenticity from Lloyd in his mouth, turned, and ran down the aisle to Pete. That's when Kringle, Pete, Mr. McManus, Miss Winkelplex and even Pastor Finn saw Rudy. He jumped up onto the stage, dropped the letters at Pete's feet, gave a bark, spun around in a circle, pounced his front paws in front of him and barked again. Then Rudy sat down.

Outside, the Airlords were found.

"Hey, what do you kids think you're doing?!" spoke a voice. The voice had startled the Airlords to such a degree that they wobbled off their trash cans and fell to the snow. By their heads, they recognized the sheriff's boots. But when the Airlords looked up, it wasn't the sheriff they saw. It was Mr.

Riggelsworth.

"M-Mr. Riggelsworth," said Johnny, confused as to why Mr. Riggelsworth would be wearing Sheriff's Jones' police uniform.

"Well Johnny, it's actually Deputy Riggelsworth now. I got myself a new job. Pretty swell huh? Now son, do tell me what on Earth you all are doing out here looking through that window? I heard about you all peeping through the bathroom window. What sort of adventure are you on?"

*

It was the sign Pete had prayed for. He recognized the fake Letters of Authenticity even before he picked them up. And so did Mr. McManus.

"What the heck? What is this?" said Mr. McManus as he stepped back to grab the letters. Pete put a strong arm out. He kept his arm out as he bent down, picked up the letters and handed them to Kringle. Pete then gave Kringle a nod that spoke that they should tell the truth about the furniture, toys *and* the cross. Kringle understood.

Kringle held up the fake Letters of Authenticity, walked over to the podium and began to explain to the confused bidders about how they'd been had. Kringle told them about the junkyard, about the orders Mr. McManus gives Pete and him, about how Pete and he had crafted everything they had seen and have ever seen in *Bonne Affaire*. He also told the befuddled crowd that Pete had crafted the cross.

Furious, Mr. McManus pushed by Pete and stuck his finger in Kringle's face.

"Liar! This is all a lie! A lie I tell you! Someone get the sheriff to remove these dreadful liars from here!" hollered Mr. McManus.

The back doors exploded open.

"Stop right there," said Sheriff Jones, followed by Deputy Riggelsworth and all of the Airlords. Ellie was astonished that her boys were with the sheriff.

Mr. McManus also looked astonished.

Sheriff Jones and Deputy Riggelsworth came up on stage. Deputy Riggelsworth immediately handcuffed Mr. McManus. As he did, a wind came in from people leaving the Town Hall, blowing Mr. McManus' black top hat off his head; it rolled in a circle by Kringle's feet.

The crowd grumbled half confused and half angered.

"Okay, calm down everyone, calm down. Now listen, we just had some news come to light and it seems that what Mr. Kringle is saying is true," said Sheriff Jones, trying to calm the crowd down.

"The toys are fakes?" a man screamed.

Kringle stood by the sheriff.

"They are not fakes, just the story Mr. McManus said about them are. Pete and I made them."

"Well, I don't want mine any more; I won't pay," screamed a woman.

"No one has to pay for anything," said Sheriff Jones. "The Auction will not bind the bids."

Disgusted people began to get up and leave.

"Take him away Riggels," said the sheriff. "Miss Winkelplex, may I have a word?" said Sheriff Jones, as he began to handcuff her as well.

"Looks like you're the one who's going to be slam-clicked," said Deputy Riggelsworth to Mr. McManus as he and the sheriff brought both Mr. McManus and Miss Winkelplex out the back door.

Most of the fortunates had already left the Town Hall. They grumbled and made threats. Also exiting through the back door was Mrs. McManus explaining to the Twins what had happened. She looked relieved as if a huge weight had been lifted off her shoulders.

The Airlords joined Kringle, Pete, Pastor Finn and Rudy on the stage. And Ellie and Flo came down from the rafters to join them.

"Where did Rudy get these?" asked Kringle.

"We broke into Mr. McManus' house," said a proud Billy with an equally proud group of Airlords beside him.

"You what?" asked Ellie.

"Well, cook a goose with a candlestick, nice work kiddos," said Flo.

"How did you even know about these papers?" asked Pete.

"Oh, we were listening to you outside The Workshop window when you were making the toys," said Johnny.

"Ya, you said that you needed the papers so that people would believe you," said Billy. "And how they couldn't or wouldn't without them."

"Ya-ya, so we just went and got them for you," said Murf.

"It was hard; we went down the chimney," said Terrance.

"You what?" asked Ellie.

"Us Airlords stick tagethah ya naw?" said Ramona.

"Well, all I know is that you all did it," said Pete.

"Boy oh boy kids, you sure are Airlords," said Kringle.

"Well, what a pretty little spoonful of miracle," said Flo. "Kringle and Pete, what then are you going to do with all these toys now? You know, now that all the people just got up and left them?"

"We have an idea," said Kringle.

Ellie smiled.

What we all love most are the big snowflakes. We spot one and we chase it. These bigger snowflakes simply stand out to us among the smaller wild ones that whip by. Hovering, they slowly canopy down, rotating above us with moonlight illuminating sparkles inside their tips. Some say that the wisest snowflakes find the view below so gorgeous that they decide to slow their descent. These friendly flakes take the hand of the younger, more nervous flakes. They talk to them, calm them and explain to them the beauty, their beauty and the miraculous life that is in store for them.

This particular snowflake floating down was the grandest of them all that New England night. It moved up with the wind; then fell slowly rotating slightly. This fluffy flake seemed weightless, exhibiting *ballon* in a *grand jete* on the dotted sky. Looking down with delighted eyes, this snowflake took the hands of a few smaller flakes and together they decided to, ever so softly, fall on the red hat of a young toymaker who pulled a sleigh that held an abundance of toys inside a big red sack.

Poof.

The Moon kissed the Sun that night. Their eclipse lit the way for Kringle and Pete. Bundled in his layers, wearing two perfect size nine shoes that Kringle had saved to give him that night, Pete tied up his red sack full of toys, slung his cross over his back and headed to Mr. Thomson's church-barn to deliver this first gift that night. Kringle waved Pete goodbye as he headed the opposite way down Commonwealth Street.

Kringle stopped and stood at the end of Bridge Street watching Pete make his way past the homes of Hamilton. He looked down at Rudy by his side, rubbed his forehead, buttoned his red jacket, brushed the white fur on the cuffs of his sleeves that Ellie had sewn on to cover the many burn holes, put on his red hat, tied up the big red sack full of toys, then began to pull his sled down Commonwealth Street to deliver the toys to all the good boys and girls of Hamilton.

The town was quiet. The night was angelic. Kringle and Rudy visited home after home as the families inside slept warmly in their beds. Kringle would stop, open his big red sack, pull out a few toys, leave them by their doorstep and then move on to the next home. The McCulloughs, the Greys, the McKools, Miss Magnolia, all the children in her class, even Mrs. McManus and the Twins; everyone in Hamilton received something special that night - to feel noticed, loved and of course fortunate, even if it was for just one day.

When Kringle was finished, he headed back up Bridge Street. There were still a few toys left in his sack. As he walked with Rudy by his side, Kringle soaked in the beauty of the dancing flakes, the beauty of the Moon kissing the Sun, the beautifully bending birches that looked to be bowing to Kringle, and the charm of the small makeshift home that kept Kringle's love warm inside. Kringle stopped to look at Ellie's home before coming to her door. He had taken Mr. McManus' black top hat and placed in on the snowman outside the home. Rudy sat, then turned his head north, for he heard the robust breath first. Then Kringle gazed north as well. Down the small rise, walking into the junkyard, were Basher, Dazzler and Comet. Basher waited until Dazzler and Comet were under the tarp of the plumbing pile before he took a last look around and then entered himself. The deer family had finally found a home with a safe heart.

Kringle slung the rope around his shoulder and headed toward Ellie's home. He soundly knew that he had chosen the correct path at the crossroads of his life. He felt peace within himself. Kringle pulled out the last toys in his sack, held them in his arms and walked up the porch stairs with Rudy. But, when Kringle got to the top of the porch stairs, before he could lay the toys down on the doorstep, it slowly opened. It was Ellie. She looked heavenly. Glowing. And dressed in a simple white dress with a red sash around her waist tied in a bow. Kringle looked at her; the falling flakes behind him reflected in her blue eyes. Ellie held Kringle's small model ships – the Nina and the Santa Maria. The firelight bounced behind her. And two hidden pairs of eyes gazed down upon Ellie and Kringle from above.

"I told you he was a good guy Johnny," whispered Billy.

"I believe in him now Billy; I believe in him now," whispered Johnny back.

Kringle and Ellie stared at one another. The two smiled with their mouths *and* their eyes. Kringle thought Ellie to look like all the joys in this world inside one woman. Ellie thought Kringle to be a magical miracle. Ellie stepped out. The Boone boys smiled to one another.

Outside the snowflakes fell upon them. Ellie placed one of her hands on Kringle's cold red cheek and kissed him.

FEEL FORTUNATE

It was the morning that changed everything
    And all through the town
Children who dreamt magically
    Had their little wishes found

Gifts laid on door steps
    Were a magical winter sight
Morning eyes widened
    For life had taken a new light

Families that struggle so,
    Close together now sat
And if even for one day,
    Each one felt fortunate

Word spread quickly
    Who made this magic in us jingle?
It was the two men who lived in a workshop
    Honest Pete and Kristopher Kringle

THE END

David McWane was born in Hamilton, Massachusetts and raised in a first period farm house surrounded by history. He graduated from the Berklee College of Music in Boston and is the lead vocalist, lyricist, and song writer for the band Big D and the Kids Table. As a touring musician David has traveled throughout the world. During his travels he has recounted the places he visited, the people he met and the experiences he had in 3 books of poetry and a tour documentary. This is his first novel.

Other books by David McWane

The Gypsy Mile

Let The Poets Come And Stop Me

Biting Lightening, Bloody Mary

The Modern American Gypsy: Travels with David McWane

davidmcwane.com

www.ingramcontent.com/pod-product-compliance
Lightning Source LLC
Chambersburg PA
CBHW022205010726
47493CB00002B/414